PADDY COLMAN

PADDY COLMAN

JOHN BRUCE BOYCE

Order this book online at www.trafford.com
or email orders@trafford.com

Most Trafford titles are also available at major online book retailers.

Printed in the United States of America.

ISBN: 978-1-4669-0534-4 (sc)
ISBN: 978-1-4669-0533-7 (hc)
ISBN: 978-1-4669-0535-1 (e)

Library of Congress Control Number: 2011961005

Trafford rev. 02/09/2012

 www.trafford.com

North America & international
toll-free: 1 888 232 4444 (USA & Canada)
phone: 250 383 6864 ♦ fax: 812 355 4082

CONTENTS

Prologue

One week before 9-11, I was on an airplane flying out of Montevideo with my brother Tom. During the flight, we discussed ideas for screenplays. I suggested an interesting premise I had been considering – one that concerned the story of Uruguayan independence.

In the early years of the nineteenth century, all the nations of Latin America, with few exceptions, fought against Spain and were ultimately successful in freeing themselves from Spanish rule.

One of those exceptions was Brazil. During the Napoleonic war, with the Iberian peninsula nearly overrun by the French, the King of Portugal and his family lived in Rio de Janeiro. After the war he left his son to rule Brazil when he returned home. Rather than wait to become king of a small European nation, however, the son decided to declare himself emperor over the vast South American empire. His father was powerless to prevent it.

Another exception was Uruguay. It had also been successful in throwing out the Spanish, but its citizens then became subject to occupations by

Argentina and Brazil, both of whom coveted their little piece of land. This was something the Uruguayans would not allow without a fight.

Uruguay's national hero, José Artigas, was a remarkable man. His story is tragic, however. It would end in exile and bitter defeat, his country still under control of the Brazilians.

It would take another man, one of Artigas' captains, and just as remarkable in his way, to realize the dream. Juan Lavalleja returned to his country with thirty-two volunteers to begin what would seem a hopeless military campaign against the Empire of Brazil. The unimaginable success of these men sealed their glory in Uruguay, where they are known today as the thirty-three immortals.

I thought it was a great story. Tom did too, but he pointed out something that was very disappointing to me. People in the United States couldn't care less about Latin American wars of independence.

He was probably right. So what should I do?

Our father used to say, "Show me a revolution and you'll find an Irishman." Ironically, the national hero of Chile, Bernardo O'Higgins, is exactly that, and the man who led Argentina's revolutionary navy, Guillermo Brown, may have been also.

I like to think he was. It helps prove what my father said.

So I created Paddy Colman, the fictional Irish hero of my screenplay. He would tell the story through his eyes and perhaps it would have a better appeal to North American tastes. Almost everything that happens to him in my work is based in fact.

Two years later I submitted my screenplay. It was rejected.

Tom was very consoling. He said it might not have been the screenplay itself, but rather the subject matter. He also said my age may have been a factor. I had to list it on the application and Hollywood types are currently convinced that young people make the best screenwriters.

So he suggested I write a novel instead.

I resented that suggestion; but then suppose he was right.

So here then, is my novel – a historical romance (of sorts).

Reading this book may be easier if I say something about aspects of the region beforehand. It is the great pampas, that huge grassland that extends across northern Argentina, southern Brazil, and encompasses all of Uruguay.

The GAUCHO – Most of us know them already, the cowboys of South America. Uruguay alone has almost three times as many cattle as people and four times as many sheep. Most of the gauchos' gear is familiar to us, even though what they are called may not be. There are two exceptions.

Gauchos prefer loose fitting pants over the tighter ones worn by the cowboys and vaqueros of North America. They are called bombachas and they actually have their origins in Turkey.

One of the tools they use that is definitely not found among the North American cowboys' implements is the boleador. This is probably because these were not originally Spanish, but native to the local indigenous peoples. We know them as bolos.

A very ornate boleador. Those used in real work are usually
made of smooth round stones wrapped in rawhide.

The Gaucho barbeque is called a parillada, loosely, "stuff from the
grill". A good example of what the parillada is like can be found in the
South Brazilian steakhouses in major cities across the United States.
There are several great chains. Some even dress their waiters like gauchos.
However, these chains don't serve all the things found in South American
parilladas, such as tripe, brains, and various organs. Some things take
getting used to.

Just about everyone, then and now, drinks YERBA MATE, pronounced
zhehr'-bah mah'-teyh. It is made from a grass that grows in the region
(some call it an herb, but it's a grass). It is drunk from a hollow hard gourd
(the mate) through a silver plated metal straw and strainer, the bombilla,
pronounced bome-bee'-zhah. The mouthpiece of the bombilla is plated in
gold and is said to prevent the spread of contagious germs.

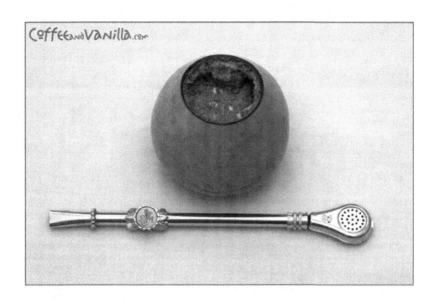

A simple mate filled with yerba mate and waiting for some hot water to be poured in. The bombilla is shown below. The more elaborate mates are stained and polished with the rim finished in ornate metalwork. I have even seen a few covered in stretched seamless untanned leather with very short hair – bull scrotum.

Lastly I want to mention the TORTAS FRITAS pronounced tor'-tahs free'-tahs. Literally translated it means fried cakes but it is really nothing more than fried wheat dough and is exactly like the Mexican sopaipilla. It is served the same way, with honey, and is almost always available, around the clock, in Uruguayan households. If one visits a Uruguayan in his home and is not offered tortas fritas, he must not be held in high regard.

CHAPTER ONE

Stranger in a Strange Land

Able seaman Patrick Colman sat alone in the busy sun filled plaza of Montevideo. He was young and fit, although a bit on the slender side. Since most of the inhabitants of this relatively new city were of European stock, he would have blended in well, except he had some striking differences.

For one thing, he had the red hair common to people of the Emerald Isle, not the bright orange variety, but the darker kind tending toward a deep reddish brown. It framed a face that, by most of the world's standards of the day, had to be judged as handsome. Its features would allow him to remain so even as he aged into his later years. These characteristics alone would have set him apart from the rest of the people in the plaza, but as an English sailor, he also wore his uniform – the dress blues.

His bench faced the great cathedral, and except for an occasional movement of his head, Colman sat perfectly still. The casual observer might have supposed him to be napping, or at the least in a semi-trancelike state, devoid of any active thought.

But his mind was racing.

Colman made his trip to the plaza every day—expressly to spend time in the cathedral. Recent events had troubled him so deeply that he felt he now required whatever consolation and comfort the cathedral might provide.

On a previous day, as he sat in his now familiar pew, he glanced up from his thoughts and saw a young woman turn to leave. Her shoulder length hair was a deep black, so common to the Mediterranean nations – black like a raven's and just as lustrous, but her face was as fair as any in England.

Colman was immediately taken aback as she walked up the aisle. Perhaps "taken aback" was a term far too mild. He was stunned. She was the most striking woman he had ever seen.

Immediately he knew that his vision would haunt him for days—perhaps weeks to come. But he had the maturity to know that his mind would soon store her beautiful image mercifully in some recess, to be drawn upon from time to time throughout his life only as a pleasant memory of the past. *Two ships passing in the night,* he thought to himself.

And that might have been the case had he only seen her that one time. But the next day she was at the cathedral again. In the following weeks, Colman came to realize the woman was a regular visitor – as regular as he. Very quickly he adjusted his own schedule to coincide with hers.

So now he sat waiting on the plaza bench for her arrival. He had not been aware of it at first, but soon it was undeniable. She was becoming an obsession. She was the fire that now had his mind racing while he sat so quietly.

Although not a zealot, certainly by Navy standards, Colman could still be described as a religious man. He often considered that someone might have been set aside in the eternal scheme of things expressly to share his life; set aside, perhaps, even before the foundations of the world were put in place.

But were these ponderings actually based in theology or simply some personal wishful lunacy. Did they have their origins in Christian religion or were they vestiges of earlier classical beliefs that placed so much stock in "the fates"?

Yet there was enough scriptural evidence. Colman fully understood that much of the basis for his beliefs came straight from Milton's "Paradise Lost". Written a century and a half earlier, he now questioned whether Milton had been inspired or simply wrote a good story.

He was being foolish, he suddenly thought, and he became disgusted for having allowed himself to become a victim of his own hopeful desires. He determined right then to set such thoughts aside.

But what if it were true?

What if providence had carried him to a different world in another hemisphere to realize all the things God intended for him? Were that true, should he now turn his back on it? Surely he would regret the decision for the rest of his life.

So he sat in the agony of his thoughts. Then, from nowhere, he was delivered from his pain. Without knowing how, all his hopes seemed suddenly possible. Now in the warm afternoon, his thoughts of her prompted a smile.

*   *   *

The brilliant sunlight that filled the large open plaza was a striking contrast to how gray it had been in the dreary days of the previous four months. The coming of spring, now coupled with his thoughts of this woman, made the world suddenly beautiful and full of promise. Colman watched the parishioners enter and leave the cathedral. Anxiously he hoped that soon the woman would appear.

And then—there she was. As he watched her approach the portico, Colman wondered what might have affected her so deeply that she took time each day to come. Privately he hoped the English were not a part of it.

He watched her walk into the cathedral. To prevent others from suspecting that he waited in the plaza just for her, Colman remained on the bench for what he thought to be an appropriate amount of time. Then he also arose and went in.

The woman was kneeling in one of the front pews, passing the beads of her rosary through her fingers. Colman genuflected and moved to "his" own pew more to the rear.

He offered a quick and trite little prayer, his conscience admittedly ashamed. Reasons for his visits to the house of God had now changed somewhat. No longer did he come to worship only, and he was certain the Almighty was aware of it.

Colman sat back in his pew, meditating. He was pleased that, for the moment, he was capable of keeping his thoughts worthy of the scrutiny of the Lord. But soon his mind began to roam from things spiritual back to his world now, so foreign to the one he knew only a year ago, and back to the people of Montevideo.

Their customs were so different from the English. They were Spanish, but no longer really Spanish. There was something in the Americas that transformed colonials into peoples of entirely different races and heritages. And they became different from each other according to the region in which they lived. In the places where the Europeans actively intermarried with the natives, the populace had mutated into entirely new breeds—mongrel perhaps by European standards. But each was destined to be unique, and in some ways hardier than its predecessors, as a mixed breed dog or horse might be hardier than his thoroughbred parents.

It was how quickly the cultures had changed into something no longer European that had amazed Colman.

As to be expected, the indigenous people had their influence on this new culture. The colonists readily adopted much of their clothing, ate their food, and incorporated many of their words into their own vocabulary.

World trade had also influenced the local dress on the Rio de la Plata. Local cattlemen, called gauchos, were very fond of their bombachas, baggy woolen trousers brought in on ships from Turkey. Whatever the original intent had been for the garment, its hardiness and comfort made it quite appropriate for the working of cows.

Colman forced his conscience back to present surroundings once again. He gazed upon the sculptured saints and icons around the cathedral and again he found comfort. Here an Irishman had more in common with the locals than with his mates. He was Catholic and so were they. The cathedral was not overly done by baroque European standards. The architecture could still be identified as Mediterranean, but its austerity was akin to the Irish and Colman liked that too.

The woman rose now and slowly began to make her way to the exits in the rear. Colman watched her from the corner of his eye. After she had passed, he waited only a few seconds more. Then he rose to follow her.

Outside the building, he paused briefly to build the courage he would require to approach her directly. It appeared he had all the time he needed as he watched her tarry in the plaza. But now he became concerned that he would not be able to find the courage he so desperately sought. However, not following through frightened him even more, and this new panic caused him suddenly to call out to her.

"Senorita!"

The woman turned and stared at him, but she said nothing.

"That is, senorita, I presume."

She turned back quickly and began to walk away.

"Please," Colman begged.

The woman paused, and then slowly turned once again to face him.

"Is that the limit of your Spanish, Englishman?" she asked.

"Please, senorita. May I speak with you?"

She stood in silence for what seemed to be at least a minute, obviously in thought. It was unnerving. But then she nodded. "Only for a moment," she said.

"Shall we sit?" he asked.

"No!"

The response was abrupt and brutal. A cold wave of new self doubt flowed through Colman. Then she softened her reply.

"I do not know you", she said. "It is only proper that we remain as we are."

"I truly beg your forgiveness," he began, "but I visit the cathedral quite regularly, and I have noticed that you too come here often."

The woman now seemed startled. "You have been watching me?" she asked.

"Only from a distance, and only because I find it curious as to why someone as young as you would come to the cathedral so often," Colman lied.

The woman stared at the ground and said nothing.

"I am seaman Paddy, that is, Patrick Colman," he volunteered, "of His Majesty's ship *Vigilance*." Colman thought he saw a faint smile cross her lips.

"Patricio?" the woman responded.

"That's right."

The woman looked at him intently. Paddy felt it might yet be too impetuous to ask her name, so he waited. After another uncomfortable period she again spoke. "My name is Tereza," she said. "Tereza Ferrando."

"That is a beautiful name," Paddy said. Inwardly he winced at his awkwardness and how silly his words seemed.

Tereza blushed. "I must go," she said.

"May I speak with you again?" he asked brashly.

Once again Tereza was slow to respond.

"Yes, I believe so," she finally answered.

Paddy watched as Tereza walked down the side street. Along the way she turned back once and smiled at him.

*   *   *

In the opening years of the nineteenth century, the demand had been great in England for teachers of the French language. Students ranged from the brightest of the diplomatic corps to the lowest of the Royal Navy—the average able seaman. Everyone believed a working knowledge of the language might serve him well in a new Europe, forever changed by the revolutionary French.

But French classes were full and the cost was always high. Paddy became one of a smaller group, then, who selected a less sure path and began studying Spanish. Whether Spain was to be an ally of the English or the French, he believed a knowledge of Spanish might be useful in his future on the high seas. It might even influence a possible assignment to warmer climates, maybe even the Indies. Now on the Rio de la Plata, he was happy he had made the decision. Here now he had the opportunity to apply what he had learned with actual Spanish speakers.

His efforts were also bringing him other benefits. Though Colman was definitely not a linguist, his new abilities helped him become a part of the small staff of the *Montevideo Star*. The English established the newspaper (the first ever in Montevideo, as it turned out) to help with public relations and counter adverse propaganda. This assignment allowed Paddy and his coworkers the opportunity to spend much more time in town than the rest of the crew. When winter came and Antarctic storms rolled in, the newspapermen suddenly found it necessary to spend even more time at the press (and the warm building) rather than return to the cold damp ship.

The assignment was also what had allowed Paddy to attend mass regularly. The surroundings were comforting and the mass was just as it had been on the emerald isle – down to each Latin word.

Now on his way back from the cathedral and Tereza, it took Paddy only ten minutes to reach the print shop. Already his co-workers were laboring at their tasks.

"Good of you to join us, Mr. Colman." The sarcasm came from James Burke. Burke had hair the color of Paddy's, but he wasn't Irish. Actually no one really knew exactly what Burke's origins were. He was a handsome man, though not nearly so good looking as Paddy, and he was slightly heavy, his large frame covered with solid muscle.

"My apologies, sirs," Paddy replied. "I shall surely try not to make tardiness a habit."

Robert Driscoll, the other member of this technical triumvirate, chimed in. "The truth is you are our fastest typesetter, Paddy. The sooner you are here the earlier we can all retire."

"Were that really true, Bobby, I dare say you would not speak to me in the callous tones I am presently subject to." Paddy said.

No one called Driscoll Robert. He was Bobby to everyone. He had a boyish face and dirty blond hair. He was plain and slightly built. And he was a good friend. He just seemed like a Bobby.

"Oh it is true!" Burke assured Paddy. "And your feeble responses won't get you off so lightly. You are spending far more time at the cathedral now than ever before. You're not becoming holy on us, are you?"

"Do you never question the nature of things, Jimmy? Do you never feel the need to ask the Lord for just a small bit of guidance in your life?"

"I am a sailor in His Majesty's Navy." Burke replied. "I've all the guidance I need."

Paddy smiled. Among the crew, Burke would be the last to call himself a sailor in His Majesty's Navy. Of all the lamentations men voiced over having been "shanghaied" into the navy, his was the loudest and most frequent – so much so that Paddy worried he might at some time be thrown into the brig.

Burke's story was also the most unique. While the others claimed to have been deceived in one fashion or another in London or a port city in England (usually when they were drunk in some public house) Burke said he had been seized off an American merchant ship on the high seas.

The English were known for the practice of taking the sailors they needed from foreign vessels. The claim was that the Navy was taking back deserters, and most of the time they were. But the Navy always took what it needed and sometimes the supply of deserters simply was not there. Many innocent men who had never set foot in England previously had been "impressed" this way.

And Burke might have been one of them. His accent was definitely not English, at least not from the wharves nor any of the coastal towns, nor from the north. It didn't ring of the traditional Scottish, Irish, or Welsh either. He had been in the Navy long enough to absorb enough of the English ring that one might identify him as an Englishman, but it just wasn't quite there. No one could really determine what his origins were.

"Do you not think our little paper would be more successful were we to print it in Spanish?" Paddy asked.

"We already have a greater circulation than we imagined we ever would," Driscoll said. "Besides, we don't have all the necessary type, what with the tilded n's and the accented vowels."

"I imagine the Spanish could muddle through the print without tildes and accents," Paddy laughed.

"Well then, maybe soon we could print a special Spanish edition. But you will have to draw double duty – translating and typesetting," Driscoll joked.

"It would be an honor," Paddy said.

"So, what is it really that keeps you from the shop, Paddy?" Driscoll inquired. "You haven't stumbled on the Dons' hidden stash of gold, have you?"

Paddy's reply was quick.

"Damn it, Bobby!" he yelled. "It would be well for you both to get out of this stinking little hole from time to time and discover the city! After months of numbing cold, we've actually had a number of very pleasant days. Today was most glorious! If you'll take time to look out the window, gentlemen, you will find that the spring is wonderful"

"It was a nice day," Jimmy replied thoughtfully. "I would think the more glorious days of the season are still yet to . . ."

He halted abruptly.

"Paddy, are you involved?"

Paddy thought for a moment; despite his hopes he really wasn't, and it would have been simpler just to say no, But Burke's question caught him off guard—and he took a little too much time to think. He realized his extended silence was as good as a confession.

"I hope to be," he said.

"Watch yourself, Paddy." Driscoll warned. "If the captain catches wind of this you'll be confined to the ship."

"And what kind of a Navy permits a man to pass time with prostitutes but will not allow him a legitimate sweetheart?" Paddy retorted.

"The English navy kind," Burke replied. "The captain believes you can get in trouble with sweethearts."

" . . . and not with prostitutes?"

"Well that would be trouble of a different sort . . . and not so long term."

"The type is set!" Paddy announced with a bit of resentment in his voice. "I'm going back to the *Vigilance*." On his way out, he closed the door with a little more force than usual.

"We would do well to keep this our little secret," Driscoll said. "We won't find another typesetter nearly as quick as Paddy."

"Agreed," Burke nodded.

*   *   *

Paddy sat in the plaza at what was becoming his customary bench early in the afternoon of the following day. He was somewhat content. His first conversation with la Senorita Ferrando had turned out better than he had expected.

Still, there was enough worrisome content in what had been said to cause him an uncomfortable night. Sleeplessly he rehearsed in his mind how he would greet her again. He practiced many different approaches and tried to imagine what her responses might be. In almost every case, the outcome was bad.

He began to worry, if in hindsight, she might have found him far too forward. He knew Spanish customs and manners were very different from the English and in many ways much more restrictive, especially when a young man wanted to meet a young woman. He understood fairly well their system of chaperones.

Now, as he lie in his bed and had time to ponder what he had done, it was becoming obvious that he had been a complete bumbling idiot the day before. As the night progressed, he invented new demons of the mind. Now he felt strongly that he should be cautious with Tereza and take things much more slowly, but then he knew he could not. His deepest fear was that he knew the *Vigilance* would not stay in port long enough to allow him to follow the proper Hispanic protocol.

Fortunately, as it usually does, the light of day chased most of the demons away. One fear was dispelled when, at her usual hour, Tereza again arrived at the cathedral.

She remained in the plaza for some time but never appeared to look his way even once. Then, at the steps in front of the doorway, she finally turned, looked directly at Paddy, smiled, and immediately entered the building.

"What was the significance of that?" Paddy asked himself. He decided it would be better for the moment not to go in. He spent his time on the bench still searching for the right thing to say. He realized he was no surer of himself now than he had been the entire night before. When Tereza finally came out, he still had not come to a resolution.

She paused and looked his direction again.

Paddy remained seated but nodded slightly.

Tereza turned and took several steps toward her home.

Then she stopped, turned, and looked at him again.

Of course, you fool! Paddy thought to himself in disgust. *A Spanish lady isn't simply going to saunter over to you.*

Paddy rose and walked over to where she stood. "I beg your pardon, Senorita Ferrando," he said.

"How are you today, Mr. Colman?" she asked.

"Oh, I'm fine. And how are you?"

"Fine, thank you".

The formalities were most awkward and Paddy searched for some better words. "Uh, would you like to go over to a bench and sit down?"

"No thank you. Not at this time."

Paddy wondered if he had actually winced. "Forgive me for being so clumsy, ma'am, but I simply do not understand your customs . . ."

Tereza interrupted him, "When the English seized Montevideo many friends were killed."

The abrupt change of subject took Paddy by surprise, but he recognized this immediately as a matter that had to be addressed.

"I am so sorry ma'am. Me and my mates, we only follow orders." He thought for a moment. "Were any of those friends someone special?"

"All were special," she said. "They were my friends. But there was one. I was very fond of him. And from that day I have hated the English."

This is not going well at all, Paddy thought.

"I imagine no one here likes us very much." he said, looking around at the people in the plaza. "Thank you for taking time to talk to me."

The expression on Tereza's face indicated that Paddy's remark both disappointed and frustrated her.

"You have been straightforward with me," she said. "So much, in fact, that it surprised me. When you said you had been watching me . . ."

"I said I had noticed you," Paddy interrupted. "I am sure of it. I chose my words carefully so not to offend you."

Tereza put a finger on his lips to silence him. It was startling, electric even, and it shut him up very effectively. She looked quickly over the plaza as if to see if anyone had been watching. When she was sure no one had, she put the finger to her own lips.

Paddy was speechless and amazed at how effectively her message was communicated.

"The truth is I had also taken notice of you," Tereza confessed. "It was odd to see an English sailor in a Catholic cathedral, and I wanted to believe that this was the only reason I found you interesting. But in my heart, I knew I would have noticed you anyway. You are not an ugly man and I thought I could see that you were also different from the rest."

Paddy wanted to stop her and say he was just like the rest, but he couldn't. Not now when it seemed he had an inroad.

"You see how you have conflicted me. I do not know how I can explain an Englishman to my family," Tereza continued.

Paddy smiled broadly, "Then tell them I'm Irish."

Tereza scowled. "If we are to be friends, do not make fun of me. You have presented me with a very painful problem."

"But I am Irish!" Paddy insisted. "English mothers don't name their boys Patrick! That is why I come to the cathedral. I am also Catholic. Tell them I was abducted and forced into the English navy."

Tereza raised an eyebrow. "And would that be true?"

"All except the last part," Paddy laughed. "And even that is almost true."

"What is your family like?" Tereza asked.

"I have no family – or none that I know of. I was orphaned at a very tender age. I was told that in Ireland my father fought against the English. He paid for his folly with not only his own life but that of my mother as well. If I have any brothers or sisters I am not aware of it."

"Is Patrick Colman your name from birth?"

"I believe it to be," Paddy replied. "It is the only name I have ever known."

"Well then, maybe someday you can find the brothers or sisters you may have. If the church in Ireland is as the church here, there must be records," Tereza volunteered.

"That would be many years down the road and many thousands of miles away," Paddy said. "Right now my life belongs to the navy."

The sentence was more revealing than Paddy would have wanted and Tereza turned away.

"We are foolish believing we can be friends. When the English leave you will be gone—and I will have only a memory."

Then Tereza stopped.

Now it was she who felt she had said far too much. It was not right to reveal so much of one's feelings too quickly. From Paddy's point of view, however, she had said just the right thing. He could feel himself becoming more attached to this woman with every breath.

"It will not be so," Paddy assured her. "I would return when my enlistment is done. Tereza, you are the finest thing I have ever set eyes on."

It might have been better had Paddy avoided his last comment. It was obvious the instant he said it and it was confirmed by the quick look of rebuke Tereza gave him.

"You are an English sailor," Tereza retorted, "and you know nothing of me as a person. How many women in how many ports do you say such things to? Who knows, the church may be as good a place as any to find women. And a woman who needs the comfort of the saints, one who is hurting inside, surely she would be the most vulnerable!"

Both understood the stakes in this fledgling relationship. They began to see that both were desirous to make it work. But the possibility that the Royal Navy could leave at any moment and Paddy with it made them hurry their questions and express their fears that, in different times, would have been left for much later.

At this moment Tereza was certain it was she who had pushed issues much too far. Paddy indeed perceived a side of her he wasn't sure he could enjoy. She seemed to have a temper. For now, however, he would attribute it to her frustration with him.

"In the orphanage I was raised by nuns," Paddy said softly, "and one thing they did was teach me moral standards. As yet I have not known a woman. And while certainly there are many English sailors who frolic in every port, and zealously strive to keep their reputations tarnished, surprisingly there are many of us who do not."

Tears formed in Tereza's eyes, but she was able to keep them from flowing down her face. "Forgive me, Mr. Colman," she said. "It appears the sadder experiences of my life are, at this moment, revealing themselves in my outburst."

Paddy reached for her hand. She allowed him to take it, but still only briefly.

"I know we have only spoken to each other these last two days," Paddy said, "and then just for a short while. But in those few things we shared I feel I am coming to know you quite well. I would feel more at ease if you called me Paddy."

Tereza looked around once again. "Maybe we should leave the plaza. Will you walk me home?"

"Surely," he responded.

Paddy took the street side as he walked alongside her. Desperately he longed for her to take his arm but he knew it was too early even for that. From what had transpired in the plaza, however, he comforted himself in believing that perhaps Tereza also longed to take it.

"Well, then, Patrick," she said. "You may call me Tereza."

"Tereza!?"

"Or Tere, that is short for Tereza."

"Terry! Just like the English," Paddy smiled. "It may take a while before I become comfortable calling you Terry."

Tereza returned his smile. "Tereza will do."

"How will your father feel about me?" Paddy asked. "Is there any chance I might find favor with him?"

"You will not have to worry about that," Tereza replied. "My father is dead. It is my brother you must win over."

"How old were you when your father died?"

"It wasn't that long ago. Before he died, Luis, my brother, was a very happy boy. Unfortunately the burden of responsibility that fell on him has made him bitter."

Paddy was unsure whether it was better to deal with Tereza's brother rather than with a father. He found it wise to learn as much as he could about him.

"For a while he tried take my father's place," Tereza continued, "as a gaucho, but the estanciero was not pleased with his work and he dismissed Luis. Then we came to Montevideo where my uncle got him a job working at the docks."

"You are not from Montevideo?"

"I am from Minas. It is a town some distance east of here in the hills."

Tereza spoke for most of the rest of the walk home. It was not a long conversation for the house was not too far from the plaza. When the two arrived at her street, she asked Paddy to follow her no further, so he watched from the corner as she walked to her house. Once the door closed behind her, Paddy turned and made his way back to the *Montevideo Star*.

*   *   *

The viceroyalty of La Plata was nowhere near the homogeneous state Paddy had imagined it would be. Geographically it was huge, spreading from Brazil and Alto Peru down to Cape Horn and from the Andes to the South Atlantic.

Politically it was divided into provinces along lesser geographical features. Still those features were significant enough to separate one people from another, at least to the extent that different cultures had evolved. In some cases the separation (and therefore the difference in culture) was only slight, but where the boundary was as wide as the Rio de la Plata and as swift as the Rio Uruguay, the differences could be considerable.

Much of the difference was only a mindset. But it had developed over decades and was just as real as any difference which was visible.

The easternmost province of the viceroyalty lay between the Atlantic Ocean and the Rio Uruguay and was called La Banda Oriental—the Eastern Strip. Its inhabitants were known simply as Orientales, or Easterners, and Montevideo was their capital city.

The city occupied a prominent peninsula on the east side of a deep and compact bay. The hill for which the city was named rose on the shore opposite the peninsula and was topped by a small fortress. Outwardly Montevideo may have appeared well protected, but aside from another small fort in the city located at the bay's entrance, its only wall cut across the base of the peninsula, separating the city from the rest of the mainland.

The other exposures, the bay, the inlet, and the Rio de la Plata, were guarded only by water, and as the English proved, Montevideo was vulnerable from the sea.

Paddy had been captivated by the city. It was an unusual mix of rudimentary frontier and civilized Europe. There could be no doubt that this was a new city. Plumbing was primitive compared to that of the older European communities. But being new, much of the past mistakes of the old world could be avoided. The cathedral's bell towers dominated the skyline. Paddy knew, however, that with time, as in Europe, larger buildings would one day obscure the sentinels.

He paused when he approached the door of the print shop, not quite ready for what he knew awaited him on the other side. *Well, let's face the music,* he thought. Then he went in.

Burke started in on him right away.

"It is so very kind of you to call on us, your Lordship," he called out.

"Once again, sirs, my apologies," Paddy said softly. "I am afraid I have fallen subject to another glorious day.

Bobby Driscoll looked up from his work but said nothing.

"You really must find some time to enjoy a little of it," Paddy continued. There is not enough appreciation in this world for the curing tonic of springtime."

"I know the animals seem to like it," Driscoll said. Now he was no longer looking up and Paddy understood he was perturbed. "Could it be you have been influenced somewhat by their seasonal tendencies, Mr. Colman?"

Burke perceived Driscoll's displeasure too and sought to soften the atmosphere with a lighter remark that still addressed the issue Bobby had put on the table. "I see now why the captain is so against us having sweethearts," he interjected. "They tend to take us away from our work far too much. Prostitutes are much better."

"I will not even try to tread the profane roads you two wallow in," Paddy responded. "The lady I escorted home today is – well—a lady."

"Listen to him now!" Burke joked. "Saint Augustine himself, above all the hungers we lesser beings are subject to."

"That is not what I am not saying, Jimmy," Paddy replied. "But I find myself only able to consider this woman on the highest and purest of levels."

"And you are telling us you have not thought once about how nice she would be warming your bed," Driscoll inquired.

"I'm telling you that what I have considered is how nice it would be to have her with me, constantly by my side, and as my wife."

"As your wife!?" Burke laughed. "Paddy, this is Bobby and Jimmy you're talkin' to.

Paddy understood the intent of the message. Burke had just accused him of being less than honest with them and Paddy responded with a look of wounded incomprehension. "Have you never held anything so pure and in such high regard that you dared not think any evil of it for fear it might shatter like fine crystal?" he asked.

"My word," Burke cried in mock astonishment. "It is the woman who's a bloody saint—worthy of the right hand of the Virgin herself."

"Shut your mouth," Driscoll scolded, "before you profane yourself! I do believe the man is serious – that or he's daft."

"I am serious," Paddy said resolutely, "and you're right, Jimmy. I suspect the woman is a saint."

"I fear you are headed for a bitter disappointment, Paddy," Burke counseled. "Even if this woman were all you imagine her to be, who can tell what the future holds for any of us in South America? We have but a shaky foothold on the continent at best."

"I believe we're here to stay," Paddy responded. "In all the British military, Popham and Beresford were the greatest examples of incompetence, and in spite of them we still took the cities. I think we would be in Buenos Aires yet had we better commanders. When the admiralty replaced Popham with Auchmuty it proved England's resolve to remain here. And she needs to be here if only for the commerce, to say nothing of the wealth the land holds."

"Wealth?" Driscoll remarked dubiously. "It is pretty much understood all the gold is in Peru."

"Who is to say?" Paddy asked, "And besides, there is more to wealth than gold. It is a wide unexplored land, and there may be spices and plants here that will yield a man a fortune."

"We already have markets for tobacco and potatoes". Driscoll said.

"And chocolate, and sweet potatoes!" Paddy added.

"That's true," Driscoll agreed, "but I don't like sweet potatoes—and neither do the locals apparently. They seem to be preferred more on the North American continent."

"Nevertheless, Paddy's point is right," said Burke. "There are fruits and flavors in the tropics that are marvelous, but they do not travel well. If you are going to be a wealthy man you have to get the product to Europe before it rots. Now that is where the money would be."

"Even if what all you say is true," Driscoll said, "it may be a difficult task to wrest the land away from the Dons. Surely you have not forgotten that our first encounter with the locals was supposed to be largely ceremonial while they handed us the keys to the city?"

Paddy ignored the comment. "General Blackhouse should arrive here within weeks to reinforce Beresford, and if they still can't get the job done, General Whitelock is coming with even more men," he reasoned. "Surely now that must indicate the extent of England's resolve."

"Regardless of her resolve, England's chief concern must still be Napoleon," Burke argued, "and the fighting here will not get any easier. Do you think it is the Spanish we are fighting in South America?"

"Well, of course!" Paddy responded.

Jimmy did not say anything at first, and he appeared to be gathering his thoughts. Bobby decided to drop out of the banter altogether and just sit back and enjoy it. He had already concluded he was not at his friends' level in discussions such as these. He was just not as quick.

When he revealed this opinion to Paddy on an earlier occasion, Paddy kindly told him that he simply did not take the time to observe things around him. Paddy might have been sincere, but Bobby wasn't buying it.

Now as he was waited for Jimmy to say something, he glanced over at Paddy, and Paddy, surprisingly, seemed somewhat puzzled this time.

"Fifty years ago the English threw the French out of Canada." Burke began.

"I do not need a lesson in recent history," Paddy remarked.

"Oh, yes you do", Burke countered. "And when you see what we are truly up against, I am willing to bet your enthusiasm will be on the wane."

A look of slight concern now crossed Paddy's brow, and he settled back in earnest to hear what Burke had to say.

"Everyone believes the English fought the French in that conflict. In truth, the war was fought between the English and their allies and the French and their allies." Burke explained.

"Of course, the colonials. But they were English and French," Paddy said.

"And what of the thousands of indigenous people who also fought on both sides?" Burke asked.

"Subjects of the English and French crowns, depending on whose side they were on," Driscoll volunteered.

"Perhaps so," Burke said. "But all, be they colonial or indigent, considered themselves apart from the Europeans. They were Americans. They did not consider the conflict really theirs. It was the Thirty Years War spilling over onto their continent."

"Then why did they fight?" Paddy asked.

"Because, in part, they still did consider themselves loyal subjects," Burke replied, "but mostly, and this is the key, they fought to defend their families and their way of life."

Paddy thought for a minute. "And you believe it is the same here?" he asked.

"Ask your lady," Burke replied. "See if she considers herself Spanish. I dare say she has never set foot on the Iberian Peninsula; neither she, nor her parents, nor even possibly, her grandparents. She harbors no thought of returning "home" someday. This is home. She is an American."

"She will say she is Oriental," Paddy said.

"Oriental of course, then Platense, maybe then American. Last and most definitely least, if at all, Spanish." Burke stated resolutely. "This war with Napoleon has accelerated Spain's declining control in the Americas. And once the people here discover they can govern themselves, you will see firsthand just what loyal Spanish subjects they really are."

Paddy sat back in his chair and studied Burke in a new light. There was no mistaking it now. Everything he had claimed about his impressment had to be true, otherwise how could he have been able to speak so resolutely and with such authority on this matter? Jimmy too was an American.

"Then the fighting here can only become more intense," Paddy said.

"That's right," Burke replied.

CHAPTER TWO

Marooned

Two weeks had passed since Paddy first had the courage to introduce himself to Tereza. Since that day he came to the plaza early and waited. If he had been successful before in concealing his fondness for her, by now all discretion surely was lost.

The two could be seen entering and leaving the cathedral at the same time. Some days Paddy would even accompany Tereza back to her home. Frequent visitors to the plaza now had ample opportunity to see them together.

Secretly Paddy wondered whether some grief might come to her because of what he was doing now. If so, she would never tell him. He was certain of that.

As if on schedule, Tereza rounded the corner of the cathedral and came into full view. Paddy could almost sense her presence now even before he could see her, or perhaps it was simply that he perceived the soft unique cadence of her footsteps.

Yet he had heard that husbands and wives, in long and happy marriages, often developed a sixth sense. They anticipated the other's thoughts and moves quite accurately. There were times that they felt impending dangers to the family. It was even said, in some cases, that wives of sailors at sea knew the very moment their husbands had met their deaths, even if half a world away.

Once again Paddy felt foolish. He still was looking for a silly sign. Now he was irritated for allowing himself to continue to enter into these idle daydreams with no definite purpose. Abruptly he dismissed all this current line of thinking.

The two barely knew each other, hardly long enough for such phenomena to occur, if they ever did at all. It was more likely he glanced so frequently toward the corner where Tereza would appear that she could not possibly surprise him, even if she had made a conscious effort to do it.

But over time, a pattern developed, unplanned and unrehearsed, but as precise as if it had been. Without hesitation, Tereza would glance Paddy's way when she arrived, and smile. Then she would proceed on into the cathedral. Paddy would wait a minute or two longer, still seated at his bench appearing to read the latest edition of the "Star".

It was a weak ruse at best. Surely the citizens in the plaza already guessed he knew the "Star's" contents far too well to take that much interest in it.

As she always had, Tereza still walked to the front, genuflected, and knelt in a forward pew, praying fervently. And just as before, Paddy sat some distance behind in what had become "his" pew to offer up his own prayers.

But where before his prayers had been dutiful yet somewhat hollow, now they were deep and meaningful. Now he begged for forgiveness and sought redemption from his sins. Now he asked for guidance and the strength he needed to become a man worthy of this woman. He prayed for Tereza and her family. He prayed for her and himself, that they might one day be at ease with each other and perhaps enjoy the mass in the same pew.

Never before had he understood how compelling the need for prayer could be – or how it would help ease his deepest of fears. Yet as he prayed, a dark recent fear emerged still from somewhere deep within – the fear that in the end, all would be for naught. The two would be separated forever by forces neither could possibly overcome.

Paddy looked up. Today Tereza remained in the cathedral until the priests arrived for mass. He wondered what had caused her to stay. Could it be she had additional prayers to be offered or was it her need to partake of the sacraments? Could it be she was struggling with some of the same emotions that now tormented him so terribly?

Whatever it was, he suddenly realized it actually made him happy. This would allow him to enjoy a little more time with her.

After communion, he accompanied Tereza once again down the now familiar street toward her home. This time, however, Paddy decided to put forth a new question, one that had been bothering him for some time.

"Tereza," he asked. "Does your family know about me now?"

Tereza smiled and looked straight ahead. "Oh yes," she replied. "All of Montevideo knows about you."

Paddy was stunned. A few seconds passed before he continued. "And how do they feel about me?" he asked.

"It is me they are not happy with," she responded honestly. "It has nothing to do with you, except, of course, that you are an English sailor."

Paddy reached for the right words but they were not there. Finally he said the only thing he could think to say.

"I'm sorry."

Tereza stopped. She turned and put her hand on Paddy's cheek. "It could be worse," she said. "For an Englishman I think they actually do like you – a little."

"What can I do to improve my situation?" Paddy asked.

"Nothing. For now you must remain obscure and let me continue to overwhelm them with all your good qualities," Tereza said.

"My good qualities?"

"Oh you have a few – the rest I have to invent," she laughed.

"Invent?" Now Paddy was a little put out. "Well, you know I actually do have more than a few. You just have to know me better to discover what they might be," he insisted.

"Well, maybe I can begin today," Tereza smiled.

"Today?"

"My brother has gone to Minas to help a man with his cattle. My mother went with him so she could visit some of her friends there. Today we will have some time alone," she said.

Paddy began to wonder. Maybe this woman was not quite so saintly as he had imagined. Well, he would not have any part in proving it otherwise. He would not destroy his world as he had now created it.

"Are you asking me to spend some time with you?" he asked.

"Of course," she replied.

Paddy swallowed. "Tereza, when we get to your house, I cannot go in."

"You see," Tereza giggled. "I'm learning more about you already. Had you acted differently, you surely would not have gone inside. I would not have permitted it. Now I believe maybe I can trust you."

Paddy looked up. He had been so absorbed in the conversation that he had taken no notice of where they were. They had already arrived at Tereza's house.

"I only want to share some yerba mate with you," Tereza said. "That is all. Won't you please come in?"

Paddy thought for a moment, then responded.

"Very well".

Tereza unlocked the door. In minutes she had a fire going in the masonry oven built right into the wall. Presently she set a teapot on one of the grated openings on top. Paddy had fully expected some of the smoke to spill through those openings into the room, but the oven drafted so well that all the smoke rose up the chimney.

"Won't the dock foreman miss your brother?" Paddy asked.

"I don't believe so," Tereza replied. "For some reason the work at the docks is very slow right now."

Of course! Paddy suddenly realized. *The fleet must be approaching.*

Tereza had revealed more in that one sentence than the Royal Navy would have wanted anyone to know. And only Paddy was in a position to put all the pieces together and understand the significance of it. The reconquest of Buenos Aires was imminent, and to control the flow of information, the fleet would be stopping all merchant vessels on the high seas.

In its war against Napoleon, Britain's nearest ally in South America was Portugal. Paddy guessed correctly that the ships being detained were either sitting at anchor in the Atlantic waiting for permission to continue on into the Rio de la Plata or they had been redirected to the Brazilian city of Porto Alegre.

Steam began making the teapot sing, and soon Tereza brought it into the small parlor with two mates and a platter with what appeared to be little biscuits. Paddy was impressed by the grace she maintained in carrying all she had.

She put the platter and teapot on a small table beside him and handed him one of the mates. It looked as though it was filled to the brim with bits of dry grass. It smelled like it too. Each gourd had a solid silver straw called a bombilla tipped with a gold mouthpiece. She poured hot water into his gourd until it covered the "grass".

"You must wait a while before you sip the yerba mate," she said.

Paddy nodded.

"Soon I also must also go to Minas and visit my aunts and cousins," Tereza said.

"How soon?" Paddy asked.

"Not right away," she smiled, "but soon. Besides my family, I have a really good friend there I must see."

"Is he someone I need to worry about?"

Tereza laughed.

"You silly man," she said. "My friend is a woman, Ana Monterroso. She lives nearby and we have been friends almost since the first day I came to Montevideo, but she has gone to Minas to visit her novio. He is the man Luis is helping."

Paddy and Tereza spent the next half hour talking about Tereza's family in Minas. He could feel himself steadily becoming drawn more to her and he longed to kiss her. He wondered what she was thinking of him. Outwardly there was not the least indication that she felt as strongly. Then suddenly, she began asking questions that showed she might.

"Paddy, How do you feel about this place?" she asked.

"About your house?"

"No, about the city; about our country."

"I like them very much, Except, where I come from, March is the first month of spring, so it has been difficult adjusting to the seasons of the southern hemisphere. And I didn't know it could get so cold here. I have never liked the cold. Not that I am unfamiliar with it. The cold is bone chilling both in Ireland and England."

"Do you miss Ireland?, Tereza asked.

"I only have a few faded memories of the place," but I remember it to be nice."

"And England?"

"Well, yes and no. England was both a blessing and a curse. I was already an orphan when I was four. An English officer stationed in Ireland took pity on me. It was he who had arranged for my care in a Catholic orphanage in London. Through his act of kindness, I was delivered from the sufferings that lay ahead for so many of my countrymen."

"What a kind considerate man!" Tereza commented.

"Yes, he was. But he died before I was fifteen and when I reached that age I was no longer allowed to stay in the orphanage. Those were the rules. They gave me some money but it was soon gone and I suddenly found myself struggling out on the streets of London. Then I was unwittingly 'recruited' into his majesty's navy."

"And they saved you!!??"

"I suppose," Paddy said. "At least I would not starve. But in the navy, the winters are especially bad. The ships are very cold and the sailors fight a continuous struggle to keep just some of their clothing dry.

He laughed. "But it always appears to be a losing effort. There were weeks when I wondered if I would ever wear anything warm and dry again in my lifetime."

"I cannot imagine having to live like that," Tereza said sympathetically.

"Well, I knew it had to get better, and when we sailed south to patrol off the coasts of Africa, I believed perhaps I would find the relief I was so desperately seeking."

Now Tereza let Paddy talk. He seemed to want to let her know a little more about himself and she hoped to discover along the way how he really felt about South America and what the English had done there.

"Through most of the journey my expectations had been fulfilled. It was only when I was assigned to duty on deck or up in the yardarms, during a storm, that I would get cold. Other than that I stayed warm."

"Did you see any action?" she asked.

"We sailed down the Atlantic and moved along the Gold and Ivory Coasts toward the Cape of Storms. But our encounters with the enemy were rare and always uneventful. The ships we saw quickly took to flight. I thought some could have been overtaken, but our pursuit always seemed half-hearted. Don't misunderstand me though; all of us on board were most grateful for this lack of combat."

"The Commodore kept the squadron lingering around the Cape for several weeks. Then suddenly, we sailed due west out into the South Atlantic. The quick departure from Africa was a total surprise and questions and rumors began to circulate. Am I boring you with all this?"

"No," Tereza smiled.

"Well, for all his faults, the old man always had the pulse of his crew. At last he revealed the true purpose of our mission. The lengthy maneuvers off the African coast were intended to dispel any possibility that local spies might surmise what the mission was. It was hoped they would be think the fleet had gone home or perhaps had sailed on into the Indian Ocean."

"The English high command believed the South Americans had come to despise decades of Spanish rule. If that were true, we all thought they would welcome the English as their liberators."

"But that was foolish!" Tereza finally said. "Why would anyone believe we would welcome the English?"

"Reports from informants indicated you might, but looking back on it now, it all does seem very silly. But that is what we believed. Of course, the joyous reception did not materialize. On the contrary, the battle for Buenos Aires lasted a full week before the city was subdued."

"And here in Montevideo, the fighting was unlike anything I had previously imagined. Sailors and marines in the streets were attacked by men, women, and servants alike fighting from the roofs of their houses."

"I was one of those," Tereza confessed. "Of course, most of the women did not go to the edge of the roof to fight, but we helped reload muskets and then, when the ammunition was gone, we carried things up to the roof to be thrown down. That is when my friend was killed, shot in the head. I cradled him in my lap and his blood flowed onto my skirt as I wept over him."

"Tereza, I'm so sorry!"

"Do not be! I missed him and I miss him still, but only as a dear friend. I thought I loved him, but now I see what I felt for him was not nearly what I feel for you now."

Paddy looked for the words, but now they all were awkward. "Since then, we have tried to build a good relationship with the people. The "Star" is a part of that. But our effort has become even more difficult since the English were driven out of Buenos Aires. We had to regroup in Montevideo. It has been far from the best of circumstances."

Tereza could sense Paddy was beginning to hurt inside. She had learned most of what she wanted to know so she changed the subject.

"Ana has not been too happy with her novio lately," she began. "It is a good relationship, but I honestly do not know how it is going to end. These last weeks he has been keeping himself current with the present situation in Buenos Aires," Tereza remarked.

Again Paddy was startled. Had the upcoming operation been discovered?

"He says the viceroyalty is anticipating much less support from Spain now in light of its difficulties with Napoleon," Tereza continued. "The possibility exists that we will be on our own for a while, at least until King Carlos is restored to the throne."

Paddy was relieved. The secret still appeared to be a secret. "And how does Luis feel about all that? He asked"

"He does not like it. The Porteños always have treated us Orientales as second class," Tereza said. "Our only redress was with the Peninsulares. But now if they cannot govern La Plata, we may be in for some hard times."

"It cannot be all that bad!"

"Perhaps not, but Luis believes Juan is right. Luis says he would have much more work here on the docks if it were not that Buenos Aires is the capital city of La Plata."

"And why is that?" Paddy asked.

"According to Luis, Montevideo is a perfect harbor. It is deep and sheltered and its approaches are not treacherous. He says Buenos Aires is just beach and shallows. They must build long wharves out into the water to accommodate the ships. Then they must rebuild them each time a strong pampero blows in from the south and knocks them down."

"Luis makes sense," Paddy commented. "Montevideo is also well protected from pirates with forts in the city and on the cerro."

"Ana's novio said that too," Tereza added.

Paddy's mind raced. Loss of commerce is a serious issue anywhere in the world. When the cause is a political one, the resentments that linger are not only understandable, they can boil over into outright conflict. He wondered what other issues might exist between the Orientales and the Porteños.

"Is there any smuggling?" Paddy asked.

"Oh yes," Tereza replied, "From Colonia to Maldonado – and beyond, but the ports on the Atlantic are less desirable and the conditions there much more unpredictable."

"If the English were in control, they would not be so stupid as to use Buenos Aires as their main port of call. Would the people here be happy for that?" Paddy inquired.

He was looking for any small assurance in an ocean of uncertainty. Soon confrontation between the English and the locals was almost certain once again. With it might come the end to the future Paddy now hoped might be possible. But Tereza's response to his question stung.

"Replace one European power for another? A colony will always be a servant to its mother country, whoever she is."

"But like a mother, she is there to protect the colony." Paddy retorted.

"Oh, is that true?" Tereza asked. "So where is Spain now?"

"There are good mothers and then there are bad ones." Paddy paused and took time to compose himself. "Tereza, I would rather that there be no contention between us. I care about you far too much."

"Take no mind of me," Tereza said. "We live now in an uncertain world. When I was a little girl things were always the same. I thought it would always be that way. Then when papa died, everything changed. Because of Napoleon, the Spanish have become more militant, and yet they are less capable of managing affairs or even protecting us. Then, when the English came, it seemed like the end of the world had come with them."

"But we can provide a stability to things, Tereza, and make life much more secure," Paddy contended.

"Who can say," Tereza went on. "Princess Carlotta is now married to the Portuguese heir to his throne, and we wonder if it might be the Brazilians who will rule over us next?"

"I wouldn't worry too much about the Portuguese, or the Spanish, not right now anyway. The French have overrun both their countries."

"You do not know what you are saying," Tereza argued. "Because of this war the Portuguese Royal Family, with the Princess Carlotta, are living in Rio de Janeiro. They have taken control there and appear to like it."

"They are here in the Americas?" Paddy asked.

"Right up the road," Tereza replied sarcastically.

Paddy rose and handed the mate to Tereza. "Miss Ferrando," he said. "I must take my leave. Please forgive the English for whatever pain we may have brought. I truly had hoped we all might have been able to realize a brighter future together." He took her hand and bent to kiss it.

Tereza deftly clasped the back of his neck and placed her mouth on his. It surprised Paddy completely, but he did not recoil. No—he meekly succumbed. A feeling of joy, contentment, and peace overwhelmed him. If it were possible and within his reach, he would have remained there for a very long time.

But Paddy knew it was not possible. Many events were quickly coming to pass that could easily destroy everything for everyone. He pulled away.

"Tereza," he said. "I believe I am in love with you."

"Tereza smiled but said nothing. Then Paddy turned and ran off down the street.

* * *

There was excitement in the print shop the following day. Paddy had decided it was best to stay quiet about what was happening now between him and Tereza. The boys probably thought he was progressing better with her than he actually was anyway. He would not be able to stay silent for long, however. It was not so much that Jimmy and Bobby would drag the facts out of him, but as the men worked, their conversation would make it necessary for him to reveal them.

"I suppose you are quite happy now, Mr. Colman, since it seems we three may not be going to Buenos Aires," Bobby snickered. Jimmy looked up with a grin.

"What are you talking about?" Paddy asked. "Is the mission cancelled?"

"You do not know? Paddy, if what we hear is true, this little band is indeed blessed above most," Bobby replied. "Beresford is leaving a small force here in Montevideo to keep the peace. Talk has it that he has ordered us to remain here too and keep the paper going so that an air of continuity might be maintained."

"And how long were you going to keep this from me?" Paddy asked.

"We honestly thought you knew," Jimmy chimed in. "If you could treat this post more like an assignment and less like an extended leave, maybe you would be around long enough to pick up a little on the scuttlebutt. Of all the men to have on a newspaper staff, you have to be the least informed on matters than any in the entire crew."

"On the other hand," Bobby laughed. "He probably is the best informed about what is happening among the natives."

"Aye, that he is," Jimmy agreed.

"Perhaps I am," Paddy said. "I can tell you there is more to our being in this part of the world than we have been told, and it could get a lot hotter than any of us know."

"What are you talking about?" Jimmy asked.

"I'm saying that old man Popham may have known a lot more than we gave him credit for," Paddy said. "The entire question as to who reigns in Iberia may be settled here in South America."

Bobby and Jimmy said nothing. Paddy was pleased with himself at how well he had stunned them both. "Right now the royal family of Portugal resides in Rio de Janeiro and the sister of the Spanish prince is with them, wife to the heir apparent," he said.

"How do you know all this, Paddy?" Bobby asked.

"Maybe it might be a good idea to be friends with the locals!" Paddy replied.

"So our little jaunt may not be such a sideshow, after all," Jimmy reasoned. "And that would better explain why Beresford and Whitelocke have come with so many reinforcements."

"It won't be a sideshow if we are successful," Paddy said. "England will have a future presence in South America for a long time to come. In all the world, here is where she holds the least influence. And yet all that could soon change."

"If we are successful here, and Nappy is defeated in Europe, we could go down in history as one of the major factors of this war," Bobby declared. "Of course if we are not successful, we will be considered only as a minor affair and soon forgotten. Have your local friends given you any idea as to how difficult this might be?"

"Do you think I discuss military secrets with them?" Paddy responded with some displeasure. "There is one thing though. All is not roses on the Rio de la Plata. The Porteños see themselves as the outright rulers of the viceroyalty, since their city is the capital. It does not sit well with the Orientales, and I imagine the feeling might be the same in the other provinces."

"Whether this dissention you describe is real or not, they will still unite against a common enemy," Jimmy assured them. "This won't be sweet."

*　*　*

Eight thousand miles away, President James Madison of the United States of America was meeting privately with James Monroe, his Secretary of State.

It was the secretary who had asked for the meeting, and it was he who spoke first regarding a matter that troubled him.

"Mr. President," Monroe began. "I have met with the Spanish ambassador and he is very concerned about current events in South America."

"What is happening in South America?" Madison asked.

"The ambassador reports that the British are there, on the Rio de la Plata," Monroe responded.

"That is not good news," Madison said. "What opinion do you draw from this?"

"Without more facts, it is difficult to come up with one strong solid opinion," Monroe replied.

"Of course. Let me ask then, why would the English take this course of action when they are so pushed by the French in other sectors? Do you suppose they might be taking advantage of the Spanish situation there in order to expand their empire?"

"It is hard to say, Mr. President," Monroe replied. "But that is not an unreasonable assumption."

"Napoleon has set Europe on its ear," Madison stated firmly, "but France's efforts with republicanism have not gone at all well. Still, her revolution has all the crowned heads worried. They wonder if what occurred in France might happen in any of their own kingdoms – could their necks be next?"

"It is most unfortunate for everyone that France could not fulfill her commitment to democracy," Monroe replied. "But to the extent we remain true, the world will still have one example that a republic is possible."

"What is happening in South America is most vexing," Madison commented. "At every turn the British appear to go out of their way to push us – and with impunity, from impressing our citizens into their navy to now securing this foothold on the Rio de la Plata."

"We are powerless to do much against them, Mr. President. Their navy can take them anywhere in the world and their military, in my opinion, is still unparalleled."

"Everything you say is correct," Madison said. "But we may not be so far removed as we think from being as capable ourselves. Our strong fleet of merchant vessels already travels the world. The capability the English have is within our reach. All we require is a little time – and the will."

"The will mostly to spend the money," Monroe laughed.

"We will have to find it sooner than later, I fear," Madison said. "The situation in the Americas is quickly becoming ripe for its people to free themselves. What road will they follow then—one of monarchy or one of democracy? Whatever they chose, once they are independent, they must be allowed to develop within their separate spheres—without fear of another European power coming in and taking over."

"I would not discredit those regions too much, sir. When they are free, it may be more difficult that it appears for any European power to reassert itself," Monroe said.

"You are probably right. What chance did the world give us in our own revolution? Still, it will be well for us to become strong – strong enough to help our neighbors should they require it. Until then, we must strengthen ourselves for our own selves' sake. We simply cannot allow England to continue pushing us around."

*   *   *

Paddy returned to the *Vigilance* late that afternoon with both Jimmy and Bobby. The ship was alive with the rumors of the day. It was known for certain now that the reinforcements needed had anchored off Maldonado. But they only remained long enough to recover what men were available there. Just a handful of soldiers were left in that coastal town to maintain order. The fleet was already on its way to Montevideo.

The operation had to move quickly now. The same sources that brought the news of the reinforcement's arrival at Maldonado could just as easily carry the news on to Buenos Aires. It was in this excited and somewhat confused climate that the three printers received a confirmation of their most welcomed news.

Jimmy notified the other two. "Well mates, what would be the best thing that could happen right now?" Jimmy asked, smiling.

"The Dons in Buenos Aires surrendered without a fight!" Bobby offered.

Jimmy looked a little perturbed. "Yes that would be great. It's not going to happen, though. I'm afraid this thing is going to be nasty." He paused and looked at Bobby and Paddy, smiling.

"Well?" Paddy asked. "Are we going or not?"

"It's been decided. We're definitely not going," Jimmy said.

"Jimmy, this is something you had best not be jesting about," Bobby threatened.

"Strike me down if I am," Jimmy laughed. Then he turned to Paddy. "Bobby and I can handle the paper, Paddy. Why don't you take this opportunity to spend some time with your lady?

41

"Are you being serious, Jimmy?" Paddy asked.

"Of course!"

"I don't know. I wouldn't feel right about this when at the same time others are going off to possibly get killed."

"Paddy," Jimmy reasoned, "this may be a Godsend. Can you think of a better opportunity?"

"She is going to Minas. Can you be without me that long?"

"We'll manage."

"And what about you, Bobby?" Paddy asked, turning Driscoll's direction. "How do you feel about this?"

Bobby was smiling ear to ear.

*   *   *

The cold hard winter that had everyone complaining so much seemed long ago now. It was summer and Minas in the summer is warm. No, it is hot! Still, everyone there told Paddy it was better to be in Minas up among its surrounding hills than in other parts of the country.

Tereza had introduced Paddy to all she knew, good friends and mere acquaintances, and he found them to be mostly a cheerful and very friendly people.

During the day, Paddy would join Luis and ride out to one of the estancias where Ana Monterroso's novio worked. Ana's novio was Juan Lavalleja – the man about whom Tereza had spoken, and he looked perfectly suited to ride a horse. So did Luis for that matter, and Paddy wondered how out of place he himself must have looked, a sailor between two gauchos.

Paddy took to his horse naturally enough, and he was grateful he had not been given a plug. Aside from the few embarrassing moments in the beginning (the ones that had to occur when a new man unaccustomed to riding was given a mount such as his) he was pleased. It was the quality of his horse that helped him better understand the kind of men he was among. They had considered him much more than the object of a few laughs. They had judged him to be capable enough to adjust to his new environment quickly and Paddy did not disappoint. Soon he was one with them. Well, almost. While he learned quickly, there was much to absorb and some skills simply would not come quickly. He could see that with the boleador, he would have to spend more than a few weeks to become skilled at that thing.

The boleador was an amazing device – simple, but so very effective – deadly even, if handled skillfully (or unskillfully). It was one of the locally crafted items that the newly arrived Europeans quickly adopted.

It was made with three round stones wrapped tightly in rawhide that had been soaked and dried so that the leather became as a skin around them. Each was fastened with a braided rawhide tether, the opposite ends tied together. A skilled gaucho could bring down many kinds of animals with it, including cattle.

To use it, a gaucho held one stone in his hand and whirled the boleador overhead, finally throwing it at a target. Once it left the his hand it would splay out, each stone separating itself from the next and spinning until the target was struck. Then the tethers would wrap in on themselves, converging the stones at great speed until they made contact with the object. If that object were a cow's leg and the ankle or knee were struck, a bone could be easily chipped, or worse, it could be shattered. With cattle the boleador was used sparingly.

West of the Rio Uruguay, the gaucho counterparts of these magnificent men called the device the bolo. This slight change in terminology only proved what Jimmy had already said, each territory was developing its own identity, be it ever so subtle, right down to the language itself. Each was becoming a people different from the other.

Paddy marveled at the skills of these men. They were so adept at maneuvering their large animals – not at a gait or a trot, but running full out. The art was Spanish for certain, he thought, but it takes the huge spaces of the new world for it to be developed to this level. He imagined the scene repeating itself throughout the two continents many times over, wherever there were cattle and flat open land. The dress, and maybe some of the implements, might vary, but the skill level would be just as he was witnessing here. Where in the old world were there horsemen such as these? Perhaps the Cossacks on the Steppes.

Paddy studied the differences between Juan and Luis. Juan most assuredly was the most accomplished but Luis looked good on a horse. Maybe had he spent less time on the docks in Montevideo and more time in the rolling hills around Minas, he would soon be just as good. Shortly Juan rode over to where Paddy sat.

"So, Irishman, what do you think?"

"I'm impressed, Paddy replied truthfully.

"The best part of today comes this evening," Juan laughed.

"This evening?'

"Tere did not tell you?"

Juan jested. He knew she hadn't. She had wanted Paddy to be surprised.

"Tereza has said nothing," Paddy responded.

"Just as well," Juan smiled. "There will be no disappointment then from too much anticipation."

"What is going on?" Paddy asked.

"A parrillada," Juan replied, riding off, "and a dance."

Paddy watched him as his image got smaller. Juan Lavalleja was a natural leader. Tall men with deep voices sometimes lead simply because by their stature they are imposing, but Juan had become a leader in spite of the fact that he had neither of those characteristics. He was a little shorter than average and his voice was a little high. But he was a leader because those that followed him knew he was deep in the things that really counted.

*　　*　　*

The Ferrando house in Minas was a beehive of excitement. Everyone there knew tonight was going to be special.

"So, has Paddy behaved?" Tereza asked.

Because of her mother, Paddy's own brand of morality, and to keep the locals from talking, it had been arranged before the trip to Minas that Paddy would stay with Juan Lavalleja. Paddy had actually been relieved on hearing this. He knew he would be uncomfortable in the presence of Tereza's mother and he was quickly learning that it was difficult to maintain an excellent relationship if the couple were together too much of the time.

For the very same reasons Ana too had stayed with Tereza in her childhood home. She had rarely been away from the city and this was an adventure for her.

"A perfect house guest, Juan says," Ana replied. "And with you, does he behave?"

"Better than I would like," Tereza admitted.

"I see," Ana smiled. "I am beginning to wonder what sort of tigers we have chosen for ourselves. But we will be blessed for it, you'll see. In fact, I believe we already are."

Tereza gave Ana a puzzled look.

"They do not misbehave because they hold us in high regard," Ana continued. "We are their ladies."

"Indeed!" Tereza retorted sarcastically.

"Believe it," Ana smiled, "or don't believe it. It doesn't change the truth of it. Do you think Paddy will enjoy the parillada?"

"I do not know," Tereza laughed. "I have never seen him in a social setting other than the small dinners we have had."

"So you do not know if he can dance?"

"I suppose I don't," Tereza giggled.

Ana laughed. "Then we'll see tonight, won't we?"

"Well, I'm sure he won't know how to dance the Pericón."

"You will have to teach him," Ana responded. "How many tortas fritas do we have?"

"Over two hundred," Tereza replied.

"And honey?"

"The ladies say we have more than enough honey."

"More than enough?" Ana sighed, "Well then we had better fry some more tortas."

* * *

Summer evenings in Minas are most enjoyable. The air cools quickly then seems to level off – heaven made for a fiesta in the campo. Hours before the sun had set Paddy caught the faint scent of freshly butchered bullock roasting on the parrilla. Then the day's activity began to die down – earlier than usual, Paddy noticed.

The more conscientious gauchos were slipping off to clean up before festivities began. Some of those who remained began what would eventually become a large bonfire. Paddy could sense the excitement building.

Soon wagons from town began to arrive, and boys not yet old enough for working cattle removed tables and chairs and set them some distance from the bonfire. The mothers and sisters of these boys followed, spreading the tables with the food and dishware brought from home. The activity seemed almost choreographed in its precision, and it was apparent that it had been performed many times before.

Paddy searched the trail intently. He was surprised when he finally saw what he had been wanting to see. It was Tereza with Ana sitting in the wagon beside her. Paddy smiled. He had never pictured Tereza as anything but a lady and yet here she was, expertly driving the team of mules that pulled the wagon.

He was still smiling when Tereza pulled the wagon up beside him. Paddy said nothing.

"What are you grinning about so much?" Tereza asked.

"I had no idea you could handle a team so well," Paddy replied.

"I handle many things well," Tereza teased. "There is still much about me you do not know."

Ana raised an eyebrow.

"There is plenty of time for all that," Paddy shot back. "A voyage of discovery is not completed overnight".

Now Ana raised the other eyebrow. "Here, Paddy," she interrupted. "Help us with the food."

* * *

The shadows of the fortress on the hill crept slowly across the bay toward Montevideo in the late afternoon. The citizens, however, were not taking in that particular view, lovely as it was. Their attention was drawn to the huge English fleet, recently arrived and sitting with sails very loosely furled outside the cove.

"Why do they not enter the harbor?" a young boy asked his father.

"Maybe they do not intend to stay for long," the father replied, "if we are lucky."

All eyes were now on an undermanned long boat approaching the shore halfway up the peninsula. The helmsman and a partial compliment of rowers were navy men, distinguished by their blue coats. A small band of red jacketed marines accompanied them. Other than they the boat was more than half empty.

When it was beached, two of the oarsmen jumped out to pull her further ashore. They waited patiently while the marines disembarked and quickly ran up the street toward the cabildo where the small force left behind had been garrisoned. Two of their number turned down a side street toward the print shop.

*   *   *

The knock at the door surprised both Jimmy and Bobby. As soon as Bobby answered the marines entered the room.

"You are ordered aboard the *Vigilance* immediately," the senior marine blurted out. "The fleet is departing for England.

"What?" Jimmy countered. "What about this equipment?"

"Leave it!" the marine said. "Where is the other man?"

"Paddy?, He's out of town," Bobby replied.

"Out of town? What is he doing out of town?"

"He is with his lady," Jimmy replied.

"Who authorized this?" The marine asked.

"I suppose I did," Jimmy replied defiantly, "as master of the keep".

"Do you know where she lives?"

"He kept that pretty well a secret," Jimmy said.

"He is probably still in Minas," Bobby volunteered. The thought made both men suddenly worrisome. The consequences would be more than serious.

"The best we can do is leave a note," Jimmy suggested.

"Make it quick!" the marine said. "We need to get back to the ship".

Jimmy began scribbling a message. "It is a real shame, to be leaving all this equipment behind," Bobby commented.

"How does this sound?" Jimmy asked. "Paddy, It seems things did not go well in Buenos Aires. Orders are to return to England immediately. We are stopping at Maldonado to recover the men left behind. Get there as quickly as you can!"

"Fine enough!" the marine said impatiently.

"What if he doesn't make it?" Bobby asked.

"Well then, he can go into the printing business." Jimmy replied.

"Until his majesty's navy comes back for him," the marine laughed.

"Well, maybe they won't!" Jimmy yelled.

"At the least he will be labeled a deserter, that's for sure," Bobby said despondently.

Jimmy nodded. Within a minute the print shop was locked up and the four men were making their way back to the boat. The note rested in an obvious place on the press, waiting for Paddy's return.

*　　*　　*

Night had fallen on Minas and moonlight bathed the land all around except where the huge bonfire raged. In that area, the light it produced was so bright that the presence of the moon was not even noticed. Whatever attention that was drawn skyward by the people enjoying the fiesta was caused by the small glowing bits racing up from the fire itself.

Another attraction that caught the revelers' eye was the Englishman. Paddy had spent the early part of the evening partaking of the joys of the parrilla, and everyone wondered how he would like it. The meats, having been slowly cooked on the open fires, were more delicious than any he could recall at home.

Even the taste of the more unusual organs, harvested from the great animal slaughtered earlier that afternoon, were not too objectionable. Paddy drew the line when it came to brains and testicles, however. *He would have to acquire a taste for such things over time,* he thought, *maybe.*

At the moment Paddy felt that he was being wise to hold off dancing while he ate. He could use the time studying the different dances and becoming familiar with the steps. It was only when he was somewhat sure of himself that he ventured over to where Tereza had been talking to the other ladies, waiting for him.

"It's about time," she said.

"I needed the time to learn the steps," Paddy replied. "You don't want me putting you to shame now, do you?"

"Oh I don't think you will do that," Tereza said.

"Prepare to be surprised," Paddy threatened.

The dance began simply enough and Paddy started to feel he might actually be able to get through it. Somewhere in the fourth stanza however, he missed a step. The music pressed on while Paddy's mind slowed and struggled to identify the place where he had become confused. Quickly he was two steps behind, then three.

Had he only been dancing with Tereza, they could have stopped for him to think through all of it. But as with many dances with their roots in Western Europe, each participant was a part of a team, usually of eight, but sometimes comprising of all the dancers. Each relied on the other.

Soon many people were bumping into each other and losing their own steps. The musicians played another three or four measures before they realized the dancers were no longer in sync. Then as each gave up in turn out of frustration or laughter, the music dying a discordant death.

Tereza was laughing, as were all the others.

"See?" Paddy said. "There truly is no limit to my capacity to create an embarrassment from any circumstance."

Maybe we will save the Pericón for another time," she smiled.

*　　*　　*

When Sunday came Juan found himself alone preparing to attend mass.

Paddy was already at the chapel waiting for Ana and Tereza. Paddy still had been somewhat concerned at the impression his uniform might make, but it was the nicest thing he owned and he was, after all, still a sailor in his majesty's navy.

He had never enjoyed mass as he did now in Minas. The church was no cathedral, but it was a substantial chapel. Juan and Ana hoped to be married there and Paddy thought it might not be a bad place for him and Tereza should he be so fortunate to see that day come.

He knew all too well why he was enjoying life so much now. With Tereza at his side he could see it being fulfilled as it was intended to be.

Again Paddy sensed the solid and reassuring feeling that comes with being Catholic. The mass and the catechism were exactly the same wherever a traveler ventured. This was especially true of the mass, since it was always in Latin.

Whether the ceremony was moving or not, it was always a happy time when the mass ended. Before mass, parishioners arrived sporadically, in small numbers, and tried to be as pious as they possibly could. They offered up their prayers and anticipated the holy sacrament. But afterwards everyone would leave together.

In a small town like Minas, most of the people took time to socialize with those they hadn't seen since the week before. Families would come in from many miles away, both to worship and enjoy the company of their good friends in town. A banquet of sorts was prepared and eaten in the afternoon.

It was during this banquet on this particular Sunday that the rider suddenly raced in from Montevideo. He did not approach at a lope, but closed quickly at a full gallop. His horse was so lathered it was obvious he had been ridden very hard all the way.

Juan rose and went out partway to greet the man. Only a few sentences were spoken before both he and the rider hurried over to the diners.

"Paddy, the fleet has returned to Montevideo," Juan announced.

"Then I must be going," Paddy said.

"No, señor," the rider interrupted. "The fleet did not stay. They recovered the soldiers there and departed."

"What . . . to where?" Paddy asked.

"From what was said, it is fairly certain they are returning to England," the rider replied.

"What are you going to do, Paddy?" Tereza asked anxiously.

"I have to go to Maldonado. Perhaps I can intercept the fleet there."

"I believe it is too late, my friend," Juan advised.

"Maybe not. The fleet must stop to pick up the garrison. It is my only chance," Paddy said.

"And if you find the fleet there?" asked Tereza.

"I will have to leave with it," Paddy replied.

"But what about us?" Tereza cried.

"You do not know the English Navy, love," Paddy explained. "If I am not back aboard the *Vigilance*, I will be labeled a deserter, and sooner or later, I will be hunted down."

"Then it is as I always feared!" she screamed. "I was a fool to let you convince me it could be otherwise!"

Paddy reached for her, but Tereza turned away.

Juan intervened, understanding the urgency of the moment. "You will need a fast horse," he said. "I will saddle you one."

"Thank you, Juan," Paddy replied. As Lavalleja hurried off, Paddy turned to Tereza once again.

"Take heart, my love," he said. "What we have is far too great to be destroyed by anything as small as the English Navy."

"I am not so sure," Tereza replied in her tears. "Paddy, I am very afraid."

Paddy stood motionless, fully comprehending that nothing he could do or say could lighten the moment.

Mercifully Juan returned quickly, and with his help, Paddy was soon on the road to the coast. Forcefully he put thoughts of Tereza aside as best he could, but his last image of her tearful face, and almost to the point of collapse, would torment him the rest of his life, he was sure.

Paddy began to appreciate what a good friend Juan had become. He realized now that an outstanding horseman was much more than just someone who could ride. The speed that Juan was able to call upon to prepare this mare was another sign of his ability. Selecting such a good horse as this, still another.

"I could give you a stallion, lightning fast," Paddy remembered Juan saying as he rode off. "But this horse is almost as fast and has something the stallion lacks – constancy."

Not constancy, Paddy now thought to himself, *Heart! She will go on when it would appear there is nothing left.* The thought would have brought a faint smile to his face except for the gravity of his present circumstances. Could it really be that he had seen Tereza for the very last time?

An hour passed and Paddy saw in the distance the curiously shaped mountain called the Pan de Azucar. Something between a hill and a real mountain, it was surely not as famous as the Pan de Azucar in Rio de Janeiro, but this one more closely resembled its namesake, he thought. The mountain taunted him as the minutes passed and it still appeared no closer.

In spite of this frustration, Paddy was grateful for the mountain, for now he could estimate where he was along this road simply by its apparent size and location relative to him.

Another hour passed and Paddy was on now the east side of the Pan de Azucar. Mercifully its size shaded him and his horse from the afternoon sun. But the lowness of the sun in the sky worried him further. He could see the day was becoming quite late.

Soon he would see another large hill rising up as a landmark alongside the Rio de la Plata. The road would lead him toward it, where he would turn to the left at its base and ride on into the town of Maldonado.

It was twilight when Paddy finally reached the outskirts. Maldonado was not a large town and within minutes he was at the water's edge. Near the horizon he could see the English fleet, already under full sail. It was disappearing toward the Punta del Este, the peninsula that defined the boundary between the Rio de la Plata and the South Atlantic.

His heart sank. In less than an hour they would be out of sight for good.

One of the few dockworkers still on the wharf approached him. "They did not stay long, Ingles," he said.

"Just enough time to recover the garrison, I imagine," Paddy responded without looking up.

"They hardly furled the large sails. The smaller ones they just allowed to be tossed in the wind on their slack." The dockworker waited but Paddy did not speak. "Do you have a place to stay?" he asked.

"Where do you think they will anchor?" Paddy asked.

"That would depend on their supplies, I should think. Most likely they will need to be provisioned. They could anchor at Porto Alegre, perhaps. But I believe they won't stop until they reach Rio de Janeiro."

"Do you believe I could catch them?"

"I think not," the dockworker responded honestly. "Overland you have a small advantage in speed. But both man and beast must rest, and a fleet sails twenty-four hours a day."

Paddy did not respond.

"Are you hungry?" the dockworker asked.

"Yes."

"Then come to my home. My wife has prepared a fine guisado."

"Thank you," Paddy said gratefully.

"What would your plans be now?" the dockworker asked. "You may stay with us for a few days if you wish."

"You are most generous, friend, but I must return to Minas."

After all that had happened, Paddy now had time to concentrate on those things that were good. Fortunately, after the quick meal, he had a full moon and his horse could easily see the road ahead. They traveled at no more than a walk now. The horse needed rest and Paddy was able even to find some sleep in the saddle. He realized then that they both needed to stop and rest alongside the road until morning. Perhaps he should have taken the dockworker up on his invitation to stay the night. It was the poor judgment, he rationalized, of an overtaxed mind.

He and the mare would not be in Minas until late the next day now. But the concerns of the future died away as Paddy drifted off into a much needed sleep. Soon he would be back with his Tereza.

CHAPTER THREE

Revolution

In the town of Colonia del Sacramento, just across the Rio de la Plata from Buenos Aires, Captain José Gervasio Artigas stared into a mirror on the wall of his small quarters and made some final adjustments to his uniform. Outside on the parade ground, Lieutenant Rafael Otiguerra stood in full dress with the garrison Artigas commanded standing at attention. The Captain had planned to make his beloved Blandengues Corps his life's career, but now the task before him would be a sad one. His Corps was a shining example of the Spanish military in the Americas, and he was proud to be a part of it.

A few final adjustments to his hair left Artigas unsatisfied, but he had run out of time and he knew he really could do no better. A thousand thoughts ran through his mind as he stared into the mirror one last time. Then he suddenly turned and walked out onto the parade ground.

"Attention," Otiguerra ordered as a matter of habit, and the garrison stood even straighter than before. The captain went through his requisite review in a slow and methodical manner that gave no indication of his eagerness to get to the pressing matter at hand.

"At ease, gentlemen," Artigas finally ordered, and the structured sound of the men assuming a more comfortable yet still regulation position echoed across the open ground. A long pause followed.

"Men," The Captain began. "I am certain all of you have been concerned with recent incidents within the viceroyalty. We have witnessed these past weeks' events with consequences that before long will surely touch us all—events of such significance that, rather than have them posted, I have chosen to speak to you about them now."

Artigas paused and stared at the ground as his mind sought the exact words to convey his thoughts. The heat was becoming noticeably oppressive now and the waiting men were visibly uncomfortable. Finally he redirected his attention back to them.

"It has been my great honor to command the Blandengues Corps," he continued. "I personally regard our action against the British at Buenos Aires as our finest moment. In the years I have been in the Corps, we have amassed a record that, given the time and the place, is as fine and enviable as any military unit in the world. I consider myself most fortunate to have been numbered with you."

Some of the men's faces now revealed a bit more interest. A few even appeared puzzled. Numbered? Why was the captain speaking in the past tense?

"Spain has appointed a new governor," Artigas continued. "His Excellency Javier Elío will now direct her affairs on the Rio de la Plata. However, Elío has not been given the title of viceroy, though he will be expected to assume all viceregal authority. The government in exile, it seems, will not name a viceroy until a Spanish king once again sits on the throne in Madrid."

"In response, Buenos Aires has chosen not accept Elío as governor since he has not actually been named to that position by the king himself. The city, in the meantime, has determined to govern both itself and its surrounds until the king names a governor. The new interim government of Buenos Aires also has declared it will also not permit Governor Elío to take his seat there. So until matters improve, Elío has decided he will govern the Viceroyalty of La Plata from Montevideo."

"Buenos Aires alone has forced this state of uncertainty upon us all. Its government is now officially held in contempt by the Spanish government in exile. All participants have been charged with treason".

The men in the ranks looked at each other in astonishment and Artigas waited patiently for their full attention.

"Finally, as of noon today, I will no longer be your captain. I am resigning my commission."

A pronounced groan rose from the gathered company.

"As you were, men," Otiguerra ordered.

"Understand that this decision has been most difficult for me," Artigas continued. "I have sworn an oath, both to the corps and to Spain. I have never been disloyal to either. To be true to itself, the corps must always be uncompromising and constant. But the Spain that it serves has changed, and I fear the repression it is already beginning to impose here on this continent may soon become intolerable."

"The corps must side with the crown regardless of how the crown behaves. My cause, while in this office, has always been to safeguard the rights of the citizens and uphold their individual liberties. Those two promises were woven within the oath I swore, both to Spain, and to the corps. But now I have come to a crossroads I would never have thought possible. I must choose what I believe to be the greater cause in the oath over the lesser. I must chose the rights and liberties of the citizens over all else."

Artigas began to move slowly up and down the ranks, as if he were still reviewing the troops. his pace, however, was deliberate and labored as he looked each man in the eye. It was also very disquieting to many of them. It seemed as though he were trying to perceive the innermost thoughts and allegiances of each individual soldier. When he was finished, he returned to his place in front of the unit.

"What is the greatest gift of God to man?" Artigas asked.

The garrison remained silent.

"This question is not rhetorical. I need an answer," Artigas insisted.

"Salvation," volunteered a meek voice from within the group.

"Most assuredly," Artigas smiled. It was not the answer he wanted, but it was correct, and he knew how to make it work.

"But how is salvation gained?" he continued. "Men must be free, totally free, to be totally tested – and men must be totally free even to hope for a complete and lasting joy. The hour has come for each of us now to decide for ourselves whether or not this principle is true, and if it is, just how deep is our conviction to it."

"This afternoon Lieutenant Otiguerra and I will cross the Rio de la Plata and offer our services to the government of Buenos Aires. In the days to come, I can assure you that, whether you like it or not, each of you must also decide which path to follow. Whatever is your choice, I wish you and your families well."

Artigas turned and walked back to his quarters. "Sergeant, dismiss the corps!" Otiguerra shouted.

* * *

Paddy had come to love the summer in the southern hemisphere, but as he looked into the night sky he could not deny he missed not seeing the greater and lesser bears that always remained below the horizon at these latitudes.

Yet the new celestial objects on this side of the world that replaced what could not be seen more than made up for the loss. The compact

Southern Cross shone brilliantly – even drawing attention away from the always spectacular Orion. But the Magellanic Clouds, two nearby nebulae outside the Milky Way, impressed him even more.

Four years had passed since he had come to South America, and now Paddy had become accustomed even to the reversed seasons. His life had changed beyond what he could have possibly imagined. Married to a woman who completed him more than he thought possible, he was the father of two very fine children. His life was full.

Katy was the oldest. She not only resembled her mother in her outward beauty but she also had Tereza's inner spiritual beauty as well. They had named their second child Luis, after both his grandfather and his uncle, but almost all who saw him declared he was the image of his father. Everyone called him Luisito so he would not be confused with Tereza's brother when they were both in the same company.

Paddy smiled as he sat at his desk. He looked around the print shop and reflected in amazement at how blessed his life had become. The shop was certainly one of those blessings. Since the navy had purchased the place legally, a Montevideo court granted Paddy the property and its holdings, being that he was the only remaining representative of that navy. It was a gift from the city, really, and Paddy knew it. The judge considered how the shop could best be put to use and found Paddy most capable of seeing it done. In doing so the judge admonished Paddy to use the shop not only for his own benefit but also to serve the community.

Without the additional help that Jimmy and Bobby had provided, however, he was not in a position to continue maintaining the *Montevideo Star*. Instead he printed broadsides for the local officials and he had enough advertising business to enjoy an adequate life.

A sound at the door brought Paddy back out of his thoughts. It was Tereza with the children.

"How are you, my love?" Paddy asked as she entered.

"Wonderful, my darling." Tereza responded.

"We are going to Punta Carretas," Katy interrupted happily as she ran to her father's lap.

"Punta Carretas? Were you planning to go without me?" Paddy teased.

Katy frowned but her smile lingered.

"Ana is here," Tereza said. "She wants to go on an outing where we can talk without being uninterrupted. The children wanted to go swimming so I packed a meal. Do you have time to go with us?" she asked.

"I would truly love to go, Love, but I have to print a broadside for the governor," Paddy answered. "Besides, if you want to talk uninterrupted, what would I do?"

"Watch the children!" Tereza laughed. Then she became more solemn. "It has been so much better here since Elío came to Montevideo,"

"Yes it has," said Paddy. "I pray this lasts, but I mistrust Buenos Aires. Now that they see they can actually govern themselves they have become less and less concerned about restoring the king to his throne. Instead they appear to be more ambitious about extending their influence over the rest of the continent."

His words made him pause as he suddenly realized that what Jimmy had told him years before might truly be on the verge of unfolding before him. Tereza could see he was deep into his own thoughts and remained silent. It worried her some but she had been married to him long enough to know that when he was like this, it was best not to interrupt him.

"I do not expect them to leave us alone for long, especially since they have seen how well we have accepted the new governor here," Paddy finally continued, and almost as an afterthought he added, "How is Juan?"

"Juan is tending cattle in Minas, as usual. Ana has become somewhat concerned about him though."

"He is not losing interest in her, I hope."

"No. He has just been very preoccupied by the present situation."

"We all should be worrying it to some degree,"

Paddy smiled. "But not today! Go and have a good time. I'll see you later this afternoon."

*   *   *

It was on that same afternoon when Captain José Artigas and Lieutenant Rafael Otiguerra walked down to the dock in Colonia. They waited for the launch that would ferry them across the narrowest part of the Rio de la Plata to Buenos Aires. Shortly, the Blandengues Corp arrived to offer their last respects and bid them farewell. Artigas passed among his men for what he knew was the very last time, shaking their hands and offering light quips in a circumstance that did not lend itself to light behavior.

Otiguerra spoke briefly with the crew of the launch, ostensibly to assess the current climate of affairs in Buenos Aires. In truth he was buying Artigas a little more time to say farewell. When the crew began to become impatient he returned to where the corps stood standing around the man who had commanded them for so many years. Most of the men had never known another leader.

"Captain, the launch is ready to depart," he said.

"Then we must not keep it waiting," Artigas replied. He turned to the men on the dock.

"Fare you well, my dear friends. I truly hope to see each and every one of you again someday in the not too distant future."

The two officers descended into the waiting launch. As it pulled away, the men on the dock offered one final salute with a loud cheer.

* * *

February 12, 1812. In the early dawn, a small band of gauchos on horseback approached the Arroyo Asencio. Dismounting, they quickly began to build a fire and heat water to prepare their yerba mate. Within half an hour another group arrived, followed by another. When it was ready, the mate was shared among them all much as coffee is shared in other parts of the world. Well over 100 men were assembled at the arroyo when the last group arrived. A few wore the uniform of the Blandengues Corps.

After the comfortable period of greeting and small talk, scribes who had been preappointed for the task before them sat down at portable tables, ready to record the proceedings of this seemingly unlikely gathering. Pedro Viera, a man whose bearing and dress would have revealed him already to be a natural leader, rose to address the men.

"It is very good to see so many assembled here today," he began. "I had wondered who it would be who would respond to our invitation. I am especially honored to see Ramon Fernandez of the Blandengues Corps and some of his men with us. Tell me, Captain! Are we to be arrested before we even begin this business? "

"Have no fear, Pedro. Those you see here are with you," Fernandez smiled. "But be duly warned! If we in the corps know of this gathering—without having been sent the invitation, by the way—you can be certain there are others without invitations who also know of it. If you do today what I expect, they will not be sympathetic to your actions and would just as soon see you lined up on the gallows in Montevideo."

Viera nodded. "Thank you for that cheerful admonition, Captain. So then, let us quickly be about our business."

"For some time I have felt myself being pushed inextricably to where we are, here and now. The time of consideration and assessment is past. This is the hour, and this is the place. Venancio, may I have the pronouncement?"

Venancio Benavides, Viera's capable aide, handed him a prepared document. Viera reached in his vest pocket and retrieved his eyeglasses.

"Over the course of the past few years, the Kingdom of Spain has become incapable of minding the affairs of state over her vast empire. This has allowed her locally appointed ministers to become tyrants where they would, and many have imposed upon her loyal subjects new and unbearable burdens," he began. "Not since the grand inquisition have honorable citizens been arrested without charge. Unjust duties and taxes are now imposed by the king's ministers without prior review and approval by the local authorities. Worse still, soldiers are now quartered in our homes without our consent, and some have committed unspeakable acts of atrocity."

Shouts of outrage and protest arose from some of the men.

Viera held up his hand. "Whether you know of it or not, it is true and fully documented," he shouted.

With the descent subdued, he returned to his reading.

"There appears to be no end to this despotism and for this reason it will be tolerated no longer. We are here assembled to pronounce against it. We will not live under this tyranny, and should it be necessary, we are resolved to take up arms. Viva la libertad!"

"Viva!" some in the group shouted.

"Viva la causa!" Viera responded.

"Viva!" the men repeated. All were shouting now.

"Viva la revolución!"

"Viva!"

An impetuous few, including Benavides, rushed the tables and grabbed the first copies of the newly transcribed document, the ink barely dry. They mounted quickly and rode off, shouting independence and freedom. They were soon followed by the many others.

*   *   *

Tereza awoke when Paddy stirred in their bed. Normally she would simply turn and go back to sleep, but this time Paddy was repositioning himself so often she could not. She waited patiently for half an hour as he tossed restlessly.

At first she thought he only was having trouble getting comfortable, but as he continued in his efforts she began to worry.

Finally she spoke, "What is it, love?"

"How long have you been awake?" Paddy asked.

"Long enough to know there is something troubling you," Tereza replied.

It took a few seconds for Paddy to choose his words.

"Do you remember how we talked this afternoon—about how good our life is?" he asked.

"Yes."

"And yet how delicate our situation may be?"

"Yes." Tereza replied.

"Before you returned from Punta Carretas, a courier brought me copy for a broadside he wants me to print," Paddy said.

Again there was a pause. "Tereza, it is a pronouncement."

"A pronouncement! Against the government?" she asked.

"What else?" Paddy replied. "And I do not know what to do."

Tereza's response was immediate. "You must take it to the governor right away".

"I know what I must do," Paddy said, "but whatever I choose, it will appear I will have sided with someone. For the sake of my family, I have preferred to remain neutral throughout this growing unrest. Now, if I print the broadside, we will suffer retribution from the government. If I do not print it, the retribution will come from the revolutionaries."

Tereza sat for a moment in silence, and then she rose and crossed the room to the armoire. Paddy watched her as she began to dress.

"What are you doing?" he asked.

"I'm going to the cathedral," Tereza responded.

*   *   *

Paddy was at the Cabildo as soon as it opened for business early the next day. He explained his purpose to the guard at the door and showed him the order.

"Take this pronouncement to the adjutant's office and explain the matter to him. He will tell you what to do," the guard said.

As soon as the adjutant became aware of Paddy's problem, he was ushered directly into Governor Elío's office. From the papers on the governor's desk it was clear that he was right in the middle of important matters.

"Yes, what is it," he asked impatiently.

"Governor, allow me to present Mister Patricio Colman," the adjutant said. "He is the owner of the print shop and he has brought a matter that requires your immediate attention."

"As if I didn't have enough of those already," Elío growled. "All right! I'll hear what he has to say."

The adjutant saluted and left the room.

"So what is it, Mister Colman?" Elío asked.

"I received this last evening from a client. He wants me to print it. I believe you should read it first."

Paddy placed the pronouncement on the governor's desk.

"So the populace is rising up in rebellion," Elío commented as he read it.

"I would not go so far as say the populace," Paddy responded, "a few revolutionaries, maybe."

"You are probably right." Elío said. "How can I soon forget the warm response from the people when I first came to Montevideo, and how they came to my defense when Buenos Aires wanted my head?"

"But times can change quickly," he continued. "The world is crazy now. The sooner Napoleon is stopped and the monarchs are restored to their proper thrones, the sooner we can return to normal and put all this foolishness behind us."

"Yes, your Excellency," Paddy responded.

"Concerning this pronouncement," Elío continued, "I want you to print it. It is going to be printed anyway, whether or not you are the one to do it, and I certainly do not want to endanger your family further. The man who brought it will not be prosecuted and it is prudent that the rebels not know you came to see me, so be cautious when you leave. Now thank you for coming."

"Thank you, Excellency," Paddy said gratefully.

*   *   *

The small fleet floated slowly and silently in the predawn darkness down the Rio Uruguay. It was nothing more than several large boats and it was still dark when they beached on a sandy shore at Calera de las Huerfanas near Colonia. One hundred and fifty-eight men disembarked, leaving only the remaining boatmen to row quietly back to the other side of the river. The neighing of the horses and the metallic response of arms being moved about revealed quickly that this was a military expedition. When the preparations to move inland were completed, the men gathered around their captain.

"So now we are here," José Artigas declared. "at last we touch the soil we have sworn to liberate! During the next few days there can be no rest. We must strike hard and fast."

"Tomorrow before our presence is discovered we will attack the garrison at El Collá. With our success there we shall begin to build our army with those here who would be numbered with us. They are here. I know it – and they number in the thousands—the common, the hardy, campesinos, gauchos, even as yourselves. We shall draw them to us as a watermelon draws flies in the summer's sun.

*   *   *

Midmorning found Artigas' small force moving purposefully along the dirt road toward El Collá. Soon the little town could be seen in the distance.

As the men slowed their approach, a pack mule suddenly brayed. The advance halted and every ear listened for some response from the town. Everything remained quiet. Most of the men interpreted their actions as the result of unjustified jitters. There would be nothing unusual about a mule braying, especially in the morning.

Artigas motioned the men forward once again. Now many began to wonder just how close they could actually approach the town before someone in the garrison was alerted of their presence. Certainly before long just the noise of feet and hooves on the road would awaken someone.

At last even the General reckoned that the gamble to close the distance any further was becoming too great a risk.

"A la carga!" Artigas suddenly shouted.

The small group of battle hardened Argentines charged into the town swiftly. They hit the building housing the Spanish garrison hard and surprise was sudden and complete. The ensuing battle was all one sided and it became evident to Artigas' men that few if any of the outmanned Spanish had ever been in a real battle. Those who made a stand were quickly shot down.

The more cowardly fled, still in their night clothes, through the rear doors and windows, only to be mowed down by Argentines already in position outside. Only the detachment stationed at the stable in the far end of town had any chance. They quickly mounted and rode out of town, but a group of Artigas' mounted men spurred their horses to chase the survivors down.

"Let them go!" Artigas yelled. "The time has come for our presence to be announced."

"Lieutenant Otiguerra?" he shouted.

"Yes Sir!"

"Station a small picket line outside the town and have the rest of the men get some sleep. I want to be moving again before the sun rises tomorrow."

"Yes Sir," Otiguerra responded.

*   *   *

The next morning Artigas was true to his word. He exited the cuartel while it was still quite dark and found his men already waiting – the dutiful Otiguerra holding the reins to his horse. He mounted his stallion and leaned forward, looking into the faces of each of his men.

"What happened here yesterday is a good omen," Artigas declared. "Now . . . , let's take Montevideo!"

"The men looked at each other, confused and concerned. Suddenly Otiguerra smiled.

"Viva Artigas!" he cried.

"Viva Artigas!" the men responded.

Artigas did not wait for the gritos to die out. He spurred his horse and headed east out of town. Otiguerra followed right behind, as did the men.

The first several hours were uneventful and the journey became so quiet and routine that the men began running out of things to say to each other. They had come to that part in a long journey where even those who say things just to break the silence now said nothing for a few moments. It was as if Artigas had been waiting for this moment. He motioned Otiguerra forward.

"We are being followed," Artigas said as Otiguerra approached him.

Otiguerra spun his horse around. Sure enough, far in the distance a band of armed men were coming up the road.

"Sharp eyed bastard," Otiguerra thought to himself and smiled.

"Lieutenant! I want you to take three men and parley with these hangers on," Artigas ordered.

"Yes sir!"

Under a white flag of truce, Otiguerra led a party of hand selected men back toward the unknown force. Artigas watched warily as they approached and began to speak and gesture. Everything he had anticipated about this mission had developed just as he had expected when he was back in Buenos Aires – everything up until now.

Hopefully his plans would still unfold as he anticipated on down the road to Montevideo. But now, at this moment, he began to worry. He had not envisioned this, and now an uneventful trip to the capital clearly more probably would not occur. Surprises could come at any time from any direction during this period, and he could not come close to anticipating even in a small way what they all might be.

Fear of the unknown is the most powerful and unreasonable fear of all, he thought to himself. Then suddenly his squint widened as he watched the entire group ride toward him.

Otiguerra smiled broadly and waved his arms over his head. Artigas heard his men reach for their weapons and he motioned for them to remain quiet.

"You are a prophet, my captain!" Otiguerra yelled. "Come greet the first fruits of our new army."

As the men drew near, it could be seen that many of the faces among them were also at the Arroyo Asencio.

* * *

Paddy was setting type for a broadside when Tereza entered the shop. She was not smiling.

Ana and Juan Lavalleja came in just behind her. Of the three, Juan was the only one who appeared to be cheerful. Paddy perceived something was up, and it appeared he might be in for a solemn if not rocky discussion about it. As yet he did not know what it could be, but he was sure he was about to find out. He rose to greet them.

"Juan, it is so good to see you again," Paddy declared.

"As it is you," Juan replied. "The pronouncement you printed looks magnificent – a work of art."

Juan's words surprised Paddy. "It was a commission," he said, "and the Governor bade me to print it.,"

"The Governor? Is that so?" Juan asked curiously. He decided not to make an issue of it. "Well, you printed it. You set the type. You must have read it!"

"Yes."

"And what did you think?"

"Think?" Paddy asked.

"About what it said!" Juan was smiling but his tone showed a degree of impatience.

"Juan is joining the revolutionaries," Tereza interrupted softly.

Paddy was surprised. "Juan, have you thought this thing through?" he asked.

"What is there to think about?" Juan replied. "The hour is here. We actually have the opportunity to free ourselves. North America was only the beginning. I tell you Paddy, right now this entire part of the world has the chance to sever all bonds of Europe from Hudson's Bay to Tierra del Fuego."

Paddy waited for Juan to finish before he spoke. "But right now you and Ana have so much to live for," he said. "What will she do if you are killed? And when you marry, you will have a family to think about,"

Juan shook his head. "What greater gift can a father give his children than a world where they are truly free?" he countered.

"Luis is going too," Tereza interrupted again.

Now a flash of anger crossed Paddy's face. "Did you talk him into this?" he asked Juan.

"Tereza's little brother is his own man," Juan responded. And he IS a man now, capable of making up his own mind. He has thought this matter out more clearly than it appears you have."

"I must look after my family," Paddy said in disgust.

*   *   *

The scouting patrol returned to the advance force of Artigas' small army, a force that now numbered many more Orientales than Porteños. The corporal commanding the patrol rode directly up to the General.

"What is the news, corporal?" Artigas asked.

"The Spanish know we are coming, sir." he replied. "They are ready and waiting. They have been reinforced with so many I don't know where they all sleep—and they are very well armed,

"Well then, we will truly see now what we are made of," Artigas declared grimly. "Lieutenant Otiguerra, inform the men that we are going on a forced march."

"Yes sir," Otiguerra's response was automatic. He turned his horse and began barking orders to the other lieutenants and sergeants. Within a minute the army was preparing for a full mobilization.

Soon the lieutenant was back at Artigas' side.

"Montevideo surely knows we are in the country now," Artigas said. "I do not want survivors telling them how close we are."

"I understand, sir," Otiguerra agreed.

Artigas studied the sight unfolding before him. His men were moving down the road in especially good order considering how little they had drilled. They were in good health, and the General knew he could thank a growing company of camp followers, that desperate group that most generals considered an unavoidable nuisance.

Artigas knew better. There were many times when the camp followers did get in the way, but they were dutiful and devoted to the soldiers. Most were the wives and sometimes the children of his men. Some, of course, were girlfriends, most of whom hoped to become wives. A few were no more than prostitutes, that forlorn group of women who simply by their appearance stained the rest with the same reputation.

Regardless of who they were, they would see to the best of their abilities that their men had the necessary provisions. And they would share the risk of possible defeat and its consequences in order to do it.

Artigas turned to Otiguerra once again.

"I want enough men on each side of the town and in the rear to stand guard. Have them in position before the main body attacks. Their mission is clear. No one escapes!"

"Yes sir," Otiguerra replied.

All the men moved out quickly now and disappeared down the road, leaving the camp followers behind to follow with the equipment and wagons.

Several hours had passed before Artigas' army reached the perimeter of Paso del Rey, but it was not until the outriders galloped back signaling for silence that most of his men realized just how close they were.

"Lieutenant" Artigas called out.

"Yes, Captain," Otiguerra replied.

"Deploy your men. They have a quarter hour to get in position – and in total silence. We must have complete surprise!"

"Yes sir!"

Otiguerra rode off, followed by his band of hand picked men who would systematically execute any Spaniard trying to avoid capture.

Seconds after they disappeared, the remainder of the men began to move into position.

The fifteen minutes that Artigas had given Otiguerra seemed like an eternity. Most of the men left behind felt that he was giving his lieutenant a little extra time just to be certain all would go well. But finally Artigas motioned for the attack.

Almost immediately the patriots drew fire from the sentries. Then a full volley exploded from the military compound, revealing that the unit obviously had been waiting in advance. In light of this revelation, Artigas was amazed that Otiguerra had been successful in getting his men in position without being detected. The Captain would have to give him a citation.

But he watched in apprehension as he saw some of his men fall. They had taken their first casualties, undoubtedly with some fatalities, and now the question would be how the men would respond. To his relief and satisfaction, his men continued to surge forward in one mass. They reached the compound before a second volley could be fired.

The charge overwhelmed the Spanish. A few held the line and fought boldly with swords and sidearms, but most panicked and looked for a way out.

Many ran down the side streets into the trap already set by the flanking forces Artigas had previously deployed. They were killed with musket fire. Those who chose the main road for their escape were similarly dispatched by the men waiting there. As Artigas listened from the center of town, the gunfire abated only to be followed by the sound of the clash of cutting and slashing arms.

When it was almost quiet, Artigas shouted as no one had heard him shout before.

"Otiguerra! Otiguerra!"

Artigas' faithful lieutenant rounded the corner two blocks down the street and quickly galloped up to him.

"Lieutenant Otiguerra? Have any escaped?"

"I believe not, sir," Otiguerra responded. "We had them covered very well."

"Prisoners?" Artigas asked.

"Twelve. How shall we dispose of them, sir?"

Artigas' face revealed an irate disappointment that his orders had not been followed to the letter. Then he thought better of it

"Keep them under guard, Artigas ordered. "I intend to be in San José by tomorrow night. We can incarcerate them there."

"Yes sir."

*　　*　　*

Paddy took his time returning home from the shop. The day had not gone well and every effort, even that to get up and go home, was easily procrastinated. When he arrived it took some time for him to make up his mind to go in.

Ana was there. And to Paddy's relief, Juan was not.

"Good evening, preciosa," Paddy said to Tereza in a low voice.

"Hello, my love" Tereza replied.

"How is Juan doing, Ana?" Paddy asked.

Ana sobbed and turned her head.

"Juan has left," Tereza said. "He told Ana he was going back to Minas."

"Oh Come on! Our argument was not all that bad!" Paddy laughed.

"It wasn't because of the argument," Tereza cried in frustration. "He discovered that Artigas is in the Banda Oriental. He is recruiting some of his friends and plans to join him."

"Who is Artigas?"

"He used to be Captain Artigas, the commander of the Blandengues Corps," Ana sobbed. "Now he is bringing an army to Montevideo."

Paddy's face became even more solemn. "He's a military man?"

"Yes."

"Tereza, you must go away with Ana!" Paddy said. "You must do it now and you must take the children with you. Go to Minas for a while!"

"What? But why . . ." Tereza asked bewildered.

If Artigas is successful, he will lay siege to the city, and whether or not he bombards it, should Elío not surrender quickly, many will die."

"But what about you?" Tereza asked.

"I will be alright," Paddy assured her. "I can swim to Punta Carretas if I ever need to get out. In the meantime, I will have to keep the shop open so the Spanish don't think I suspect something."

"Is he able to do what he says?" Ana asked Tereza.

"Oh yes," Tereza smiled, looking at her husband in admiration. "He is a powerful swimmer."

"I had to be," Paddy laughed, "just in case the ship sank."

Now even Ana laughed.

"When should we leave?" Tereza asked.

"Where is Artigas now?" Paddy asked in return.

"They say he is approaching San José," Ana volunteered.

"San José? Then you must leave as soon as possible. If Artigas faces no opposition he could be here in as little as two days," Paddy said seriously.

"Very well, my love," Said Tereza. "And you be careful!"

*   *   *

In Buenos Aires, the news of Artigas' progress in the Banda Oriental was not met with joy everywhere. Mariano Moreno, the present director of the young government, walked the corridors of the Cabildo with Manuel de Saavedra, the man who would eventually succeed him.

"Artigas is moving through the Banda Oriental much more quickly than anyone has expected," Moreno declared. "Already he has established himself in San José, and he is not that far from Montevideo itself. Moreover it would appear he now may have already gathered enough men to send a force east to occupy Maldonado."

Saavedra decided it would be wise not to reveal his mounting concern so quickly. "It is good to see the revolution going so well there," he said.

"Perhaps," Moreno commented, "but if Artigas' successes continue, he may not see a need for any additional help from us. Right now, in all of his army, there are only 150 Porteños. We could lose the Banda Oriental as easily as we lost Paraguay."

"If that is so, it might be wise to move Rondeau's army to Montevideo now," Saavedra suggested.

"I think so," Moreno said. "I believe we require a higher presence there." He took a minute to consider his options while Saavedra patiently waited. "I shall order General Rondeau into the Banda Oriental immediately," he finally said, "regardless of his present preparations."

"To be effective," Saavedra reminded, "he will need the support of a sizeable army. If his force is not overwhelming, Rondeau may have difficulty assuming power."

"Then he shall have it," Moreno declared, "and once he is in the field, we will have Artigas reassigned. He can command the local militia only."

"Are you convinced that this is wise?" Saavedra asked. "Such an action might lead to a full scale revolt among the Orientales."

"I think not," Moreno said confidently. "Artigas will submit to this, and his troops will follow him. I do not believe he is fully prepared, as of yet, to commit treason."

CHAPTER FOUR

Las Piedras

San José was the first sizable town Artigas had occupied. Thankfully, contrary to all his fears, it had not been strongly defended. Still, more patriots fell in this engagement than any so far, and one was the captain's cousin. The weather had changed and was symbolic of the current feeling in the camp, rainy and miserable. In spite of the all the successes, now it was time to mourn the fallen.

The weather was not doing its part in helping morale, that up to this point had been unbelievably high. To avoid the effects his personal lament might have on his little army, at least in part, Artigas kept to himself in his headquarters. There he poured over maps and reports in preparation for the conflicts yet to come. He suddenly heard a knock at the door. It was not unexpected.

"Come in," Artigas ordered.

"You called for me, captain?" Otiguerra asked.

"Lieutenant, I have here some very promising reports," Artigas replied. "They indicate there are local stores that we may be able to commandeer. Since the Spanish have yet to leave the protective walls of Montevideo, I want you to take this present opportunity to lead a patrol into Sauce and Pando. Find those supplies. And send my brother Nicolas into Canelones. It has been confirmed there is a large quantity of livestock there. I need him to requisition them."

"Yes sir," Otiguerra replied.

*   *   *

Early the next day, Rafael Otiguerra and his small band of raiders left San José. Before noon they approached the town of Sauce. Some distance behind a couple of sets of teamsters were playing a serious game of pushing their teams to an undetermined limit while yet assuring they would have enough left in their oxen for the return trip to San José. They leaned a little on the side of speed since it was imperative to get in and out of Sauce as quickly as possible. And there was a good chance they could secure fresh draft animals in the town.

Otiguerra's patrol approached Sauce quietly. He signaled the attack and the Orientales immediately broke into a full gallop. A surprised Spanish sentry fired his musket wildly toward them, the ball flying high over their heads, and shouted the alarm.

"The rebels are upon us!"

The little Spanish force responded more quickly than Otiguerra would have liked. Most of the soldiers there were cavalry, and they had obviously been informed that the patriots were in San José. They were in a high state of readiness with their horses already saddled. There was time enough to mount up and meet Otiguerra's attack just outside the town.

The forces were equally matched, and shortly the battle broke down to a classic cavalry skirmish with the slashing of sabers mixed with some pistol fire. For several minutes there seemed to be no clear advantage on either side. Otiguerra began to worry less about obtaining the supplies in Sauce and more about extracting his men with the minimum of casualties.

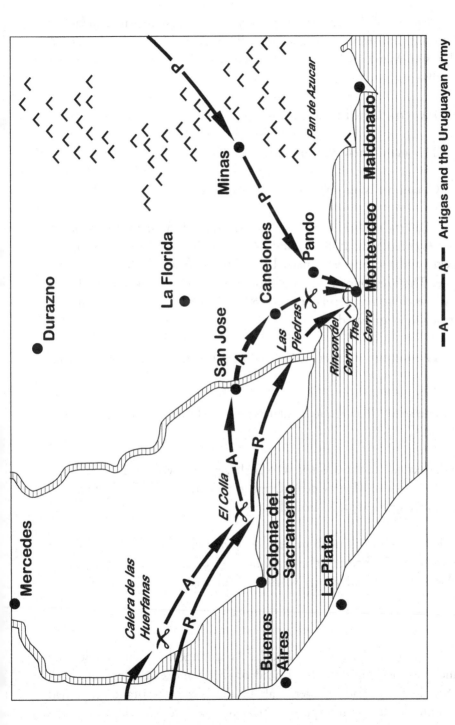

ARTIGAS' FIRST CAMPAIGN - 1813

—A— Artigas and the Uruguayan Army
—R— Rondeau and the Argentine Army
—P— The Portuguese Army

Then one of the new Orientales began to execute repeated audacious feints and charges into the Spanish, inflicting much damage at great risk to himself. As men fell around him, his companions took heart and began the rally.

Otiguerra turned to his sergeant.

"This man is new," he commented. "Who is he?"

"Corporal Rivera, sir," the sergeant replied.

Otiguerra studied Corporal José Rivera with admiration. Now the other Orientales had all responded to his example. The battle turned quickly and the Spanish finally broke into a panicked flight back into Sauce. They regrouped at a warehouse where they took refuge. It was heavily built and an excellent place to make a stand. Even so, a white flag of truce soon appeared.

How well are we prepared to accept prisoners?" Otiguerra asked his sergeant.

"I believe we have enough men to do it safely, lieutenant," the sergeant responded.

"Select two of the Spanish who are less gravely wounded to ferry their casualties back to Montevideo," Otiguerra ordered. "Allow them to depart once our wagons are fully loaded".

The move was as much strategic as it was humanitarian. Care for their wounded would hamper the Spanish forces occupying the besieged city and right now any advantage would be beneficial in this campaign.

*   *   *

At almost the same time, Nicolas Artigas and his men were leaving Canelones, herding over 2000 head of sheep and cattle in route back to San José. He had wondered about the lack of resistance they had encountered. It was unexpected. Next to San José, Canelones was the largest town in the area and much closer to the capital. But he decided not to worry about it.

Nicolas turned to Sergeant Roberto Nalerio, his second in command. "All our tasks should be so delightful, Roberto," he commented.

"We have been most fortunate, Lieutenant," Nalerio replied. "In all our endeavors . . ."

Nalerio's sentence was suddenly cut short. From a rise to their left, an overwhelming Spanish force appeared—abruptly and in full attack. The Orientales made a desperate attempt to settle their now agitated livestock but this quickly proved impossible. They would not be able to maintain both order with the herd and fight the Spanish at the same time.

The misstep was pivotal. Only a few shots were fired before the Orientales were forced to surrender. No one escaped.

Back on the rise the Spanish commander watched a private ride back toward him.

"What is the report, private?" he asked.

"You have a complete victory, Captain. Except for some minor wounds we have suffered no losses—and you have a prize."

"I can see that, private," the commander commented.

"It's much more than the cattle, Captain," the private smiled. "You have captured Artigas' little brother, Nicolas."

*   *   *

In Montevideo, Paddy watched from his home. The rain was coming down once again after a brief respite. News of the actions at Sauce and Canelones had just reached the city. *It was good to be in the printing business,* he thought to himself. *The news usually arrives there quickly.*

85

Good? he rethought the idea.

Tereza joined him at the door. "The day seems appropriate in light of the news," she said.

"When the rain stops, you must leave immediately," Paddy said. The area is becoming very dangerous now and the siege could begin at any moment."

"With all this rain, the roads could be treacherous," Tereza said. "Would it not be better to wait until they dry out a little?"

"No!" Paddy retorted. His tone was almost harsh. "I will accompany you most of the way but you have to leave now!"

"But how bad could a siege be?" Tereza asked.

"That depends on how long it lasts," Paddy replied. "I have not experienced one personally, but I know men who have. First comes the hunger, then starvation. Death soon follows, and the bodies will either be burned, probably in the plaza, or they will be thrown over the walls or in the Rio de la Plata. They will probably be dumped in the river into minimize the stench and flies and to prevent the rebels from catapulting them back into the city.

Rats will run uncontrolled and eventually they will become the only remaining source of food. Those who survive starvation will be plagued by disease and more deaths will follow, until the city finally capitulates or no one is left."

"It sounds horrible," Tereza commented.

"It will be," Paddy confirmed. "And as unreasonable as it sounds, a bombardment would be merciful, for in spite of the deaths it inflicts, the surrender it accelerates actually saves lives."

* * *

In San José, the rain that had begun early in the afternoon now continued to come down hard. Artigas sat at his desk, pondering a newly arrived dispatch when Otiguerra appeared at the door, soaked. Ordinarily the lieutenant would have waited outside the door and politely knocked, in spite of the weather. Artigas sensed this was something serious.

"May I enter, Captain? I have some bad news." Otiguerra said.

"Of course, lieutenant," Artigas replied. "Does it concern Nicolas?"

"Yes sir. "

Artigas braced himself. "Is he dead?"

"No, Sir. He is not dead. Some new men have just come in from Minas. They report that his force has been defeated at Canelones and he has been taken prisoner."

"Is he still in Canelones?" Artigas asked.

"I do not know," Otiguerra replied, "but one of the men from Minas would like to speak with you. He says it is urgent and he may be able to tell you more."

"Have him come in, Lieutenant."

Otiguerra exited the doorway and Artigas returned to study his dispatch. But his heart was not in it and in seconds he simply sat waiting for his lieutenant to return. Otiguerra was back in less than a minute with Juan Lavalleja. Both men were now thoroughly soaked.

"Captain," Otiguerra began. "I present Juan Antonio Lavalleja, from Minas."

"Lieutenant Otiguerra tells me you have some information," Artigas said, dispensing with the formalities of introduction.

"It is not good news, I fear," Juan said.

Artigas responded harshly. "The dispatch I hold informs me that I will no longer command when General Rondeau arrives. I can accept that. I knew this when I left Buenos Aires. But now they give me command only of the local militia. This, after we have gone so far and gained so much."

"Now I discover my brother Nicolas is a prisoner," he continued. "Today is the day for bad news, Señor Lavalleja. So let me have all of it!"

Juan began his report. "Recently the Spanish have gained a much better knowledge of the strength of our forces. They intend to hit us hard very soon."

Artigas' gaze narrowed. "Senor Lavalleja, how is it you come by this depressing news?"

"My novia has a good friend who lives in Montevideo. Her husband is a printer and as such he is in a position to receive much information, a lot of it confidential. He has assured me that when the time comes, even under siege he can get word out of the city."

"If what you say about a Spanish attack is true, we must prepare immediately. I will not wait for them here in San José where they can position themselves around us," Artigas declared. "We will meet them in the open between here and Montevideo."

"What is your rank, Senor Lavalleja?" Artigas asked.

"I have none," Juan replied. "I suppose I am just a private soldier."

"Did you lead the men who came with you?"

"They look up to me."

"Then you will be a corporal, in charge of those men," Artigas ordered.

"Thank you sir," Juan said gratefully. He could not help but think of how distressed Ana would be when she heard this bit of news.

"Now corporal, how is it you know so much about the disposition of our patrols?" Artigas asked. "Your novia's friend surely did not have ample time to learn of it from the printer and then communicate it through her to you. My first thought is that you could very well be a spy, sent here in the service of the Spanish."

Juan was quick to reply. "When the men you sent to Maldonado defeated the Spanish garrison at Minas, they told us where you were. We wanted to be numbered with you, so we came. It was the people in the towns we passed along the way who told us what had happened to your patrols. And now that we are here, we see almost your entire army must be made of men such as us."

Artigas smiled.

"So it is."

Now his countenance became more serious. "Can you tell me just what happened at Canelones?" he asked.

"The patrol you sent was doing well," Juan replied. "They had rounded up many cattle and sheep when the Spanish surprised them."

"How many cattle and sheep?"

"Several thousand head."

Artigas was astonished.

"The patrol put up some resistance," Juan continued. "But they were overwhelmed. In truth, they probably fought longer than intelligent men should have."

"Now this is the Nicolas I know," Artigas declared. "You are not a spy, corporal. Return to your men."

"Thank you sir," Juan said, and with that, he ran out into the rain.

"Lieutenant Otiguerra, see that the papers on Lavalleja's promotion are drawn up," Artigas continued.

"Yes sir," Otiguerra replied.

"And tell the men to prepare to move out immediately."

"Immediately?" Otiguerra questioned. "In the Rain?"

"We cannot wait," Artigas responded. "The supply train can stay here in San José until we call it up."

"Yes sir."

*   *   *

It had ceased raining the following morning and Paddy spent no extra time in getting his family on the road. His wagon was stopped at the city gate – something that was very unusual. It only reinforced his opinion that he was doing the right thing. The Spanish sentries went through his things and found them to be exactly as he had declared.

"And what is the purpose of this trip?" one of the sentries asked.

"Word is that the city may soon be under threat of siege," Paddy replied. I am seeing my family as far as Solís."

"You may be right," the sentry admitted. "I wish more families would take the opportunity to get out. How long do you personally intend to be away from the city?"

"When I know they are safe I will return immediately and continue to run the print shop." Paddy replied.

The sentry appeared dubious but he shrugged his shoulders and sent them on their way. Paddy was grateful for the lessons learned in the British navy. A straightforward answer more often than not resulted in a minimum of harassment even when the answer could be somewhat revealing.

At the crossroads the family was met once again by more sentries. One held up his hand to signal Paddy to stop.

"The road north is closed today," he said.

"I am headed east toward Minas," Paddy replied. "Is the road to Pando still open?"

"Yes it is," the sentry said. "Do your best to make good time. There could be trouble here soon and I believe the farther you get down the road, the better off you'll be."

"Thanks," Paddy said genuinely. He swished his whip between his two horses' heads and they bolted forward.

When they were out of earshot, Paddy turned to Tereza. "Did you notice the condition of the road to San José?" he asked.

"I wasn't paying any attention," she replied.

"It was deeply rutted and pock marked," Paddy said. "A large force has left the city, either last night or very early this morning. I believe they may be en route to engage Artigas. Had they departed any later than when they did we would probably not have been allowed to leave."

Tereza crossed herself.

*   *   *

Artigas' army moved slowly down the road toward Montevideo. He considered it a blessing that the storm had passed and the rain was gone. But though the sky was a deep blue now and the sun was bright, the ground was still boggy.

Otiguerra rode up to him. The horse labored and sent jets of water and fine mud in all directions as his feet struck the earth. "Damned mud!" he cursed. "It does not help our advance, Captain."

"Be grateful for it, Lieutenant," Artigas responded. "If we find the Spanish, it will be our ally."

"Do you believe the Spanish have left Montevideo?" Otiguerra asked.

"I am almost certain of it. Have you not noticed there have been no travelers coming our way?"

"I cannot remember even one." Otiguerra said.

"There are none! The Spanish are coming—and anyone they encounter along the way is being detained."

Otiguerra stood in his saddle and squinted intensely down the road. "Someone IS coming," he declared.

Artigas opened his spyglass. "It may be one of our patrols," he commented, signaling a halt.

"It is one of our patrols!" Otiguerra smiled. "It is Manuel Oribe".

"Saludos, Manuel!" Otiguerra shouted, hailing him with an exaggerated sweep of his arms. Oribe approached at a gallop without returning the greeting.

"Captain, the Spanish are less than an hour away," Oribe cried.

"How many are they, Corporal?" Artigas asked.

"A sizeable number, I would say between one and two thousand at least. To me it looked like an army"

"Then we must get the men far off the road," Artigas ordered. "Take the side toward the sun."

Otiguerra immediately began carrying out the order. Once off the road, the men, animals, and wagons struggled through the mire. It was not until they had gone some 800 meters that Otiguerra ordered them to turn and take up positions.

Still on the road, Artigas monitored the progress in surprised admiration. His little army was young. It had been operational for just a month, but already he only had to give the order and it was as if Otiguerra had read his mind as to exactly what he wanted. Of course, his second in command had been with him for . . . how long had it been?

Artigas turned to his spyglass once again to the road to check for the Spanish. They still could not be seen, but they were there, and they would be on them soon enough. Oribe had reported it and he was not a man who was easily excited. When he perceived that the grunting and yelling had begun to subside, Artigas rode over to where his men now waited.

"A well executed command, Lieutenant," Artigas congratulated Otiguerra. "Quick and efficient."

"The distance may have made it appear so, General, but with this mud it was very difficult," Otiguerra responded.

"Good! Remember that then!" Artigas said. "Ride with me, Lieutenant. I will address the men."

"Yes Sir!"

Artigas and Otiguerra passed in review along a somewhat ragtag battle line.

"Men," Artigas began. "Until now our parties with the Spanish have been mere child's play. But we have bloodied their noses often enough that they now appear to be taking us a little more seriously. Do not expect them to be such gracious hosts today."

"Take note of the sun. It is at your backs and the Spanish will be looking into it. Remember too the difficulty you had in moving here from the road. We will let the Spanish close on us now through this same mud—and then we will strike them."

"When we do, our cavalry will ride to face them on horses of the estancia—horses that know what it is to be driven hard through mud like this. The Spanish ride on groomed military horses better suited for the parade ground."

Artigas could see some whispering and nods of agreement among his men. In spite of what would otherwise be a lack of discipline, he ignored it.

"When I give the signal," he continued, "Shout like Indians. But hold your attack until I give my command. When it comes, hit them with all your fury."

A single "Viva Artigas" came from somewhere in the ranks. Many responded in turn with their own Vivas. Artigas immediately glared his displeasure to the men and signaled for them to hold it down before the grito gained momentum.

*   *   *

Some distance down the road, the Spanish commander, Captain José Posadas, motioned for to his second in command, Manuel Mena, to come up.

"Yes, Captain Posadas," Mena inquired.

"When we are between Las Piedras and San José, we must be more watchful for rebel patrols." Posadas said. "I am not at all pleased that we have no good information as of yet on the size of their force."

"I would not worry too much about it, Sir," Mena responded. "The prisoners we took said they have no more than 100 professional soldiers. The rest must all be recent volunteers. I am quite confident our Royal Marines can handle any situation."

"That would be more reassuring if we were fighting ship to ship," Posadas said. "But I imagine you are probably not be too happy with your command either."

"What? Parolees?" Mena laughed. "Almost all are professional soldiers—and the reward of a pardon is far too good to be endangered by a foolish act of cowardice now, I would think."

"Most of those who were arrested were charged with desertion already . . ."

A shout from the ranks interrupted Posadas, and drew his attention to the patriot army suddenly seen waiting in the distance.

"Damn it!" Mena cursed. "If they had any artillery we would have been decimated before we knew it."

"Still, it appears they are not disposed to come down to us, Posadas commented. "Form the ranks and prepare to attack."

Mena rode back through the troops. They began to form up on the side of the road to attack. Posadas rode along the column with concern on his face. As he reviewed his men he could find nothing that would indicate that they were ready for the battle ahead.

When he was as satisfied as he thought he could be, he gave the order. "A la carga!"

The men opened what would become a very difficult half mile advance across the boggy field. Much of the mud, recently turned over by the Orientales, was now more than ankle deep. The only sounds to be heard were the labored breathing and grunts of both men and horses and the sucking of the mud around their ankles.

Across the field the Orientales waited in silence as they watched the awesome battle line approach. Then Artigas raised his arm. As commanded, the Orientales began an incessant shout.

"Hold fire until I lower my arm," Artigas yelled. Otiguerra rode along the line relaying the order. At 50 yards sporadic shots were fired from the Spanish line despite their officers' efforts to maintain order. With his arm raised Artigas made an inviting target and several shots whirred past his head. He lowered his hand, perhaps somewhat earlier than he would have wanted, and the Orientales released their own first volley. The Spanish prepared to respond, but before they were set, the mounted cavalry of the Orientales charged into their ranks.

Without waiting for the command, many Spaniards fired their muskets as soon as they had reloaded into the oncoming cavalry and several riders fell. What Spanish cavalry there was began to valiantly counter the attack, but as Artigas anticipated, their horses struggled wildly. The patriot horses appeared to have much less difficulty, just as he had said.

The lines merged and the fighting became hand to hand with pistols and sabers. The patriot foot soldiers advanced quickly now to join in. As Artigas watched, his focus was drawn to two of his men in particular. Again Rivera slashed through the Spanish with no apparent regard for himself. Not far away Juan Lavalleja was duplicating Rivera's effort. It was as though they had become fanatics.

Soon the Spanish line began to crumble. At first only a few panicked and broke—then a few more. Suddenly it collapsed in a full terror and the Spanish ran for their lives back to the road, the Orientales hewing them down along the way. Once the Spanish had regained the road, Artigas ordered a halt to the patriot pursuit. Lieutenant Otiguerra rode up to him.

"Captain," Otiguerra shouted, fighting to restrain his anger. "Let us finish this work! We can destroy them all now!"

"We must attend to other things, Lieutenant," Artigas yelled. "Return to San José and bring our people up to help bury our dead. I will take what men we have here and go on to the cerro.

"Would it not be wise for us to wait for General Rondeau's arrival?" Otiguerra asked.

"He can catch up with us. When the dead are buried send those who are at San José on to the Rincón del Cerro," Artigas ordered.

"Yes, Captain."

*   *   *

The vanguard of the defeated Spanish army passed through the city gate of Montevideo later in the afternoon. Paddy had purposely positioned himself there in order to receive the very first news of the battle. Now, the first hand knowledge that the Spanish had lost filled him with mixed emotions.

He wondered if Luis and Juan were still alive. He was glad that his family was now safely on the road to Minas. Whatever had happened in Las Piedras, those things were now a part of past history, no matter how recent. Now he was dreading what lie just ahead. Within a day, surely no more than two, the siege would be upon them.

*   *   *

Tereza, Ana, and the children were just beyond Pando when word came of the great victory at Las Piedras. While the women were thankful for the joyous news, their first thoughts were of their loved ones who surely were on the field of battle.

"It seems not knowing might be more severe than having the worst confirmed," Tereza commented.

"I don't believe that to be the case," Ana responded, "but this is surely as much as I can bear for the time being."

As the little cart moved on up the road, the two women found it impossible to think of anything else, and yet what they were doing was utterly futile. The only relief, Tereza knew, would be news confirming either the best or the worst. Paddy would surely write as soon as he received word.

Or would he? With Montevideo under siege, there probably would be no mail. News of Juan might come if he wrote to relatives in Minas, but what about news of Luis? He could no longer write to Mrs. Ferrando.

Tereza's mother had died a couple of years earlier. It was most likely her first opportunity to learn anything about Luis would be when she saw Paddy again at Punta Carretas.

*   *   *

That evening in Montevideo, Governor Elío angrily faced Captain Mena in the cabildo.

"And how is it that the Royal Marines can be defeated by an army of peasants?" Elío yelled.

"We were not prepared to fight such a battle, Excellency. Between tigers and tunas, if the battleground is the sea, you bet on the tunas."

Elío was visually disgusted with the lightness of Mena's poor attempt at philosophy. "In light of the fact that I have lost over half my army and its leader, I would prefer that you dispense with any frivolity."

Mena's demeanor became much more morose. "General Posadas condition is unknown," he said. "He chose to stay with the wounded and the rear guard to allow the rest of us a chance to return to the city. I believe he wanted to be the one, if he survived, to surrender his sword to Artigas."

"That was damned foolish of him!" Elío said. "Re-impress the convicts and . . ."

"The convicts gave all they had." Mena interrupted. "And those who survived the battle, if they are here with us, have not deserted . . ."

Mena's retort was interrupted in turn by a courier who burst without knocking into the room.

"A thousand Pardons, Governor," the courier said, short of breath, "but Artigas is on the cerro."

"Can the news become any worse than it already is?" Elío cried.

"It will be difficult for him to take the cerro without artillery, Governor," Mena reminded Elío.

"No, captain," the courier said. "Artigas already has taken the fortress. He surprised the garrison completely and simply walked in.

"I am surrounded by fools!" Elío shouted. "With the guns from the fortress, it now appears Artigas now has secured his artillery."

In disbelief Elío and Mena climbed the stair to the roof of the cabildo. Elío peered through his spyglass across the inlet of the bay and saw the dimly lit but unmistakable flag of the Northern Provinces flying from the fortress walls.

"This is intolerable," the governor cried. "Now the port is at their mercy. We must retake the cerro immediately!"

"I am not certain it can be done immediately," Mena said.

"Come now, Captain," Elío said in mock jest. "In the cerro the rebels do not have the mud to help them. That was their great ally at Las Piedras, was it not?"

Posadas glared at the governor. "Our force is much diminished from what it was this morning," he said, "and that of the enemy grows by the hour.

Elío glared at Mena but dared not counter the rebuke. The awkward silence hung in the air until it was broken with the appearance of a second courier.

"My humble apologies, Governor," the courier began. "I bring a message from the forces on the cerro."

Elío's face reddened even more as he grabbed the dispatch from the courier's hand. As he read he became more enraged.

"Artigas demands we surrender the city or he will lay siege," Elío shouted. "Captain, just how many men do the rebels have?"

*　*　*

Later that evening Artigas met with twelve of his officers in the commander's office at the fortress on the cerro. Included in this group were Otiguerra, Lavalleja, Rivera, Oribe, and Venacio Benavides. Juan and Rivera were the only ones there who were not officers, but their invited presence was significant. The elements of Artigas' future staff were now beginning to take shape.

"I have Governor Elío's response to our demands," Artigas began. "He will not surrender the city. Therefore, I am ordering a siege. "

"Lieutenant Otiguerra, First Corps will take positions opposite the city wall from the bay to the Plata," he continued. The order so surprised Otiguerra that he could not avoid raising an eyebrow. Artigas did not miss it. "I know your men will be spread thin, Rafael, but they will be reinforced both from here and from the Rincon del Cerro tomorrow."

Otiguerra nodded obediently. He knew the Captain was entrusting him with this great responsibility because Artigas felt he could be trusted. And the Captain rarely called him by his first name.

"I am reserving third corps for a siege of Colonia, Artigas continued.

Now the men began to murmur. Just how thin was he going to stretch them?

Artigas ignored the muted outburst. "Lieutenant Benavides, you will take the third corps there. I am aware that a few more men would make your task less difficult, but Buenos Aires is just across the river. If your forces can cut the Spanish off on the land side, we will deprive them of all communication to the outside. This must be done."

"Yes sir!" Benavides replied.

"Men, all this appears very ambitious, I know, but I expect General Rondeau at any moment. His arrival will make all our efforts much less difficult"

*　　*　　*

At the print shop Paddy entered into a personal project that he felt duty bound to undertake. When he had been in the Royal Navy, he had read all of the instruction manuals and pamphlets that had been issued to him. Many had to do with combat strategies including how to fight a man hand-to-hand. Some were manuals that taught proper drilling procedures. Others informed the sailor on how to wear the uniform. Beyond these, there were many more manuals that had to do with topics which could become necessary depending on the time and the place. One had to do with survival in case the sailor was separated from his company in enemy territory. A second gave instructions on how to survive if abandoned or marooned. A third one, and this is the one Paddy was trying to recall now, had to do with how to survive during a siege.

Sadly all of Paddy's manuals went back to England aboard the *HMS Vigilance*. He would have to do everything from memory and he hoped his memory was good.

The result was a manual that was surprisingly well executed. It began by emphasizing the immediate need to regiment food consumption. It continued on into other areas that the reader could find personally objectionable or outright disgusting. Many would swear they would starve first before they would follow some of the instructions in Paddy's publication.

Paddy's instructions were on the street within a day. In the cabildo Governor Elío was enraged when he first read it. A publication such as this could do a lot of harm, up to and including inciting a panic. After a few minutes, however, he realized that Paddy had just done the city a great service that could save a few hundred lives. Who could really tell at that moment? All the signs indicated a dreary outcome.

*　　*　　*

When General Rondeau finally arrived at the fortress on the cerro, he set his advance guard up to bivouac around the base of the fort. Then he entered with his staff to speak with Artigas.

Artigas smiled when he saw him. "It is so very good to have you here at last, General Rondeau," he said.

"I am grateful for your warm reception, Captain. I had expected one that would be somewhat different."

Rondeau paused. "I presume you have been informed of your new position," he said.

Artigas' smile disappeared.

"Commander of the militia—yes sir, I've been told," Artigas replied.

"Captain Artigas," Rondeau said. "You have performed brilliantly – more than brilliantly; you have exceeded our highest hopes! Such success should be repaid tenfold. But the government has become suspicious of the personal ambitions of all its successful soldiers. You must understand, that after putting so much into the effort to liberate the Banda Oriental, Buenos Aires does not want to lose it to an usurper."

"Am I the usurper they suspect?" Artigas asked. "Are we not here all fighting for the same reward, General—freedom?"

"Truly," Rondeau responded. "But the government envisions this freedom as a strong single nation from Alto Peru to the Atlantic, and it includes the Banda Oriental. It foresees a nation strong enough to counter the Brazilians in any eventuality."

"The United Provinces of America?" Artigas asked.

"Maybe," Rondeau replied. "It is not an overambitious dream, Captain. It is the natural evolution of the Viceroyalty of La Plata."

"The Orientales have served the viceroyalty since the beginning, General, and almost always to their own detriment," Artigas said. "Come with me!"

Artigas and Rondeau left the office and climbed to the rampart facing the city. In the distance the Spanish flag could be seen flying from the cabildo near the cathedral.

"Look across the bay into Montevideo, General," Artigas said. "This is the finest harbor for a thousand miles. It is deep and excellently sheltered. But the merchants here are not allowed to develop this port. All merchandise must go through Buenos Aires where merchants there can realize the profits."

There was no response from Rondeau.

"How do Corrientes, Entre Rios, and Santa Fe regard this grand United Provinces?" Artigas continued.

"Response has been favorable," Rondeau replied. "Most people prefer being part of a larger secure nation than a smaller threatened one.'

"Should the Banda Oriental become a part of the United Provinces, it must only be as an equal to Buenos Aires," Artigas declared.

"And do you speak for all the Orientales?"

"I do at this moment."

"Then perhaps the government's fears are not so unfounded."

"I have done nothing to raise the suspicions of the government, Artigas said, "except to drive the Spanish before me."

"That is true. I am too poor a politician not to know I need you with me now. You are still my second in command whether or not Buenos Aires decrees it.

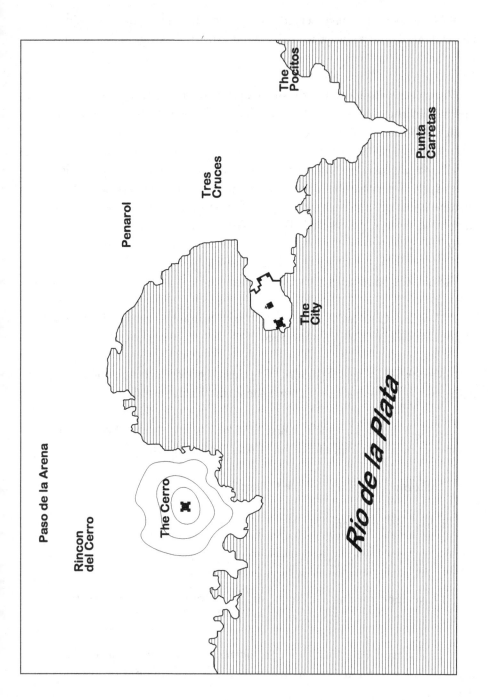

MONTEVIDEO ENVIRONS

* * *

Six days later, Artigas and Rondeau moved about the troops at the Tres Cruces encampment. Tres Cruces had been selected as siege headquarters expressly due to its location. The two officers were checking preparations for a possible assault on the city when a courier rode in from San José.

"Captain Artigas," the courier shouted. "A dispatch from Colonia."

"Give it to the General," Artigas yelled back. "He is in command here now."

Rondeau's face revealed a trace of irritation at Artigas' comment, but he had not been out of order. The Argentine general took the dispatch from the courier and began to read it. Suddenly a pleasant look of astonishment crossed his face.

"Colonia has fallen," he said softly. "The dispatch is from Benavides who is now in the city."

Shouts of joy and laughter immediately spread through the camp.

Artigas himself was beaming. "How do you think Buenos Aires will find the militia now, General?" he asked.

Rondeau laughed.

* * *

In Minas, Ana sat weeping alongside a table in Tereza's home. The news had come in bits and pieces, but the only names in the dispatches were those of the fallen.

"No news of our loved ones is good," Tereza reasoned. "Who would think to send a list with the names of known survivors? For if the names we sought were not there it would cause more grief than what we have to bear now."

"That makes sense," Ana laughed. The laugh was genuine but still had enough in it to show that Ana was not fully consoled. "Imagine how angry I would become if Juan's name did not appear on that list and yet he was still alive!"

"The longer we go without word," Tereza said, "the more convinced I become that Juan and Luis are alive,".

CHAPTER FIVE

Betrayal

Two days later, it came. The letter that both Ana and Tereza had so desperately sought was from Juan. After the introductory sentence (where he expressed his love for Ana whom he missed so much) he confirmed that Luis had survived Las Piedras and was safe. The joy in the Ferrando home was indescribable for a brief moment. But then as she continued to read, signs of concern began to show on Ana's face.

"What is it?" Tereza asked.

"Juan is a corporal now – and he has been named to Captain Artigas' general staff."

"But that has to be good news," Tereza exclaimed. "Now that he is on the captain's staff, surely he will be grouped with the officers in a more secure place."

Ana looked at Tereza with both doubt and exasperation.

"Tere," she said. "This is Juan we are talking about. Now he will feel it even more necessary to lead his men by example. And how do you suppose he was able to impress the general so, a mere corporal, that such an improbable thing could even happen? He must have done something, or perhaps many things, that were foolishly courageous. Knowing Juan, even if Artigas orders him to remain in a safer place, I doubt he could do it!"

"Courageous, perhaps," Tereza responded. "But if he were foolishly courageous I doubt Artigas would have named him to his staff."

*   *   *

It had been two weeks since Governor Javier Elío sent his reply to Captain Artigas that Montevideo would not be surrendered. Now visible results of the siege were becoming evident within the city and they were sobering. The first noticeable change was the sudden lack of new perishable food being brought in from the outside. Fresh fruit disappeared from the markets altogether as they did not keep well. Ignoring the ominous future it portended, this one thing appeared to be, at most, an inconvenience. Still, it was impossible to look out over the walls at the abundant strawberry fields in the distance and to the peach and citrus orchards alongside and not long for them. No one yet understood the relationship between the lack of vitamin C and scurvy, or how a craving for a particular food might be the consequence of a deficiency of some nutrient that food contained.

No one knew even what vitamins were. Every malady was believed to be a sickness. Nothing was known about deficiencies. Only the English knew that there must be some connection. It led to their peculiar policy of stocking their ships with limes and ordering the sailors to have one every day. The Americans, still unfamiliar with the benefits of this practice and worse off for not adopting it, derisively began to call their English counterparts "Limeys".

The next item to go was the vegetables. For a while the few milk cows in the city continued to give milk, but as their food supply diminished, they stopped giving and ultimately they were slaughtered for their meat.

New wells were dug, but the water was brackish. The lack of food, the bad water, and the growing unsanitary conditions all led to a disastrous increase in sickness and death that always accompanies a siege. The first to succumb were the children and the aged. The children's small bodies allowed disease to spread quickly and the frailty and weakness of the elderly made them less immune.

As conditions worsened, Elío saw the need to call his staff into the cabildo for an unscheduled meeting.

"The situation is already as bad as I imagined it could ever be," he began, "and Seville appears powerless to help us in any way. The entire continent of South America is in revolt now and Spain does nothing. It seems her presently military effort is directed solely to avoid falling to the French completely at home."

It was Manuel Fernandez, one of Elío's senior counselors, who dared open a dialogue with the Governor. "The war in Europe is taking some intriguing, and almost unbelievable turns, Excellency. There are reports that the English are now in Spain, actually fighting alongside as an ally. And in order to drive the French out, they have sent the finest of their generals."

"Even were that true," Elío countered. "It would take six months to a year for it to be of any benefit to us, and we do not have that amount of time."

"Then perhaps it might be wise to come to an agreement with the rebels." The unthinkable suggestion came from Juan Soria, another of Elío's counselors. "The people are suffering greatly now and they will be starving in another week. The hospitals are already overflowing."

"You are talking surrender!" Elío shouted. The outburst was not planned theatrics. It was totally spontaneous. Then the governor calmed himself and sat down slowly.

"No, not quite yet," he said softly. "As it is certain we cannot expect Spain to deliver us, I have already sent a secret communiqué to the crown prince of Portugal. I am asking him to come quickly to our aid."

The room filled with groans of surprise – then silence. Finally, the bold Fernandez spoke again.

"The Portuguese? Why not simply turn the city over to the rebels now and save ourselves some time?"

"In the past, Spain and Portugal have not been cordial. I know this," Elío admitted, "but as it has been observed, Napoleon has made friends out of enemies in Europe and enemies out of friends."

"The Portuguese do not want to lose their colonies in America any more than we do," he continued. "A successful revolution next door to Brazil definitely will not be of any benefit to them. Watch and see! The Portuguese will come. And since our Princess Carlota is now the wife of their crown prince, it is most probable that Portugal will return the Banda Oriental to Spain when this business is done."

* * *

When it arrived in the Royal Portuguese Court at Rio de Janeiro, Governor Elío's written appeal was accepted with guarded optimism. King Joao read the dispatch several times over, thinking through all the possible intrigues and ramifications it might hold. Then he summoned his son Pedro to the king's chambers.

"The Banda Oriental has always been the natural extension of Brazil in the south," the king ranted. "That is very clear should one bother to look at any map! We have always desired it for that reason alone. And now Governor Elío invites us right in."

"But I am certain he will want it back when matters improve," Pedro smiled.

"Certainly he will!" the king laughed. "But let us concern ourselves with that little matter when the time comes. I am not too sure that Spain will be capable of reclaiming any of her colonies, even the little Banda Oriental, after the war in Europe ends."

"Have you considered how large an expedition would be required in this effort?" Pedro asked.

"I plan to call General Da Souza to lead 5000 men." The king replied. "This force should be more than anything the Spanish or Orientales have, and they will be much better trained."

*　　*　　*

It had become a recent ritual. Governor Elío and General Mena climbed into the bell tower of the cathedral just as twilight was deepening. It was the perfect hour to still see over the walls and fully assess the enemy's strengths and weaknesses. All the objects visible during the day could still be seen clearly together now with the campfires that would be kept burning throughout the night.

"Has fear made me more irrational, or is the number of campfires actually growing?" asked Elío.

"There are more," Mena confirmed. "Now that the rebels know we cannot possibly retake Colonia or Maldonado, many of those men have returned."

"Yes," Elío agreed. "And new recruits join the rebels by the day."

"That is also true, Excellency," Mena said.

"I am beginning to question why it is we even come up here," Elío confessed. "There really is nothing we can do, and the new revelations only serve to depress me further."

"Whatever the situation, it is best to be well informed of it," Mena advised.

"Surely," Elío replied.

Deep in thought, the governor stared off into the distance. "We are accomplishing nothing here. If it were possible to obtain a truce that guaranteed the lives and liberties of all those involved, and give us both the opportunity to go off and live the rest of our lives quietly as private citizens, should we do it?"

"We swore an oath," Mena reminded him.

"Yes we did," Elío concurred. His attention was suddenly drawn to the right.

"Hmmm, what is this here? There appears to be one lone campfire on Punta Carretas."

*   *   *

From the south shore of the city, someone else was also watching the fire. Paddy Colman had come to this place every evening for the past several days. Tereza was to have returned from Minas and she was late. Paddy could only imagine what difficulties she might have encountered. When she arrived she was to signal by lighting a fire on Punta Carretas. Could this be her?

It was time to take a swim.

Paddy removed his clothes down to the minimum and placed them behind a large boulder near the water. Then he entered the river. It was cold – much colder than he had expected. He dog paddled out from the shore to minimize the noise, then he turned east, swimming freestyle.

Things seemed wrong from the onset. First, there was far too much moon. If it truly was Tereza on the point, Paddy would have to coordinate rendezvous times with her more carefully in the future. The wake he created might be seen from the shore. With this much light it would not be difficult for anyone short of a blind man to determine that something was out on the water. At best the observer might think it a sea lion or dolphin. At worst he might actually come to investigate.

The second problem was not as immediately apparent as the first, but soon Paddy realized it was of much more concern. He was becoming fatigued far too quickly. What was happening to him? Only a few months ago this would all have been child's play.

Then it was suddenly obvious to him. Of course! How long had it been since he had truly had a good meal? He was not replenishing himself. Now he was becoming fearful of succumbing even before he reached the shore. Surely this was not the way it would all end!

Paddy kept the locations of landmarks ahead present in his mind, as best as he was able. Ordinarily that would have been no problem, but now too much of his time was spent concentrating on individual strokes and performing mental calculations on how many would still be needed. And he was conscious that his mind was becoming dull.

It took everything he had within him to reach Punta Carretas. From her position hidden in the greenness away from the beach, Tereza suddenly appeared, running over the sand toward him. Lying on the ground, Paddy weakly raised a hand.

"What has happened to her arms?" Paddy wondered in his confused state. "I can't see her arms."

When she came close, Paddy saw that her arms were shielded by the several thick and warm blankets she carried.

"Oh my wonderful wife," Paddy said softly. He was hardly understandable because of his shuddering. Tereza covered him and embraced him, kissing his face as he slowly warmed.

* * *

In the town of Bagé in southern Brazil, the townspeople looked on in wonderment as the large Portuguese army marched south through the narrow streets. This would be the last night this army would spend in their homeland. Already the high ranking officers had found billeting in the finer houses. The main body of officers set up camp in the plaza, and the rank and file bivouacked at the south end of the city. By nightfall tomorrow they would all cross into the Banda Oriental.

* * *

The new day was beautiful. Paddy and Tereza sat up in the grass just a few yards from the beach on the west side of Punta Carretas. Behind them rose the dense green vegetation of a still pristine forest. They gazed out over an uncharacteristic blue of the Rio de la Plata that flowed on a still day under an even bluer sky.

It had been years since Paddy and Tereza had been truly alone together. Now with the children in Minas, they could see that under the right circumstances they really had not changed that much. They laughed as much as they ever had and kidded each other. There were only two things that kept them from becoming totally lost in the joy of the moment.

For one, Paddy knew this was a special moment in time. These occasions were much less frequent now and he conscientiously took time to appreciate what was happening to him. It detracted somewhat from a complete spontaneous joy, but he wanted to remember the details of this day for the rest of his life.

The other was the specter of the city itself looming on the peninsula at his right. Except for a wisp of tell-tale smoke, the city seemed to be totally at peace.

"Montevideo looks as it always has from here on the point," Tereza remarked. "In my mind I can visualize the buzz of the people and pigeons in the plaza."

"I don't believe they are there right now," Paddy said. "That is where they burn the dead. The plaza has become a crematorium."

"I cannot imagine the tragedy that is unfolding inside," Tereza confessed.

"I am so glad you left when you did."

"Why don't they just give up?"

"There are a lot of reasons, and they don't seem that significant now, but they have to do with patriotism, duty, and honor."

"Foolishness," Tereza commented.

"Perhaps," Paddy replied. "But if laying a siege succeeded easily, there would be many more of them – and more suffering."

"Give me a kiss!" Tereza ordered.

Paddy gladly complied as they lay on the grass. He became totally absorbed in it. Tereza might have too were it not that one eye looking over his shoulder and past his temple toward the city beyond.

*   *   *

Outside the walls of Montevideo, the activities of the revolutionaries had become routine and deliberate. They all now understood that they had settled into what was becoming a very long siege. The tranquil setting was suddenly disturbed by the approach of a hard riding courier. He did not jerk the reins until he was nearly on top of Rondeau's headquarters. In one motion he was off his horse with a dispatch in his hand.

"A most important message for the General,"

"Come inside," said the sentry.

Rondeau looked up from his campaign desk.

"What is it, private?"

"A message from Melo, sir."

Rondeau read the message and sat expressionless.

"Thank you, private," he said.

"Do you have a response, Sir?" the courier asked.

"If I did, I do not believe there will be anyone there to receive it. I am ordering you to remain here. Go get some food, Private."

"Yes Sir. Thank you, sir!"

Rondeau looked up into the faces of his staff.

"A very large Brazilian army is approaching the town of Melo. By now they may already be in the city and I would expect them to be either in Minas or Maldonado very soon."

"I believe it will be Maldonado," Artigas volunteered. "There they can be resupplied from the sea."

Rondeau nodded.

"Lieutenant Gomez!" he shouted"

"Yes sir," Gomez replied.

"Send couriers to both Minas and Maldonado immediately," Rondeau ordered. "If the garrisons have not been overrun I am ordering them to withdraw—and have another courier on hand to take a written dispatch to Buenos Aires."

"Yes sir," Gomez replied. He saluted and left the tent.

Rondeau looked at his officers crowded into a place that now seemed very small. "In light of these events, we must adjourn for now," he said. "We will reconvene this midafternoon. Lieutenant Otiguerra?"

"Yes sir.

"We must send our ablest spies to scout all along the Melo road," Rondeau ordered. "Assemble a unit large enough for a continuous communication with us. We must have a constant knowledge as to where the Brazilians are."

"Yes sir."

"Dismissed, gentlemen," he said.

The men slowly filed out. Before the last man had left, Rondeau was already sitting down at his desk to pen his dispatch.

* * *

Captain Artigas and Lieutenant Otiguerra sat in Artigas' tent on either side of the campaign table. If anyone understood the captain, it was Rafael. He studied Artigas' face as the news of the Portuguese invaders was being revealed and he immediately knew the man was both distressed and brooding – and already thinking about how to counter the new set of circumstances.

Within minutes they were examining a small map of the area.

"It has become more urgent than ever that we take the city now—before the Portuguese arrive," Artigas stated bluntly. "Inside its walls we can maintain a foothold against them until reinforcements come. We won't starve. Admiral Brown can supply us from the sea."

"He would have to do it from the La Plata side rather than the port side," Otiguera countered. "And it will be dangerous. The shoals are rocky and the ships would still be within cannon shot from both the cerro and outside the city wall."

A noise at the tent flap hushed the conference.

"It is Corporal Lavalleja, Captain," Juan called out. "May I enter?"

"Surely Juan," Artigas replied. "It is very good to see you."

Juan came into the tent with Paddy and Tereza behind him.

"Captain, I want to introduce you to my wife's closest friend," Juan smiled. "Tereza Ferrando de Colman and her husband, Patricio."

"Oh yes, the Irish sailor you told me about in San José," Artigas responded.

"Yes Sir," Juan answered. "But now he is no longer a sailor. He is a printer."

"Of course. Welcome to you both," Artigas smiled. "We have been looking forward to speaking with you and learning what conditions are like now within the city."

Juan nodded for Paddy to speak.

"Patricio?"

"Well, Captain, the siege is beginning to take its toll on the city," Paddy began. "The population is now well beyond the first effects of it. The hospitals are more than full with the sick and dying and the people are becoming resentful of the Spanish. They believe that some of the Peninsulares eat better than they themselves, or worse, better than their children.

"Should we be prepared to quickly come to their aid if they launch an uprising?" Artigas asked with some hint of hope in his voice.

"I do not sense that they have come to that point yet," Paddy replied, "although I could be wrong. I do believe the Spanish think it is a possibility, however. It can be seen in their faces. I worry more about what they might do should they come to allow their fears to govern them."

"They may already have done it, Patricio," Juan said.

Paddy gave Juan a worried look.

"What Corporal Lavalleja is saying, Mr. Colman," Artigas interrupted, "is that the Portuguese at this moment are headed here from Brazil with a force that far outnumbers both ourselves and that of the Spanish. Could it be they have been invited in?"

"But that makes no sense," Paddy countered. "The Spanish must know the Portuguese will never leave!"

As soon as he said it, Paddy realized it made perfect sense. And he was suddenly impressed by his first lesson on how Captain Artigas' mind worked.

*   *   *

The following day, Manuel de Saavedra entered Director Moreno's office in the cabildo in Buenos Aires.

"You wanted to see me, Excellency?" Saavedra asked.

"I just received a dispatch from General Rondeau in Montevideo," Moreno said tersely. "He claims that the Portuguese have invaded the Banda Oriental. He also states that their force is reported to be insurmountable."

"This is some very bad news, Excellency," Saavedra said.

"Manuel, we have a duty to quickly resolve how to counter this action," Moreno said.

"If Rondeau's report is to be considered accurate, and I see no reason to doubt it, then we really have little hope of holding the Banda Oriental, and none of taking Montevideo," Saavedra declared.

"It could be we have undertaken a challenge beyond our capabilities, Manuel. Lord knows it would not have been the first time. But let us examine this situation from a positive perspective—if there is one.

If, for the time being, we abandon our efforts in the Banda Oriental, for the first time we could concentrate all our forces in Alto Peru. Then once we achieve our purposes there, we could return to Montevideo in full force. This news may not be as bleak as it first appears."

*   *   *

"Captain Artigas?" The voice came from outside his tent. "It's General Rondeau."

"Come in, General!" Artigas replied.

"I bring some most distressing news, I'm afraid," the General said solemnly.

"Buenos Aires will not reinforce us?" Artigas guessed.

"They have nothing left with which TO reinforce us," Rondeau replied. "Our armies are spread all along the frontier from Chile to Brazil. Above all else, Buenos Aires is determined to continue the campaign in Alto Peru—They want us to negotiate a truce."

"A truce?" Juan shouted.

"Corporal!" Artigas yelled. "You are out of order!"

Juan took his seat.

"I have already sent a representative to Governor Elío to begin the talks," Rondeau continued. "The Portuguese are also sending their own delegation. No one wants further bloodshed if it can be avoided. For now the Portuguese army will remain in Maldonado."

Now Artigas became agitated.

"General," he said sharply. "I have left dead Orientales, AND PORTENOS, from the Rio Uruguay to Las Piedras—for this? They died believing they were fighting for something; they died believing their sacrifice had meaning. And now we honor them by negotiating a truce?"

"You need not redress me, Captain!" Rondeau shouted. "My passion here runs as deep as yours. I have been telling my soldiers there is no higher cause. Now I must appear to turn my back on all of it. But I am a soldier and a loyal soldier obeys the orders of his superiors."

Artigas was smart enough to remain quiet after that outburst. Besides, the General's comments were true. It took a minute for Rondeau to compose himself.

"Moreover we must all think as rational men," Rondeau softly added. "With the Portuguese here, all hope is lost unless we are greatly reinforced—and those reinforcements will not be coming!"

The men look at each other in disgusted silence.

*   *   *

"Juan lost his temper today," Paddy said. "He yelled at General Rondeau in front of the entire command staff."

Tereza and Paddy stood together outside the camp at Tres Cruces under the shade of a lone Ombú tree.

"Will he be alright?" Tereza asked.

"No one took any action against him, not then at least" Paddy replied. "I believe Rondeau fully understood his anger and Artigas might even have been a little proud of him, though it was he who rebuked him."

"Juan needs to learn to curb his anger," Tereza said.

"Does his temper ever affect his relationship with Ana?" Paddy asked.

"No, not at all," Tereza replied. "He is always a perfect gentleman with her, but his passions can take control of him sometimes in other affairs."

"So it is with all of us, at times, with deeply held beliefs."

"Will you go back into the city?" Tereza asked.

"I do not believe there really is any good reason to go back now," Paddy answered. "The risk is far too great and the city will be open soon anyway when the Portuguese come to occupy it."

"What will you do then?"

"Once the Portuguese are here, let's return to Minas and get the children," Paddy suggested. "Ana will probably be ready to give them to us. Then when we come back to Montevideo, we can resume our lives."

"That would be wonderful," Tereza smiled.

*　*　*

The little cart carrying Paddy and Tereza plodded slowly towards Minas. They had taken enough of their belongings to allow them to spend a month in the town. The trip itself lasted four hard days and Paddy knew a single rider wearing out a good horse could be there in one. That frustrated him. He was also concerned about how quiet the journey had been. Earlier trips to the town had been pleasant because Tereza, with her light conversation and laughter, made them so. Not this time.

"You haven't said much this trip," Paddy remarked.

"There is so much . . . ," Tereza began, and then she thought for a minute and rephrased what she was going to say.

"I know I mustn't worry, but I am beginning to believe the tranquil world of my childhood is gone forever now. It seems we face only a threatening uncertainty today and I wonder how long it will be before the fighting begins all over again."

"Well, with the Portuguese now in Montevideo we are no longer at war, and while this has not turned out well for the Orientales, you should be happy at least that peace is at hand." Paddy said.

"I am," Tereza said, but that was all. She sat staring pensively at no one thing on the horizon. It was Paddy who broke the silence.

"I have been thinking too, Tere," he said. "And I wish I could tell you something that would bring you some comfort, but I fear the Orientales will not stand the Portuguese presence for long."

"Not with men like Juan especially – and now Luis too, maybe" Tereza said. There was more than a hint of bitterness in her voice. It surprised Paddy.

"I believe they would follow Artigas to a certain death were he to order it," he said. "The Captain has a charismatic hold on his men, that is for certain!"

"I do not know why they cannot be more sensible – like you are, Paddy,"

Tereza's comment stung and caused Paddy a moment's pause.

"What gives Artigas his ability to lead his men is that he has a talent for drawing out of them that which they never quite knew they had inside. He touches their innermost sensibilities and appeals to their deepest beliefs. Once they are exposed to that, he polishes them by finding exactly the right words—revealing that which was always most sacred in them. It is not a talent he practices to perfect. These are things he feels himself and the words come because they are from his heart, and as it turns out, exactly the words he needs."

"Is that what is happening to Luis?" Tereza asked.

Again Paddy thought for a minute. "Jimmy Burke once told me there is something unique to the Americas. He said it is not a natural thing for the people here, born here and destined to die here, to be governed by magistrates thousands of miles away. They will grow increasingly resentful of it, even if they are being governed justly."

Paddy stopped there, but it was an awkward place to stop. Tereza knew there was more. "And?" She said.

"Ultimately they will revolt," Paddy continued. He wondered if he had mistakenly opened Pandora's box. This was going to do nothing to ease Tereza's concerns.

"Jimmy assured me that once the fighting starts, there will be no going back. He called it part of the American character and from what I have experienced these past few months, I think he may be right. The provinces will not be Spanish much longer regardless of the sacrifices required. And I believe even Brazil may not be destined to remain Portuguese."

"Many lives will be lost," Tereza commented.

"Maybe."

"And who will the Banda Oriental belong to?" She asked.

The conversation that had been lacking most of the journey now had become so focused that almost without realizing it the cart had pulled into Minas' central plaza, the large chapel in the background.

"That is where Juan and Ana want to be married," Tereza said. "Look, it is so tranquil here it seems like nothing has changed."

Paddy was grateful for the change of subject. He did not know who the Banda Oriental would belong to, and he did not want to say so.

*   *   *

That evening Paddy and Tereza sat quietly in the front room of the Ferrando house. They were "guests" of a dinner that Ana had planned weeks earlier. Juan promised he would try to be there but he had not yet arrived. The children would be going to a friend's house so it would be just the four, if and when Juan did arrive.

Tereza asked Ana if she could help. Ana assured her she had everything under control and it would not be right to leave Paddy all by himself. So now in the front room they sat quietly with Paddy studying Tereza's far off gaze.

"Still worried, Love?" Paddy asked.

"The fears I expressed today are still there," Tereza confessed.

"I did not do a very good job of easing them," Paddy admitted, "and they are not foolish, Tereza. I know the present calm will not last. But whatever follows, we must hope it will pass quickly and without too much suffering."

"When it comes, I know Juan will be in the middle of it – and probably Luis," Tereza said. "They have become obsessed."

"You speak as if you see them as two boys, grown up but still playing soldier. They ARE obsessed, Tere, but they are not obsessed with war. They deeply believe in what they are doing."

"What did the Spanish ever do to us that now we must despise them so?"

Tereza's words cut deep. Paddy knew she had not forgotten what he had told her regarding what Jimmy had said. Could it be she just did not want to accept it as possibly being true?

"We had our homes and our families," she continued. "We looked forward to living out our lives as fully as possible. Even Juan and Luis must know that their loved ones depend on them and suffer when they are away."

Suddenly Tereza's frustration turned into an angry outburst directed squarely at Paddy.

"It was all so peaceful here before the English came!"

Paddy had to respond to this attack.

"The English were not the cause of this revolution, nor were they the catalyst for it," he said. "That pot was already coming to a boil long before the English ever arrived. They were only the harbingers of what was to come."

Luisito came into the room and walked over to where Paddy was sitting. Paddy was grateful for he needed an opportunity to change the subject. He smiled at his son who now stood beside him and he put his arm around the boy.

"What is your sister doing?" Paddy asked.

"She is with Ana helping in the kitchen. The food will be ready soon."

Tereza looked at her two "boys" and used the scene as a chance to put the conversation back on track. "It is more than Juan and Luis," she said softly. "I worry that you will ride off with them too someday."

Paddy was ashamed. Now he saw that Tereza's concern had not been so much for herself, but for him. He watched as Katy approached carrying a tray of food that still was a little too much for her. Paddy smiled and tightened his one armed embrace around Luisito.

"I have far too much to live for right now," Paddy explained. "I never imagined I could be so blessed! So you needn't worry. Now that I am here, I can't be going off and getting myself killed."

Ana came into the room, and though she was jovial, her speech revealed some consternation.

"That man I love!" Ana laughed. "He promised he would be in Minas by tonight – well, no matter. We will have fun in spite of him."

"The food looks wonderful, Ana." Tereza said.

"I know Juan would be here if he could," Paddy added. "It is difficult to even imagine what might be happening in Montevideo in light of recent events."

"Time for the two of you to go over to the Gubitosi's" Paddy told Katy.

"Alright, I love you ma'," Katy said. She and Luisito walked out the door and off toward the neighbors' home. Ana looked down the street. There was no sign of Juan.

"Well the day is not yet over – and Juan is not one to make light promises to me, at least, not until now," Ana smiled. "He may still come."

"We will make an effort to leave him some food," Paddy laughed. Paddy's jest was met with polite but forced smiles.

"Paddy, will you ask the blessing," Ana requested.

Everyone bowed their heads and Paddy began the short Catholic blessing on the food he had learned so long ago from the nuns in London. He was not quite finished when a disturbance came to the door. Juan was home.

"Welcome home, Cielo," Ana smiled broadly.

"Hola, preciosa," Juan replied. "Paddy, Tere."

The two nodded.

"You look very tired. Sit down and eat," Ana ordered.

"It all smells so good," Juan said. "I regret coming in so late but the horse really labored the last part of the trip. I needed to remove the bridle and saddle and cool him down a little when we arrived. Added to that, there are a great many things happening now. It is good we are all here because there is so much that should be discussed."

127

It was not what Paddy wanted to hear.

"Is it bad news Juan?" Ana asked with a worried expression on her face.

"Right now it appears to be. But it is too early to tell what might happen."

"What IS happening in Montevideo?" Paddy asked.

"It seems the Portuguese intend to stay a while," Juan replied. "And the Porteños are eager to pull out."

"Pull out?" Paddy asked indignantly. "After so much effort and sacrifice they simply mount up and go home?"

"We must face some difficult facts, Paddy," Juan explained. "The Porteños ARE the revolution right now in the southern half of the continent. We cannot help them. Our hands are more than full right here and Paraguay feels content enough to only sit and watch."

"And?" Paddy asked.

"The revolution is not going well in the west. The Porteños are spread far too thin."

"What will happen to Artigas?" Paddy asked.

"The Portuguese do not want him here, that's for sure. Buenos Aires has offered him a minor post in Entre Rios – alcalde of Ayuí."

"Will he accept it?"

"He almost has to," Juan continued. "If he remains in the Banda Oriental sooner or later he will be killed. I can tell you this much though. He is none too pleased at how things have played out. He is threatening to take his army and whatever families who will follow him."

"To Ayuí?" Paddy asked.

"Yes"

"Juan, what do you mean to do?" Ana asked.

"I intend to sit here and counsel with you, Amor," Juan smiled. "But I will be honest. I am leaning toward following the Captain."

"But what about us – all we have worked toward?" Ana cried.

Tereza gave Paddy a telling glance. "Juan," she yelled. "How is it you could simply go and leave Ana to—to so much uncertainty?"

"Tere, this may not be the right time or place," Juan replied.

"Oh no? You wanted to discuss . . . so let's discuss," Tereza insisted. "How many Orientales, especially those with families, do you believe will truly follow Artigas into Entre Rios when they finally come face to face with what they are actually leaving behind?"

*   *   *

The scene was one of organized chaos. One month after the Portuguese had come, the former enemies now mingled together at the city gate at Montevideo—Spanish, Porteños, Portuguese, Brazilians, and Orientales—all struggling to reorganize themselves. Outnumbering all of them were thousands of civilians preparing to leave. From a distant rise Artigas and Rondeau watched the activity on horseback with somber faces.

"Peace is here, General," Artigas commented. "Is it all you expected?"

"This is nothing more than a vision of capitulation without it being called that," Rondeau replied grimly. "But the treaty is the best we could hope for, given the circumstances – and many lives have been spared."

"Nothing has changed" Artigas grumbled. "All our gains are Spanish once more and our troops are compelled to leave."

"As are the Portuguese," Rondeau reminded him, "and that is much more than we had expected. I am grateful that you accepted the post as alcalde of Ayuí."

"I see it for what it is, General—a bribe meant to keep me from making trouble," Artigas said. "My Orientales had already determined to continue the siege regardless of the terms of the treaty, and that would have been a disaster."

"It would have been catastrophic," said Rondeau. "It is good the people follow you to Ayuí, but I fear they face many difficulties ahead. The trip will be hard, and when you get there, how will you provide for these people? It might be better that they remain here. You must already know they cannot expect help from Buenos Aires."

"I cannot force them to stay—nor would I. The people saw us as liberators. They have suffered much more than anyone of us in the hardships of the siege. To stay in Montevideo now would be to surrender all remaining hope."

"Let the Spanish rule over themselves," Artigas continued. "Let them grow their own food and run the port by themselves. Our exodus will be difficult, but we will survive. We take our herds with us. It may be the Spanish who find it truly difficult."

"God be with you, Captain," Rondeau said, "and may you prosper in Ayuí."

"Thank you, General." Artigas replied. "I do not expect us to be in Ayuí for long. When we feel we are ready we WILL drive the Spanish from the Banda Oriental, with or without Buenos Aires."

As they talked, the very first of Artigas' followers began pulling out with their families, passing through the great city gate and turning north along the road to Las Piedras. For the next several months, tens of thousands of Orientales, a great portion of the southern part of the country, would follow in a great exodus northwest toward the Rio Uruguay. The journey would be difficult, as General Rondeau had predicted. The weather would be bad, and crossing the Rio Uruguay would be hazardous.

*   *   *

That same afternoon outside Tereza's old house in Montevideo, She and Paddy loaded their own wagon. The children helped with the smaller items.

"Will there be room for the china dinnerware?" Tereza asked.

"We probably have room but unless we protect it, I do not believe it will survive the journey," Paddy replied.

"How would we protect it?"

"We should have hired a carpenter to build a box with compartments. But there is no time now." Paddy said.

Tereza said nothing, but she slowly sat in the doorway and began to sob. Paddy walked over and put his hand on her shoulder.

"Tere, we'll take the dinnerware, he said softly. "If we are careful we can probably get through the trip with no breakage. We can tell the children to ride up front or they will have to walk along beside the wagon. The only time they will be allowed in the wagon is when it is time to sleep."

Tereza looked up and smiled sadly. "We can't expect them to do that if it rains," she said. "I am just being silly."

"No you're not," Paddy said. "The dinnerware represents the things that make life sweet. Why not empty a trunk and put the dinnerware into it. We can wrap each piece with an item of clothing we will not wear along the way. The things in the trunk that we do use can be put unto blankets."

Now Tereza was embarrassed. "I have no right to expect you to entertain my frivolities when there is so much more to do," she said.

"Oh my sweet love, Paddy said gently. Do you not know it is the women who make life worth living? The fiestas, the banquets, special decorations for special occasions – none of that would exist were it not for women. And to do that, they need their tools. The dinnerware is one of those tools. Now how could I expect you to sweeten my life and not allow you the tools you need?"

Tereza smiled and looked up into Paddy's eyes. "I love you," she said.

At that moment Luis rode up.

"We must hurry, Paddy. The Captain wants us to begin leaving the city my mid afternoon. He hopes to have most of the wagons in Tres Cruces and the campfires burning by sunset."

"We are about ready, Luis."

"You and your horse appear very tired, Luis," Tereza said. "Take time to have some water."

"There is no time, Tere. I still have many families to attend to."

Paddy and Tereza watched as Luis rode off. In the distance he stopped to encourage another family that was still packing.

*　　*　　*

Late in the afternoon, before he made his way to the city wall, Captain Artigas passed one last time along the streets of Montevideo. Along the way he contemplated all he and done and what the final consequences had become in spite of it. Here and there he saw piles of the possessions that people, at the last minute, had decided they could not take. Some Portuguese soldiers were already rummaging through many of the items.

Some looked at him in disdain and a few times he heard snickering as he passed.

Eventually he reached the city gate – the famous Ciudadela. He dismounted and stood for a moment, looking at the road ahead.

CHAPTER SIX

Exodus

Tereza had never before been so far from home. And yet her family was passing along a road already familiar to many of the men who had served with Artigas in the recent campaign. This time, however, they were going back the way they had come. It had all the earmarks of a retreat, or worse, a journey into exile.

She tried to remain stoic, and to her credit most of her moments were good ones. She treated the journey like a grand adventure that might hold the promise of new discoveries for both her and her family. But sometimes, usually around twilight, she would come to grips with the reality of things, that all she had, all she owned in this world, was riding in the wagon with her. In those moments it took all her strength to keep from coming apart emotionally.

She had married her Irishman for better or worse. She had to admit, however, that on her wedding day her head was filled only with better when she considered her future with him. Paddy was strong and so level headed. He would provide.

But now as she watched him talking with the other men, he seemed no more self assured than any of them. He seemed no more capable than any of them. It was obvious. No one knew what the future held now, not even Paddy. The future appeared only bleak and desolate to almost everyone except those who still put their faith in Captain Artigas.

She would have laughed at the irony between their still hopeful comments and the obvious actuality of their position, were she not so afraid.

*   *   *

Within a week, General Rondeau and the Argentine army had also withdrawn from Montevideo. Rondeau made it a point to ride at the head of the column while his men made their way along the coastal road toward Colonia. From that position he could establish the pace of the withdrawal, a pace that was unusually slow. But he had also put himself at a disadvantage. In this position he could not quickly assess any problems or difficulties within his ranks, everything being behind him.

So it was that he was unaware of a rider quickly approaching him on horseback, not until he heard the hoof beats.

"General," the young officer shouted, "Is there no way we can hasten this withdrawal?"

Somewhere within him Rondeau smiled. Only a junior officer would have acted so brashly without considering the possible repercussions. Perhaps even a senior officer had put him up to it. Outwardly there was no indication the general was smiling. His face was a stern as it ever was.

"Is there a problem?" Rondeau asked.

"The men have long since begun to grumble, and in truth, we are having nearly as much difficulty at this snail's pace than we would in a forced march."

"I can appreciate the difficulty, soldier, and you must know already that I alone am the one responsible for our lack of progress. I want to minimize the physical wear on the men, animals, and equipment. They all must be in the best condition possible for our campaigns in the west."

"I understand, Sir."

"It's more than that," the General confided candidly, "I want to give Captain Artigas every opportunity to avail himself of our offer of help. I fear he has little understanding of the travail that may possibly await him and his people."

"Yes sir," The officer replied. "My apologies. I will inform the men."

The young officer spurred his mount, but before he had put thirty yards of distance between them Rondeau called out to him.

"Lieutenant!"

"Yes sir. "

"Tell the men if we do not hear word from the Orientales by tomorrow night, we'll speed up the march."

*   *   *

The Orientales now moved in a great exodus toward Salto on the Rio Uruguay. The caravan was not one single unit, but rather it flowed sporadically in individual groups of wagons and animals. The sheer mass, however, left very few places along the route where it did not appear to extend as far as the eye could see.

There were more cattle and sheep making the trip than there were people. Also included in the number were untold quantities of hogs, goats, and poultry. Tending these animals only added to the hardship of what had already become a very difficult journey.

Happily one early fear was unfounded. Artigas and his officers had anticipated that riding herd on so many pigs and chickens might be an unending nightmare for the Orientales. But the animals seemed to sense that they belonged on this expedition; either that or they had a strong herd mentality. The result was a surprisingly organized procession of living things.

But it was not altogether a happy procession. The trail was strewn with broken carts and wagons, the carcasses of dead animals, and cast-off possessions that families had finally considered not worth carrying any longer. Frequently there would be a fresh grave. Mothers seated in wagons nursed their newborn in the heat.

When the weather turned bad, life became even more miserable. It gave rise to pneumonia and worsened the conditions of those with the consumption. Many had only recently suffered the rigors of the siege. They were not in the best of health. The death toll rose frightfully but the procession did not stop. The concern was ever present that Portuguese benevolence might change in a heartbeat and they would ride down upon the hapless travelers in their most vulnerable situation.

* * *

"Your Excellency, Governor Vigodet has arrived."

From his desk in the cabildo, Javier Elío looked up and nodded. This day would be his last in the chair he now occupied. Gaspar Vigodet had finally come from Spain to replace him. The aide who announced the new governor and had seen Elío's agony over the preceding months was overcome with grief, but he stood motionless as Vigodet entered. Elío rose from his desk.

Elío forced a smile. "Governor Vigodet. Welcome to Montevideo," he said. "It is good to see you here at last."

"I am astounded and gratified that the city is still in Spanish hands," Vigodet responded, his voice dripping with obvious sarcasm. "Or should I say, in Portuguese hands."

Elío was stunned by Vigodet's opening salvo.

"For months Montevideo has suffered under an intense siege by a superior force," Elío said. His voice was terse but restrained, and he tried to control any tremor. "When it became clear that no help would be coming from Spain, it was the Portuguese who kept the city from falling into the hands of the revolutionaries. Now they have signed the treaty and are committed to return home."

"Governor Elío, it is no secret that the Portuguese want the Banda Oriental," Vigodet said. "That has not changed. They have always considered it to be theirs. And while we may argue that it is ours due to the line of demarcation set forth by his holiness, it is just as reasonable for them to regard this land as the natural southern limit of Brazil—which we all know they do. You are naive if you Believe the Portuguese will leave, or that neither they nor the Porteños will no longer be a threat to us."

"Buenos Aires will always be a threat to us until it is forced to accept allegiance to Spain once again! We all know that," Elío countered. "The more immediate threat, however, is a man named Artigas. He was the first who brought the recent crisis to Montevideo and under the present set of circumstances he has departed a very disenchanted man."

"I know about this Artigas already," Vigodet said, "and make no mistake about Buenos Aires. The city must be dealt with harshly when

Spain resumes her place on the continent. They not only have abandoned any desire to return to mother Spain, they also have designs on controlling the entire viceroyalty. This in itself makes Artigas an invaluable asset to them. And with their help, should he later decide to return in force, I believe he would be much better prepared than he ever previously was."

"Buenos Aires is most cunning and treacherous," Vigodet continued. "Even at this moment they make overtures to us to greet us with a proposed treaty, while all the time they continue preparations to drive us off the continent."

"Artigas appeared quite humble a few days ago," Elío said candidly. "He looked soundly defeated. But I still know he will shoulder a major part of any future preparation against us."

"Be certain of it," Vigodet warned. "From what I have read of the man, I have had my doubts that he can be bought off so easily as it appears he has. I do not think him capable of it. Yet as alcalde of Ayuí, it may be that he has done exactly that. The Porteños want him to behave and this position is his reward. Still, if I am to follow my intuitions, I am certain he will yet be back."

The new governor had Elío's attention now, so Vigodet continued. "As we have been arguing over these things, the current state of affairs has become clearer. It well may be that I do owe you an apology. Since it is true, as you say, that Spain is helpless at the moment, until Buenos Aires reels in this Artigas it might be best that our Portuguese allies remain here for a while, whether or not we like it. In the meantime, through diplomatic circles, we might explain how Artigas' demise could benefit not only the Portuguese but also the Porteños."

*   *   *

A mad scene of confusion greeted Paddy and his family as they approached the riverbank south of the Salto Grande. The refugees ahead had been waiting many hours as weary ferrymen strained to get them all across a river as powerful as the Ohio.

There were two ways to cross. Many had chosen to cross at the falls themselves. As cascades go, these were hardly worth mentioning – no more than rapids in an outcropping of rocks that kept the water level upstream at a somewhat higher level.

The second way was by ferry some distance downstream.

When the ferries were on the water, the cables used to move the craft across were pulled sideways from the force of the current. When the boats were berthed, the cables dragged the water due to their extended lengths.

Both crossings had their degree of danger, but to Paddy, this was the safer of the two.

"I anticipated some confusion at the river," Luis said, "but I didn't imagine anything like this."

"Study the scene closely, Luis," Paddy advised. "The chaos appears only in the organization along this side of the river, and even here some order persists as to who boards the ferry next. The boatmen are doing far beyond what might be considered the best they can."

Luisito interrupted.

"Mama, may we play with some of our friends while we wait?"

"I would prefer that you not," Tereza replied. "It is much too easy to lose you when our time comes to cross."

"It will still be quite a while, Tere," Paddy said. "We may not cross until tomorrow."

"What do you think, Love?" she asked.

"I believe they will be alright if they do not wander off," Paddy said. "If they stay close to that ombú where we can see them, we can quickly call them back when our time comes. It would be better for all of us than to have them to remain in the wagon all day."

"I'll see if some of the other children might want to come," Tereza said. "Perhaps if I go along with them many of their parents will feel comfortable about letting them go."

"They will when their children become too much of a bother," Paddy laughed.

Tereza gave Paddy a wink. Then she left the wagon and skipped up the rise with Luisito and Katy toward the ombú tree. Paddy watched her in admiration and thanked God for the woman he had married.

"Once we are on the other side, I believe the remainder of the journey should be uneventful," Luis said. "Ayuí is only some five leagues from here."

"Maybe it is only the size of this river," Paddy said. "But I am suddenly overcome with a sense that I am leaving my home."

"How could that possibly be?" Luis asked. "But then, if you are no longer an Irishman, maybe it is time to stand up for the Banda Oriental."

Paddy smiled at Luis. "I'm not sure I've the grist to be a patriot, Luis," he said.

*   *   *

The lengthening shadows signaled the approach of the end of the day. Throughout the afternoon the Colman wagon moved slowly within the procession, drawing nearer to the head of the line at the riverbank. Paddy had been right. Other mothers also grew tired of sitting and went to tend their children at the great ombú. That gave Tereza an opportunity to return to the wagon for a while with the comfort that her children were safe.

And Paddy was happy to have her back. He realized that among all the things about her that pleased him, what he enjoyed most was just having her by his side.

141

One thing that could be said about the Ferrando family, they were communicators. The conversation was light and humorous among Tereza, Luis, and Paddy, and it made the afternoon pass quickly. Now there were only a handful of wagons between them and the ferry.

"Call the children, love," Paddy said. "We want to be ready should our time come."

Tereza gave Paddy a peck on the cheek and exited the wagon.

"It is remarkable that the ferrymen have any strength left," Luis said, "considering the number of wagons already on the other side."

"Necessity can be very cruel, but she is a most efficient disciplinarian, Luis," replied Paddy. "The ferrymen know their work is urgent and they will continue until it is too dark to see. But I am beginning to worry, that with the fatigue, mistakes are more possible. We have all been most fortunate up to now."

"I would prefer to be on the other side of the river tonight," said Luis. "We could get a good night's sleep and then be on our way to Ayuí refreshed."

"You may be disappointed," said Paddy. "Have you noticed it has been some time since a ferry has returned?"

"That's true," Luis responded, "and the ferrymen appear to be preparing the boats on this side for the night."

"It is just as well,' said Paddy. "It would be most unfortunate to experience a mishap now that we are so close to the end. Things will go much more efficiently tomorrow morning once we are rested."

Luis looked back toward the ombú and saw Tereza returning with the children.

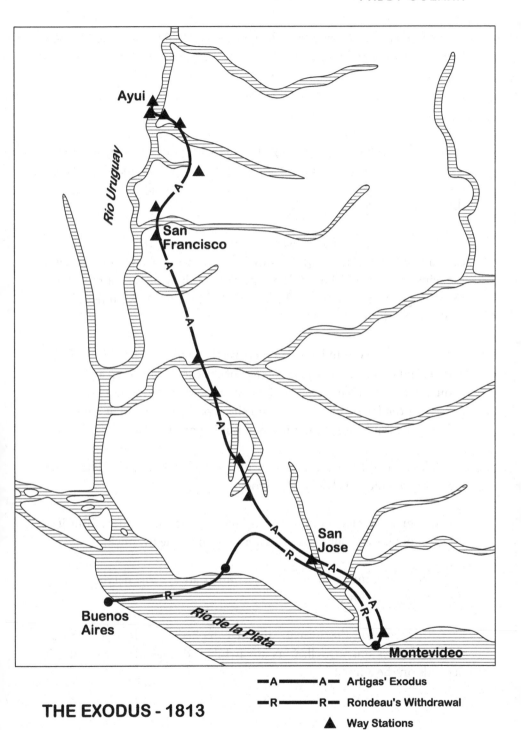

THE EXODUS - 1813

—A———A— Artigas' Exodus

—R———R— Rondeau's Withdrawal

▲ Way Stations

"My sister will be happy with the news," he said. "She does not like being on the water and the darker it becomes the more fearful she would have been."

*   *   *

The ferrymen were up early the following day and began moving wagons across the Rio Uruguay as soon as there was enough light to see the opposite shore. By sunrise Paddy and Tereza had already maneuvered their wagon to the ferry landing.

The men on the ferries were experts at loading the team and they coordinated efforts along with Paddy, who still sat in the wagon seat with the reins in his hands. Low rails on the sides of the vessels kept the wheels of the wagons from slipping off the sides. Still, the work was intentionally deliberate and careful.

When a ferry was fully loaded there was little spare room. The children and pets sat on or in the wagons on top of the cargo. Able men among the company of Orientales helped as best they could while the ferrymen gave orders. As the ferry pulled away from the slip, Paddy smiled at a member of the crew near him, a well built man pulling on the cable.

"Have there been some storms upriver?" Paddy asked. "The water seems higher and a little stirred up today."

The man laughed. "Oh I've seen much worse," he replied. "But it is rough enough for us all to pay closer attention to the livestock."

"They do seem agitated. Are the animals always this nervous during the crossing?" Paddy asked.

"It depends on the animal," the man replied. "Cattle and sheep do alright—horses not so well. Cats are awful, and dogs . . . well again, it depends on the animal."

"The team appears to be settling down a bit now," Paddy said in a relieved tone. He looked back to Tereza in the wagon. "How are you farin' love?"

"I will be happy when we are across" she muttered.

"I must say I'm feeling somewhat sad looking back at the old shore. This move is beginning to take on the look of permanence about it," Paddy commented.

"I feel it too," Tereza said.

"Do not worry yourself too much, Patricio," Luis smiled. Captain Artigas has given his word we'll be back."

"I wouldn't be too certain of it," Paddy counseled. "Time has a way of cooling the ardor in men's hearts. Things can change."

"Not in this," Luis replied resolutely.

In spite of all their attention to safety, the ferrymen chose to forgo one precaution because of time – time they did not have. Ordinarily they would secure each cart and wagon to the boat, but the ramps that were now raised in the front and back and the side rails would have to suffice. For a day and a half all had gone as hoped.

Then suddenly, in the ferry next to theirs, a team became startled. Men rushed to calm the animals and they appeared to be in control. But then in one motion the team bolted backwards into their wagon. The force of the blow sent it up onto the side rail where it teetered for a few seconds. Men desperately strained to drag it back, but in spite of their efforts, the wagon slowly began to roll farther on and finally spilled into the river, pulling the horses in behind.

It was now clear to the Colmans that the driver in the wagon was a woman. Besides the heads of the struggling animals, only she and two of her small children could be seen in the water. Amid the chaos and the shouting it was quickly confirmed that no man had accompanied her on the trip.

Luis suddenly jumped into the river.

"Luis!" Tereza screamed. For a few seconds she sat watching in terror. Then she collapsed into the wagon over a pile of her belongings. "Oh Luis! No no no Luis!" she cried hysterically.

People on both ferries were now shouting together so nothing could really be understood. Paddy knelt over Tereza and held her tightly, but there was nothing more he could really do or say. They both watched the forms in the river appear and disappear as they were swept downstream. Already Paddy knew this outcome was not going to be good.

*   *   *

Within a half hour the ferry was berthed on the opposite shore. A few women accompanied Tereza and the children to a nearby shelter. Paddy looked in their direction. He felt helpless, and he knew at this moment the women could do a much better job in this matter than he. But Paddy had to do something, so he hurriedly returned to the ferries to help offload the wagons.

"This was not good," the burly ferryman said, "not good at all."

"It is going to affect me and mine for a long time to come," Paddy responded.

"We had been so fortunate on this crossing. I was beginning to think God himself had a hand in it," the ferryman commented.

"Now we see He has not," Paddy said bitterly.

"Sadly, there was little hope for the woman and her children," the man said, "none at all, really. Once it became obvious his cause was lost, I had hoped the man, at least, would have tried to reach the shore."

"Not this man," Paddy said. "He would not have given up on them, not even when he no longer had strength to stay above the water."

"How can you be so sure?" the ferryman asked.

"I am married to his sister," Paddy replied. "I know the man – that is, I knew the man."

The ferryman bowed his head and crossed himself. "Just the same, we will send men downstream to look for them until they are found, one way or the other."

*   *   *

Several months had gone by when Paddy rode from his little rancho some distance away into the town of Ayuí. All his European clothes had now been replaced with gaucho garb. A boleador and two rawhide rope hung from his South American saddle. As he entered the town he caught sight of Juan Lavalleja making his way into the makeshift cabildo. Paddy shouted out and Juan waited for him to ride up.

"How is the cattle business, my friend?" Juan asked.

"Not too good!" Paddy laughed. "It appears everyone around here has plenty already."

"At least we will not starve," Juan smiled. "I have been summoned to a meeting with the Captain. Let me see if they will allow you in."

"It would be good to see them all again," Paddy said, "but if they don't permit it, I'll talk to you more the next time we have the chance."

"How is Tere?" Juan asked a little more somberly.

"Honestly, she hasn't been the same since Luis died, "Paddy replied, "and I want the old Tereza back."

"How is Ana? He asked."

The exodus had also changed the relationship between Juan and Ana. Not having any place to go, she lived with Juan now. For him, this new situation created another problem. His father now saw Ana as a lose woman and he counseled Juan to leave her and find a lady more worth marrying.

Ana was Juan's lady, but until things became more secure he would not marry her. It left Ana wondering just how deep his devotion truly was, but she had gone too far to turn her back on him now.

"Ana is fine, Juan said. "I am most fortunate to have a woman like her. You too, Paddy. Tereza leaned a lot on her brother after their father died and she was very close too him. I'm sure you could see it."

"See it? I worried that there was something unusual about it for a while."

Juan smiled. "Underneath she is a strong woman and she will be fine. Right now she needs your strength. Somewhere, further down the road, you may need her. Life works that way."

"Perhaps," Paddy remarked.

Juan paused and nodded toward the door of what could loosely be called the cabildo. "Come on in. Artigas still speaks of you and I feel certain they will let you sit with us. You just may find it interesting. Anyway, I want to talk to you later today so I need you to go along with me."

Paddy smiled apprehensively. "How long do these things last?"

The two entered the building. Artigas was sitting at the head of the table. Rivera and Otiguera were also there, and there were two new counselors that Paddy did not know. Manuel Oribe was a part of Artigas' staff now thanks in a large part to his valor at Las Piedras. The other man was a Charrua Indian, Andres Guacaray, who from first appearances seemed to be quite capable. The captain called him Andresito.

"I hope I have not been presumptuous, Captain." Juan began. "Is the meeting too sensitive for a friend to attend?"

"It is a meeting of my commanders," Artigas said with a scowl. Then his face brightened. "But for Mr. Colman? Not at all."

Paddy was amazed and gratified at the Captain's statement.

"I am surprised you remember me, Sir," he said.

"The man who swims from Montevideo to Punta Carretas – and at night, no less. How could I forget?" asked Artigas. "Yes, do come sit with us. It may be we will need a man of your talents in the days to come."

"I question why would you need an Irish family man?" Paddy wondered aloud.

Your countrymen have distinguished themselves over the entire continent against the Europeans. I am aware of two men in particular who are becoming legendary – General Bernardo O'Higgins in Chile and Guillermo Brown, admiral of the Porteño navy. Perhaps you know him.

"I have only heard of him," Paddy stammered.

"Be that as it may," Artigas replied. He turned to address his staff and Paddy took a seat. "My spies are telling me that there has been much intrigue along the Rio de la Plata regarding what to do with me."

"How is that, General?" Rivera asked.

"While it seems they can agree on little amongst themselves, one common belief they share is that all would be better served were I not around."

"Not around? Would they be so audacious as to murder you, sir?" Rivera continued.

"Assassination is such a brutish activity for gentlemen. A much more round about and acceptable process is being fashioned. The Spanish and Portuguese are pressing Buenos Aires to have me declared outlaw with a charge equal to treason."

Now it was Juan who spoke, "Then they truly want your head!"

"Oh it's not so bad as that," Artigas laughed. "They would be perfectly willing to simply have me shot."

That brought a bit of subdued laughter out of the group.

"Fortunately for me," Artigas continued, "there still exist Porteños who see some use for me, all thanks to the Orientales I command. Even now they are preparing to send General Sarratea with a vanguard of supplies up to Ayuí in preparation for our return to the Banda Oriental. We are to support General Rondeau, who is being sent to Colonia, to march with his army once again on Montevideo. Officially Sarratea and I are to share command, but do not be misled! In truth he is to be our overseer."

Although just a visitor, Paddy felt compelled to speak. "Captain, you must lead your army into the Banda Oriental now, before Sarratea returns with the remainder of his train. The Orientales cannot allow Rondeau to take Montevideo alone or we will all become mere policemen under the Porteños."

"You are a very astute man, Mr. Colman." Artigas commented.

Now Otiguera spoke. "Begging your pardon, Captain, I must speak up on behalf of my men. It isn't that help from Buenos Aires is not appreciated, but none of us wish to sacrifice ourselves once again for gains the Porteños might later negotiate away. Already there are those among us who have sworn they will not fight alongside them."

Artigas smiled. In the last campaign his little staff was nothing more than a collection of dutiful aides. Somewhere between then and now they had become counselors.

"Is that true?" he asked. "And how do your men feel. Lieutenant Guacaray?"

Andresito rose from his chair. "My Charruas will follow you into hell, Captain."

Artigas took a seat. "Gentlemen," he said, "I thank you all for your straightforward talk. It has compelled me to respond with the same candor."

"The situation is such that we must work with Buenos Aires, but I will make it known to them what we expect in this campaign. Those of us who choose not to participate can watch the Bonairenses take the land alone and administer it as they want. Who is to say that General Rondeau is not already in the Banda Oriental?"

*   *   *

In the early nineteenth century, world events became world knowledge in any area served by the trade routes, even if the news traveled slowly. So it was that the British Empire decided to pay a visit to the Royal Court of Brazil in Rio de Janeiro. At his request, the British ambassador, Lord Strangford, was permitted an audience with the Portuguese monarch, King Joao. Acceptance of the request was not totally from courtesy. The King had a keen interest in what the ambassador had to offer. After the opening niceties, Joao took no time in getting down to business.

"Lord Strangford," he began, "you are aware, are you not, that we have been in negotiations with Buenos Aires regarding the affairs in the Cisplatine—not to any great success, I'm afraid."

Strangford got the message, loud and clear. Good diplomacy requires a great deal of knowledge of the area and an ability to instantly pick up on "other things" that are being said in a sentence.

"By the Cisplatine, I assume you are referring to that region known as the Banda Oriental."

"Come now, Lord Ambassador," chided the King. "You know we have always referred to it by that name. When the Pope so graciously split the continent, the Cisplatine fell into an area where the Spanish could lay a claim on it. But look on any map! It is the natural extension of southern Brazil."

"It is a reasonable argument," Strangford said diplomatically. "Perhaps both sides are asking too much and relinquishing too little, your highness."

"Already we have conceded more than I ever thought we would without any considerable return from Buenos Aires, King Joao declared. "I cannot concede more."

"Your Highness, I also have been in communication with Buenos Aires, and while they would not want me to reveal it, our spies are saying they intend to invade the Banda Oriental once again and occupy it in force."

"Are you prepared to tell me something I already do not know?" the King asked.

"Perhaps. They are willing to allow Montevideo to remain a Spanish stronghold if Portugal removes its troops voluntarily and declare itself neutral to affairs on the Rio de la Plata."

"And you found this to be plausible?" Joao asked. "Were the Portuguese to leave Montevideo, Buenos Aires can take it at its will. The Spanish are far too weak to defend it."

Now Strangford needed to do some deft diplomatic dancing, but he had anticipated this response and was prepared to dance.

"Spain is indeed finished in the Americas. It is only a matter of time. But when the Spanish are gone, you, the last European power standing in South America, will only have to contend with Buenos Aires."

"Their current situation is precarious," Strangford continued. "At present General Belgrano leads the Porteños in a campaign against the Spanish in Alto Peru and General San Martin has another army fighting in Chile. The Porteños are spread far too thin."

"Should this be true, once Buenos Aires removes Spain from the region, we should be able to easily retake the Banda Oriental without any other foreign entanglements."

The ambassador took the wording "foreign entanglements" correctly to mean interference from England. He decided to skirt the issue without making a direct promise. "Retaking Montevideo for yourselves at that time might require far less Portuguese lives than defending it for the Spanish now. It is something to consider, Highness."

"So it is."

*   *   *

"'Evening, love."

Paddy entered the Colman house outside Ayuí after a hard day. Tereza was preparing the evening meal over a rustic fireplace with Katy and Luisito helping her with table setting.

"How was your day?" Tereza asked coldly.

"What is there to say? When you work with cattle, one day is much like all the rest unless you break something."

"Is this the way you thought it would be when we married?"

Paddy did not like this line of questioning, nor the tone in which it was being delivered. "That is not a fair question," he replied. "A lot of things have changed since we first met."

"And have these things affected what we have between us?"

Now he was becoming angry. What had he done to deserve this? It took some effort, but he chose to reel in his emotions. "I don't believe so," he replied. "Have they affected you?"

"I try to believe they haven't, but . . ."

"Is this about Luis?" Paddy interrupted.

Tereza looked up from her work.

"Is that what you think?"

"It doesn't take a seer to show how you have changed since that awful day. I suppose that's understandable, but these emotions you harbor now have gone on for so long I am beginning to sense you hold me accountable for what happened to Luis."

Tereza began to cry.

"I have tried very hard to believe nothing could have been done," she said. "I was so proud of you for swimming to Punta Carretas time and again, but when Luis drowned you did nothing."

Now Paddy lost control.

"There was nothing to be done!" he shouted. "Luis knew that when he went in, but being Luis, he had to make the effort – and for what? Now he is dead. Had I tried to save him we would both have been lost that day. Is that what you are asking?"

"I don't know," Tereza cried. "My grief has overpowered any ability to see clearly – I know that. I honestly cannot even begin to think about what it is I really want."

"None of what has happened, from the beginning when your father died, up until now has not been good for us." Paddy's tone was softer now that he better understood. "We should be able to live in a world both safe and stable where we can plan our future, but we do not have it now."

"Will we ever have it again?" she asked. "I wonder now if we really ever had it before."

"Yes we did," Paddy said. "And we will have it again. But for now we must put our hearts into working to perfect the things we still have. We cannot give up. We owe it to Katy and Luisito."

Tereza nodded and smiled. "And so you work the cattle, day after day, in an effort that seems will go on without end."

"Yes, for now I do," Paddy replied. "But I know if I do not act in some way soon to affect a change, this might well go on forever, just as you hopelessly see it now."

A look of alarm crossed Tereza's face. "What are you saying, Paddy?"

"I'm saying it may be time to take a stand. We belong back on the other side of the river."

"Are you saying you may become a patriot?" she asked.

"Has my image in your eyes fallen so far that you cannot see the possibility?"

"No, I can see it – and I am afraid."

*   *   *

Maintaining a revolution in the southern half of the continent kept the cabildo in Buenos Aires very busy. The business of this particular day would put the matters of Chile and Alto Peru aside and be directed only to matters on the other side of the Rio de la Plata. Director Moreno would meet with his Generals, Saavedra and Rondeau, who had been chosen to direct the effort. He allowed Saavedra to open the formalities.

"General Rondeau," he began "we have called you here to report on the recent campaign in the Banda Oriental."

"Had we been given more support, the report might have been happier," Rondeau said dryly.

"You and Captain Artigas achieved far beyond anything we had hoped," Moreno interjected, "but we could not send you more aid because of the deteriorating conditions in Alto Peru."

"You preferred to dedicate our efforts to far-off Alto Peru instead of against the Spanish forces right across the Rio de la Plata," Rondeau said. It was more a condemnation than a statement.

"There is much to consider when we deploy our forces," Moreno replied. "In the early days of the revolution we thought we could go anywhere and take anything. Paraguay showed us it would not be so easy."

"The strength of Spain in the new world is in Peru," Saavedra added. "Bolivar has had much difficulty there, but there is evidence now that his fortunes are turning. Now while we wish him well, we cannot allow Bolivar to sweep through Peru, and on into Chile and Alto Peru. We must maintain a presence in that part of the continent or the Northern Provinces might also be lost."

"And Buenos Aires would become a small insignificant nation," said Moreno, "provided it too is not eventually overrun by the Colombians—or the Brazilians."

"By then the Brazilians might well be entrenched just across the river," said Rondeau.

"We will act to counter Brazil," declared Saavedra.

"When you decide the time has come," said Rondeau, "I recommend that Artigas be a major component of the operations."

"We are all aware of Artigas' abilities," replied Moreno, "and apparently so are the Spanish. Vigodet has actually requested that he be declared outlaw. General Da Sousa goes further. He wants us to declare him a traitor."

Rondeau broke out in laughter. "For what?"

"What does it matter for what? There are no grounds for the charge," Moreno smiled, "but treason is a capital offense."

"Then they want us to kill him!" Rondeau yelled.

Saavedra nodded.

*   *   *

Within days, General Sarratea, a marginal military officer but a fine politician, visited Artigas at his headquarters on behalf of the government of Buenos Aires.

"Since I received word of your coming, General, I have been looking forward to speaking with you." Artigas said. "Something of a grand scale must be at hand if Buenos Aires sends a man of your stature all the way to Ayuí to see me."

"That is correct, Alcalde. And I can see what I have heard about you is not unfounded," smiled Sarratea. "It is my unpleasant duty to make you aware that Portugal is pressing the government in Buenos Aires to have you declared a traitor!"

"I already know of it. And have come to arrest me?"

"Hardly," Sarratea laughed, "although Buenos Aires has never really been comfortable with you. You are too independently minded."

"This business is about independence, General," Artigas said sternly, "both of nations and of individuals. And while Buenos Aires will not declare me a traitor, I understand they are willing to have me declared outlaw provided Portugal withdraw its troops. Since that might not necessarily mean my execution, Portugal has declined."

Sarratea looked up from his mate. "Rumors I'm sure. In spite of Buenos Aires' discomfort with you, they are not unappreciative of all you have achieved. Even now they propose to provide you an army of 5000 men to return to the Banda Oriental. With your Orientales your force will be greater than the army the Portuguese have there now."

"Am I to have complete command of this force?" Artigas asked.

"Again, your intuitive nature is very acute, Alcalde," Sarratea remarked. "No, General Rondeau will meet you at Montevideo with his army, and he will command the campaign as before. I am to be attached to your force."

"Since you are a general, you will then be in command."

"Well then, maybe I have some good news. That which you suspect is not true," Sarratea replied. "You are to be promoted to the rank of general. You are authorized to make your lieutenants captains if you desire it. We are to command together, but I have no misunderstanding as to our individual talents. You are the strategist and you will be the director of our operations."

"Then your purpose must be as a spy," Artigas continued, "to report my actions and attitudes to Buenos Aires."

"Joint command will be difficult for us both, Sarratea admitted. "I do not enjoy my assignment. Did you know Portugal has also threatened a blockade if you are not declared a traitor?"

"And executed!"

"And executed!" Sarratea agreed. "It is not a bluff, the blockade is already underway. Buenos Aires remains true to you, but they expect fidelity in return."

"Then we understand each other, General. I look forward to going back to the Banda Oriental. Once the Orientales return, be assured they will not leave again."

"I understand. And you be assured this time we are committed to take Montevideo," said Sarratea, "and keep it. We are working with the British to pressure the Portuguese. The Spanish in Montevideo will not last long without support from Brazil."

*   *   *

At Rio de Janeiro, Ambassador Strangford was once again back in the Royal Court of Brazil, this time at the invitation of the King.

"Lord Strangford," King Joao greeted him. "Perhaps you already know our most recent talks with Buenos Aires have now broken down completely."

"Yes, I heard," Strangford replied. "As I have already said, perhaps you have been asking too much, your highness, when just a little patience and tact would give you exactly what you want."

Immediately the King Joao sensed that Strangford was going somewhere with that remark. "Could it be you have a proposal?" he asked.

Strangford smiled. "Once again, I have been in communication with Buenos Aires," he said. The King raised an eyebrow. Strangford actually expected a much stronger reaction.

The ambassador's assignment encompassed most of southern and eastern South America and it was generally expected that he call on many of the seats of government. But while he gained a broader understanding of the pulse of the continent, no single government confided in him too deeply for fear he might play one against the other. He could also reveal sensitive secrets to a potential enemy. Both of these things Strangford was about to do right now.

"You have my word they will be back in the Cisplatine before we enter the next season," he said.

"And they want us to just leave!" the King said angrily. "Do you still believe that if they are successful they will allow the Spanish to remain as they have promised?"

"No," Strangford said. "Not now."

"Then, are you suggesting that we could then take the Cisplatine without any outside interference?"

The King was still fishing for the assurances he needed, this time more directly, that England would not become involved, and while Strangford was reasonably sure she would not, he did not take the hook. "It is something to consider," he replied.

"My son—the prince—could face some problems with his little Spanish wife were we to go in that direction."

"I would think once Princess Carlota fully understands the embellishment her kingdom is to receive, she will be more receptive," Strangford said.

The King, understandably, nodded.

*   *   *

The message arrived within weeks. Once received, the demoralized Portuguese army began almost immediately to prepare to evacuate Montevideo. From the gate, General Da Souza and Governor Vigodet watched scenes of soldiers outside the city wall kissing tearful sweethearts. The less fortunate, who had no sweethearts, fought with their packs or with teams of animals,

"This evacuation is insupportable, General," Governor Vigodet cried. "You sign our death warrants with it."

"I am most regretful, Governor," Da Souza responded. "Were it my decision, we would stay. But I have my orders."

"But this makes no sense," Vigodet argued. "Portugal has always been committed to seeing that the American colonies are maintained, for the sake of all the European powers mutually."

"That is true, but in this particular matter a stronger participation from Spain had been expected," Da Souza replied, no longer able to conceal his irritation at Vigodet's continuing lament, "but Spain has not responded. If Spain is ever going to provide more in the defense of Montevideo, she should do so now."

"You know that is impossible," Vigodet said bitterly.

"Then if Spain cannot maintain her colonies, the time may have come for her to withdraw."

"Spain cannot be expected to abandon colonies she has spent three hundred years to develop," Vigodet shouted.

"Perhaps she could turn them over to another European power," Da Souza suggested, "in sale or for safekeeping."

"Portugal perhaps?" The Governor said coldly.

CHAPTER SEVEN

The Return

In spite of Artigas' best efforts, military procedure at Ayuí had become very unmilitary. His soldiers now spent most of their time simply trying to provide for their families on the harsh plain, and that included most of his staff. He kept his permanent staff intentionally small now, and it became more expedient to give a directive to only one or two and have them relay it on to the others.

To counter the lack of discipline this was sure to cause, Artigas still held his regularly scheduled meetings at the cabildo. The little building was never intended to be the seat of local government. But in spite of its diminutive size, it still was one of the larger buildings in the area. So the Captain chose it as his headquarters and it became known as the cabildo simply by default.

Much of the time there was no military reason, except to maintain some degree of morale and discipline, to even hold the meetings. They became little more than a means for the officers to become updated on goings-on in the community. Quite naturally then, the protocol lapsed into something that was far from rigid. So on this occasion, when Artigas actually rose from his chair to address his staff, everyone took note.

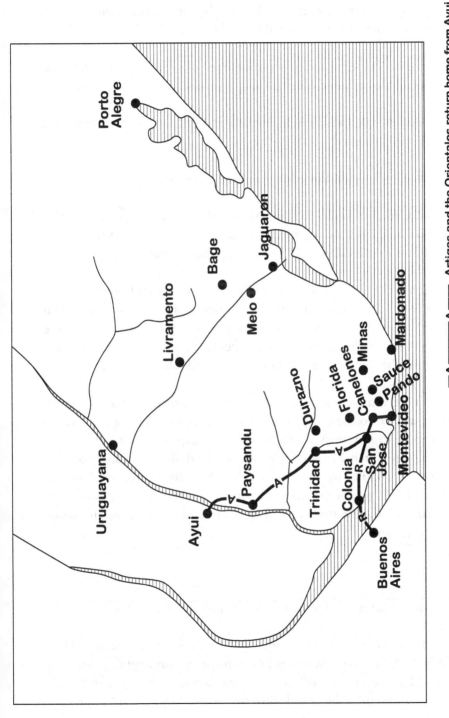

ARTIGAS' SECOND CAMPAIGN

A —————— Artigas and the Orientales return home from Ayui

R —————— Alvear's and Sarratea's route to Montevideo with the Argentine army

"My dear faithful officers," he began. "You may inform our brothers that we will now be returning to the Banda Oriental."

The men let loose a spontaneous outburst of joy. Many had questions. Artigas smiled and raised his hand to quiet them.

"General Sarratea is bringing an army to this very place to be united with us," he continued.

Now the joy was followed by a unified grumble.

The Captain's smile did not wane. "I foresaw the possibility that this news might not be warmly received," he said, "but to drive out the Spanish, we must avail ourselves of every possible resource."

There was an uncomfortable silence. Then Lieutenant Otiguerra spoke up. "It is not that their assistance would not be appreciated, Captain, it will be! We just do not wish to sacrifice ourselves once again for something Buenos Aires might negotiate away afterward. Already there are those among us who say they will never fight alongside the Porteños."

"But we must work with Buenos Aires," Artigas countered. "I will make it known to the Porteños what we expect in this campaign. Those who choose to stay in Ayuí, rather than participate in this fight, might very possibly watch Buenos Aires take the land alone. I assure you that under those conditions, they will surely rule as they want. Patriots who prefer that WE govern the Banda Oriental can come with me. And let me add that it is possible that General Rondeau and his army are already on our beloved soil."

*   *   *

"When the army pulls out of Ayuí, I intend to be with it."

Paddy's declaration was sudden but not totally unexpected. From what he had said recently, Tereza knew the revelation might come at any time. Still, she always thought casual conversation between her and Paddy might ease into the subject and allow her time to adjust.

"What about the farm?" she asked.

"See if you can sell it. Try and get a good price if you can, but sell it just the same."

"But this is all we have!" Tereza said.

Paddy leaned forward in his chair. "I have thought through this very carefully," he said. "Artigas is committed to return to Montevideo and he will do it soon. Without Portuguese support, the Spanish will fall quickly. Casualties should be light, if any"

"What about us, the children and me? What about our livestock?"

"You'll have to sell the livestock too. We will need as much hard money as we can get. When this is done, I hope to go back to doing what I did before we left."

"Do you think the press is still there? Maybe someone else has it now."

"Perhaps. But it may still be there unused. We'll just have to see."

"Paddy, why are you doing this? Why are you turning your back on the children and me?" Tereza asked.

"I have suffered long, thinking about what I would say when this moment arrived and how I would say it," Paddy replied. "When Katy and Luis look back on this period of our lives, they will remember that almost everybody they knew were involved in this struggle, directly or indirectly – just about everybody. But their own father was not one of them."

"I will remind them that a live father is much better than a dead hero," Tereza said.

"That may not always be true," Paddy replied. "Consider this, a father who died courageously is better than one who has become a live coward."

"I do not see you as a coward. Do you see yourself as one?"

"I really do not know! Up until now I thought that it was the wise thing to stay out of this conflict and see after my family. But through it all I have been beset with feelings that I should be with the men."

"You do not have to prove yourself, Paddy," Tereza shouted.

"I don't think that is my problem. I just feel I should be with the men."

"So it's duty then!"

"You make me feel noble."

"I don't mean to," Tereza said. "You also have a duty to your family."

"Of course, you are absolutely right!" Paddy sighed.

"No, damn you. You are right. It is your duty, and only now have I realized it fully."

"Am I that convincing?"

"It is not you, It's Ana."

"Ana?!?"

"I watch her. I watch her every day. She has sacrificed her whole life for Juan and his ideals. I know she wants a little of what I already have – a husband, home, and children. It may be something she will never have. In the meantime, she does whatever she must until that day finally comes."

"Juan is a lucky man," Paddy said.

"Yes, and you deserve to be as fortunate as he."

"Tereza, don't . . ."

"Just listen to me. I have been far too selfish. You deserve a woman who will support you in your ideals, as hazardous as they might be. I will no longer resist you in this. I will do more. I'll mind the household wherever it is and I'll support you however I can, but Paddy . . ."

Tereza paused there.

"What is it, love?"

"If you are killed, I will never forgive you!"

*   *   *

At the fortress on the cerro, Spanish soldiers watched from the battlements as the Army of the Northern Provinces approached Montevideo. The Captain of the Guard squinted uneasily into his spyglass.

"Governor Vigodet was right," he said. "Now that the Portuguese are gone, the rebels are back."

"How many men do you believe there are, Captain?" his corporal asked.

"Several thousand at least, surely more than enough to take this place – and quickly. Signal the city that the enemy is here."

"Yes, Captain," the Corporal replied.

It required more than another hour for the ranks of General Rondeau's army to form up just outside the range of the cannon on the fortress walls.

"Captain," bellowed Rondeau.

José Culta, rode up to where Rondeau sat on his horse. "Yes, my General."

I will remain here with second corps and lay siege to the fortress," Rondeau said. "The rest of the army is to follow you around the bay to Montevideo."

"Yes, General."

"I expect the cerro to fall by Christmas—surely no later than New Years Day," Rondeau continued. "In the meantime, you and the remainder of the army shall maintain the siege of the city until you receive further orders."

*   *   *

Artigas' army of Orientales was still plodding along the western road toward Montevideo when a single rider came galloping toward them. He had been sent ahead earlier on a strong fast horse to gather as much information about the situation as he could.

"What is the word from the front, soldier?" Artigas asked the rider.

"General Rondeau's forces have already surrounded the city. They foiled an escape attempt by the Governor, but by the worst of luck, he was able to flee back behind the city walls."

"What about the fortress."

"The cerro remains under siege," the rider replied, "but it is believed the Spanish there no longer have food."

"Captain Rivera!" Artigas shouted. Within seconds José rode up to his side.

"Yes, General."

Both men were smiling. Events of the past several weeks had surely turned in their favor. As Sarratea had promised, the government in Buenos Aires decided to promote Artigas to the rank of general, but only after considerable discussion. Then when it became clear that Sarratea was not nearly ready to move his army to Ayuí, Artigas was ordered into the Banda Oriental without his Argentine support. The decision was a painful one for the director, and it was made over much objection from his government.

Among the Orientales it was questioned whether the Porteños would remain true to their word—that when Sarratea finally caught up with the Orientales, the two men would still share command.

"Shared command," Artigas smiled to himself. It was a joke and he knew it. To strengthen his position, he immediately promoted his senior officers to the rank of captain. Then they raced toward Montevideo, fully intending to stay ahead of Sarratea all the way.

"Take an advance guard into Paso de la Arena and prepare camp there," Artigas ordered. "I want a council of war as soon as I arrive with the main force. Things are happening very quickly now in Montevideo and we cannot afford to miss this party."

"Yes, sir," Rivera replied.

*   *   *

Artigas' main force arrived at Paso de la Arena a day later than Rivera. Even before his soldiers could begin to unpack, Rivera's men greeted them with hot water for their mates. Artigas and his brothers, together with Otiguerra, Juan Lavalleja, and Andresito walked to the campaign tent where Rivera stood at the entrance.

"Did you have a hard journey, General?" he asked.

"It was as tiresome as a forced march can be." Artigas replied. "You look rested, though."

"You gave me a small force of strong men."

"What is the news from Montevideo?" Artigas asked.

"The city is still expected to fall at any time," Rivera replied.

"Not before we can be a part of it I hope."

"No sir, Rivera said, "And Sarratea?""

"There's been no sign of him. We are not going to wait for him, though," Artigas declared. He dismounted and entered Rivera's campaign tent with the rest of his staff. Inside they took their seats around a small table Rivera had already set in place.

"Tomorrow we will move to Tres Cruces," the General said. "When we last came to Montevideo, we were the conquerors—We, the Orientales. Now we may have arrived too late to be of any true importance."

"I know Buenos Aires," he continued. "Should they believe Spain was defeated solely through their efforts, they will believe they alone are entitled to rule in the Banda Oriental."

"Well, I have not come this far only to change one ruler for another," Rivera grumbled.

"None of us have, José," Artigas assured him. "At Tres Cruces, I want a meeting arranged with representatives from every major town council. When this thing is over, me must stand united as a nation."

The General took time to look at each man individually, as if updating his assessment of them all.

"The importance of these representatives' presence cannot be overstated," Artigas affirmed. "They must be the most esteemed of men in their communities!"

The men sat in stunned silence. Juan was especially surprised. He never had any thought that an idea such as this was even being considered by the General. Yet it had to be in Ayuí that Artigas had begun anticipating the coming problems and thinking of ways to counter them.

The solution now seemed so simple and obvious there could be no other. The officers would not resolve the issue, bickering among themselves, nor would the armies that might oppose each other. Artigas had decided to enlist the people themselves through their locally elected leaders. They would add the necessary validity to the effort. At the same time, it would also become much more difficult for the civilian sector to remain comfortably seated on the fence.

Was he the only one who could see though this thing all the way? Lavalleja looked around the room. No, they all saw it. Every man was looking at the General both in astonishment and admiration.

"To do this, we must dispatch riders at once," Artigas said.

Otiguerra jumped from his seat. "We will see to it, General," he shouted.

*　　*　　*

It was either the height of optimism or the height of folly. If there was one thing Paddy had learned in his majesty's navy, for battle plans to be successful, they must first be simple. That was not to say there had to be plenty of contingencies still to counter the unexpected.

Ana and Tereza had already come into the camp along with the children before they continued on to Minas. Artigas had asked the people of the exodus to return from Ayuí as quickly as possible. In doing this he explained that he required a show of force from them all, since he had already told the Porteños that the Orientales would return and never again leave.

Whatever the reason for Ana and Tereza's quick arrival, Juan and Paddy were happy they were there. As the children played, the adults discussed what Artigas was about to try to do.

"The plan is far too ambitious, Juan," Paddy said, "and far too involved – especially when there are so many, even in our ranks, who are more than anxious to see it fail."

"Perhaps," Juan said, "but we will never really know unless we at least try. And if do we achieve the impossible, how wonderful would that be?"

Again Paddy remembered Jimmy's words, and now he saw them exemplified in the form of the friend standing before him. Deep down, Paddy too would like to think it could happen. No! He had to be the voice of reason and counter this lunacy that had its hold on the otherwise reasonable people of the Americas.

"Juan," Paddy retorted almost mockingly. "You are so sober minded, so level headed in so many things, how can you allow yourself to be so easily seduced by all this?" The prize is too important to be put at such risk!

"No!" Ana interrupted. "Juan is right! If there is any possibility that this dream can be realized now, then we must try! We must! How is it you cannot see this?"

Now Tereza took a turn. "Paddy sees it well enough!" she yelled back. "He is here, isn't he – taking his place among the soldiers? And he knows how I feel about it!"

"I genuinely hope the General is successful," Paddy said softly. "I have sworn to be at his side until we have thrown the Spanish out, regardless of what lies beyond. But I know there will be stumbling blocks all along the way. Most will be placed in our path intentionally by those who would see us fail, and anyone of them can bring down the entire plan."

*　　*　　*

The first of these stumbling blocks rode into the encampment at Tres Cruces two days later.

General Sarratea entered the camp at the head of a substantial force. If there were any ideas about his ingratiating himself to the Orientales, they could not be discerned early. Salutes and words of greeting from the Orientales were returned by minimal gestures and a harsh stare. When he arrived at Artigas' headquarters, he dismounted and walked in without announcing himself.

If Artigas was surprised, he did not show it to his staff.

"General Sarratea," he said warmly, "We have eagerly anticipated your arrival."

"I wish I could be as cheerful as you, General," Sarratea said gruffly. "But as I entered the camp, I saw an army totally unprepared for combat. The discipline and preparations here are deplorable."

"General," Artigas replied, "this army has been on a forced march almost constantly since we crossed the Rio Uruguay. Our supplies and support are still somewhere up along the road. We cannot settle in for as of yet we do not know whether we are to remain in Tres Cruces or be shortly ordered to the city wall itself. Moreover, the men need rest."

"Really? I have been informed that rather than use this time in military preparation, you have become involved in political intrigues," Sarratea charged. "Do not presume that the course Buenos Aires has laid out for the Banda Oriental, or this entire region for that matter, will be diverted!"

Now Artigas became obviously agitated. "Buenos Aires is carrying the revolution to every corner of the continent which is not contested by Bolivar himself. It is a highly honorable effort. Nevertheless Buenos Aires is only able to do all this with the cooperation of the patriots from those many regions who are rallying to the cause."

"The revolution would not be where it is now were it not for Buenos Aires," Sarratea countered.

"Nor for the efforts of those patriots," Artigas said, raising his voice. "I do not minimize what Buenos Aires is doing, but I have already said we will not exchange domination by Spain for domination by Buenos Aires."

"This is precisely the attitude that has Buenos Aires concerned", Sarratea yelled.

"There is none here bolder than General Artigas!" Jose Rivera interrupted. "And none has been more successful in taking the fight to the Spanish. Beyond that, when the battle is joined, he is there in the thick of it among his men. Can that be said of Rondeau or Sarratea?"

"That is enough, Lieutenant," Artigas shouted.

"Begging your pardon, General," Rivera responded. "We must not allow these presumptuous bastards to run over us. Our sacrifices have been far too great to permit it!"

"Lieutenant Rivera, you are dismissed!"

Juan had never seen the General so upset. Rivera stood frozen for a second, obviously shaken by the General's blast. Then he stormed out of the tent.

"That man will have to be disciplined, General," Sarratea said.

"General," Artigas responded in a quivering voice, "there are a handful of men on whom I rely totally, some because they have been with me from the beginning, and some, like Captains Lavalleja and Rivera, because I need their abilities in battle. If I am to lose any of these men, it will not be due to the decision of a disciplinary court."

"General Rondeau will receive my report", Sarratea threatened.

"Then he will also receive mine," Artigas fired back.

*   *   *

The two sentries manned their station along the picket line somewhere midway between Tres Cruces and the city wall itself. At 3:00 am they kept their fire burning brightly, which silhouetted them very well for anyone who might want to take a shot at them. It was dangerous business, but necessary, as it allowed everyone—them, the Spanish on the walls, and the observers in their own camps—the capability of seeing not only the extent of the picket line but any possible disturbance anywhere along its breadth. On clear nights the fires could easily be seen even from the cerro.

Men assigned to be sentries on the line were advised to keep laughter and horseplay to a minimum and to be constantly vigilant for any approaching force. It was not a difficult order to obey, for while an attack by the Spanish was not a serious consideration due to their limited numbers, a small raid or worse – snipers – were not out of the question. In this tension that ebbed and flowed, depending on the mind's imagination, the two sentries heard the unmistakable sound of an approaching horse.

"Halt and identify yourself," shouted Corporal Manriquez.

In the darkness came the response. "I am a Spanish courier and I approach no further. Are you Oriental or Porteño?"

Corporal Manriquez looked at Private Sanchez in surprise. What kind of question was that?

"Oriental," he volunteered.

"Then I bring a message for General Artigas. It is from the governor. He trusts you will respect the confidentiality between these two men until General Artigas deems otherwise.

The sound of something hitting the ground in front of the sentries made both men jump. The sound of the courier's horse galloping away followed. The dim glow of the firelight revealed the object to be a diplomatic pouch complete with the Spanish royal seal. Private Sanchez cautiously retrieved it.

The pouch did not go directly to the General, not at 3 o'clock in the morning. The sentry felt it more prudent to disturb Captain Otiguerra's sleep rather than Artigas'. Rafael better understood the situation and he knew the General would be more upset if he had not been advised of the pouch until the following morning. He dressed and made his way to the General's tent.

Artigas sat in silence for almost a minute after he read the dispatch. That was very uncharacteristic of him and it took Otiguerra by surprise.

"I'm going to require some time to sort all this out," Artigas said. "Schedule a council with my captains for this evening."

"Yes, General," Otiguerra replied.

"And Rafael,"

"Yes?"

"Be discreet! This meeting is only for Orientales."

"Yes Sir."

*   *   *

Artigas decided that when he met with his captains they would not be crowded into a campaign tent. The General requested and was granted the use of one of the larger homes in the area thanks to a grateful patriot family. Keeping this a secret from the Porteños was a major accomplishment.

The staff met around a large table and even wine was served.

"I received a communication last night from Governor Vigodet," the General began. "It seems in some way he has become aware of the strife that exists between General Sarratea and myself. There may be spies among us, so watch what you say and do in camp."

The men looked nervously at each other around the table.

"Because of this strife, the Governor has made what I am sure he considers a very enticing offer."

Artigas paused – expressly for dramatic effect.

"What is it he wants, General?" Juan finally asked.

"He proposes that the Orientales join with him and the Spanish to drive the Porteños out. If we are successful, the Banda Oriental would then become the permanent seat of the Viceroyalty of La Plata. Montevideo will be the capital and all world commerce bound for this region would be routed here. Our army would become the armed force in this region, in Spanish service of course, and I and my officers will be rewarded beyond what we can dream."

The council sat stunned. Finally Rafael Otiguerra spoke.

"What is it you want, General?"

"I have never declared anything other than my commitment to freedom. That has not changed. Apparently the governor believes we can be bought."

Suddenly, one of the guards entered the room unannounced.

"General Artigas. General Rondeau has been seen approaching the camp."

"Usher him in when he arrives," replied Artigas.

"Could he possibly be aware of the governor's offer?" asked Rivera.

"I do not know," the General said calmly. "We will have to see."

Artigas and his small staff waited in the silence of their thoughts. An agonizing twenty minutes passed before Rondeau, Sarratea, and a good portion of their staffs entered the now crowded room. Artigas rose from his chair.

"Do you see," General Sarratea blurted out. "He convenes these meetings regularly and sends no reports on their transactions."

"Welcome to Tres Cruces, General," Artigas said warmly.

"Thank you, General Artigas." Rondeau would be both candid and direct. "This visit will not be a cordial one. It comes as a result of some very distressing circumstances."

Artigas' captains glanced at each other. *This could very well be the end,* Juan thought.

"I remain your humble servant," Artigas replied.

"I have never doubted it," said Rondeau. "Nevertheless, you have been subject to some bad commentary—more than anyone has a right to. The motivation for this commentary, I am convinced, comes in a perceived fear more than an actual threat."

"Begging you pardon, General," Sarratea interrupted, "the government is truly concerned. They fear the Banda Oriental might choose to leave the United Provinces and become an independent state, much like Paraguay."

"In all the time you spend in the circles of government," Rondeau said spitefully, "have you never seen that its members are suspicious of everyone—including each other? I am convinced a more worrisome body of men does not exist."

"My apologies, General," Sarratea said meekly.

"This is my second campaign with General Artigas," Rondeau continued. "I have never seen him do anything disloyal. On the contrary, he is a most successful field commander. It may be this success that is the basis for Buenos Aires' fears."

"I cannot abide dissention in my camp," he said. "I am therefore ordering your resignation from this campaign, General Sarratea."

The men sat stunned amid an uncomfortable silence. Finally Sarratea spoke up in a definite defiant tone, "Yes sir. You will have it immediately," and he abruptly departed the room.

"You have done a bold thing," Artigas said. "The ramifications could be severe."

"I doubt it," Rondeau replied. "While the directory in Buenos Aires may appear to be a collection of fools, I believe them wise enough to judge between the character of Sarratea and those of ourselves."

* * *

The weather was pleasant on the peninsula of Punta Carretas. From a sheltered grove of trees, Paddy, Tereza, Juan, and Ana watched the children wade in the waters of the Rio de la Plata. Looking over the water toward the city, extending peacefully out on the neighboring peninsula, brought back thoughts of the previous siege. From a distance, it was still difficult to imagine that there might be people suffering there at this very moment. Paddy remembered though. It hadn't been but a few years earlier he witnessed what pain and sorrow the last siege had brought.

"The seals are playful today," Tereza said as she watched a herd on the point. "Do you think we might see some whales?"

"It's not likely, Love," Paddy replied. "We would need to go to Maldonado for that. If you have a sharp eye you may see some dolphins though."

"Do you believe in divine intervention, Paddy?" Juan asked. The questioned piqued Paddy's interest.

"I believe in God," Paddy said. "I am not sure as to how much he involves himself with the affairs of men."

"Well, consider this," Juan continued. "Yesterday Artigas appeared finished," A betting man would have wagered that he was."

"Quite possibly," Paddy agreed.

The women listened intently. They had already heard what had happened at Tres Cruces.

"And yet it was General Sarratea who was finished," Juan said, "stripped of command and sent packing back to Buenos Aires. Now Artigas alone commands the Orientales, the city has yet to fall, and we are on an equal footing with Rondeau and the Porteños."

"And what do you think Buenos Aires will do when Sarratea gives them his report?" Paddy asked.

"Katy, Tell Luis to stay close to the shore," Tereza yelled.

It was Ana who spoke before Juan could reply. "Do you believe he could cause much trouble?" she asked.

* * *

King Joao sat reading at his desk in the Royal Court at Rio de Janeiro. His attention was focused on one particular dispatch that had just arrived from his chief of police. Most of the intelligence gathering for Brazil was handled through the police rather than the army and this was a regular update for the King. While there were no specific facts presented, the chief expressed his opinion as a consequence of all the bits of information coming into his office from all over South America. His opinion was alarming.

> "The intent of the revolutionaries in Buenos Aires is to misrepresent our court while promoting themselves as the better option in Montevideo", one part of the dispatch said. "Their ambition is not confined to Montevideo, but also to the expansion of their revolution into the provinces of Brazil when the time is right.

> Your loyal servant,
> Paolo Fernandez de Vianna,
> Chief of Police"

The king put the dispatch aside and remained sitting at his desk, thinking. After a considerable amount of time he rang for an attendant.

"Yes, your majesty:

"Ask the prince to come here," the King ordered.

* * *

At his headquarters at Tres Cruces, General Artigas also found time to pen some letters. One particular piece of correspondence had two purposes. He first needed to get his own ducks in a row should he need them down the road. His second purpose was driven by a genuine regret that there had been an altercation with an unsatisfactory ending. Regardless of who was at fault. General Sarratea was, after all, only obeying the orders he had received from Buenos Aires.

"13 of February, 1813

Esteemed General Sarratea;

I deeply regret the events that have prompted your departure. Be assured that Buenos Aires need not fear my efforts so far as the freedom and welfare of all the United Provinces remains our objective.

Since the day I declared against Spain I have been persecuted, not by the Spanish, but by those who would call themselves my allies. Despite this, I have never felt inadequate to the task. The freedom of the Américas shapes my agenda. It forges my single desire. No future circumstance will alter my position.

I am bound by my own reputation never to do otherwise. Justice and reason guide me, so I always know which choice to make. I also know that a well placed lance could take my life at any time. Should this happen,

I intend to die incorruptible. It is honor that forges my
character and it is honor that sets my course.

General Jose Gervasio Artigas"

*　　*　　*

On the surface it appeared that the dismissal of General Sarratea
had quick and possibly devastating effects. Within weeks General Carlos
Alvear arrived at General Rondeau's headquarters—on very short notice.
He had come to replace Rondeau with several thousand additional men.
This spectacle was viewable from the city walls, and once he had been
informed, Governor Vigodet himself watched the procession that was
taking place.

"General Alvear. You are prompt," Rondeau said in a chilly greeting.
"Only now have we received word of your coming."

"Once Buenos Aires made the decision, I was dispatched immediately,"
Alvear replied. "My men were preparing for the campaign in Alto Peru.
They are as surprised as you that they find themselves here."

"Do you know the reason I am being recalled from the field?"

"As a strategist, your talents are highly regarded," Alvear replied.
"Belgrano needs you to help work out final details for the push into the
Andes."

Both Alvear and Rondeau knew his statement was only half true.

"And the campaign here?" Rondeau asked.

"Buenos Aires wants it finished immediately," Alvear replied.

General Rondeau looked around and examined the military spectacle
that now surrounded him. "We certainly have enough men for the task,"
he commented.

"More than you know, General," Alvear replied. "Admiral Brown is bringing the navy to provide a truly effective blockade."

"Had we dedicated this amount of effort the first time we were here, we could have driven the Portuguese out," Rondeau said. His tone was bitter.

"At the loss of many men, General," Alvear responded. "I believe this result will be much better."

"Perhaps."

*   *   *

That same afternoon Governor Vigodet met with his staff in the cabildo of Montevideo.

"It was I who first accused Governor Elío of being deficient in his duties" Vigodet began. "Had I been more aware of his circumstances, I would not have acted so harshly. The situation here now is much worse than it was back then. What must Spain be saying about me?"

"Is it possible that we might appeal to the Portuguese once again?" asked Manuel Fernandez, Elío's old counselor. Only Elío had been sent back to Spain. The rest of his staff had remained in Montevideo to serve the new Governor.

"The Portuguese will be content now simply to allow us to wither and die." It was Vigodet's opinion, of course, but an obvious one. "When the revolution has spent our adversary, the Portuguese can then return for an easy conquest."

"Then we must appeal once again to Spain," a now somewhat agitated General Posadas declared. He had suffered an embarrasing defeat at Las Piedras against far fewer men than he was facing now. Repatriated in a prisoner exchange, he could not bear another.

"I am afraid that Spain is no better prepared now to send us troops than she was when Elío was here," Vigodet said. "Her recent gains against the French have only been made possible with England as her ally. No, in truth the effects of the war in Europe has actually weakened her more."

"What shall we do then, Governor?" asked Fernandez.

"I see few options," the Governor replied. "Even at the height of her power, the English still could not hold her colonies in North America . . . and they had a huge navy and retained a large body of loyalists there. Spain has none of those advantages here."

"The citizens here have shown no inclination to rebel," Fernandez remarked.

Posadas laughed. "The citizens in the city?" he said. "How would they rebel? What weapons do they have? Whether from cowardice or regard for their families, these will remain docile, but I assure you they are not ardent loyalists!"

"Well then, we cannot expect them to stay complacent much longer," Vigodet added. "We have little food, and rightly or not, soon it will be perceived that we are hoarding that for ourselves. When they see their children starving, that will be the end of their cowardice."

Vigodet stared at the tabletop, saying nothing.

"My apologies, gentlemen," he said after a pause. "There is no reason to prolong what is inevitable. I will open talks with the rebels to discuss the terms of surrender."

CHAPTER EIGHT

Almost There

General Artigas began to think he might have to beg the church for a large enough room to house the representatives of the town councils who were now arriving daily. But unlike the priests in Mexico or even just across the river, the priests in the Banda Oriental were not so eager to commit treason as of yet. In the end, however, his aides were able to secure a large room in the community of Peñarol, not too far from Tres Cruces.

At last he would confer with these representatives in an opening forum that would set the agenda for a series of additional meetings in the coming days.

"Gentlemen,' he began, "I am encouraged by your full and prompt response. It is only through this kind of effort that we will be able to set a beneficial course for the Banda Oriental."

Joaquin Suarez, one of the representatives from San José, immediately raised a question.

"Would it not be better to discuss these matters after the present conflict is ended?" he asked. "We may then have a better perspective of the direction we are headed."

It was a legitimate concern expressed by the man who would quickly become one of the strongest civilian leaders in this revolution. Artigas anticipated the question, although he did not know who it would be to raise it, and he already had a response.

"I know Buenos Aires," Artigas replied. "It will be too late when Montevideo falls. If we do not solidify our position now, the Porteños will quickly position themselves to rule over us, regardless of our objections."

"How can you be sure, General?" asked Suarez.

"They desire the Banda Oriental, not as an independent Province, but as the northern half of their own province. Buenos Aires then would be centered within this new province rather than on the edge of the present one. Maritime competition from Montevideo would be effectively eliminated and there would then be no immediate threat to itself from a distant Brazil."

"If what you say is true," Suarez continued, "then how can we possibly prevent this?"

"We maneuver for full provincial status now, equal to that of Corrientes and Entre Rios," the General replied. "Then within this confederation we push for semi-autonomy. Buenos Aires still struggles with what form of government they will finally have. Some within the directory are even talking about establishing a new world monarchy."

"And what form of government would you prefer, General?" Suarez asked.

"A republic," Artigas replied.

Joaquin Suarez looked at the General dubiously. Everyone admired the possibility of a republic, but was it feasible? It seemed its very nature, rule by the people's elected representatives, was its weakness. "That may be an unattainable ideal," he remarked. "The natural evolution of a successful republic is empire. Rome proved that, France has proven that, and the North Americans appear to be headed to that same end.

The men nodded.

"The North Americans do indeed appear to be engaged in empire building," Artigas agreed, "but still today their elected representatives and leaders come and go on a timely fashion through regularly scheduled elections. Let us not look on that nation as an empire yet. It has no emperor. It could be that it is evolving into exactly what is needed to secure the rights of man – a large strong republic capable of contending with the true empires of the world."

Slowly Artigas won over the great majority of the delegates. In the coming weeks the plan he had kept in his mind for so long was germinating. Committees were formed to discuss and resolve issues. It quickly became apparent that the two forces in the proceedings were José Artigas and Joaquin Suarez and they conferred often. It was a perfect mix, one from the military and one from the body of private citizens, each with a growing and enduring respect for the other.

Secretaries were constantly transcribing the proceedings. Slowly the vision began to take shape—a totally new republic to be called the United Provinces of America – the South American equivalent of the United States of America. The full vision included a nation that would fill the continent. It would take a lot of convincing. Already Simon Bolivar had unveiled his counterpart vision, Gran Colombia, and of course, there was the matter of Brazil. Well, maybe Brazil need not be included. It might be well to have a true American empire in place to show the people how not to do things.

Finally a vote was taken by a show of hands and there were congratulations all around for the new delegates elected to carry the vision to Buenos Aires.

*   *   *

It was a beautiful morning, the kind that made each man glad to be alive, in most cases, regardless of his present circumstance. Yet today there seemed to be more. There was a different spirit in the air, a feeling that was almost physically palpable.

Or maybe it was just the absence of the usual noise. In the strange quiet of this particular morning an old man sat puzzled on his usually familiar bench in the plaza in Montevideo. But age had dulled his senses and he was confused that the normal sounds and activity of the place were missing. Shortly a young boy entered the plaza from a side street, rolling a hoop. The old man motioned for him to come over.

"Young boy, Where is everybody?" the old man asked almost pathetically.

"They're all at the wharves, the boy replied. "The Spanish are leaving."

"The Spanish are leaving?"

"Yes, and when they are gone there will be a great celebration in the plaza."

The old man smiled. "Like the old days," he said.

The young boy shrugged his shoulders. "I suppose so," he said, not knowing what the "old days" were that the man was taking about. And with that he ran down away toward the harbor.

* * *

As the sun approached midday, the sentry looked out from the city wall. He saw in the distance the first column of many approaching from the Tres Cruces road and he smiled. The sentry was expecting this.

In gratitude for being at the General's side from the beginning, Captain Rafael Otiguerra rode triumphantly at the head of the column. His company would be followed by that of Captain Rivera, then Lavalleja's, Andresito's, Oribe's, and the rest of the Orientales. Following them would come the Porteños.

Surprisingly the order that the Orientales enter first was penned by the hand of General Alvear himself and the Orientales were grateful for it.

When Otiguerra reached the Ciudadela he looked up at the sentry and smiled. The sentry wore the uniform of the local constabulary. The Spanish really were gone.

"Who approaches the gate?" the sentry asked, almost in a laugh.

"Captain Rafael Otiguerra," came the reply. Otiguerra's smile was a broad grin now, "And the Army of the Orientales."

"You may pass, Captain Otiguerra", the sentry shouted down.

The gate opened and the Army of the Orientales entered, moving with difficulty through the sea of joyous people lining the narrow streets.

When Paddy entered with Lavalleja's company, he was overcome with emotion. The joy was infectious. Perhaps, after all, it was possible. Maybe Juan's dream could be realized. It could even be that God actually was looking down on them and guiding their affairs with His own hand.

In the plaza, Otiguerra ascended the steps of the cathedral. He turned toward the joyously screaming crowd and raised his arms triumphantly. The people responded in a mighty roar.

*   *   *

The tense discussion between Director Moreno and Saavedra in Moreno's office in Buenos Aires had to do with the document now lying on the desk.

"Victory in the Banda Oriental is only days old and already Artigas sends a hand picked delegation with a list of demands," Saavedra shouted. "In his success he has become even more arrogant."

"The gentlemen in this delegation say they are the elected representatives of the town councils." Moreno said. "Four are priests, and the fifth is an officer from the old Blandengues Corps."

"Artigas' henchmen all the same," muttered Saavedra. "The man is driven by ambition."

"Hopefully his ambition will be revealed in the document," Moreno suggested.

"I have read the document," Saavedra sneered. "They demand full civil and religious freedom, equality, and security for everyone in every province. It requires that both the local and central governments operate under these principles."

"They're fearful of the old days," Moreno commented. "That's understandable, and these points all appear reasonable."

"They prefer three independent branches of government, provincial autonomy with regard to internal matters, and the abolition of military despotism by means of constitutional checks."

"Someone has been studying," Moreno smiled.

"The last point is the most galling, Saavedra complained. "It demands that Buenos Aires be excluded from consideration as the federal capital."

"Now that is insane!" For the first time there was some excitement in Moreno's voice. "And where else would the capital be then—Rosario, Santa Fe, . . . Montevideo?"

"Buenos Aires is the only obvious choice, Excellency," Saavedra said, "if only for its size and accommodations alone. And they all know that. It may be that they believe if they cede this one point, the most extreme of their demands, they will be able to keep those that are more reasonable. Or it may be, as you say, Artigas is becoming more dangerous by the minute."

"Something may have to be done about him."

* * *

Paddy returned to the print shop. His duties as a soldier required many hours of the week, however, and now his business suffered because of it. Nevertheless, between his contracts and the small pay the army now received (thanks to Buenos Aires), his family was able to get by. The threat of war was greatly diminished, now that the Spanish had surrendered, but a new air of uncertainty hung over the city. No one really knew in what direction Montevideo would go now. The elected representatives of the Banda Oriental were poised to take their plan for the United Provinces to Buenos Aires, but there were hardly any who believed all the points would be accepted without opposition.

Juan Lavalleja, on the other hand, spent his time taking care of affairs as General Artigas saw fit. The new set of circumstances that presented themselves after the fall of Montevideo made for more than a full day for the General's staff. In military matters, Artigas relied on Otiguerra, Oribe, and Andresito as much as he did Lavalleja and Rivera. It had become obvious, however, that when it came to those things which were political, Lavalleja and Rivera were the most adept. So Artigas leaned more on them in those efforts than he did on the others.

And Juan's work was laudable, especially in light of the present troubling events in his life. Whatever the reason, Lavalleja's father was suddenly making himself more bellicose than normal. Before the exodus Paddy didn't even know him, but then the old man's resentment of Ana became apparent when the she and his son took up residence together in Ayuí.

They kept that arrangement now that they were back in Montevideo, and Juan's father turned up his arguments against her, threatening to disown Juan if he did anything as foolish as marry the tramp.

The man actually had nothing materially of consequence, but Lavalleja valued the times he had shared with his father in the now distant past and he hated the current ostracism.

The turmoil strained Juan and Ana's relationship, and that, in turn, spilled over into Paddy's life with Tereza. She was Ana's true friend and she was quick to take Ana's side in her contentions with Juan.

Paddy appealed to the women that they try to understand the burdens under which Juan was laboring. It fell on deaf ears and he regretted having even gone down that road. So it came as no surprise when Tereza announced she was taking the children to the Ferrando home in Minas earlier than had been planned. Ana would also be going with her for who knew how long – but long enough for the men to contemplate what was most important in their lives and finally come to their senses.

"Fine!" thought Paddy, "it will help ease the stormy atmosphere around here for a while."

His hostile attitude lasted half a day. When Paddy went home that evening, the emptiness there was almost unbearable. He wondered why. It surely wasn't the fighting with Tereza that he missed.

Yet as long as she was there, the promise remained that one day they would renew what they had before, when conversations with her at the end of the day lifted his heart. He also understood, for the first time really, how important the company of his children was, and how sweet.

So what now? What had all the efforts of the past two years achieved?

*   *   *

"Thank you for seeing me, General," Artigas said gratefully.

General Alvear looked up from his desk in the cabildo – the same desk that Rondeau, Vigodet, and Elío had previously occupied.

"How could I not?" he replied. "You and General Rondeau have experienced far too much together for me to be less gracious, my friend."

"I have with me some points of order that the people . . ." Artigas began. Alvear was quick to interrupt him.

"Before you begin, General, I have received some good news from Buenos Aires."

"Yes Sir?"

"The government has recognized the Banda Oriental as a full province within the United Provinces." Alvear said.

"That is excellent news, General!" Artigas responded. "It is one less thing we will need to discuss here."

"There is one thing." Alvear looked up and almost winced. "They have named Nicolás Rodríguez Peña as the interim governor."

"A Porteño?" Artigas shouted. He paused to get himself under control. "No! The governor must be from here!"

"He is only the interim governor, General," Alvear assured him, "to establish order in the transition."

"Or to establish a firm grip around our collective throats," Artigas replied. "Trust Buenos Aires? That leopard cannot change its spots!"

Once again he had to compose himself.

"In what capacity are the Orientales to function under Governor Peña?

"Except for communications with Buenos Aires, you will be in charge of everything, from commerce to affairs within the interior," Alvear explained.

"And if the Orientales do not agree?"

"I do not anticipate a rebellion, General," Alvear said, "but there will be enough troops here to enforce the law."

"An army of occupation you mean! So this is the sovereignty Buenos Aires has planned for us."

"Be forewarned General," Alvear admonished, "We have come too far to have everything destroyed by a little treason now."

"Do not threaten me, General," Artigas responded. "I could go to my gauchos and Charruas and overnight raise an army formidable enough to drive your occupational force into the Rio de la Plata."

Now Alvear spoke more softly. "It is not meant as a threat, General, but a warning. I am duty bound to issue it."

Artigas was also speaking more soberly. "For the moment, the Orientales will strive to work within the limits Buenos Aires has so graciously set for them."

*   *   *

Months followed, and conditions had become just as Artigas had expected. His constant protests to the government in Buenos Aires against the way it managed affairs in the Banda Oriental now made it dangerous for him to stay in Montevideo. The peril increased, and finally he left the city and began moving from town to town.

So it was that he rendezvoused with his captains, Otiguerra, Lavalleja, Rivera, and Oribe in the little town of Canelones. This was as close as he dared approach the capital in an effort to still provide a short easy trip for the others. The alcalde had set aside a small obscure room in the cabildo and here the General described the recent events to his captains—and outlined his plans to counteract them.

"Gentlemen," Artigas began, "the recent weeks have not been favorable to us. I have learned that Buenos Aires has assembled a provincial congress – one that significantly did not include the Banda Oriental. I am certain they had one singular purpose—the destruction of the successful work between us and our fellow provinces."

"How can you be sure of this, General?" Otiguerra asked.

"The conference was so large that it could not be held in any hall of government," Artigas explained. "It took place in the Chapel of the Chacra of Maciel, on the banks of the Arroyo Miguelete. A great many more delegates participated than just the members of the assembly."

"What do our delegates report?" Rivera asked.

"The delegates of the Banda Oriental have yet to be seated in the government, and as I already inferred, they are the only delegation not invited to the recent congress."

"Then this must be interpreted as a direct affront," Juan commented.

"Most certainly," Artigas confirmed, "and unless this course can be altered, I fear it must ultimately end in armed conflict. Our people have endured too much to meekly submit. Only a benevolent change will prevent it. For now we will watch how Governor Peña minds his affairs, but we must begin to prepare for the worst.

"To further distance myself from Montevideo," Artigas continued, "I am moving on to Belén on the Rio Uruguay. From there I intend to go on into the neighboring provinces and attempt to repair whatever damage has been done by Buenos Aires."

"What do you require of us?" Rivera asked.

"We must not allow Buenos Aires to usurp our rights," Artigas replied. "Any attempt to further impose their will on our freedoms must be met with force. But be secretive in whatever you do! Be subversive! I do not want a war breaking out here while I am somewhere in the northern provinces."

"We understand, Sir!" Rivera said, and the others voiced their united support.

Now the General's speech became eloquent. It was evident that the words were written earlier and rehearsed, intended for the scribe's pen and the ages. But they were his words directed to his captains and he was entirely genuine as he spoke them.

> "My dear friends, any authority I might have comes through you and ends with you. The people will be in full possession of their rights. No despot or dictator will rule here. This must be the fruits of all my concerns and anxieties, and the prize of all my labors."

* * *

That evening Paddy Colman heard a knock on his door.

"Tere!" he thought.

But it wasn't Tereza. Instead Paddy was surprised to see Juan Lavalleja standing there.

"Juan!"

"May I come in?"

"Of course," Paddy replied.

The two sat in the front room.

"I saw the General today," Juan began.

"Artigas is in Montevideo?" Paddy asked.

"No," Juan replied. "I went to meet him outside the city – Jose, Rafael, Manuel, and me."

"Where was Andresito?' Paddy asked.

"Captain Guacaray is away with his Charruas, I Believe. I really do not know exactly where he was but he was not there."

Juan's response was abrupt and sounded somewhat irritated. Paddy interpreted it to fatigue and the fact that Juan could not get down to what he really wanted to say because of Paddy's small talk questions. He sat back and waited for Juan to continue.

Juan spoke about what had happened at the convention at the Chapel of the Chacra of Maciel and the fears Artigas expressed because of it. As the story unfolded Paddy found it all very interesting and probably intended to be much more confidential than Juan was treating it now.

Then suddenly the real purpose of Juan's visit became clear.

"Have you heard from Ana?" he asked.

"No," Paddy replied, "not even from Tereza. I believe they are very put out with us."

"With us?!! Why? What have you done?"

Paddy smiled. "I may have defended you a little too much, I'm afraid."

Juan let out a small string of profanity, followed by, "I am sorry you are being drug into this, my friend."

"What I said had to be said," Paddy responded. "If Ana is going to leave you she should at least know how much you love her." Then he paused. "Juan, why don't you marry her?"

"I want to marry, Ana," Juan confessed, "but what can I offer her now? I know women. They say that they can live with very little, but soon they become very depressed if they do not have at least a few fine belongings."

What Juan said rang true, but Paddy knew he still had a strong argument.

"She was with you in Ayuí. How many 'fine belongings' did you have there? And did she complain?"

"No," Juan replied, "Ana would not complain. But she would if ever the conflict ends—and there is one thing more. I cannot think of how her life would be in this present circumstance should anything suddenly happen to me. She deserves a full life with a good husband at her side."

"Do you think she loves you so much she would never remarry?"

"I know she loves me very much," Juan said. "But that by itself would not be what will keep her from remarrying."

"No?" Paddy asked. "What would then?"

"Respect," Juan said. "Respect for me, for the Patria, and for the name 'Ana Monterroso de Lavalleja."

It was a sobering thought, and Paddy immediately knew Juan was probably right here too. There was still one last argument. "How much of a factor is your father?"

"I honor my father," Juan said, "and I love him, but he alone will not prevent me from marrying my Ana."

"She is not your Ana yet," Paddy said. "Not entirely. You need to marry her. And believe me; it would really help me with my lady."

"From what the General says," Juan responded, "things are likely to become very tense very quickly. But when this thing is over, if I am still around, I will marry her – and she is my Ana!"

* * *

It was a crisis, and it did not need to be. Governor Nicolas Peña knew the Orientales were a factor in this thing, but for the present they were controllable. It was Buenos Aires that was really pushing the issue and for reasons Peña did not fully understand. If he dug deeper in the matter, he feared he might not like what he would find.

Regardless of what the reasons were, Peña had his part to play, and his orders. For the moment those orders were the reason he now met with General Alvear and two of his subordinates, Captain Soler and Captain Dorrego, in the cabildo in Montevideo.

"Governing the Banda Oriental has not been a simple matter," Peña complained. "Rather than being regarded as allies, we are now resented as occupiers."

"I am more convinced now Artigas is behind all this contempt," Alvear declared. "He has infected the people."

"While I have resisted it in the past, it may truly be that Artigas must be brought down," Peña agreed. "He and his followers could destroy the very establishment of a true United Provinces."

"It is sad. He cannot be trusted because he himself distrusts Buenos Aires," Alvear said. "He still feels we betrayed him when we negotiated the armistice with Elío and the Portuguese."

"But surely he knows there were no other options there," Peña said.

"Even so. This time he believed the Orientales would be allowed more self rule. As we have not yet permitted it, he considers this also as a betrayal."

"If we do not deal with Artigas now," Peña said, "we must surely face a full rebellion in the future."

"I have considered that," said Alvear. "Suppose we invite Artigas to discuss the transfer of power. When he comes, we could destroy his forces and have him arrested."

"One last betrayal," Peña muttered.

"It must be done," Alvear said adamantly. "This is a dirty business, Governor, and immediately after this meeting I intend to send Captain Soler along the coast to secure everything between Montevideo and Colonia."

"The men are already prepared, General," Soler interjected.

"Captain Dorrego will be assigned the task of destroying any resistance in the central regions of the country," Alvear continued. "It could be a difficult mission."

"We are up to it, General," Dorrego said confidently.

"Well then, if that was the true purpose of this meeting," Peña said, "that all here fully understand the will of Buenos Aires, there is nothing I really can do to prevent this course of action. One thing though, it must be quick and decisive. I am certain nothing will solidify the people more than a prolonged effort that is less than overpowering."

"The Orientales will be no match for my regulars, Governor," Dorrego stated.

"Guard against overconfidence, Captain," Alvear warned.

* * *

Tereza ran anxiously to the door when she heard the knocking. Could it be that Paddy had come for a surprise visit? She was terribly disappointed when she opened the door but she stoically tried not to let her disappointment show.

"Hola Juan," she smiled.

"May I speak to Ana?" Lavalleja asked meekly.

"Wait here in the front room," Tereza said, "I'll get her."

Juan waited for a very long time. As he waited, he began to feel some resentment. Maybe Ana was making him wait out of spite.

What Ana was doing was arguing with Tereza about whether or not to see him at all. It was a poor argument because all the same time Ana was doing her best to make herself very presentable, and she did a very good job. When she came to the front room, she was beautiful.

"Hello, Love," Juan said.

"Hello Juan," Ana said somewhat defiantly.

Juan did not say anything in response.

"Well, what do you want?" Ana asked.

"I was thinking," Juan said, "that maybe we should get married."

"Is that when you truly want?"

"Oh yes!" Juan replied.

"And how is it you have come to change your mind now?" asked Ana.

Tereza made a slight gesture to signal Ana to be less hostile, but Juan was already responding graciously.

"Some nights ago I woke up and suddenly realized I might really lose you."

"What about your father?"

"I will deal with him," Juan said. "There is one thing, Ana. We cannot get married in Minas, nor in Montevideo."

"Why not?"

"Because of what my father might do."

"Then you are still afraid of him!" Ana yelled.

"Not of him," Juan replied, "but of what he might do. I was thinking we could get married in La Florida."

"La Florida?"

"Yes," Juan replied. "It is not too far from Montevideo and yet it is far enough that rumors would not quickly get back to my father."

"I will need time to think about it," Ana said.

Tereza was stunned. Her two friends were so close and now Ana was the reluctant one. Juan grabbed his hat and walked quickly to the door. "Thank you for your time, ladies," he said with a degree of anger in his voice.

"Please come again Juan," Tereza shouted, realizing as she said it how foolish it sounded.

*　　*　　*

It was a brisk and thoughtful walk that led Juan Lavalleja back to his temporary headquarters in Minas. He was surprised to see Captain José Fructuoso Rivera was waiting for him.

"José, what brings you to Minas?"

"Artigas has been invited to meet with General Alvear," Rivera said. "There they are to discuss the admittance of our delegates to the General Assembly."

"I should feel encouraged about that, but I am not." Juan responded.

"Because Buenos Aires promises nothing that she does not later rescind," Rivera continued.

"That is part of it, Juan said.

"Still, is not Artigas the one man who would achieve success in these discussions?" asked Rivera.

"Yes he is," Juan agreed. "I am always amazed at what the man is able to do. But I really do not believe he will be successful, not now, in this matter."

"We must be prepared for any outcome, Juan," Rivera warned.

*　　*　　*

Outside Marmarajá, a lone rider whipped his stallion as if it would help him run any faster than he already was. The rider periodically looked back over his shoulder to see if he was being pursued, but he saw no one.

Someone was there, but beyond the rider's view. It was not the distance that kept him from seeing them, but the obstacles. On the winding road they were kept hidden. But they were close.

The rider knew it, and he did not slow to a gallop as he entered the small town. This drew the attention of those along the street and all eyes were on him as he rode up to the military headquarters and dismounted his lathered horse on the run.

Captain Rafael Otiguerra was startled as the rider burst into the room.

"Captain, a large force of Porteños is only minutes away," The rider shouted.

"We have received no notice of any operation in this area," the Captain replied.

"I believe this is meant to be a surprise, Captain," the rider said excitedly. "They appear ready for a fight."

Otiguerra jumped from his chair.

"Alert the men!" he shouted.

In less than a minute the garrison was struggling to prepare for the immediate battle. Many were saddling their horses while others assembled their battle gear, but there really was no time. Before all but a few could complete their tasks Dorrego's Porteños were upon them. A general onslaught of Orientales began that could not be stemmed, and Otiguerra watched as his men fell around him. It was quickly becoming obvious that a retreat had to be ordered before the entire garrison was slaughtered.

Otiguerra turned to his aide. "Have the men break ranks," he shouted. "Each must see to himself and his family. We will regroup with Rivera."

The aide wasted no time. "Break ranks! Break ranks!" he shouted as he rode off.

A panicked pursuit ensued. Quickly a Porteño lieutenant rode up to Captain Dorrego.

"We have them on the run, Captain, the lieutenant cried. "Shall I order the pursuit?"

"No, Lieutenant." Dorrego laughed. "Let the lucky ones tell their friends what to expect from us now."

So it was that the first military encounter between Porteños and Orientales was a resounding victory for the Porteños.

*   *   *

For the next two weeks Dorrego chased after his next prey, José Rivera's company, which was drawing him across the southern half of the Banda Oriental. While he did not pressure his men excessively, the Porteño Captain was still able to slowly close in on Rivera near Guayabos.

Dorrego had been right. Word had spread quickly about the slaughter at Marmarajá, but the effect was far different from what he had expected. More than that, he was unaware that Juan Lavalleja was receiving reports on his movements through a small but efficient network of spy-scouts that relayed the information back to him on horseback.

Also unknown to Dorrego, new volunteers were filtering into Otiguerra's depleted garrison from throughout the country. That, together with small groups of reinforcements sent by Artigas, made his force formidable once again.

And Dorrego did not know where Otiguerra was.

Scouts kept Otiguerra constantly advised of Dorrego's position and that allowed him to rest his men more than he could have been able to otherwise. His mission for the moment was to parallel Rivera, and be ready to launch a surprise attack should Dorrego decide to engage Rivera's army. As Otiguerra had few roads available to him in this effort, the going was difficult at times. It was while his little army was trying to negotiate a particularly bad stretch of land that a scout rode up to him.

"Captain Lavalleja reports Dorrego is in Guayabos. He wants to know if you would be able to launch an attack on the Porteños there."

"Has he considered other options?" Otiguerra asked."

"He may ask Rivera to turn and execute a frontal attack," the scout replied.

"Dorrego has been pursuing Rivera a good while, Otiguerra said, "and he may have scouts reporting their movements. Any sudden change in Rivera's routine could alert Dorrego of a possible trap."

"Yes sir."

"As of now I believe he is unaware that I even have a force, Otiguerra said. "Tell Captain Lavalleja we will attack Dorrego before noon tomorrow."

"I will advise the Captain," the scout answered and rode off.

* * *

The following morning Dorrego's regiment mounted up in the town of Guayabos in preparation to continue his pursuit of Rivera when suddenly a far off shout ring out.

"Orientales!"

The cry threw the Porteños into a frenzied panic. They struggled in a desperate effort to arm and position themselves for the imminent thrust, but within seconds the Orientales were already pouring through their ranks, shooting and hacking. Despite a brief, stiff resistance, the Porteño position was obviously hopeless from the start. They broke and took flight, including Dorrego and his aide.

The tables had been turned! The chase now was frantic. But over time, Dorrego and a small band of exhausted survivors, were out of harm's way and able to slow down on the road to Corrientes.

"How many are still with us, Lieutenant?" Dorrego asked.

"About fifty, sir." Replied the aide.

"Fifty! A total disaster. How could I have allowed myself to be so surprised."

No one would have believed it possible that Otiguerra could recover so quickly from the thrashing we gave him at Marmarajá," the aide said.

"No! There is no excuse, Lieutenant," Dorrego shot back. "And after this disgrace, I see no possibility of advancing my career."

"Looking at us right now, could we be ready to attack Otiguerra within a week?" the lieutenant asked, "Like Otiguerra has done?"

Dorrego studied the scene of misery and failure around him. "No," he replied. "It is finished for us. Otiguerra's new troops crawl out from beneath the rocks. We have no such convenience."

*　　*　　*

In Montevideo, there was panic in the cabildo as the Porteño staff workers rushed to pack records and belongings. Amid this chaos Governor Peña talked with a staff member.

"Dorrego was a fool!" he lamented. "He was exceedingly disdainful when he left this place. Did he think the Orientales were simply going to turn tail?"

"It is a most unfortunate outcome, Governor," the staff member said.

"Unfortunate is not the word!" Peña shouted. "It is a disaster. I cannot yet comprehend the shame of being ordered to leave the Banda Oriental. One defeat and we slink away."

"It is reported that, out of all Dorrego's regiment, less than a hundred men reached Corrientes."

"What is the message we send to the rest of America?" Peña continued. "Do not worry, Spanish, Buenos Aires may send an expedition to the Andes, but they cannot even defeat the Paraguayans or the Orientales next door. And General Bolivar! The help you were expecting from the Rio de la Plata? I would not count on it if I were you."

"We will be victorious in the west, Governor. Then we can rededicate all our efforts here."

"Let us hope so," Peña remarked.

*　　*　　*

One week following Peña's lament, the Army of the Banda Oriental marched triumphantly into the plaza to the applause and shouts of a cheering crowd in Montevideo. General Artigas and his captains, Lavalleja, Rivera, Andresito, Benavides, Oribe, and Otiguerra each led their individual companies in the procession. When he reached the cathedral, Artigas bounded from his horse and walked quickly up the steps to address the people. The crowd became quiet to hear his words.

"Orientales!" the General began. "We have come to the end of this segment of the long road toward the fulfillment of our goal." A mighty cheer roared spontaneously from the crowd, and it took almost a minute for Artigas to damper the response, in spite of his obvious efforts to do so.

"I am not a prophet," he continued, "and I cannot foretell what lies ahead as we continue down this road. But know this—there are those on the continent who still desire our little strip of land."

Now the cheers turned to cries of defiance.

"I believe in the United Provinces, bound together for the mutual good, but each minding his own affairs at home. Let the people of Corrientes govern themselves!"

The cheers commenced once again.

"Let the people of Entre Rios govern themselves!"

Now the cheers increased.

"Let the people of Santa Fe govern themselves!"

The noise was louder still.

"Let the people of Buenos Aires govern themselves!"

Still louder.

"And let the Orientales govern themselves in the Banda Oriental!"

Now the roar was deafening. Artigas struggled to quiet the crowd.

"Our neighbors, however, have dreams of empire. The great Simon Bolivar even sees South America one day as a single empire, with or without Brazil. Neither would abide for long the existence of a separate Banda Oriental."

Now the crowd became quiet once again.

"I know the men of the Banda Oriental," Artigas continued. "I know their character. I have fought alongside them and I stand in awe at their deep and abiding dedication to our cause. That dedication persisted even when, at times, all seemed lost."

"I also know the women," he continued. "They are as stoic as any on earth. I have seen them suffer during the great exodus. Rather than complain, they endured, and in spite of their own discomforts, they struggled to ease the suffering of those around them. They cared for our wounded. They cried over our dead. They bore our children and tended to them. And through all of that they still took time to see that our army was fed."

"In all soberness, we as a nation must come to terms with the fact that we are small. There is no assurance that we can be successful in repulsing outside attacks against us. But let those who would come know that we are not weak, and any effort to conquer the Banda Oriental will be at a cost so high and dear for the presumptuous conqueror that he will regret ever considering it."

Now the cheers rose once again.

"It is because of all this that I will continue to work with the leaders of the northern provinces," Artigas promised. "Together we must build an alliance so powerful and so united that no army will dare come against us."

Louder cheers.

"When that day finally comes, we can live in peace and security. Only then can we determine for ourselves the course of our own destinies."

Artigas stepped away. He and his captains made their way through the crowd toward the cabildo. The people, however, remained in the plaza a long time afterwards, laughing, singing, and embracing.

*   *   *

A month passed with no activity along either the Brazilian or Argentine borders. It began to appear that perhaps the Banda Oriental might be allowed to govern itself after all. Juan Lavalleja used the occasion to gather with his fellow officers at Florida. He had come to do the one thing that he had put off for far too long. All the rest had come to celebrate finally his wedding to Ana Monterroso.

The Colmans were there too, and many had come a long way to be a part of this event. There was only one glaring absence. The elder Lavalleja was not at the wedding. Juan's father had not been invited.

And he did not even know the wedding was taking place.

CHAPTER NINE

The United Provinces of America

It was a bright afternoon when the wedding party emerged from the chapel. Select officers of Jose Rivera's company gave the newlyweds a military salute at the front doorway. The couple seemed equally as happy as any who had known each other for much less time than these two.

After all his procrastination and expressions of doubt, Juan now looked genuinely content. As for Ana, this is what she had wanted for so many years. And now here they were – El Señor y la Señora Juan Lavalleja.

Following the ceremony, as soon as the festivities began, Juan proceeded to mingle with his men and fellow officers. This was a glaring break from tradition where the couple would sit together as long as guests continued to pass by to bid them well. It was a prearranged agreement between the two. As a consequence of his deeds in the recent campaigns, Juan had become somewhat famous and popular, and it was feared the reception could last all night should they do things traditionally.

Ana would have enjoyed being the center of attention in a long reception line. On the other hand she was now free to walk and talk with her friends as well, and that meant spending much of the time with Tereza. It also meant that Paddy had to endure several hours of woman talk, centered on children and plans for future households. He could do either that or impose himself on the men.

Paddy preferred to have been with the officers, but he did not yet consider himself truly part of that group. He knew full well that there were many still who considered him not only a nuisance, but a nuisance foreigner as well. It was regrettable in one sense, because as the overlying theme of all their conversations would be what possibly awaited them in the near future. Paddy was sure in some areas he had a little better knowledge than most about the subject and he definitely would have had his part to contribute.

The changing political world had always been a major topic in the Royal Navy. Surprisingly, the discussion usually was a well informed and educated one, even among the crew. Due to the apparent success the United States was having with its new form of government, and the recent events in France, all of Europe was talking.

Ships from the young but impressive American merchant fleet were now seen in ports all over the world. Her fishing fleet was just as impressive, descending on waters older European nations always saw as theirs alone, both historically and traditionally. Disputes naturally arose that could only be settled by treaty.

The amount of timber the new nation had at its disposal to build so many ships in such short a time was sobering. And it seemed that America was totally dedicated to putting out to sea. Yet just as many Americans were expanding the country inland and westward into the new lands between the Appalachians and the Mississippi river granted them by the treaty of Paris. There was no mistaking it—the Americans were building their own empire.

The French were just as surprising. Out of the ashes of chaos and nightmare that their revolution had become, the country stabilized under the capable hands of Napoleon Bonaparte. The ruined economy was revived dramatically. People now not only had enough food on the table, but money left over to buy a few nice things – many for the first time in their lives. It made Napoleon very popular. It also created the perfect climate for what educated men feared most, a dictatorial empire, the terrible ultimate result of forays into "republicanism".

So the French were also becoming an empire, but one in the more traditional sense, with an actual emperor at the helm. Their armies suddenly seized most of Europe and affected future events throughout the world for centuries to come. That future was now the speculation of nobles and scholars in the few remaining "free" European courts. The speculation passed quickly and amazingly intact down to his majesty's admiralty, then to the ships' captains, on to the junior officers, and even down to the crews themselves.

After an hour had passed, Juan found his way to where Paddy was standing.

"Well my friend," Juan said, "it seems I'm in it for good now!"

"Like so many of the rest of us," Paddy replied. "But you and I have an advantage many others do not. We both were lucky enough to have found very good women to support us."

"That we did," Juan laughed. "I was a fool for not marrying Ana earlier. You know I came very close to losing her."

"It definitely appeared so. But you may not have been so close as you believe, Juan," Paddy remarked. "Even now I do not think you understand how fully Ana loves you."

It was clear that Juan was becoming uncomfortable with the current conversation. "So what do you think the possibilities are for a permanent peace here?" he asked.

"I'm afraid I agree with the General," Paddy said. "Both Brazil and Buenos Aires covet this piece of land and each suspects the intentions of the other. I am sure we will be called upon to defend ourselves soon."

"Earlier in my life, I would never have anticipated a possibility such as this, one where we would be fighting our own neighbors. It reveals how ignorant I was back then."

*   *   *

At that very hour, in the Royal Court in Rio de Janeiro, King Joao and Prince Pedro strolled along the long corridors discussing the Banda Oriental as a part of the matters of state.

"Unlikely as it would appear,' Joao remarked, "the Orientales are now in complete control."

"So the apple has ripened," replied his son.

"And is ready to be plucked," the King added. "Yet should we invade, who is to say Buenos Aires would not be ready to intervene once again?"

"They might, if they were able. But I do not believe the Porteños are capable of it at the present," the prince said. "They have committed their armies totally to the Andes. It is, in part, why they were not able to counter their recent reversals at the hands of the Orientales."

"Yes, that has to be it!" The King admitted. "Still, I am astonished at what has transpired. Artigas' leadership must truly be remarkable for the Orientales to have realized such a success."

"His abilities are as good as they appear, father, and he must be regarded as a definite menace, a threat to the entire region, as much to Brazil as to Buenos Aires," Pedro said.

"Nonsense! He leads the smallest province on the continent," the King retorted. "What real threat can he possibly pose?"

"The threat is one of new ideas," answered the prince. "He is said to carry on his person a copy of the Constitution of the United States. He considers it to be the one form of government with any chance of providing the people self rule. And he seems very inflexible in this matter. As he continues in this fanaticism, he is slowly pulling the provinces between the Andes and the Rio Uruguay away from the influence of Buenos Aires. Already Santa Fe has declared its independence. This act and those that may follow are key in Artigas' apparent plan to establish a new United Provinces outside the realm of Buenos Aires."

"Ordinarily I would regard anything to Buenos Aires' detriment as a blessing", King Joao said. "But you are right. This rush to republicanism must be considered a threat to us all. Would it be possible to assemble an adequate force to invade the Banda Oriental within, say, a month?"

* * *

General José Artigas wasted no time implementing the plan he had earlier laid out before his captains in Montevideo. Secretly he had sent invitations to the directors of the various provinces of the old viceroyalty to meet. He did not invite Buenos Aires.

The plan took him to the westernmost city of the Banda Oriental, Paysandú, where he would open a conference of representatives from the other provinces.

In the local cabildo, after a certain amount of open discussion among the dignitaries, Artigas rose to address the group.

"Distinguished emissaries," he began, "I thank you for your prompt and favorable response to our invitations—and a special thanks to the town council of Paysandú for the use of their facilities."

"We have called this conference to discuss two issues."

"First—We are all acquainted with the manner in which Buenos Aires imposes its will on each of us. We allowed her armies to march through our lands to fight against the Spanish in Paraguay, Alto Peru, and Chile. We allowed it because we understood that we are all fighting the Spanish in a common cause."

"But in truth, the cause is not common. Buenos Aires uses us only to her advantage, as much now as she used us in the days of the viceroyalty, only now to be cast aside when we no longer benefit her."

Murmuring broke out among the delegates. Some nodded in agreement.

"In the Banda Oriental," Artigas continued, "it was the blood of Orientales that flowed in our struggle to drive out the Spanish. Then, when it became inconvenient for the Porteños, we were left to the mercy of the Portuguese. I tell you, Buenos Aires sees itself as destined to rule over us, and we must not allow it!"

The murmuring grew louder and Artigas raised his hand to quiet the group.

"The second issue is coupled with the first. The future will be here before we know, and we must now ask ourselves, 'How will we be governed?'"

"Some among us would exchange a European monarchy for an American one, and there are many who would happily step in and be the monarch. Be not deceived! Most of those who favor such a plan do it for their own ambition and not for the good of the people. They see themselves in the upper echelons of a new American aristocracy, sucking off the labors of others."

"Ashamedly, most are the Creoles—my class. Placed on a lower social level by the Iberian born Spanish, they now reach for the top, all too happy to deny mestizos, mulattos, Indians and Negroes that status which they themselves were once denied."

"To justify this outrage, they reason that these lesser unfortunates are without education and therefore incapable of governing themselves."

"How can we then say to them, 'Come fight alongside us in our common cause as brothers. Come bleed with us, and die with us,' and then when the fighting is done we would have no part of these people except as they can benefit us as our servants?"

Artigas took a long thoughtful pause.

"I have fought alongside all these men. I have eaten with them, slept with them, and used the latrine alongside them."

Artigas paused for the laughter he expected.

"What some men say of these unfortunates is true. They are not well educated, except for a special few. But they can reason with the rest of us. They want what we all want, to live happy lives and to raise their families—to see their children live better than they did."

"We have an opportunity here to create a world that is better for all our peoples – and the key to all this is the establishment of a republic."

More murmuring followed this remark. Artigas raised his hands to dispel it.

"I have heard the arguments. Experiments in Europe have failed. But while the French could not keep their republic, even for a decade, Rome endured as one for more than two hundred years before it succumbed to the evils of empire. For now, I would accept two hundred years."

"And what good have we gained from any European example? The lesson learned is that to guard against empire, we must hold in check those who would rule over us. The North Americans appear to be having some success with this, and I am convinced that it is in limiting their leaders' powers, by law, that they accomplish it."

"We can do the same! And if we are successful, should Europe ever consider colonizing this part of the world again, she would face two strong bulwarks of liberty in the Americas, one in the north, and one in the south."

*   *   *

When he left Governor Peña alone in Montevideo, General Alvear returned to Buenos Aires triumphant. He was so popular, in fact, that in a very short time he himself had become the Director of the General Assembly. When word arrived of the fall of the Banda Oriental, however, his ride on that wave of good fortune came to an abrupt halt. This news was so disastrous that Alvear was quickly replaced by a new director, Alvarez Thomas.

The talented Alvear, however, would not disappear into the night.

The outgoing Director used the little time remaining to him by cleaning out the opulent desk as he awaited the arrival of Director Thomas. After he had done all he felt he could do, Alvear sat waiting at the desk in thought. A thousand images and vignettes raced through his mind as he considered the events that had brought him to this moment. His ponderings ended abruptly by a polite knock on the door.

"Come in," Alvear said softly.

Director Elect Thomas came into the room and stood before Alvear at his desk.

"Please take my seat," Alvear said rising.

"If you will not be too uncomfortable, Director Alvear," Thomas said. "Remain at your desk for a short time more. I will sit here."

The new Director took one of the visitors' chairs.

"Director Alvear," Thomas began "I hope you understand, assuming your office was not something I have desired nor aspired to."

"I do not believe that could have been avoided." Alvear said. "Events of the day have dictated it. The people hold me responsible for the loss of the Banda Oriental, and it appears now that the Northern Provinces might also be lost."

"It is very sad," Thomas said earnestly. "No one could have done more for his country than you. We have all underestimated Artigas. But I do not believe the Northern Provinces admire the man so much as they respond to his message."

"For what he has accomplished, I admit I still admire the man, but I must say his message is very dangerous," Alvear confided.

"Of course it is," Thomas agreed. "It is an open door to mob rule. But if we do not remain strong or alter our own position somewhat as to what form of government must take, we may well lose the provinces. What then? Brazil would become the only great power on the continent, capable of consuming each smaller province separately—one at a time – and at her leisure."

"Her dreams of empire are no secret," Alvear said.

"Definitely not!" Thomas said adamantly. "But I am certain that the provinces desire a solid security against outside invaders almost as much as they long for self government. And here is where our position is much stronger than that of Montevideo."

"What do you intend?" asked Alvear.

"We have established contact with each of the provinces to propose a new plan," Thomas said.

"Does it include a republic?" Alvear asked.

Thomas nodded. "This is where Artigas has forced our hand. But if the republic should fail, a monarchy, or perhaps an oligarchy, could quickly follow."

"After much internal strife and suffering, I fear," Alvear remarked.

"It is only through strife and suffering that a monarchy could be realized," Thomas declared. "Otherwise the people would see no need for one."

Alvear thought for a moment on what Alvarez Thomas had said. "It is important that you present your plan quickly."

"We have already begun," Thomas responded, "and we have learned from Artigas' example. Rather than hold his conference in Montevideo, he held it in Paysandú. That eased the traveling for the delegates of the Northern Provinces.

"And when you present your plan, where will you hold your conference," Alvear asked, "Rosario?"

"In Tucumán," Thomas replied.

"Tucumán?" Alvear cried. "Good Lord! Why not just hold it in China?"

Thomas smiled. "What better way to show the other delegates we have no real aspirations over them. The farther from Buenos Aires this conference is, the less it will appear it is being run by Buenos Aires."

* * *

It was the first continuous peace in many years for Montevideo and the entire Banda Oriental and it was now more than four months old. During this respite, the Colmans and the new Lavalleja family took time to enjoy outings on the beaches of Punta Carreras. The women packed baskets for the days' activities and the Colman children were as excited as children always are about the fun they expected to have.

This particular day was acceptably nice, somewhat warm with a slight blustery wind, but it could have been worse. Tereza looked at the water with some concern. It was choppy and she admonished her children not to go too far out.

"Juan and I are going down the beach a ways, Love," Paddy said. Tereza looked at him contemptuously. The families had come to Punta Carretas for some fun, but these two would never allow themselves to put away their concerns, even for a few hours

She was right. When they were some distance down the beach, Paddy asked the first question of many that were bothering him.

"What do you hear from the General?"

"I do not hear much," Juan replied. "I know he's somewhere out west talking with leaders of the Northern Provinces."

"Has he been successful?"

"I haven't heard," Juan answered honestly.

"It would not be too absurd to believe there is a lot of intrigue taking place throughout this part of the world right now," Paddy said.

"You are probably right," Juan replied. "With the General's intense effort to advance his program, you can wager there are others working to defeat it."

"The people here have quickly become very comfortable living without the constant fear of some impending threat," Paddy commented.

"They are fooling themselves," Juan said. "We will not be allowed to enjoy these conditions too much longer."

"We will definitely have to fight again," Paddy agreed, "very soon. I am sure of it."

"The question is, against whom," said Juan.

Paddy nodded. "What irony," he laughed sarcastically. "We thought if we defeated the Spanish, that would be all. But now we have driven them completely from this part of the continent, and we are threatened still. The Spanish only survive now in remnants in the west and the north. Their position is truly hopeless. I honestly do not know why they do not go ahead and lay down their arms and spare the lives of so many men."

"It is a hard thing to turn from 300 years of controlling the continent," Juan commented.

*   *   *

"Father, May I come in?"

It was very unusual for anyone to interrupt the King in his own bedchamber, even if it was a member of the family. Prince Pedro's presence truly startled the old man.

"Pedro is that you?" the King asked.

"Yes Father, the prince responded.

King Joao gave out a boisterous laugh. "Damn! This must really be important," he said.

Pedro did not return the King's lightheartedness. "Two letters have come to the court. They indicate the time might be right for operations into the Banda Oriental," he said. "The first is from minister Viana in Buenos Aires."

Pedro handed King Joao the letter and he read through it quickly, a scowl slowly developing on his face.

"The minister paints a bleak picture," the King said. "The rush to republicanism appears more serious than we may have imagined. He even anticipates a mob rule that would astonish even the French."

"The other letter is from Tucumán," the prince said.

Quickly King Joao read the second letter.

"This reads like an open invitation from the United Provinces for us to invade the Banda Oriental," he commented.

"The provincials have now resolved that Artigas should be removed, but they prefer that someone other than themselves do it," the prince said.

The King smiled. "And who do you suppose they would like that someone to be?" he asked.

*   *   *

The appointment was prearranged. Juan Lavalleja had a meeting scheduled later in the day with General Artigas and his staff to discuss the events of the Paysandú conference. Always anxious, Juan wanted to speak with Paddy first. He had come to consider "his Irishman" as good counsel in political matters. He arrived at the plaza early and waited half an hour for Paddy to arrive.

"Whenever you want to talk," Paddy said when he arrived, "it almost always indicates trouble."

"Possibly, I know nothing for sure," Juan responded, "but deep inside I feel that the road is going to be very perilous and it is coming quickly."

"Is there anything to justify this feeling?" asked Paddy.

"Nothing at all," Juan replied, "only a deep sense that things are not right. I was hoping with your experience you might be able to show me where I might be right—or wrong."

"What experience?" Paddy asked. "All I have done is serve in the Royal Navy."

Juan rebuked him. "Don't be funny," he said sharply. "We both know you have become a contributing part in developing our strategies precisely because of your service in the Royal Navy. There are much politics and intrigue there and you seem to have developed sort of an eye and ear for such things."

Paddy thought about what Juan said. "Even so," he responded, "that is now beginning to be some time in the past. The skills become less refined."

"I do not believe that," said Juan. "But whether or not it is true, I still would like you to listen to what I have to say."

"That's easy enough," said Paddy.

"The General has held meetings with leaders of the northern provinces where he has laid out for them his plan for a new nation" Juan said. "All indications are that his efforts were well received. Nevertheless, there also are indications that some of the leaders are not too quick to rescind complete control over the provinces they now lead.

"This almost sounds contradictory," said Paddy.

"It gets better, or worse depending on how you look at it," Juan continued. "Almost immediately after those conferences had ended, Buenos Aires initiated a new call to hold its own set of conferences in Tucumán."

Juan paused to let Paddy soak it in.

"And?" Paddy asked.

"You know there's more," Juan said. "But what can you deduce only from what I've told you so far?"

"Have our delegates been invited to Tucumán?" asked Paddy.

"I believe so."

Paddy thought for a minute. "Whether they have or not, this conference Buenos Aires has called has been intentionally planned to undermine the efforts of Artigas."

"That is what I think," Juan said. "and Otiguera and Rivera are also of the same mind."

"But this is only how I feel," Paddy said, "and it may not be correct – surely not enough to merit this degree of concern."

"None of us are sure of anything," Juan said, "but we all feel the same way—and the more we speak about it the idea becomes more tenable. I will let you know how our meeting this afternoon turns out.

"You said there was more," Paddy reminded Juan.

"Now I have decided it is better to tell you about that later."

Juan walked away toward the cabildo.

Paddy sensed that he was becoming somewhat the subversive. Surely it could already be seen as a breach of security for Juan to talk to him so candidly. Juan obviously considered Paddy to be one of his closest friends, not only worthy of keeping a confidence but also someone whose opinions almost always were formed from life's experiences and were based in fact.

Paddy definitely was all that, except for one small detail. His own confidant was his wife, Tereza. He told her everything that went on his life—including the things that he and Juan discussed.

Much like Juan, Paddy was certain Tereza would keep his confidence. But then he began to wonder. If each individual in turn had someone that they also felt they could absolutely trust, somewhere along the chain must be a weak link. Paddy hoped the strong link in the chain was Tereza and that the rumors and stories he passed along would stop with her.

*   *   *

That afternoon General Artigas met in the cabildo with his captains.

"It gives me great pleasure," he announced," to report that our efforts with the Northern Provinces have been most positive. There has not been a single objection from any of the delegates at Paysandú to what we are attempting to achieve."

It was Rafael Otiguerra who was courageous enough to begin the rebuttal.

"But General, the conference appears to have caught the attention of the new director in Buenos Aires," he stated. "He has already called for another conference in Tucumán. This is almost surely an attempt to undermine your current success. To counter this effort, we should settle on delegates to send to Tucumán here and now.

"Sending delegates to Tucumán would demonstrate obeisance to Buenos Aires," Artigas replied. "I am opposed to it."

"But if we have no delegates," Otiguerra reasoned, "we have no voice, no control on the proceedings. The good work accomplished up to now could all be destroyed."

It was not difficult to see the General's patience was being strained. "Captain Otiguerra," he said, "Director Thomas is returning prisoners taken from the Banda Oriental. He is doing the same for all the provinces. The purpose is that we might dispense justice on them as we see fit.

"This appears to be a very conciliatory act," Rivera commented.

"On the surface," Artigas said, "but consider the other elements of such a gesture, every one a benefit to the director."

"Some of these men are indeed political prisoners, but most are common criminals – and there are many. Thomas runs the risk of being called the Hangman of Buenos Aires. Now he has made each of us in the provinces responsible for controversial executions that might follow or sentences that must be enacted. He is sending a message that not all aspects of self government are enjoyable. He wants us to understand it well, and then maybe we will accede to the authority of Buenos Aires."

"Now, what other issues need we address?"

Juan raised his finger and was given the floor.

"General, we are receiving reports from the north that there is an increase in activity in the Brazilian province of Rio Grande do Sul, what we used to call Misiones."

"Yes, I've already heard of this activity," Artigas said, "And just for the record, let it be known that by renaming the province, the Brazilians are attempting to blur the historical identity of the region in exchange for a newer more Brazilian one."

"We believe their next objective, and one that they have never abandoned, is the conquest and occupation of what they call the Cisplatine, our own Banda Oriental," Juan said.

"So is any of this new activity military?" Artigas asked.

"Quite a lot of it," Juan responded. "Most of it," he corrected himself.

"Then we must have a better understanding of what is going on up there," Artigas said. He turned back to Captain Lavalleja. "Juan, I want you to take a sizeable force to Minas – Your company and a large number of militia – You select the men you want. Send two forward units to Melo and Cerro Largo where regular patrols can monitor the border."

"Yes, General."

"Traditionally, the Portuguese have used the Melo road to enter the Banda Oriental", Artigas said, "but we must also garrison Tacuarembó and Salto. I want the rest of my officers to return to their units and await further orders. Wherever the Portuguese choose to strike, our forces in other areas must be able to quickly move from their stations to aid those men under attack. Let us pray they do not hit us over several fronts simultaneously!"

The meeting was adjourned immediately, and as to what Buenos Aires was currently up to was quickly forgotten.

*   *   *

In the weeks that followed, the news was all bad. It was learned that the convention called in Tucumán had been very successful for Buenos Aires and all the gains Artigas thought he had in Paysandú were gone. Moreover, the Portuguese did exactly what Artigas had feared most. They attacked over a broad front at several locations. Now the general had to fully attend matters at home and could not counter any new Porteño influence with the Northern Provinces.

At Carumbé, his own army faced a Brazilian force more than twice his size.

"They are so many and we are so few," Artigas said to the one captain he kept with him, his first, Rafael Otiguerra. "General Lecor has driven us before him almost at his will. When we think we might be able to confront and challenge the Brazilians, it is little more to him than an inconvenience. We are achieving nothing at the cost of many good men."

"I would be happy to have a few Porteños alongside me now," Otiguerra admitted.

"I have been in communication with Buenos Aires," Artigas revealed. "I do not expect their help. In fact, it appears they may be actually siding with the Portuguese on this one."

"Perhaps if Alvarez Thomas were still the director," Otiguera complained. "The Porteños change leaders over there like a lady changes shoes."

"Actually it is Thomas himself who has done us this harm," Artigas countered. "It was he who turned the Northern Provinces against us so quickly and effectively at Tucumán. I believe Pueyrredón would help us if he could."

"But it was Pueyrredón who was named the new director at Tucumán!" Otiguera said.

"He is little more than director in name only," Artigas explained. "It is all he can do to hold the provinces together. The General Assembly is where the power is now, and they all want me dead. In order to keep the provinces together, Buenos Aires now must work to build a federal republic, and the General Assembly blames me for putting this notion so firmly in the heads of the provincial governments."

"Well, there is some truth in that, General," Otiguera said.

Artigas smiled but did not respond. He looked over his men and once again studied the massing Brazilian army.

"We do not have nearly enough men," he complained. "The Brazilians can outflank us with ease and with our full knowledge."

"Perhaps we should withdraw this time, sir," Otiguera suggested.

"To where?" Artigas asked. "There is no hope for reinforcements. All my captains face the same problems. The Brazilians are everywhere now. We can only hope to inflict as much damage as possible before they combine their forces near Montevideo."

"Desperate battles have been won in the past," Otiguerra reminded the General.

"And it could happen here today," Artigas affirmed. "I have never doubted the resolve of my men. If only that were enough. Should it be we do not take the day, order the men who remain to withdraw westward."

"Westward?" Otiguerra was puzzled.

"We must get help from somewhere in the Northern Provinces, Artigas declared, "and we must keep this army together. A move west will help us do that. The Brazilians could interpret such a move as our final flight from the Banda Oriental, and their true objective is still Montevideo."

"What about the other captains?" Otiguera asked.

"They will have to hold out," Artigas said. "If we do not realize some success quickly, all may truly be lost."

Otiguerra did not respond. He knew the General was not a man who was faint of heart, nor one who would betray his friends for the sake of his own safety. If he would not go to the aid of his other armies in the field, it only proved how desperate their situation was. He listened intently now as the Brazilian commanders could be heard barking orders across the field.

"By my command," cried Artigas, "attack hard and fast. We must reach their lines before the second volley."

The men watched on in grim silence as the first line of Portuguese began moving forward. Artigas gave his own signal and now both lines were advancing on each other. The cavalry followed close on the heels of the infantry. Captain Otiguerra scanned the Brazilian line for any indication that the Portuguese were about to fire a volley. As soon as he saw it, he ordered the Orientales to prepare to fire.

The volleys were delivered from both sides almost simultaneously.

The infantry executed an immediate move to provide room for the cavalry to pass through. The Portuguese second line fired their volley hurriedly and the riders were decimated, but the survivors continued the surge and reached the Portuguese before the first line had finished reloading. The two sides merged amid pistol shots. Then the battle broke down to sabers and machetes.

From his position, a sudden and uncharacteristic panic briefly overcame Artigas when he saw the Brazilian cavalry appear from seemingly nowhere and move into the battle line.

"My God," Artigas swore. "They have much more cavalry than we."

It was clear that the battle was now lost. At great risk to himself, Otiguerra charged into the raging fury to carry out the General's command, shouting to the men to begin the withdrawal to the west. It was a tragic personal embarrassment to the young captain as he watched the Orientales try to successfully extricate themselves from the frenzied mess and take flight.

Their success was minimal. The battle had been heated with both sides taking casualties, and now the Portuguese were slow to call off the killing. The retreat was quickly becoming a rout.

But once again the General had been correct. When it became clear that the remnants of Artigas' army were moving westward, General Lecor recalled his men and redirected their march back toward Montevideo, leaving the field to the camp followers who soon would come to mourn the fallen and take care of matters at hand.

*   *   *

It was not normal for Paddy to be this unsure of his own actions, but these were not normal times. He had always considered Minas to be a place of refuge for his family. Now the Brazilians were pouring in on all sides and there was a question as to whether the army coming down from Melo would still choose the coastal road. No, he concluded. They would take the more direct route to the capital through Minas.

Paddy considered all his options and decided it was safer this time for the family to go northwest to Salto. If necessary they could take refuge in Ayuí, a town already familiar to Tereza. It might be best to take Ana along too. Now as the Señora de Lavalleja, the wife of one of the Orientales' best officers, she was in considerably more danger than most women.

*   *   *

At India Muerta, Jose Rivera's regiment faced the forward column of yet another Brazilian army. Reports coming in from all over the Banda Oriental revealed the Portuguese were everywhere. The news was dismal, and from what Rivera saw across the way, today would be no different.

"I did not expect so many!" Rivera said.

"Maybe today is not the day to do battle," Rivera's aide suggested. The tremolo of fear in his voice did not sit well with the captain.

"No, today is the day," Rivera stated resolutely. "We are out of options, Lieutenant. The Brazilians already know we are here and we have a duty to slow their advance."

"But we are so thin," the lieutenant complained.

"Yes, and I dare not strengthen any section of our line for fear of completely exposing another," Rivera said. "We will attack with the cavalry and strike hard to inflict maximum damage."

"And they can extract themselves quickly," the Lieutenant hoped.

"Yes," Rivera agreed. He hoped he did not sound as if he had already conceded the battle, but he knew, in light of the obvious, that a forced optimism would only be seen as disingenuous. "The rear guard can cover our retreat."

"Sacrificial lambs," the Lieutenant said.

"We are all volunteers here, corporal," Rivera replied.

"The Brazilian's are closing fast, Captain."

"Then prepare the attack," Rivera ordered.

Rivera's lieutenant rode off. Within a minute the cavalry was moving up to the front. Rivera signaled the attack and the cavalry raced toward the Brazilian line. The abruptness of the attack surprised the Brazilian officers, who attempted to form ranks and get off a volley. Their hurried commands resulted in only a few wild shots as the Orientales reach the line.

The Cavalry hacked its way through the Portuguese infantry who had clearly lost any advantage they might have had. For a while Rivera almost allowed himself to take heart as he watched his men begin to collapse the line. But then Portuguese reinforcements, both in cavalry and infantry, responded brilliantly and the advantage began to be lost.

The Orientales disengaged themselves almost as quickly as they had charged. In a full gallop the cavalry rode past the rear guard already in place to absorb the full brunt of the Brazilian pursuit.

* * *

Captain Juan Lavalleja surveyed his own ragtag army that was now made up of only several hundred gauchos. He had never felt as unsure of the final outcome of any pending battle as he did now. The Brazilians were so strong. It was evident their soldiers were now being drawn from all over that vast empire to be concentrated on the limited resources of the Orientales.

Maybe Paddy had been right all along. Juan was alone now. His familiar comrades in arms each were in other parts of the country with their own little armies, desperately struggling to stem the onslaught in those areas. He had no one with whom to counsel. It was all on him. Even his second in command was a young newly commissioned lieutenant he had recently met and knew only as Miguel.

How nice it would have been to simply find Ana and go away together.

Well, that would have to wait.

"Here is where we make our stand, Miguel," Juan said. "I am tired of running."

"What do you think of our chances, Captain?"

"Even, Miguel, and I am not lying to you," Juan said. "We may be outnumbered, but I know these hills, and the Brazilian columns are becoming stretched. Their supply lines are strained.

"Some of the men feel we should have engaged them earlier", Miguel said, "closer to Melo."

"We would have been overrun," Juan assured his Lieutenant. "Artigas attacked the Brazilians early and each time he has been defeated. We can only hope Rivera can reinforce him or else we will be having Brazilians at our rear."

"If we are successful here," Miguel said.

"Yes, if we are successful here."

For the next ten minutes Juan's gauchos took their positions in the hills on the approaches to Minas. Then they waited.

Within half an hour the far off but discernible din of horse drawn equipment and metal could be heard, and it was becoming louder.

"Right on time," Juan said.

He raised his arm and his company of men became silent. When the Brazilians had positioned themselves to his liking along the road, Juan brought his arm down and the gauchos sprung forward in a furious attack.

It took only seconds for the Orientales to close on them. Caught completely by surprise, the Brazilians found themselves totally unprepared to counter the attack, although they greatly outnumbered Lavalleja's little force. Many were only teamsters who, in the heat of their first battle, lost their coolness immediately and fired wildly. Some found it better to disregard fighting altogether and took the whip to their teams. Some forced their way on through the fight and fled toward Montevideo. But the greater part was put to route back up the Melo road. The mounted Orientales gave quick pursuit to the stragglers. Juan knew word of what had just happened here would quickly spread, and he could not get caught by a superior force around Minas.

"Recall the men, lieutenant," Juan yelled. "We must regroup quickly."

"Yes sir," Miguel replied. Then he added "You have a masterful victory, Captain."

"Yes," Lavalleja concurred. "But it will not be nearly enough, I'm afraid."

"But it is a victory," Miguel smiled, "and the people needed one."

"Carry out the order, Lieutenant," Juan said impatiently, and Miguel rode off.

*　　*　　*

Artigas passed through the city gate accompanied by only a small squad of men. The scene was strange to the Montevideans who saw him and remembered when the General sat at the head of a large army. He entered the plaza, dismounted, and walked directly into the cabildo.

President Joaquin Suarez was at his desk when Artigas burst into the office.

"General!?" the startled Suarez cried.

"I am told that the government has signed a treaty subjecting us to Buenos Aires," Artigas yelled.

"I am seeking aid, General," said Suarez.

"Traitor! You have destroyed all we have achieved these past several years."

"The Brazilians are destroying all of that as you speak, General," Suarez reasoned. "How go things in the battlefield?"

Artigas lunged over the desk to strike Suarez down, then quickly thought the better of it.

"Your action is an insult to all many good brave friends who now sleep in our country's soil," he said.

"Many were my friends too, General," Suarez reminded him. "I am still struggling to attain a sovereign Banda Oriental, but within the new Argentine federation of provinces. Unless we can quickly achieve a victory so decisive that the Brazilians will go home, we have to fall back on the few options still available to us."

"Then I will do all in my power to bring you that victory, President," Artigas said.

"I have never doubted that you might do anything else," Suarez said. "But this may beyond any of us."

*   *   *

Word of Artigas' visit to President Suarez quickly arrived at the print shop. Paddy considered how fortunate he was to have such a large unsolicited and unpaid staff of reporters – those whose only reward was fulfilling their small role in seeing the news reached the people quickly. Then his thoughts became more focused on the present.

It is time, Paddy thought to himself and he locked up the print shop.

He found Tereza washing down the walk in front of the house. She smiled sweetly but her face revealed that she was wondering why he was there.

"Hello, Love," Paddy said.

"Hello mi Cielo," Tereza answered. "What brings you home this time of day?"

"It is beginning to look as if we might want to take the family out of Montevideo again. Our armies are facing defeat on all sides – And the Porteños might be returning."

Tereza sighed and her shoulders drooped noticeably. "Minas again," she asked.

"Not now," Paddy said. "Minas will be dangerous. If the Portuguese come from the east, this time they will not go through Maldonado. They will be coming fast straight through Minas."

"Where will we go then?" Tereza asked.

"I'm thinking of the Salto Grande," Paddy replied.

"The Salto?"

"Our money will go far there and if trouble comes that way you can take the children across the river into Ayuí. You are already familiar with it and we may still have some friends there."

"Do you think we will be there long?" Tereza asked.

"No," Paddy replied. "One way or the other, this business will be over very soon."

*   *   *

Lavalleja's small retreating force entered Canelones just after midday. He had hoped to find Captain Rivera in the cuartel there, but José was in the street, his own force in a high state of preparedness. Lavalleja rode up to him, smiling.

"Hello, dear friend," Juan said.

"Good afternoon, Captain," Rivera replied. "I heard you've been dancing with the Brazilians again."

"They were most cordial this time," Juan smiled.

Rivera managed his own weak smile. "How far away do you expect they are now?" he asked.

"Less than a day's ride, I would say."

Rivera chuckled. "Only a short while ago the world at last seemed right," he commented. "Within the hour I will move my force to Pando to confront the Brazilians there. If they chose to occupy Canelones first we may still have time to fall back to Tres Cruces."

"Should we not withdraw into the city?" Juan suggested.

"Half our men are cavalry," José replied, "and I would not subject the citizens to another siege. No, I will face the Brazilians in the open plain outside the city walls.

Juan nodded. "I will keep my forces with you," he said. "Together we are strong enough can make them pay dearly."

Rivera looked surprised. "Have you not heard?" he asked. "The General has ordered you west to the Rio Uruguay. Help him bring back the men we need to drive the Brazilians out."

"I do not believe I can leave you here," Lavalleja said.

"We both know it is the wise thing, Juan," Rivera replied.

After a long pause Lavalleja nodded once again. "God be with you, my friend."

"And with you, Captain."

CHAPTER TEN

The Cisplatine

The Portuguese/Brazilian strategy was very untraditional and very bold. Rather than take Montevideo and wait for Artigas to come, they would look for him wherever he might be.

There were three reasons for this new strategy.

First – a siege might not be easy to maintain and would come at the cost of many lives, some military but mostly civilian.

Second—Admiral Brown and the Porteño navy still controlled the Rio de la Plata and a Brazilian assault from the sea was really not feasible. On the other hand, an Argentine counter attack was totally possible.

Third – Artigas would be kept on the run, unable to rely on his disintegrating supply lines.

The plan required several necessary elements to be successful, among which were an able leader and a capable ring of spies. The Portuguese had them both.

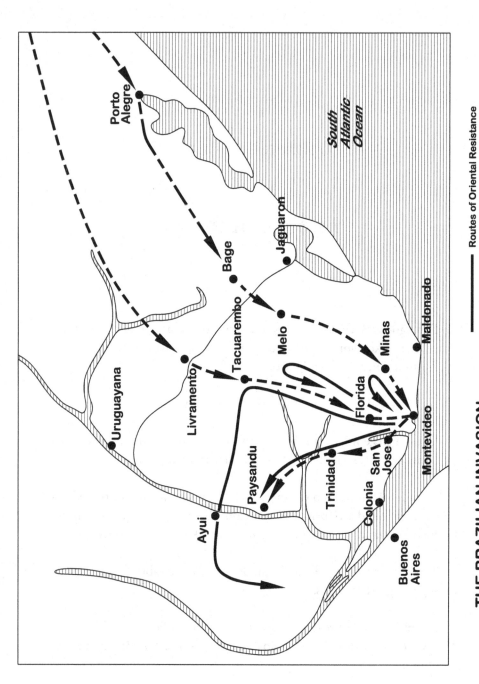

THE BRAZILIAN INVASION

Routes of Oriental Resistance
Brazilian Invasion Routes

South
Atlantic
Ocean

Porto
Alegre

Jaguarón

Bage

Tacuarembo

Melo

Minas

Maldonado

Uruguayana

Livramento

Florida

Montevideo

Paysandu

Trinidad

San
Jose

Colonia

Ayui

Buenos
Aires

General Lecor actually had field experience fighting the French in Europe and his judgment was beyond reproach. Since Lecor's quarry would be Artigas himself, the main mission of his spies would be to keep the army advised of the movements and locations of the "lesser" commands under Artigas. That would be especially true of Juan Lavalleja and José Rivera, and a plan had already been developed to neutralize those two.

It was becoming evident, if not common knowledge, that Lavalleja and Rivera were the two most competent of Artigas' captains, so it was essential that they be isolated and their commands destroyed.

This would not be that difficult. The Portuguese had guessed correctly that both the forces of Rivera and Lavalleja would be held in reserve near the General to come to his immediate aid should he need it. The solution was to send three numerically superior forces into the same area.

Each of these forces would be assigned one of its Oriental counterparts. Even if it appeared that the destruction of Lavalleja and Rivera would take too much time or prove too costly, a second plan was developed to provoke and threaten them but do nothing more. Their preoccupation with this immediate threat might then curtail their ability to support Artigas should he need it. In the meantime Lecor's force would pursue and eliminate, if possible, the wily old General.

The first encounter would come at Catalán. The Brazilians, under General Lecor's capable command, routed Artigas in a defeat that, while not fatal in itself, struck such a blow the Orientales would never fully recover. Worse for Artigas, with this defeat the ominous specter of uncertainty and doubt entered his camp in earnest for the first time.

The second phase of the patriot's spiral downward came as a result of a Portuguese misstep. In spite of their best efforts, word reached Lavalleja's camp that the General was in trouble and he was still able to move his forces out in an effort to provide relief. That alarmed the Brazilian covering force and they hit him at Paso del Cuello. Again the Orientales were defeated and, as he had been commanded to do in such an event, Lavalleja retired to Paysandú to await further orders from Artigas.

Those orders would never reach him. At Aguapey Lecor defeated Artigas again. It only took the greatest of generalship for Artigas to extract what survivor's he had left out of this debacle.

All through this dark atmosphere of gloom Artigas seethed at the recent behavior of President Suarez. Three things chafed the General most.

First—the president's actions were an outright affirmation that he had no confidence the Orientales could prevail militarily. Once word of what was happening reached his men, it would surely have a demoralizing effect on them when what they needed most was an affirmation of support.

Second—the president saw his appeal to Buenos Aires for help as the only rational course of action.

And third—the president appeared to be right about the first two things.

In a moment of deepest despair Artigas penned a letter to President Suarez.

My dear Joaquin,

While the actions of the government of the Orientales might be understandable, it cannot reflect the true will of the Orientales themselves. I have watched brave men continue to fight on and fall in pitched battles when all hope of survival, much less success, was already gone. It is freedom that drives such men, not only in the Banda Oriental, but as we have already seen, throughout the Americas.

It is most proper that a free people would prefer glory in a futile but noble cause rather than submit themselves to ignominy. As for myself, the commander of the Orientales has always shown that he loves his country much too dearly to sacrifice this rich heritage to the low price of necessity.

General Jose Gervasio Artigas

After Aguapey, Artigas fled north with the remnants of his army. It might have been out of compassion that Lecor let him go, but more probably the move was strategic. Montevideo was virtually an open city now and Lecor moved south to take it.

*   *   *

It was a somber morning the day Lecor entered Montevideo. In the plaza the banner of the United Provinces was replaced by the new green flag of the Banda Oriental under Portuguese rule. Artigas was no longer a viable threat. Rivera was bottled up somewhere north of Canelones and Lavalleja now languished near the Rio Uruguay.

Although it probably should have been otherwise, perhaps the most surprised inhabitant of Montevideo was Paddy Colman. The sight of the Brazilian soldiers startled him and he was seized by the sudden fearful realization that he was cut off from his family up on the Salto Grande.

General Lecor ascended the stairs where Artigas had stood in front of the cathedral less than a year earlier. Paddy moved near the front of the crowd of citizens and strained to hear what he had to say.

"Citizens of Montevideo. The Kingdom of Portugal invites you to take advantage of your full rights as new citizens of the Cisplatine Province in the Empire of Brazil. Portugal is working to make your lives better than you have ever known."

"We will open your ports to the world, find markets for your products, and you will have access truly for the first time to the wonderful new things the world now produces."

"The Cisplatine Province offers unconditional amnesty to all those who now lay down their arms. To those who continue to resist we say, 'Your struggle is futile. Your numbers are few.' Buenos Aires now recognizes Brazil's occupation of the Banda Oriental and they have dedicated all their forces to the liberation of Chile and Alto Peru only. At Mendoza at the foot of the Andes, General San Martin already fashions his new army."

"Return to your normal lives and have your children attend school once again. See how good life can truly be."

Paddy was sick at heart. So it was over – all the many years of struggle—and Paddy had no part in it. Well, he was only one man. What good would he have done? And Tereza was probably right – he had been the rational one.

But in his mind he could not make it work.

*   *   *

Conquering a country is one thing. Subduing it is quite another. It becomes an especially difficult task when the conqueror reaches out a friendly reconciliatory hand before the vanquished is convinced he is truly defeated.

Such was the circumstance under which General Lecor stood looking out a window of the cabildo and pondered the stagnant situation in the Cisplatine Province. At his side stood the Portuguese General Da Souza. Brazil's two ablest commanders were now in the Banda Oriental together, sent to destroy finally the pesky remnants of a revolution that had begun before Brazil ever set foot on the soil.

"Four years—and as yet we do not control the Cisplatine" Lecor complained. "Artigas still roams the countryside seemingly at will and he has not ceased in harassing our soldiers in the open fields."

Da Souza disagreed. "Everyday his forces become weaker, General, his highways more restricted. Some of his most faithful followers recently have deserted and fled across the Rio Uruguay. His days are numbered."

"Are they?" Lecor asked. "How many times have we thought we had defeated Artigas only to face him again and again? Look at us! We have treated the people here with great respect. Their lives have never been better. Yet Artigas is now a greater hero to them than he has ever been."

"Only a fool can believe there is still hope in continuing this fight," Da Souza said smiling. "We have sent overtures to Rivera, offering him not only a full amnesty, but a commission. His force, as it stands, would be designated to be the elite military unit of the Cisplatine."

"A most generous offer in light of the trouble he has caused," Lecor said.

"He is a fine soldier and has a fine fighting force," Da Souza countered. "Should it happen that he agrees to our offer, it will allow us to free a lot of troops serving here to subdue outbreaks that might spring up in other parts of the empire."

*   *   *

The Colman house was different now than it had been when first Tereza placed her hand on the back of Paddy's neck and pulled him toward her for that first kiss some fifteen years earlier. Paddy had thrived as a printer and the home was now full of new furnishings and the finer things of life.

The Colmans had changed too. Like most marriages, as the children grew older, there was a lot less of Tereza sitting in Paddy's lap in the parlor with her arms around his neck. They were parents well into their thirties now and the inappropriateness of it with growing children made it almost a thing of the past. Paddy missed it. It was a ritual that confirmed to him that this most precious of women loved him above all others. Not participating in that ritual now deprived him of her sweet tenderness – the one thing he prized above all. He was buoyed by the understanding that Tereza missed it too, but sometimes he questioned her reasons.

"Reasons!" Paddy thought. "That is a strange word for emotions that have no reason to them at all." The fading practice of the ritual also had Tereza beginning to believe she was becoming less attractive to him. His denials did nothing to ease her concerns. Paddy tried to use an example and he thought he had a very good one. He rehearsed it in his mind until he had perfected it.

"A man goes to his wardrobe where underneath the clothes his shoes and boots are kept. Among these is a pair of boots, that given the choice of keeping the rest and discarding these, or keeping these and discarding the rest, he would keep these. They are strong and durable and have much life left in them. They are also soft and supple where they need to be and they feel good when he wears them. He is comfortable in them all day. They may not be as classy or outwardly as beautiful as the others, but he values them most of all. They serve him best and it is his hope they last longer than he does."

The parable did not have the immediate effect he had hoped.

"So I am like an old pair of boots!" she fumed. She stewed for some time and Paddy wondered if he had inadvertently unleashed a beast he would never be able to subdue.

Her resentment of this parable was so intense that she thought on it for days until—suddenly she understood its meaning. There are men, like the Beau Brummels so famous in that era, who would choose the newest prettier footwear always and cast the older footwear aside.

Then there were men like Paddy. These men loved their old boots and would wear them forever given the chance. It was overwhelmingly comforting to her, but it did not ease the fact she was getting older.

Another change occurred, gradually over time, so slowly as to almost not be noticeable. But an occasional event would suddenly and briefly reveal it.

Katy and Luisito were growing and it was gratifying to see how they developed.

Katy had all the grace and charm of her mother and was beginning to catch the eye of many of the local ne'er do wells (at least, that is how Paddy saw it).

Luisito was like his late Uncle Luis. Paddy had hoped there was some of himself that had rubbed off, but it was obvious his son had many of the characteristics of his namesake. *He could do a lot worse*, Paddy thought.

* * *

The Brazilian detachment rode their mounts hard as they raced along the road to Paysandú. They did not let up even when they entered the town amid the startled onlookers.

Lieutenant Oliverio Ortiz led the group, with pistols drawn, straight to a makeshift military headquarters and surprised the less than alert guards before they could respond. Ortiz quickly dismounted and entered the building.

Juan Lavalleja looked up from his desk at the intruders.

"The struggle is finally over for you, Captain," Ortiz said. "You are my prisoner."

Ortiz waited for Juan to take it all in. Slowly he raised his hands.

* * *

"To the governors of Entre Rios, Corrientes, and Santa Fe;

I plea for your help in our noble struggle for liberty against the Brazilians in the Banda Oriental. I am confident that with my Charrúas I only have enough to hold the enemy in check, but I do not believe I can achieve victory quickly. Whatever the odds, while I live, the country must be freed of tyrants. The love of liberty is the nature of rational beings. The willingness to lose that liberty is the nature of cowards.

Excellencies, I repeat once again that in light of these unfortunate complications, the greatest help would be your support against the forces of our enemies.

Your humble servant,

General José Gervasio Artigas"

The General looked up from the letter he had just penned. The fire in his eyes was almost extinguished and there was nothing in his person that would indicate that he had any faith help would come from the governors of the three provinces. Tomorrow he would face the Brazilians once again against odds he that he already knew were insurmountable.

* * *

The men who followed Artigas battled the Brazilians heroically outside Tacuarembó on a large open plain. In spite of their valor, the battle was lost almost from the beginning. Yet the Orientales would fight on until the retreat was finally ordered.

Their force little resembled the first army Artigas had led so long ago. The old officers had commands of their own and the soldiers were darker now, mostly Indians and mestizos rather than the whiter Creoles of earlier times.

"General, I fear we must break off the fight or we shall surely be annihilated."

Artigas turned in the direction of the shout and saw Andresito running toward him. Had it been anyone else the general might have figured the man was a coward, but he could see his captain was right.

"Order the retreat, Andresito," Artigas yelled, "and have the men to regroup at Salto."

That evening Artigas camped some distance outside Salto. What remained of his army had time to rest for the first time. He exited his tent and surveyed the scene before him. Andresito had been waiting for the General but it seemed prudent to allow him some time before he approached.

"What is on your mind, Andresito?" Artigas asked.

"General, we are not fit to face the Portuguese again any time soon, Andresito said candidly.

"How many are we now?"

"About 300 sir," Andresito replied.

"No stragglers?"

"None have arrived so far."

Artigas' face reflected not only the effects of Tacuarembó, but those of all the recent defeats the Portuguese had put on all the Orientales. Andresito could see it and it worried him deeply.

"Of all our misfortunes, I am becoming greatly concerned most of all about our spirit," the General said. "How much failure can one man endure before he loses all will to fight on?"

"We will fight the Portuguese until they leave, General," Andresito vowed, "or until no one remains alive to fight them."

Artigas smiled. "If I had a thousand Andresitos I could conquer the world. We will go into the northern provinces and get the forces we need."

"Will the governors there approve?" Andresito asked.

"I will force them to approve if they will not do so voluntarily."

*   *   *

Ana and Tereza walked out of the cathedral in Montevideo after several hours of prayer followed by the holy sacrament. They stood on the stairs several minutes in conversation, then crossed the plaza and entered the cabildo.

"General Lecor." A Portuguese lieutenant said softly, "the wife of Captain Lavalleja is here to see you. A friend is with her."

Lecor was not surprised. Ana had already formally written the General for an opportunity to meet with him and he graciously accepted. "Have them come in, Lieutenant."

General Lecor smiled when the women entered. "This is a pleasure, ladies. In what way may I help you?"

"I am Señora Ana Monterroso de Lavalleja," Ana said, "the wife of Captain Juan Lavalleja, and this is Tereza Ferrando de Colman, my friend."

"I am at your service," Lecor said.

"We have come to request the privilege of visiting my husband while he is being detained here in Montevideo," Ana said boldly.

The smile quickly vanished from Lecor's face. Fortunately the appearance of kindness still lingered. It gave Ana some hope.

"I have direct and clear orders from Rio de Janeiro regarding Captain Lavalleja," Lecor stated. "He is not to set foot in Montevideo. He is to remain on board the ship that brought him here until it leaves for Rio."

"May we see him on the ship? Ana asked.

"That I cannot allow," Lecor insisted. "It is a prison ship and would not be appropriate for such a meeting."

Ana was persistent. "What will happen to Juan when he is taken to Rio de Janeiro?"

"He will be tried at court," Lecor said. "To be honest I do not believe the outcome will be in his favor. He has brought much grief to the empire."

Now Tereza interrupted. "Please General. Juan is a good man, but he is driven by his own vision of liberty that sometimes clouds his judgment."

"Is that so?" The General said reproachfully. "Señora, have you felt your personal freedoms restricted in the Cisplatine Province?"

"No, Governor, I have not," Tereza said truthfully.

"Has your life improved under the Cisplatine banner?"

"We have more than we ever had before," she said.

"Have you expressed this to your friend's husband?" Lecor asked.

"He knows it, and I am certain for the sake of his cause he would rather that the Brazilians treat us more unkindly. But regardless of how we are treated, he sees the Brazilians as invaders who have no right to be here."

"That is a pity," Lecor said. "It may very well mean his death."

Ana began to weep. For a moment she seemed in control but then her sobs overwhelmed her and her body shuddered. Tereza rushed to embrace and console her. Lecor studied the uncomfortable scene before him.

"As a soldier," he said, "I have a responsibility to myself and my men to study my enemy. You have not told me anything today about Captain Lavalleja that I have not already learned. I know he is a principled man, but there is little I can do for you."

Ana continued to weep and it appeared she was so overtaken in her grief that she did not even realize the General was speaking. Tereza, however, looked up at him but said nothing.

"But this I will do," Lecor said. "I will send you to Rio de Janeiro. There you may be permitted to argue the Captain's cause with the King. Perhaps you may even be allowed to visit your husband.

Ana looked up, nodded, and smiled through her tears.

"And I will include a letter asking clemency," he added.

Ana was overcome and fell prostrate before the General. Tereza knelt down beside her to help.

"Oh thank you, General," Ana sobbed. "God bless you." Tereza grasped Lecor's hand and kissed it.

*   *   *

The evening began innocently enough when Paddy asked Tereza if she was thinking about visiting Minas any time soon. Tereza's response was really no answer at all. She waited until the children were in bed.

Until then she answered Paddy's questions with vagaries and generalities. She could see he was becoming irritated but he did not press the matter. Paddy knew Tereza and Tereza knew Paddy. She had her reasons for being elusive. When they were alone in bed Tereza opened up to him.

"Ana is going to Rio de Janeiro to appeal in Juan's behalf," she said.

"She is?"

"I want to go with her."

"Have you thought this through, Tere? It is a very difficult journey,"

"We will not be going overland," Tereza said. "We are going by sea."

"Really! And how will Ana book passage when we ourselves may have to go into debt for you to do so?" Paddy asked.

Tereza's brow furled. "I was thinking we could pay for both passages."

"Wha . . . ?"

"The Portuguese are paying the passage," Tereza finally said in disgust.

"The Portuguese?"

"Well, General Lecor,"

"And why would he do that?"

"He was moved by Ana's tears."

Paddy said nothing.

"They were genuine," Tereza added. "Else he would not have been moved by them."

"Of course, I'm sure they were" Paddy said.

"Thank you for being patient with me, Love"

*　*　*

"How long a day will this turn out to be?" King Joao asked as he reviewed the day's schedule for the Royal Court of Brazil.

"There are many supplicants on the docket," his son Pedro said.

"Everyone needing a favor!"

"For the many who are here, you are the only person who can provide one," Pedro smiled.

The king smiled in return. "The people in the streets believe we spend our days indulging in all life has to offer," he muttered. "I do not imagine any of them would enjoy spending their day as we do, listening to the whining of others."

"Would you prefer being a man of the streets?" asked the Prince.

Joao was irritated by the seemingly disrespectful remark. "Sometimes I believe I would," he said defiantly. As he continued to scan the list, an item on the schedule suddenly grabbed King Joao's attention.

"We have women on the docket today!"

"Yes. They come from the Cisplatine," Pedro replied.

"Ana Lavalleja," the king commented. "Would this be the wife of our prisoner?"

Pedro nodded. "They have come a long way. I would rather they not be made to wait."

"Then we will speak to them first," Joao said. "I am interested in what they have to say."

Pedro motioned to an attendant. "We will see Señora Lavalleja now."

Ana and Tereza entered and curtsied. They waited for the King to speak.

"Welcome to the court ladies," Joao said. "I hope your trip has not been too difficult."

"Everyone has been most helpful, Your Majesty," Ana said. "I am Ana Monterroso de Lavalleja, the wife of one of your prisoners, Juan Antonio Lavalleja, and this is my good friend, Tereza Ferrando de Colman."

"May I present my son, the Crown Prince," Joao responded. Pedro nodded courteously.

"Ladies."

"I regret to say your husband's reputation precedes him, Señora Lavalleja," King Joao began. "You may not be aware of it, but while his name might not be familiar to the common people, my military officers know him quite well."

The first formal words from the King were not consoling ones. A look of worry mixed with fear crossed Ana's face.

"Juan is a very good man, Your Majesty", Tereza blurted out.

"He is responsible for the deaths of many of my soldiers," The King said coldly. "Most of them were also good men—many, fathers or sons of good families. Neither side can claim only theirs is defended by good men."

"Or bad ones!" Tereza replied rebelliously.

Ana gently brushed Tereza back. "Your Majesty," she said, "I have with me a letter from General Lecor regarding my husband."

"Leave the letter," Joao ordered. "I believe I already know what it must say."

"I cannot pardon your husband, Señora Lavalleja," the King continued. "It would be an insult and injustice to all the Portuguese and Brazilian soldiers who have sacrificed so much for the empire. But I will do this."

"Your husband is scheduled for hard labor in our most severe of prisons. I will transfer him to Isla das Cabras. In time he might even be paroled—and he can thank you for it."

"God bless you, Your Majesty," Ana sobbed. "May I see him?"

King Joao turned to the attendant. "Arrange a meeting for these ladies with the prisoner Lavalleja," he ordered.

*   *   *

Ana and Tereza waited in silence. There had been no special attempt to make the prison visiting room an inviting place and its stark appearance made both women wonder what the rest of the prison must be like. Soon the guard brought Juan in, still shackled.

"Juan!" Ana cried. The two embraced with Tereza at their side hugging them both. All were in tears. The guards stood back and let them have their moment.

"Oh Ana! How I wish you did not see me like this," Juan said.

Still kissing her husband, Ana spoke in soft tones, "Be quiet, my love!"

"It is so good to see you!" Juan said. "How were you able to come here?"

"General Lecor gave us an escort," Tereza said.

"Lecor!?"

"And a letter appealing for your clemency," Ana continued.

"Lecor?"

"We cannot take you home, Juan," Ana said, "but they have decided not to sentence you to hard labor."

"How goes the fighting?" Juan asked.

Ana turned her head away.

"How bad is it?"

"It is over, Juan," Ana replied fearfully.

"Over?"

"Artigas has known nothing but defeat," Ana said. "His army was unrecognizable in the last days, mostly Indians, many from Brazil and Paraguay."

"In the last days?"

"His last battle was at Tacuarembó."

"I have heard reports," Juan said. "Surely that was not the end."

"The general was left with only a few hundred men. He took them into Entre Rios where he hoped to secure help. At Entre Rios he was able to strengthen his army once again, but the governor would not help him. Artigas became like a madman. He took his army and fought the army of Entre Rios."

"Artigas was driven north to Paraguay," Ana continued. "He asked for help from the Paraguayans, but instead they put him into a forced exile. They keep him in Candalaria and pay him a captain's wage."

"And his men?" Juan asked.

"His army, or what was left of it, was left stranded in Corrientes," Ana answered. "They went back to their homes."

"So it IS over."

"Yes."

"And what has happened to Rivera?"

"His regiment is now part of the military force of the Cisplatine Province," Ana replied.

Juan could not believe it. "José has betrayed himself?" he asked incredulously.

"He received a very generous offer, Juan," Ana replied. "José and his men could have found themselves just as you are now, and the Portuguese have been good to all of us."

It was clear Juan was disgusted. "Ana. We are Orientales," he said. "The Portuguese would have us be Brazilians and call us Cisplatines. Our grand children will not speak Spanish at all. Is that what you want?"

"I want you back with me!" Ana cried in frustration.

Tereza chose not to speak. She did not have anything to say that would help and she feared if she opened her mouth, whatever she did say would only worsen the atmosphere.

She wondered now what she had expected from this meeting. Bittersweet tenderness, perhaps. It definitely wasn't this!

*　*　*

Paddy was surprised at his children – surprised and proud. With Tereza gone he knew he would be depending on Katy very much to maintain the house. She turned out to be wonderful at it. It did not matter that part of her zeal came from her desire to show her father she was capable of adult responsibilities. The fact was she was doing it.

The truth was Paddy had eaten better than he ever had. Much of the reason was that Katy wanted so much to please her father she made a point to always prepare the meals he especially liked.

She also saw to it that the laundry was done on a very timely basis. She could do this because she did not have all the other responsibilities that Tereza would have had if she were home.

Luisito was another blessing during this time. On one particular evening Paddy could see that his son was wrestling with a particular problem.

"What is it son?" Paddy asked.

"I would like to work at the docks," Luisito replied.

Paddy looked at his son questioningly, "Shouldn't you wait a few more years?"

"I think I can do it now." Luisito responded.

"Well, you're big for your age and maybe you have the strength but do you have the stamina?"

"I believe so."

"Have you already been offered the job?"

"I spoke with the foreman and he asked me to come back," Luisito said.

"You know your uncle worked the docks," Paddy said. "Come to think of it, he was just about your age when he started." It was not just an idle statement. Paddy was leading to something.

"Yes."

"And you realize if they hire you, you'll be doing the work nobody else wants and be paid lower than everyone else," Paddy counseled.

"Yes father, I do."

"Are you willing to do that?"

"Yes sir!"

"That is good to know. Your uncle was a hard worker on the docks. I don't know, it may have been because he saw himself as less than a good gaucho. But he has a reputation for dependability there even today." Paddy looked for some reaction from his son.

"But he has been dead almost ten years now," Luisito said.

"That is sometimes the way reputations are," Paddy said, "be they good or bad. You also need to know that what sounds only terrible now may become quite unbearable after a few days on the job. If it gets to that, you must persevere. You have your uncle's reputation to protect—and yours to build."

"I'll try to remember that," Luisito said sincerely.

"And try to remember also that you made a commitment to the foreman," Paddy said.

"Yes sir!"

"Now what am I going to tell your mother?" Paddy asked.

"Ma?"

"She's not going to be happy about this," Paddy assured him.

"How about you?"

Paddy thought for a moment. "I think it's probably as good a time as any," he said. "Now, what about Katy?"

"Katy?" Luisito wondered what she had to do with anything.

"You are in a position now to earn your own money for the first time. That's good, it's your money." Paddy studied his son's expression as he tried to make sense of this apparently disjointed conversation.

"Your mother depends on Katy a lot," he said, "and Katy works hard alongside her. She is older than you but she does not have the opportunity you do to earn her own money. We could never pay her what she is worth."

"Yes sir," Luisito said.

"At the same time your mother will not want her baby working the docks," Paddy assured him. "So let's sweeten the deal."

"Sir?"

"I will talk to your mother," Paddy said. "And I am asking you to share a portion of what you earn with your sister. Can you do that?'

"I suppose so," Luisito said. "How much will it be?"

"How much does it matter?" Paddy asked. "Are you taking this job to prove something or for the money you can make?"

"A little of both, I suppose," Luisito said.

Paddy smiled. "That is an honest answer. I'm thinking between a quarter and a half. Can you handle that?"

"I believe I can," Luisito said.

"No resentments?"

"I'm not sure," Luisito said honestly, "but I don't think so."

* * *

As time passed in the Cisplatine Province, Katy and Luisito had grown out of their early teen years. Luisito was true to his commitment to his father and gave his sister half of his earnings. It had to be admitted that their family had never been happier. From the Colman point of view, the Portuguese occupation of the Banda Oriental had been a blessing. But all this was about to change.

For one thing, the Portuguese were never called the Portuguese anymore, only the Brazilians. That came about when King Joao finally returned to sit on his throne once again in Lisbon and left his son Pedro and the princess Carlotta to govern Brazil.

Whether Pedro enjoyed the thought of instant power or was becoming somewhat Americanized in his own way, it was hard to say. Maybe it was a little of both, but no sooner had the old man left than Pedro allied himself with Brazilian revolutionaries and proclaimed himself "Dom Pedro" the first emperor of the new free and independent Empire of Brazil.

Portugal was helpless to do anything to prevent it. Rather than fight, soldiers loyal to the old kingdom embarked for the two thousand mile trip back to Europe. The remainder stayed to make new lives for themselves in the new nation.

The sun had set on both Portugal and Spain in the New World. Any fighting now would be among the new American nations themselves.

CHAPTER ELEVEN

The Thirty-three

For Emperor Dom Pedro and the brand new Empire of Brazil, the end of colonialism had created a new era of good feelings. As part of the celebration, many political prisoners were designated to be paroled.

In Montevideo, an aide to José Rivera entered the Captain's office at the Regimental Headquarters. He grinned but said nothing.

Rivera waited patiently for him to speak, but soon the waiting became uncomfortable.

"Yes lieutenant?" Rivera said questioningly.

"You have a visitor," came his reply.

"Very well," Rivera sighed, "Show him in!"

The aide's broad smile never waned. He walked back to the door, opened it, and motioned to the person waiting on the other side.

"You may enter," he said. And with that, Captain Juan Lavalleja walked into the room.

Rivera could not contain his joy and surprise. He jumped up from his chair. "Juan!" he shouted, and ran to embrace his friend.

"How are you, José?" Juan asked smiling.

"Good! Good! Oh what a day!" Rivera exclaimed. "I thought I might never see you again."

"It has been a long time. I was released when Brazil declared its independence from Portugal," Juan explained. "It was part of a general amnesty."

"How independent can a nation really be when the crown prince of the mother country still rules there?" Rivera laughed.

"It is not a ruse, José," Juan said, "Pedro has actually turned Brazil into a separate country, totally free from Portugal."

"But there is a deception that has been created," Juan continued, "to make the people believe they have more control of their government. In actual fact, "Dom" Pedro has installed himself as Brazil's new emperor."

"If that is true, I do not believe the Brazilians will be content to remain docile in Brazil for long. Empire is a disease. They will be looking to expand their borders," said Rivera.

"As usual, you are right, José. I believe they intend to dominate the continent," Juan commented. "The Banda Oriental is only the beginning of this bold plan. It is clear now that the final days of the Spanish in South America are very near. They are gone from the Rio de la Plata and patriot forces are driving them from Chile and Peru. When the Spaniards are gone for good, Brazil will make its move. And the Orientales will be expected to fight alongside the Brazilians as loyal subjects."

Rivera saw this as good an opportunity as any to explain his present position to Juan. "The Brazilians have been most generous with us," He began. "We could all be dead men now, the executed vanquished. But

Brazil was merciful. And who is to say really what the future holds. For now my first duty is to have you assigned to my regiment."

Lavalleja saw the suggestion as all but hopeless. "I am just released from prison, José," he explained.

"I believe I can accomplish it," Rivera argued. "At present we are in a climate of transition and reconciliation. Actually I believe there will be no better time to try. Brazil is most eager to have local disturbances subdued by Orientales rather than Brazilians."

*　*　*

Tereza finished packing the basket. In it she had placed a large slice of cheese, a loaf of bread, several peaches, a cup, some lemons, and a container of sugar. "Now Luisito, do not forget to bring this basket back," she warned. "Put it in a safe place when you are working so It will not be stolen."

"Yes Ma," Luisito said. It had been over a year since he began to work at the docks and he never failed to bring the basket home, but every day he received the same admonition still.

"And take care of yourself," Tereza begged.

"I will Ma," Luisito promised.

Tereza smiled poignantly, "I know you must be tired of hearing me tell you this, but I will always worry about anything happening to you at work," she said.

"I think the boy will be alright," said Paddy. "As much as we have preached to him, he has yet to hurt himself. It would appear he knows well enough to be careful."

"It is just that life on the docks is different than any other place in Montevideo," Tereza fretted, "I remember the language Luis brought home after he had worked at the docks only for a while. He never used that kind of language before."

"It's a hard habit to break," Paddy admitted, "but it can be done."

"Do not worry about me, Ma," Luisito said. "That is not the kind of person I want to be."

"Listen to your mother son," advise Paddy. "She knows better than you how easy it can be to start using bad language."

* * *

At the Arroyo de la Virgen, José Rivera's regiment stood at attention across a large table from a similar Brazilian force. Although Rivera had already sworn allegiance as an officer in the Cisplatine Province, this new directive came from Brazil itself on the advent of its independence. It was to be enforced throughout the Empire.

There were several reasons for not executing this order in the city. The men were told that this was a very solemn oath. As such it should be taken away from the scrutiny (and in some cases the criticism) of the population at large. Another reason, and this was the primary one, was that while the Brazilians controlled the major part of the Banda Oriental, by previous arrangement, there was still a remnant of a Portuguese force that controlled the city. This arrangement was to remain in effect until those Portuguese actually embarked for home.

So to avoid any possible problems with the Portuguese in Montevideo, General Lecor had taken his force out of the city along with that of Rivera's. Now the Brazilian commander approached the table to address the men.

"At the order of his Excellency, Emperor Dom Pedro the First of Brazil," Lecor said in a loud voice, "all provincial officers and enlisted men in the service of Brazil are required to sign the Act of Reclamation and Recognition. By signing, you renew your allegiance to the Empire and personally confirm that the Cisplatine is a part of Brazil."

Juan glanced at Rivera, but Jose's eyes were directly on Lecor and his face was resolute.

"Before you is the document, drawn up on behalf of the Cisplatine Province, the General continued. "At this time you are invited to come forward and sign."

The pause that followed Lecor's invitation lasted less than a second. It was Rivera who led the way and he quickly walked to the table to sign. Juan Lavalleja followed immediately behind and signed his name. The actions of these two were electric and if there had been disagreements or discussion among the troops beforehand as whether to sign or not, now the remainder of the corps marched to the table dutifully.

*   *   *

Only months after Juan had returned to Montevideo, it had become apparent that life working at the docks for Luisito was becoming worse than any he could have ever previously imagined. As the year progressed, Paddy and Tereza's son became less and less the happy boy they used to know. He had become dark and brooding. Moreover, the part of his income he was to share with his sister had diminished. Paddy was determined to get to the bottom of it.

It was Tereza who provided the opportunity when she suggested that Katy and she leave to visit Ana just before Luisito returned home from the docks. This would allow Paddy the time he needed to be alone with his son to discuss the issue. Paddy waited in the front room until Luisito came through the door.

"Hello son," Paddy said.

"Hello Pa," Luisito replied. "Where are Mom and Katy?"

"They went to visit Ana. How are things at the port?"

Luisito did not respond immediately.

"Well?"

"It's not going very well," Luisito replied.

"What is the matter?" asked Paddy.

"Work has increased a great deal," Luisito said, "but we receive no additional pay for it. To be fair, the foreman has proportioned the extra tasks to each of us so all share the load equally. Still, many of the men are very unhappy and there's some talk about a strike."

"Have they reduced the men's pay?"

"Not for the older men," Luisito replied, "but they have hired more new men to help with the added load. There is no additional money so they receive less than before and some of the new men who were already there, including myself have seen our pay reduced.

"And that is the reason Katy is receiving less now?"

"Yes sir."

"But you are still keeping to the agreed rate when you give her the money."

"Yes."

"Luisito, why didn't you come to me about this matter?" asked Paddy.

"I was afraid if I said anything about it you would make me quit – and I thought the situation would be temporary."

"That's a reasonable answer," Paddy said.

"What are you going to tell Ma?"

"I'm going to tell her the truth. I have to," Paddy replied.

"It is she who will make me quit," Luisito complained.

"No she won't. I'll talk to her about it."

*   *   *

José Rivera and Juan Lavalleja sat astride their horses in front of a column of foot soldiers from the regiment. The men were armed with sabers and pistols, but an unusual piece of armament hung from their belts—billy clubs – unusual except for this particular task. The regiment stood on the docks facing a company of belligerent longshoremen. Ordered by the commander of Montevideo to return to work, these men now stood with their arms crossed.

Rivera took his right hand off the front of his saddle and raised it to salute the workers. He kept it there as he spoke.

"I have been directed by the Governor to order you back to work. We do not want any trouble and we are asking you to go peaceably."

"Why should we?" asked the longshoremen's spokesman. "The port becomes busier, our workload increases, and everyone profits except us. Our pay has not been increased since the Portuguese arrived."

"Then you must speak to the governor about this," Rivera responded.

"We have," the longshoreman said, "and his response is that there are plenty of Brazilians who would be happy to come here and work for less."

"It is imperative that for now you return to work!" Rivera insisted. "I will speak with the governor myself on your behalf."

"You seek only another month's work from us," the longshoreman argued. "Even should you talk to the governor, he will never agree."

"I give you my word I will do everything possible to represent your position," Rivera pleaded. "If you do not return to work, I am required to use force, including sabers if necessary. Do not make me do this!"

"I defy you and my men defy you," the longshoreman said, "You have become the lap dogs of the Governor."

We could use men like this, Juan thought to himself.

Rivera turned toward his men. "Draw your clubs!" he ordered.

The longshoremen stood resolute. A long pause followed with men on both sides staring each other down – all except one. Luisito had hidden himself behind the men in front. He did not want Juan to see him. He had sworn solidarity with his coworkers and he feared the relationship between Juan and Ana and his parents might now present a problem, not only for himself but also for Juan. There would be no good outcome to what was about to happen, so he hid.

"Execute the order! Rivera ordered.

The soldiers fell upon the longshoremen, and most broke and ran. Those who struggled to put up a fight against the charging militia were quickly struck down. Even many who took flight felt the sting of the billy club. The soldiers pursued them into the streets away from the dock. A lesson had to be taught!

On the edge of this chaos Rivera and Lavalleja looked on in grim silence.

* * *

As she approached her home, Tereza watched the drunkard down the street stumbling toward her. A tinge of fear swept through her but she quickly dismissed it. The man could barely stay on his feet. What harm could he do? But as he drew nearer, she suddenly realized what it was she was seeing.

"Luisito," she gasped.

The closer he came, her horror increased, and she began to run toward her son. Blood had already begun to dry on the front of Luisito's shirt and his face was red with it. One eye was swollen shut. He looked up at his mother and smiled at her pathetically. Tereza stooped to provide a supportive shoulder and the two walked slowly home together.

Tereza put her son in a chair in the front room and went to the kitchen to wet some rags. When Katy entered the room, the smile on her face changed into a horrified gasp.

"Katy, go to the shop and fetch your father!" Tereza cried.

*   *   *

Back at Rivera's headquarters, José removed his cap and set it on the shelf. Just as he was sitting down at his desk, Juan entered the room. He angrily threw his cap in the general direction of the shelf, where it flew into Rivera's cap, knocking both of them to the floor.

Rivera looked up from his desk. "Unbecoming an officer, Juan," he said softly.

"The longshoreman was right," Juan shouted. "We have become puppets of the Brazilians!"

"Do you believe that I am any less distraught? I can see as well as you what is happening here!"

"Then you conceal your emotions quite well, José!" Juan said contemptuously.

Rivera took the time he needed to word his sentence correctly. "We must be patient and wait for times to improve," he said.

"Wait?" Lavalleja cried. "The Brazilian stranglehold grows tighter by the day. And sadly I see no future opportunity to cast them out."

"Definitely we are not equipped to do it now," Rivera said.

"There was a time when I was proud to be called captain alongside you," Juan said. "I regarded you no less than Artigas himself. What has happened to that man, José?"

* * *

Juan and Ana walked along the street arm in arm toward the Colman house. From time to time Juan would look at his wife and she would look up into his eyes with a worried smile. They said nothing, however, each absorbed in their own thoughts concerning the events of the day.

This was not a courtesy call, but one made out of sympathy. Juan himself was most remorseful. He understood that he was, in part, one of the reasons that Paddy and Tereza's son was in such sad shape. While he wanted Luisito to know how intense his concern was, he was almost too ashamed to enter the door.

"Juan, Ana, It is good for you both to come over," Tereza said. "Please come in."

"We are so sorry about Luisito," Ana said. "Is there anything we might do?"

"No, Ana," Tereza said. "Thank you. I have Katy and we are doing fine."

When they saw Luisito they were surprised at how bad his appearance really was. Ana began to sob.

"He actually looks worse now than he did when he came home," Tereza said. "I suspect it is the additional swelling and the most recent indications of the bruising."

"I am truly ashamed for my part in this action," Juan said. "I want you both to know just how sorry I am and I beg your forgiveness."

"Juan, you were doing your duty as an officer," Paddy said. They were not hollow words. Paddy knew first hand the inner conflicts that come from the call to duty. "Luisito and his coworkers were preparing to strike and you were ordered to put it down. You have nothing to be sorry for."

Juan looked at Paddy regretfully. "Rafael Otiguerra tells a story about Artigas, when he resigned his commission in the Blandengues Corps. The General was torn by the oath he had sworn. In it he promised loyalty to the crown and to the people, but events of the day made it impossible for him to keep both – so he chose the greater."

"I have heard this," Paddy said. "It is a part of his farewell speech to the Corps."

"Yes, it is," Juan said. "Today the same opportunity the General had was presented to me at the docks, and I chose the lesser. It will not happen again!"

*   *   *

José Rivera entered the cabildo and walked straight to the office of the Governor. He already knew the reason for his being summoned and he was not looking forward to this meeting.

"You wanted to see me, Governor?" Rivera asked.

"Captain Rivera, have you been able to locate Captain Lavalleja?" The Governor asked.

"He is nowhere to be found, sir," Rivera answered honestly.

"And his family?"

"Ana is also missing."

"So this is the way Lavalleja rewards the amnesty so graciously afforded him," the Governor said in disgust. "So be it! I declare him outlaw and charge him with desertion. Proceed with the confiscation of his properties."

"Yes sir!"

"You are dismissed, Captain."

As Rivera turned to leave, the Governor called him back once more. "Captain Rivera!"

"Yea sir?"

"I expect an accounting of his seized assets by morning. "

"Yes, Governor."

*　*　*

To anyone in Buenos Aires who saw him as they walked down halls of government, he appeared to be an insignificant, if not almost comical figure. He was dressed in an officer's uniform, and by the colors in the piping and trim he appeared to be Brazilian, although the uniform was not the standard Brazilian issue. The man was small in stature and there was little in his appearance that would have awed the average observer. He had been seated on a bench in the corridor for almost an hour, his hat in his lap, when finally a government official approached him.

"Captain Lavalleja," the government official said, "Director Rivadavia will see you now."

Lavalleja chuckled. "Rivadavia?"

The government official appeared puzzled and offended. "Yes sir. What do you find so humorous?"

"A junior officer of mine once said the Porteños change their leaders as often as a lady changes her shoes," Juan replied.

The government official smiled. "Well, that actually does appear to be true," he said.

The official and Lavalleja entered the director's office.

"Señor Director, I present Captain Juan Lavalleja," the official said in a formal tone.

"Oh yes," Rivadavia said. "Captain Lavalleja—the man who can get more out of his soldiers than San Martin or Artigas. You may not be a generally famous man, but among those who know military matters, you are legendary."

"I had no idea," Juan replied honestly.

"I can only imagine what brings you into my office," the director said.

Juan was blunt. "I want to mount an expedition into the Banda Oriental." He said.

"Once again!?"

"Once again!"

Rivadavia smiled and looked directly into Lavalleja's eyes. "You have countrymen traveling throughout the provinces asking for the same thing. A few believe they are meeting with some success. The province of Santa Fe has even chastised us for our reluctance to help and has begun to assemble its own army."

Lavalleja was intrigued. "And?" he asked.

"And then reality steps in," Rivadavia replied. "An army is expensive and must be paid. Santa Fe has discovered it cannot support the troops it already has and they have asked the Orientales to finance it. The Orientales would indeed do this were they able, but they cannot."

"Perhaps if the army could be paid now from either Santa Fe or Buenos Aires, the Orientales would repay the expenses once the battles are won," Lavalleja suggested.

Rivadavia was candid in his response. "That is a gamble no one, not even Santa Fe, is willing to assume right now," he said. "You will receive much verbal support. No one wants to speak out against a people's dream of freedom, but actual support will be more difficult to come by."

"I had not anticipated this kind of hesitance," Juan said.

"You must remember that a previous director had actually recognized the Brazilian occupation of the Banda Oriental," Rivadavia reminded him. "Also, one of our greatest fears at the moment is José Rivera's regiment. Our effort could be doomed from the beginning should his Orientales fight alongside the Brazilians. Many of our military men regard them to be the finest unit in the Banda Oriental right now."

"I expect they may well be, but Rivera will be with us when the time comes," Juan assured the director.

"He told you this?"

"It will happen!"

"Then if that is true, this is what I can do," Rivadavia said. "There are hundreds, perhaps thousands of Orientales here in the provinces. Raise an army from these, return to the Banda Oriental, and if you are successful, we will send Alvear's reserves to support you. They are presently preparing for operations in Alto Peru, but I am sure success on your part will cause the Directory to consider reassigning them to the Banda Oriental."

"The force I require will not be large," Lavalleja said. "I intend to take only the most dedicated of men."

"It could be you have chosen a very opportune time to launch your operation," Rivadavia said. "The independence of Brazil from Portugal was intended to be an amicable thing, benefiting both countries. But Dom

Pedro seems to be enjoying his roll as emperor a little too much. Apparently the Brazilians are becoming irascible hosts to the few Portuguese who have remained and they are very put out."

"How will this serve us?" Juan asked.

"I am communicating secretly with the Portuguese commander in Montevideo, a General Da Costa," Rivadavia revealed. He could see he had Juan's full attention now. "The commander feels he has lost the support of the governor and he has become somewhat marooned there. He would like nothing more than to just go home to Lisbon, and I have offered transport for him and his troops. Admiral Brown and the Argentine navy are at the ready to see him safely back to Portugal."

"Won't the Brazilians have something to say about that?" Lavalleja asked.

"Most assuredly," Rivadavia replied, "but it will be too late. It is the Portuguese who occupy Montevideo while the Brazilians control the rest of the province. Part of our agreement with Da Costa is that he deliver the Brazilian governor to us when this takes place and allow the town council of Montevideo to take charge. Our forces will replace his in the city before the Brazilians discover what has happened."

"You offer us more than we would hope to ask," Lavalleja commented. "What do you ask in return?"

"That the Banda Oriental returns to us as a full province," Rivadavia answered.

"We are fighting for our freedom, Señor Director, as we always have," Juan reminded him.

Rivadavia laughed. "And they say Artigas is finished," he chuckled, "but I see he simply resurfaces in other guises – alright, as a full sovereign province then."

"That may be a possibility." Lavalleja said.

THE FINAL CAMPAIGN

—L—— Route of the Orientales (Lavalleja)
—A—— Route of the Argentines (Alvear)
—B—— Route of the Brazilians (Barbacena)
—R—— Route of Rivera's Volunteers
—BRF—— Route of the Brazilian Relief Force

*   *   *

Within a fortnight after this meeting, a minor official in the Argentine government, Pablo Martinez, quickly made his way through the cabildo to Rivadavia's office to share some astonishing news.

"Señor Martinez," The Director said cheerfully when he entered. "What brings you into my office so early this morning?"

"I have come to inform you that Captain Lavalleja and his force have departed from Entre Rios and are presently headed downstream on the Rio Uruguay," Martinez replied.

"So soon? Where do they disembark?" Rivadavia asked.

"At La Graseada. It is an unpopulated area where livestock used to be slaughtered," Martinez responded.

"How appropriate!" Rivadavia said sarcastically. "How many are they?"

"Including Captain Lavalleja, Thirty-three, Sir."

"Thirty-three?" Rivadavia was stunned. "Thirty-three!?"

"Yes Sir," Martinez replied.

*   *   *

April 19, 1825 – In the predawn hours, the small flotilla drifted silently down an unusually quiet Rio Uruguay, keeping close to the Argentine side. The men aboard maintained order and silence as the little fleet began to move toward the opposite shore at La Graseada. As soon as the launches were beached, the men immediately began to unload horses and supplies, Captain Juan Lavalleja barking orders.

"Lieutenant Oribe, Secure the animals and see that they are pastured," he yelled," "then meet with me on the shore."

"Yes, Captain," Oribe obediently replied. Juan wondered only slightly at how Manuel would respond in his new subordinate position, but he had judged him as a good soldier who would do his duty. The Captain was determined, however, to change this arrangement as soon as there were enough men for Oribe to command.

As the men worked, Lavalleja returned to the launches and retrieved a furled banner in a leather sheath. He uncovered and unfurled the flag, and planted it in the sand, holding the pole with one hand.

Juan was determined that the banner they fought under this time make a statement. As sentimentally attached as the men were to Artigas' flag of the United Provinces, Juan knew it was time to leave the provinces behind. The provinces had already sworn allegiance to the fledgling Argentine Republic, all but one.

The new flag had three horizontal bands, red, white, and blue from top to bottom. On the center white band the words "LIBERTAD O MUERTE" were written. Soon the men filtered in from their various tasks. As they did so the crews in the launches prepared to leave. It was a scene already planned by Lavalleja. As the launches pushed off, Juan pointed toward them.

"The launches are leaving, señores," he said. "If you have second thoughts, you should swim for them now."

The men laughed.

"No. I did not think so," Lavalleja said confidently. "Not you men. We are of one mind—and one heart."

"When we were in Buenos Aires, we had many discussions on what our standard should be. Some felt it should remain Artigas' old proud banner, the flag of the United Provinces. A few Porteños thought we should carry the escarapela with us.

The laughter grew louder.

"Behold our ensign!" Lavalleja extended his free hand toward the banner. "Its words are not new, and certainly not original. They have been repeated many times in many places. But here, these words will mean exactly what they say. If victory and liberty are not won, then let no man standing here today live to give report on how it was lost."

"Many might ask how this effort will be any different from those failed attempts of the past. I will tell you how. There will be no flight across the Rio Uruguay this time to fight another day. This time it is to the death! Libertad o Muerte!"

A lone voice cried out. "Libertad o muerte!"

Then as if rehearsed, the men shouted in one voice.

"Libertad o muerte!"

Now the gritos changed.

"Viva Lavalleja!"

Then, "Viva Artigas!"

Lavalleja signaled the men to hold the noise down. "We will camp here tonight on the high ground," he ordered. "Keep the fires small and protected from view from the river. Tomorrow we move on to San Salvador."

* * *

They had done it often enough in years past that now the Orientales knew what to anticipate. Just before dawn the small force approached the little town of San Salvador. Experience had taught them that the cry of a single horse would not alarm the garrison there, since these were all a part of the normal noises of the night.

Manuel Oribe smiled as he remembered his first experience when a mule brayed under these circumstances. He was a young man then and had been almost frozen with fear, expecting an immediate volley from the darkness ahead. Now he knew it would take more than this to rouse the defenses.

The cuartel was visible from the edge of town and the small patriot force advanced quickly but quietly toward it. Suddenly Lavalleja motioned for the attack.

The surprise was complete. The Brazilians were caught just as they were rising from their beds and few had the courage to turn and fight. They ran in panic, many still in their bed clothes and most without even grasping a pistol.

It was total slaughter. Not a single Brazilian at the outpost escaped alive.

So complete was the victory that the nearby town of Santo Domingo de Soriano would receive no word of what was about to befall it.

*   *   *

The following morning four inconspicuous "gauchos" rode into the plaza of Santo Domingo de Soriano and dismounted in front of the chapel. The two Brazilian soldiers who had been patrolling the plaza took notice of the men but the sight was not out of the ordinary.

So they did nothing.

The gauchos knocked on the chapel door and soon a priest greeted them. The men spoke for a short time until finally the priest allowed the gauchos to enter, closing the door behind them. After some time had passed, a shot suddenly rung out from the bell tower and one of the two Brazilians, now standing across the plaza near the cantina, fell. The other darted out of range and quickly ran toward the cuartel.

Within a minute, Brazilian soldiers filled the plaza, trying to spot anyone in the bell tower. A few ran up to the church and beat on the chapel door.

Now the remaining 28 men of Lavalleja's force rode hard into the city and surrounded the plaza. They sealed off the exits out of the plaza and began to pick off Brazilians. From their hemmed in positions, the Brazilian garrison could not determine the full size of the force they were up against. What was evident, however, was Brazilians were falling everywhere and the attacking force was suffering little, if at all. Faced with this reality, the Brazilian commander surrendered.

Lavalleja and Oribe led their horses to the hitching rail at the cuartel.

"We will turn our prisoners over to the first town with a jail," Juan announced.

Oribe was surprised. "They will slow us down, Captain. It may be best that we kill them now."

"Then if our men become prisoners, what clemency could they expect?" Juan asked. "I want Rivera. Take four men and find out where he is."

Again Oribe questioned the order. "That will leave you with 28 men—too few to guard the prisoners," he protested. "And what if Rivera is antagonistic?"

"He won't be," Lavalleja assured him.

"Buenos Aires thinks otherwise." Oribe said.

Lavalleja's demeanor revealed that he was becoming tired and frustrated with the conversation. "Manuel, when did you become a great believer in the opinions of Buenos Aires?" he asked. "I tell you José will be with us."

From a side street a group of men rode quickly into the town. It was enough of a start that it struck a flash of fear in both Juan and Manuel's hearts. As the men approached, Oribe put the palm of this hand on his pistol handle. The leader of the group yelled out.

"Orientales! We are with you," he said, "and others are coming."

Lavalleja smiled broadly. "Gracias, hombres."

He nodded towards Oribe. "You see Manuel?" he asked. "We thought we had been so careful no one knew we were here! And more than these are on their way. That is how it has always been."

The riders rode up to where Juan and Manuel sat. "We are at your service, Captain," the leader said. "Where do you want us?"

"I am checking on that now," Lavalleja laughed. "Captain Oribe, Ask the townspeople or the good brethren from the church if they might not make arrangements for these men."

"Yes Captain," Oribe replied.

*　　*　　*

Paddy wondered how he was going tell Tereza. The news he had received through his channels of unpaid "reporters" was not good. It was clear now where Juan was—back in the Banda Oriental and coming this way. What was also becoming clear was Luisito's own hatred of the Brazilians. Worse, it was a hatred mixed with the fire of retribution and of independence. He might have been Paddy's son, but he took after his uncle. The similarities were not uncanny.

Paddy found his wife in the kitchen. He would not mince words.

"Amor, Juan is back in the Banda Oriental," he said bluntly.

Already Tereza was apprehensive. "He is?" she asked.

"Yes, he is leading a small force and he has already taken two towns in the west."

"Oh no!"

"There is more," Paddy continued. "José and the regiment are not in Montevideo. No one is saying anything but he may be on his way to intercept Juan."

Tereza began to cry. "The whole country is coming apart," she sobbed. "Who would have thought it would come to this?"

Now Paddy wondered how he was going to reveal the really bad news. Well, now he would start with baby steps.

"You know if Juan is successful he will be coming this way," he said.

"Poor Ana," Tereza replied.

"We must head for the Salto Grande one more time," Paddy continued. "We have to leave the city before a siege is laid."

"When will this insanity end?" Tereza said in frustration.

"I believe this could be the last time," Paddy replied optimistically, but then his mood became more somber. "But if it is the last time the men will know it. This time might be much bloodier than any of the others."

"Then let's go now!" Tereza said resolutely.

"There is something else you need to know," Paddy said. His voice was softer now.

It was a fear that ebbed and flowed in Tereza's heart since the beginning, when Artigas first brought his army to Tres Cruces after his victory at Las Piedras. Now her fear was to be realized. So sure she was of it that she said nothing, as if to forestall the inevitable. After a short time Paddy continued.

"Luisito wants to go with them," he said. The words seemed to burn her very soul.

"No, he can't!" Tereza said desperately. "You mustn't allow him to do it!"

"I do not think I can prevent it," Paddy said.

"Of course you can!" Tereza yelled. "You are a man and he is a boy!"

"Do you think I can watch him every minute of the day?" Paddy reasoned.

"For a while, perhaps," Tereza replied. "Then when he has come to his senses he will thank you for it."

"You are deceiving yourself," Paddy said. "He will not change his mind."

Tereza looked away and said nothing.

"There is more," Paddy said. "When we leave San José, I am going with him."

"Do not do this!" Tereza begged in a trembling voice. "I could not bear to lose you both."

"I am going to look after our son," Paddy said. "If he is hurt and I am there, they cannot forbid me to take him home to heal."

Tereza sat still for a minute, and then nodded. As poor as it was, she knew this was the best offer she was going to get.

* * *

History questions how much was already agreed to beforehand when Lavalleja led his little army into the town of Monzón. Suddenly at the plaza they found themselves facing the entire Rivera regiment. A regimental guard in a small forward company stopped them.

"Halt!" the guard ordered.

"You do your duty well, Corporal," Lavalleja said.

"Declare yourselves!" the guard commanded.

Juan dutifully responded, "Captain Lavalleja of the army of liberation. Could it be that Captain Rivera might be here?"

"I will take you to him," the guard replied.

"I am here, Corporal." Rivera yelled as he walked out into the sunlight from the shadows of an arched portico.

Lavalleja smiled. "José, old friend," he shouted.

Rivera mounted his horse and rode up to the party of men. "You are accused of desertion, Juan," he announced.

"Really? I did not think I would be missed," Juan laughed.

"The penalty for desertion is death," Rivera warned.

Lavalleja smiled. "I have an appealing counter-offer."

Rivera returned the smile. "Come inside and we will talk about it," he said.

After the two entered Rivera's makeshift headquarters, José began to speak more seriously. "How goes the insurrection?" he asked.

"It is moving along quite well," Juan replied. "We have stung the enemy with little injury to ourselves."

"And how large is your force now?"

"I cannot say, but well over a thousand men," Juan answered.

"A thousand?" Rivera questioned the remark. "Word is that you came with less than 50."

"Thirty-three," Juan replied, "but our force grows by the hour."

"My force is at your service, Captain," Rivera promised. "The men are all agreed."

"You will truly HAVE to be at my service, José," Juan reminded Rivera. "I have worried over your willingness to be subordinate to me. Especially since before it has always been otherwise."

"Will I have my own command?" Rivera asked.

"Most assuredly," Juan said.

"Then that will be enough," Rivera declared. "For discretion's sake, I was not able to evacuate my family. I must write them now and describe how the great Captain Lavalleja took my entire force completely by surprise. I hope the Brazilians will cause them no harm."

Chapter Twelve

Sarandí

My Dear Family;

It pains me to report that, much to my disgrace and the disgrace of my men, the regiment has been taken completely by surprise by an overpowering force under the command of Captain Juan Lavalleja. I am happy to say, however, that we have been treated well. I am told we are to be taken to Buenos Aires, however, and I cannot say what treatment might await us there.

Do me the favor of informing the governor of our circumstance. Please inform him also that it is the intention of Captain Lavalleja to march directly on the capital. If you are permitted, secure your leave quickly and hurry to me.

Your loving husband and father,

José

*   *   *

The army of liberation moved swiftly now along the highway between Colonia and San José. It was a genuine army now, large and complete with supply wagons, livestock, and camp followers. Juan Lavalleja, who usually rode near the front of the moving army, left his position and rode back to Rivera's column.

"I have come to believe now that, advancing east from Buenos Aires, San José is truly the key to all the cities along the coast," Juan said to Rivera. "I only hope the Brazilians are as blind to this as the Spanish were. If they are we will take San José without much of a fight."

"San José!" Rivera commented. "I am reminded now of our first time there when we served with General Artigas."

"We were mere corporals then," Lavalleja laughed. "Who among us would have realized then we would still be at this business so many years later."

"Corporals?" José laughed. "You were a corporal, I was a common private!"

"Back then we both sensed a quick victory and a free Banda Oriental," Juan commented. "Had we known then that the road was to be so difficult . . ."

Rivera cut him short. "We would have traveled it still! Look my friend, we are still here."

"And so we are," Juan agreed. "I want to occupy San José and Canelones immediately. I will place you in charge there as a vanguard until we are ready to move on. I do not believe we are as yet prepared to lay siege to Montevideo until Alvear arrives with the Argentine army, but we will send Oribe on up to scout out the situation.

"Where will you be?" Rivera asked.

"I plan to move north and set up my command at La Florida," Juan replied. "I hope from there to put in motion procedures to establish a legitimate government. With some luck we might have it in full operation before the Argentines come in and decide to take control."

"Artigas' hand still appears to be in everything we do," Rivera commented.

"Except he besieged Montevideo immediately," Juan said. "It turned out well for him, but I believe he was extremely fortunate since he was so undermanned. The Spanish did not take the opportunity to destroy him when they were most capable."

"The General made them overly cautious when he surprised them at Las Piedras," Rivera reminded him.

"The man gave us an excellent example of how to run a revolution, His vision was true and we must not stray far from it even today," Lavalleja said. "That is the reason you still see his hand is in everything we do. This time I am hoping we will be able to realize the vision."

"God willing," Rivera declared.

"God willing," Juan replied.

Oribe rode up quickly from the rear of the column.

"Were you afraid we were plotting without you, Manuel?" Juan joked.

"I have some news for you, Juan. A pair of volunteers just rode up to the rear of the column. We made them comfortable and gave them some food."

"A pair? Juan asked. "That's fairly common news, Manuel. It happens quite regularly now."

"These two are a father and his son," Oribe smiled.

"Manuel, what the hell is wrong with you?"

"The man is Irish, I would say."

"The Colmans?" Juan asked.

Oribe only smiled.

"Have them come on up," Juan ordered.

"They are really spent," Oribe said. "It appears they have been riding very hard."

"Very well, I will go back and join them then."

*   *   *

General Artigas sat outside his humble home in Candalaria, Paraguay. He passed the day as he normally did now, reading and sipping his yerba mate. For an aging man, it was a comfortable enough life. Attended by a pair of government paid servants, he watched as a third, his faithful Felipe, approach him.

"Felipe, my good man." Artigas greeted him.

"I have you a fresh yerba mate, General," Felipe said, "and I brought something you might enjoy—a newspaper from Buenos Aires."

"As always, I am very grateful for the mate," the General smiled, "but why would I want to know of things in Buenos Aires?"

"This newspaper has a story from the Banda Oriental," Felipe replied.

"Read it for me please, Felipe," Artigas asked. "It is becoming difficult for me to read for myself."

Felipe opened the newspaper to the article. "Argentinos Orientales have come together, a small group of men fully convinced that the Orientales on their own soil will rise up against Brazilian domination."

"Have the Orientales become Argentines?" Artigas asked.

"I believe that would be wishful thinking on the part of Buenos Aires," Felipe replied.

"So the Orientales are back at it again," Artigas smiled. "I am almost certain my old captains are behind this. God bless them."

Felipe looked at his boss sadly. Here the old man sat, resigned to his circumstances. The fire was still there but his understanding of his present capabilities made the scene most melancholic.

* * *

Tereza Ferrando de Colman looked across the Rio Uruguay as content as she could possibly be given the circumstances. She had to admit to herself that life on the river seemed very peaceful. In all the history of this area she had never heard of any account of armed conflict. Perhaps when General Belgrano marched his army near here back when the Argentines undertook their failed mission to free Paraguay from Spain, but that was all.

Across the river and not too far away lay the little town of Ayuí, where her family had lived after the exodus. *Had it been all she could have hoped for back then, it would not have been such a bad life after all,* she thought. She was embarrassed now for the depressed state she had maintained in her own character when they lived there and the pain it had caused Paddy. Now, able to see things from a different perspective, she began to believe that maybe this would be a good place for her and Paddy to live out their later lives.

The scene before her was restful. She watched the sky turn orange as the sun dropped low in the west. She studied how the river's flow and undulations would catch and reflect the orange and yellow glow in an ever changing yet somehow constant pattern.

Presently, when she had become concerned for her mother, Katy came out to where Tereza stood.

"Hello, my daughter," She said.

"Mother, what are you doing out here?" Katy asked.

"I am just enjoying the view," Tereza replied. "It is so peaceful here – so inviting."

"I would think you might hate this place," Katy said, "since it was here where Uncle Luis lost his life."

"Maybe earlier," Tereza said. "But as time has passed, I have come to understand that was only a part of life. We all must pass on someday and none of us knows where or when. All I want now is a place where we all can just live together in peace and enjoy one another while we may."

"And you think this might be the place?" Katy asked.

"It could be," Tereza replied. "It is so peaceful here."

"But Ma, there is nothing here."

*   *   *

Over the course of an hour, sixteen men, whose dress identified them as still somewhat humble, but yet genteel to a point, arrived and greeted each other at a waddle and daub building with a thatched roof. The simple structure shared a common wall with the chapel at la Florida, where Captain Lavalleja and his bride had wed. Distinguished by his uniform, the townspeople who witnessed the gathering readily identified a seventeenth attendee as Juan Lavalleja himself.

Moments later, Juan addressed the men now seated inside.

"Gentlemen," he began. "I offer my most sincere appreciation for your bold action in coming here today and that of your town councils for having the courage to elect you as delegates. I am sure you are all aware that they, by their action, will also be considered as co-conspirators in our great undertaking. It is regretful that we will not have the company of delegates from Montevideo nor Buenos Aires with us, but the efforts of Montevideo have not gone unnoticed. Envoys from that esteemed council are continuing to seek help for our cause in the Argentine Republic."

"I cannot yet speak for Buenos Aires. Perhaps they, as yet, are not prepared to risk the hangman's noose, even when they, among any of us, are the most secure in avoiding it."

A mix of spontaneous grumbling and laughter broke out among the men and Juan waited while they spoke among themselves regarding his comment. Then he continued.

"Here we will continue to validate the reasons and purposes of our righteous cause. The principles set forth more than ten years ago by the great Artigas, at the village of Peñarol, have not changed – and we must hold true to them as we work."

"Let there be no misunderstanding here and now! We are not so strong that we do not require help from the other provinces. Everyone of them now has only one requirement of us, that we remain united with them as a province still in the Argentine Republic. This provision must be in the document, whether we like it or not. Then when the battle is won, we will discuss it with them further."

"Be not overly concerned by this. Buenos Aires is aware that we seek our sovereignty. Whether we become an autonomous province in their nation, or we once again must fight for our rights, will depend on future circumstances that are beyond our present abilities to predict. Nevertheless, here and now, union with the provinces must be a part of this document."

Lavalleja waited for his words to sink in. The men looked at him in silence. It was clear they all understood and it also appeared that they had no misgivings, or if they did, they had no firm argument to counter what he had just said. So he continued.

"Padre Juan Francisco Larrobla, I surrender the floor to you and I take my leave. Padre, do not underestimate the stewardship that has been placed on your shoulders. Despite whatever the successes we may realize in the field, señores, our nation, as a nation, is now in your hands."

Larrobla, a distinguished Catholic priest, rose from his seat and walked to the front of the room where he took the gavel from Lavalleja's hand.

"I wish President Suarez were here," the priest told the general in a muted voice.

"You'll be fine," Juan reassured him. He formally saluted the priest, bowed to the rest of the delegates, and departed, fully confident now that that small body of men in the little room would do their duty.

*   *   *

Paddy stared into the fire. The other men in Juan's ever growing army, and even Luisito, were now off taking care of personal tasks or otherwise enjoying the respite in light conversation. And though there were men nearby all around where he sat, the brilliance and crackling of the fire had the effect that Paddy was in complete solitude.

Paddy truly felt himself alone and he interpreted this as a rare moment meant to be enjoyed. But as the fire flickered and sparked, it slowly sucked the meaningful thoughts out of him. The trance would have been a complete delight were it not for the emergence of those ancient inner fears that his subconscious usually kept well guarded in the remotest of recesses in his mind.

They were always there, lurking, waiting for the opportunity to avail themselves and take control of his being. In those rare instances when they did, it became a totally conscious effort to keep from being overwhelmed by them.

Since he first saw Tereza, his life had begun to unfold toward the contentment he now enjoyed. But he was no fool. He knew what they shared was fragile and he so wanted it to last. He had understood long ago that he could easily entertain these demons and allow them to destroy the warm times between him and his wife, or he forcibly could shove them aside.

Usually he was successful in driving them back from where they came (and it was an effort). But in the quiet of this moment, in front of the fire, he submitted to them. He agonized over his present circumstance and the possibility that either he or Luisito could be gone in a heartbeat. He wondered when he and Tereza would ever be together for any really appreciable length of time without knowing a constant gnawing dread of possible impending misfortunes.

Paddy resorted to the one source of comfort that rarely failed him. He wondered why he was so foolish not to seek this relief more often.

So he left the warmth of the fire and returned to his sheltered bedside to pray. Whether the peace that followed was heaven sent, or a consequence of wishful thinking, he could not say. But prayer always eased his fears and he believed, at that moment, he was in the company of the Holy Spirit.

*   *   *

It was an arduous task, hammering out a document intended for the world that, should events turn for the worst, could certainly bring death down on its creators. But now it was done. In the little outbuilding off the chapel at La Florida, Father Juan Francisco Larrobla stood to address the small assembly of men he had first known as a group only a few days earlier. Now, what they had wrought here, would bind them together through the ages.

"Today we put into words the principles for which the people have struggled all these many years," Larrobla announced. "To lead this struggle now, we name Juan Antonio Lavalleja as Governor and Captain General."

The assembly shouted its approval.

"In our declaration to the world, there must be no confusion that the despotic acts of Brazil has forced this move upon us, by incorporating the

Banda Oriental into its empire, and further having our people declare recognition of this. The people's rights have been usurped and trampled underfoot. Brazil has strapped the citizens of the Banda Oriental to the yoke of absolute tyranny."

"We therefore declare the acts of incorporation and recognition null and void, hereby dissolved, and to be regarded henceforth without worth."

The priest had to wait for the shouting to abate.

"We further declare the Provincia Oriental to be free and independent, from the king of Portugal, the emperor of Brazil, and from any other foreign power. We assume full and complete power unto ourselves to establish a sovereign government deemed convenient for the good of the people."

More shouts of approbation followed.

"We propose a union with the Provinces of the Rio de la Plata for the common good of all."

Abruptly the shouts were muted – not all the men were in accordance with the idea of allying themselves with Argentina. But Lavalleja said it was necessary to get her support and to get over this hurdle the delegates complied, but they all agreed that the description of the proposed union had to remain vague.

And still, union with the provinces was just a proposal. The meat of the document, independence and sovereignty, were confirmed, chiseled in stone in sentences clearly defined ahead of this mere and intentionally vague proposal. It would serve the purposes of the Banda Oriental in requiring further discussions with the Argentine Republic over the matter.

"Finally, we propose the construction of a permanent capitol building as the logical consequence of our actions here."

* * *

The cabildo in Montevideo was a building well acquainted with strife in its brief history. So much had happened, in fact, that now it seemed a long time ago when the Orientales defended the Spanish Governor Elío from the revolutionary Argentines. Shortly thereafter, the Orientales themselves, under the command of General Artigas, had become revolutionaries, and had besieged the same Elío behind Montevideo's walls.

From the Spanish, to the Brazilians, to the Argentines, to the Orientales themselves, each tenant had seen their own occupation of the building grow steadily untenable until, whether voluntary or involuntary, they were forced to vacate it. Now, for a second time, the Brazilians were seeing the early signs of this process about to repeat itself.

The present circumstance had brought the Brazilian General Lecor to meet in the seemingly accursed building with his captains, Manuel and Da Silva. Word of the pronouncement in La Florida had reached the capital, and, of course, the participants of that exercise had been immediately declared outlaw.

Those participants now were also in peril of losing their lives, just as Lavalleja and Rivera had been before them. The increasingly difficult question was how the Brazilians would be able to see to it, and for that reason it was time for Lecor to counsel with his captains

"Rather than risk a large army away from the capital," Lecor began, "I have waited for the rebels to lay siege, because this is what they have always done. Not this time, however! What could be the reasons?"

"What they are doing now is almost as effective as a siege, without running the risks of actually executing one," Da Silva replied. "Admiral Brown has successfully blockaded the port and Lavalleja controls the countryside. Neither is so near they can be noticed, but they are close enough to make it very difficult to resupply the city."

Captain Manuel had a different opinion. "General, I do not believe they have the strength to maintain a siege. If they did they would already be here. The hope they had for aid from Argentina, other than the naval support, has as yet not materialized."

Lecor nodded. "This is also what Brazil believes. Now I am being pressured by the court to leave the city and to take the fight directly to the rebels while they are weak. New reports now indicate that Lavalleja has recently split his force and the two armies are moving toward Montevideo separately. It is almost certain that Rivera leads the second unit and it would be opportune if we could dispatch each force individually."

The discussion was interrupted by a courier and the dispatch he carried would change the character of what had been said. General Lecor took a minute to read it. "Rivera has defeated our troops at Rincon de Haedo" he announced. "I want you both to assemble your men and annihilate these two rebel forces now before they can reunite and do further harm to the empire."

*   *   *

The forced march had been brutal on the Brazilians. Captain Manuel had pushed his men to their limits in order to still catch the Orientales divided. Now near the river Sarandí he could not hide his disappointment as he faced the full brunt of the Uruguayans across a broad plain.

"We have failed, captain," Manuel observed. "The Orientales have joined their two columns back into one."

"That is most unfortunate," Da Silva said. "Yet while we might surely incur heavier casualties, I am certain we can take the day against these peasants."

Captain Manuel studied the Uruguayans intensely. Suddenly he stood in his stirrups.

"They are on the move, Captain," he shouted.

"Order the men to form ranks," Da Silva yelled at a waiting lieutenant.

On the Uruguayan side Lavalleja was shouting across his advancing line of horsemen toward Rivera's position. "Forget the muskets, men. Keep them on your backs. We will cross the field quickly and fall upon them with boleadores and machetes."

"How shall we handle their musket fire?" Rivera shouted back.

"We must be swift enough that there will only be one volley—and that we will have to absorb," Lavalleja replied. "Stay low to the ground and be ready to spring once it is fired."

"Yes, General," Rivera replied.

The command quickly spread through the line. An uneasy feeling came across Paddy as he realized Juan was intending to sacrifice a portion of his army in order to save the greater part. He was not unfamiliar with the concept of expendable men. In the English navy all the drills and training were based on exactly that – absorb what the enemy had to give and win the day by giving it back harder and faster.

He never really experienced it first hand, and he always wondered how he would feel and respond should the actual moment come. Now it was here, but unlike he envisioned it. He would fight on dry land rather than a rolling deck. He looked ahead at the mounted cavalry. Lavalleja and Rivera were there in front, leading the way. "At least they are not having us make a sacrifice they themselves are not willing to make," he thought. He knew many Brazilian muskets would be aimed at these two men. They would be fortunate to survive the day!

Paddy spoke to his son in such a low tone that Luisito had to lean toward him to hear. "When the cavalry breaks, stay low – hug the ground. Once you hear the balls fly past, get to your feet and charge as fast as you are able. I will be at your side."

Luisito nodded.

Within seconds Juan shouted the order. "Al ataque!"

The Uruguayan cavalry, which had been moving forward at a trot, now broke into a full gallop.

The Brazilians had been waiting for this. Now their front line set to fire.

"Fogo!"

The Brazilians unleashed their massed volley of musket fire accurately and a sizeable number of the Uruguayan cavalry fell, but both Lavalleja and Rivera were still on their mounts. With them the rest spurred their horses on and began to hurl their boleadores into the Brazilians. The spinning flails cracked enough heads that coupled with the subsequent pistol fire the second line of Brazilians were thrown into disarray. That line faltered, and only a few of the soldiers fired their muskets, not waiting for the command.

The Uruguayans poured into the Brazilians like a tidal wave. A few of the Brazilian officers drew their sabers and vainly fought back. A few others desperately tried to rally their men in what they already knew was a futile counterattack. Most, however, had already taken flight – the consequence of an unreasonable panic when so many things go bad simultaneously. The battle was now becoming a slaughter – a mix of the sickening sounds of hacking, slashing and screams and the smells of men's blood and entrails being spilled on the plain.

Suddenly the resistance ended as all the Brazilians now broke and ran. Much of the cavalry and even some foot soldiers chased after them and Juan quickly realized that he should not have his troops separated.

"Call a halt to the pursuit," Juan yelled to Rivera.

"We have an opportunity to annihilate them," Rivera yelled back.

"Not today, José" I do not want my men split up in case of a counterattack!"

"I do not believe they're capable of that, Captain," Rivera said.

"All the same," Juan said, "obey the command."

*   *   *

Paddy looked for his son across the field of battle. He cursed himself for having allowed Luisito to get out of his sight. Up until the final moments he knew his son was at his side, but when the fighting became most heated he had lost track of him.

It did not take long for Paddy to find him. To his relief Luisito had not been killed, but he was covered with blood. At first glance, a surge of fear went through Paddy as he wondered if his son might not have been seriously wounded.

"Are you alright, son," Paddy yelled.

"I am fine, Pa," Luisito replied. "I am not hurt."

"Was the battle what you expected it to be?" Paddy asked.

"It was worse," Luisito replied, "but by the will of God I was up to the task."

Paddy was grateful. He had told his son to fight fiercely. He knew from his experience and training in the English navy that it was the hesitant man more than not who would be killed in combat.

"Did you kill anyone today," Paddy asked.

"Yes Sir," Luisito replied.

"More than one?"

"Yes Sir."

Luisito did not elaborate and Paddy did not push him. He knew that this experience would mature his son like no other. Without his even realizing it, Luisito's mind was re-sorting the beliefs and values he had learned up to this moment and re-evaluating those things of significance and those that were trivial.

It would take months and maybe years for him to realize how much he had grown today. Paddy already could see it, and he knew he would have to treat his son somewhat differently from now on.

"I had better get a letter off to your mother," Paddy said. "News of this battle will spread quickly and she will want to know that we are safe."

* * *

"From General Juan Antonio Lavalleja to the representatives of the Government of the Orientales in Buenos Aires.

The despot of Brazil can no longer expect that this province will submit to him as slaves. Yesterday the Orientales have born testimony to the world of their dear love of liberty.

On the banks of the Sarandi, two thousand select Brazilian cavalry, commanded by Colonel Bentos Manuel, were totally defeated by an equal force of valiant patriots whom I had the great honor of commanding.

I am proud to say that our men moved courageously onto an open field, ignoring the ferocity of the threatening army. Our enemies fired upon us with everything they had, but keeping their muskets on their backs, our men crouched low and advanced quickly with sabers.

When they reached the enemy, they hacked them until they broke and fled. We pursued the Brazilians for two leagues, dispersing them in full flight. More than 400 enemy lay dead and we have taken 470 prisoners, among them 52 officers. We also captured more than two thousand arms of all types, ten boxes of munitions, and all their horses.

Our losses include one officer dead, 13 officers wounded, 30 soldiers killed and 70 wounded. All, officers and soldiers alike, were valiant.

God be with you, now and for many years to come.

General Headquarters at Durazno, 13 October 1825,

JUAN ANTONIO LAVALLEJA"

* * *

There was an air of celebration all along the main avenue and in the plazas of Buenos Aires. Everywhere people were smiling. Some were laughing and even slapping each other on the back. Newspapers were bought and read as quickly as they could be printed.

In the bars and coffee houses there was one topic of conversation only—the Uruguayan victory at Sarandí. The events of the day had caused the current leader of the Argentine government, Director Rivadavia, to call a meeting in the cabildo with General Alvear, the highest ranking military officer not presently fighting in the western part of the continent.

After a few pleasantries, Rivadavia got down to business.

"It is clear that the news from Sarandi has created a new climate," he began. "The people of Buenos Aires are now demanding our immediate support of the patriots in the Banda Oriental."

It was a comment that solicited an immediate response. Alvear, however, decided to proceed cautiously.

"Well, we wanted some confirmation that Lavalleja could be successful in his own efforts," he said. "Now we have it."

Rivadavia agreed. "Until now our policy appeared to be prudent," he commented, "but now I fear Lavalleja may have seen it as indifferent and has become resentful of us."

"While it is always good to assess strategies and their results quickly after an encounter, it is also easy to over analyze them and condemn ourselves for something we did or did not do," Alvear commented. "The fortunate outcome of Lavalleja's campaign to this point is quite a bit more than we could have reasonably desired."

"But we promised Lavalleja before he departed that we would support him," Rivadavia countered. "We promised to encourage the Portuguese to leave Montevideo and to aid in their evacuation and we have done little. All success up to now has been his alone."

Alvear did not like the negative character of the Director's comments and he moved to stifle them. "You condemn us too quickly, Excellency," he said. "We did require verification that his revolution would be a popular one. Now we know he has widespread support. He has had no difficulty raising an army of locals."

"Not only an army, but apparently a highly effective one," Rivadavia replied, "and of campesinos no less. It is remarkable that these irregulars have done so well against a professional military force."

General Alvear wondered why, as the Director, Rivadavia did not take time to become more knowledgeable in military matters. Well, it was time for a quick lesson.

"The Orientales may not be uniformly dressed, Excellency," Alvear said, "but they are battle hardened. Most have been fighting for years. We must not regard them as simple militia."

"I see," Rivadavia said. "Then, if that is so, I am convinced that now is exactly the time to act—no matter how unprepared we might be. We must move the Observation Army immediately into the Banda Oriental. I will order Admiral Brown to regard any Brazilian or Portuguese ship on the Rio de la Plata as hostile. He is to sink or capture any he finds."

"The army can leave for Entre Rios immediately," Alvear said. No matter how formal he tried to appear, it was not difficult to see the new excitement in his face.

* * *

The mood was not so upbeat in the imperial court at Rio de Janeiro. The news of Sarandí prompted a meeting here too between Emperor Dom Pedro and his highest ranking military officer, General Barbacena.

The General began with an elaborate explanation for the debacle in the Cisplatine province. Dom Pedro patiently waited for Barbacena to finish, but while the General was exonerating his commanders in the field, the Emperor's patience was pushed to the limit when Lecor's name came up.

"General Barbacena," Dom Pedro interrupted, "events in the Cisplatine province have worsened to the point that it has become necessary to replace Governor Lecor.

"Lecor is a capable man," Barbacena argued. "I am sure he doing what he knows to be best for the empire."

"That may be so," Dom Pedro said, "but he made errors in judgment that has cost the empire dearly. By his recommendation we parole the prisoner Lavalleja, and now it is exactly that man who has become our greatest adversary in the region. José Rivera, Lavalleja's second in command, was in the employ of the Brazilian government, commanding the largest, ablest force in the Cisplatine. Both now fight on the rebel side."

Barbacena decided to walk down the slippery slope, knowing full well his comments would upset the Emperor. "It is argued that these actions were the results of decisions from Rio, and that Lecor was only carrying them out," the General said. "Now he is being blamed for it."

Barbacena found the long uncomfortable silence to be very disturbing. Finally Dom Pedro spoke.

"Even were that the case, Lecor failed to confront the rebels early—when they were weakest, and in spite of directives from this court."

Barbacena nodded. "That I cannot dispute," he said, "but at the time we never fully understood the obstacles he confronted."

"General Barbacena, I do not condemn Governor Lecor. I am not even saying he was derelict in his duties. It is probable that his decisions may have been the best under circumstances we do not know. But it is time for a change."

"Since December, the Empire of Brazil has been officially at war with the Argentine Republic. They not only support the rebels openly in the field, but they intend to annex the Cisplatine and declare it an Argentine province. We have taken measures to blockade Buenos Aires in order to cut off resupply across the Rio de la Plata, but this has been ineffective. As a result, Lavalleja has been able to encircle Montevideo. He is only waiting for the Argentines to arrive to begin an effective siege once again."

"Who commands the Argentines?" Barbacena asked.

"Alvear."

Barbacena raised an eyebrow.

"Am I to replace Lecor?"

Dom Pedro answered the question in a roundabout manner. "The governor at present cannot be in the highest of spirits, and this attitude is sure to be passed along to his men. I can think of no one better than you to reverse our fortunes in the Cisplatine."

"Than me? I fear you credit me far too much! I'll tell you now, no one will be able to reverse our fortunes in the Cisplatine without adequate support from the empire," Barbacena warned.

"You need not worry about that! The Cisplatine has become our most pressing matter," Dom Pedro proclaimed. "You will command 16,000 troops immediately. Many are already en route by sea to Montevideo. The remainder are being assembled in Rio Grande do Sul."

"When am I to depart?"

"A ship is waiting," the Emperor replied.

Chapter Thirteen

Ituzaingó

Dearest Wife,

Rest at ease! Your boys are safe!

I do not know what you may have heard concerning the recent battle near the Rio Sarandí, but we should consider ourselves most fortunate if all our encounters are as successful and one-sided.

Sadly, even with all the good consequences of that action, we did suffer the loss of some very good men.

But Juan and José are fine.

Yet I am beginning to fear they may not live to witness the full fruits of our labors should they continue to take the risks they do. They insist on leading at the front. While this certainly gives heart to our army, I worry that they have not considered what the opposite effect might be if either were cut down.

Please tell Ana nothing about this last paragraph.

Let Katy know how much I love her. Luisito and I miss you both very much and we long for the day when we will all be together again.

All my love,

Paddy

*   *   *

Tereza and Katy crossed the Rio Uruguay once again as they had so many times before. They took a small amount of time now to visit the friends left behind in Ayuí. These were native Argentines who had always lived in the area not too far away. Were it not for the river, there would have been many of opportunities to visit those good people frequently, but the river created a substantial barrier.

Juan's victory at Sarandí was the gift that offered Tereza this opportunity, because now it was becoming clear that whether for good or bad, an end to the struggle might finally be on the horizon. Now at this moment, Tereza felt she had to be closer to where her men were, soon to either enjoy Paddy's embrace or to claim his body and perhaps that of her son.

So her journey with Katy began at Ayuí, the first leg of a trip that would take them on to Buenos Aires and back to her old friend Ana. The women were true dear friends, friends for life, and whatever the outcome of this seemingly endless conflict, together they would rejoice or lament.

*   *   *

Up on the wall that protected Montevideo, General Lecor and his two captains looked down on the scene unfolding before them. They knew this day had been coming—and now it was here. What puzzled them all was why it had taken so long.

Mounted on his stallion, Juan Lavalleja reviewed his troops. The Brazilians were able to readily identify José Rivera and Manuel Oribe as the officers riding alongside. Much of it was for show, of course, a message to the trapped Brazilians that the end was at hand. But in part it was also to bolster the morale of the Uruguayans inside.

"How long do you believe we can hold out against them," Lecor asked.

"Possibly two to three months," Da Silva replied, "but the suffering in the meantime will be horrible by any comparison."

"And the end will still be the same," Lecor commented, "a humiliating surrender."

"An early surrender will be more humiliating than a defiant one later," Captain Manuel reminded them.

Below the wall, Captain Lavalleja was feeling more confident of the final outcome than he ever had. When the parade halted and the men left-faced toward him in unison, he smiled broadly. His little ragtag army was a well trained and well drilled formidable force now, and he bowed deeply before them. The gesture drew a loud continuous cheer.

"Compatriots!" he began, "General Alvear will arrive today. He brings with him 7,000 men. We are about to besiege Montevideo one last time and this time we are here to stay."

The men delivered a resounding chorus of vivas.

"The reward will be sweet—liberty. And for those who have been fighting since Artigas led us against the Spanish at Las Piedras, it will be sweetest of all."

"For those who watched their families suffer in the great exodus, and those who remained valiant . . ."

Oncoming riders coming in from along the bay caused a sudden interruption to Lavalleja's speech, and the captain was visibly upset.

"The vanguard of Alvear's army is just minutes away", the lead rider shouted. In light of the news they brought, Juan decided it would be wise to dismiss any punitive action against these upstarts and he turned back to his men.

"Gentlemen, prepare to greet our allies," he shouted.

The men readjusted the ranks, perfecting the line, and waited. Within a few minutes the faint clamor of an approaching army could be heard.

Lavalleja turned to Rivera. "I believe the city will fall very soon," he said smiling. "Once it does, we will drive what remains of the Brazilians back into Rio Grande do Sul."

"We have fought so long. An end to all this is almost too difficult to comprehend," José said.

Lavalleja could see Rivera still worried. "We will do it José."

It took more than half an hour for the first elements of Alvear's army to reach the camp. An Argentine captain, wearing what was obviously his most resplendent dress uniform, immediately approached Lavalleja.

"How far away is the General?" Juan asked.

"He is immediately behind us, General Lavalleja," The captain replied.

José turned toward Juan. "General?" he muttered under his breath. Well, that was good! The government of the Orientales had already declared it. Now, it seemed, the Argentines agreed.

Lavalleja seemingly ignored the remark. "Once General Alvear sees our preparations," he said, "I am certain he will be eager to join us in our endeavor."

"How can he not? The plan is well prepared and we have been most effective in already executing the preliminary steps," José said confidently.

The main force now came into view. The size of it bolstered Juan's heart. He had never seen so many men so uniformly dressed, not even the Brazilians had been able to muster a force so apparently potent. He began to wonder at José's comment. Was his plan that well prepared? It surely did not include engaging as many men as he saw before him now.

From their position in the ranks, Luisito could not help but whisper some comments to his father.

"Look at all of them," he said. "We should be fairly safe now I would think. A man could get lost within such a large force as that."

Paddy ignored the remark. His son still had not been in a battle where significant artillery was brought to bear. As yet he had not seen the devastation canister and shot could cause within a large body of amassed men.

Paddy still had time to teach his son the few precautions he could take to protect himself from those horrors, but the lessons did not have to begin today.

A huge force now entered the camp – so large it was obviously the main body. The sight of them encouraged Paddy. The soldiers all wore fine uniforms and their equipment and provisions were ample and excellently made. He knew the significance of it. The campaign across the continent was going very well and times were good in Buenos Aires. General Alvear was not difficult to pick out, mounted on an excellent horse in his own somewhat opulent uniform. He rode directly up to where Lavalleja stood with his staff.

"My compliments to your army, General Lavalleja. They do look ready to fight," Alvear said.

"They definitely are, General," Juan responded, a broad grin across his face.

"And I must congratulate you on your masterful victories," Alvear continued. "From what I have studied of Sarandí, the battle plan was brilliant."

"It was the confidence of my men in the plan and their valor on the field that won the day", Juan said modestly. "had they flinched, my story could have been far less cheerful."

"Their courage is unquestioned," Alvear added. "But let us discuss the campaign more fully once the army is settled in. I intend to take the fight north immediately."

Lavalleja and Rivera looked at each other. Did they fully understand what General Alvear had said? It simply seemed unimaginable.

"General, Montevideo is on the edge of collapse," Lavalleja argued.

"I will not become a stationary target here and be surprised by a superior force of Brazilians suddenly at our backs," Alvear replied.

"It will require very little to deprive the Brazilians of their southern headquarters right now, General!" Lavalleja explained.

"Trust me here," Alvear said patiently. "Until we truly control the Rio de la Plata, the Brazilians can retake the city whenever they wish. Our first objective must be to drive their army in the field back into Brazil, and I will need to deploy your men as I require them in this effort."

Juan was angered by the last remark. "My men are mine to command—as I see fit," he said loudly. "They follow me, General."

Alvear's bearing became visibly more stern but he did not raise his voice. "Buenos Aires has directed me to take command of the forces in this area—all the forces, and I intend to do it."

Juan prudently decided to tone down the dialog. "I support you in any effort to rid this land of Brazilians," he said, "but my men are under my command, authorized by the legitimate government of the Banda Oriental. No decree from Buenos Aires will alter that."

"General Lavalleja, The men must not see dissention here."

Juan took this not as a threat, nor even as a warning. He saw it for what it was – wise counsel. "We will talk in my tent this afternoon," Alvear advised.

From where he stood in the ranks, Paddy thought he could discern how the conversation was generally proceeding, and his emotions ebbed and flowed with its highs and lows. At this moment he was quite relieved that the two leaders seemed to have found the handle on what was appearing to be a situation that was in danger of spinning out of control.

But then Captain José Rivera almost blew the lid off.

"This is outrageous!" he shouted. "You Argentineans . . ."

Juan reeled his horse toward José and harshly signaled to Rivera to hold it down. General Alvear wisely waited as the two held a muted but obviously heated impromptu conversation among themselves. In the end Lavalleja turned his horse once again to face Alvear.

"We will meet this afternoon, General," he said solemnly.

Paddy was relieved that the pot which had almost boiled over had come to a simmer once again. He could see the expressions on both the Argentine and Uruguayan troops around him and they appeared as unsettled as he. The only good thing, he reasoned, was that perhaps the Brazilians on the city wall were even more confused than the soldiers outside the gate.

*　　*　　*

Ana Lavalleja and Tereza Colman walked to the nearby post office serving their neighborhood in Buenos Aires. It had been months since the Argentine expeditionary force had departed for the Banda Oriental and nothing new had been heard since.

It did not bode well.

The women wanted to be sure they received the mail as quickly as it arrived, so they did not wait for the postman to pin the notification on their door. The wind or a prankster might remove it (although there were stiff penalties for anyone doing such a thing).

At last, there it was. Tereza was impressed that Ana had the patience to carry the letter to the café across the street before she opened it. Her friend wanted to be sitting comfortably before being confronted with any discomforting news and the café was as good a place as any.

Because of who Juan was, Ana was well known in the neighborhood and the women there afforded every courtesy. They sat at a small table and ordered coffee, and when the waiter left Ana open the letter and began to read it in a low voice.

"My dearest Ana,

My fondest hope is that this letter finds you comfortable and in good health. I want you to know that I am well and tell Tere that Paddy and Luisito are both doing fine.

The present circumstances have caused me much consternation, however. My relationship here with General Alvear has been one of strife since first we met and it continues to this day. We now have the forces to win our freedom and he will not act! I fear years of reversals may have made the Argentines overly cautious, even in light of their recent victories in the west.

As autumn approaches I have argued with Alvear over our army's present inactivity after our recent and decisive victories. Alvear feels he must rest his troops at winter quarters in Cerro Largo near the Brazilian border.

To maintain a presence near Montevideo, I have intentionally distanced myself from him and to his credit he has tolerated this. I have installed my base of operations at Durazno. My men remain with me and this has also caused friction between Alvear and myself.

To minimize suspicions, we maintain a steady flowing dialog and discussions between us, most on how to wage war against the empire. I cannot reveal to you what is about to happen, but I assure you that plan is sound.

In spite of my differences with the General, he is a capable leader and I am comfortable with that. His regard for me appears to be the same and I know that it is this respect we have for one another that allows us to move on during these difficult days.

The government of the Orientales continues to function more independently than the Argentines would prefer. The Porteños have begun to take steps to curtail their actions. I am truly proud of our men.

I have kept the worst news for last.

José Rivera has been strongly opposed to the growing power of the Argentines and he became so outspoken that Buenos Aires finally declared him outlaw. He has been forced to flee.

We did what we could to protect José, but his volatile nature made it impossible. I have replaced him with Manuel Oribe – we all know him as a most capable man, but he is not Rivera.

My deepest love to you all.

Tell Tereza I pray for her and hers.

Juan"

Ana and Tereza looked at each other across the table.

"Juan revealed quite a bit, didn't he?" Ana commented.

"Yes, he did" Tereza replied.

"Did you take note of the envelope?"

"Someone had tampered with the letter."

"Yes," Ana said. "Hopefully it is only a curious fool, but we must devise a way to let Juan know this."

Tereza nodded.

"But first," Ana continued, "We must go to the cathedral and pray for the men in the Banda Oriental."

*   *   *

The flight to safety was not so much a harrowing experience as it was a humiliating one for a man like José Rivera. But for his brash display in front of General Alvear, he would now be commanding at least a company of men in the center of the fight to bring independence to the Banda Oriental. Instead he found himself on the last leg of a three month zigzag ordeal that brought him to Corrientes province in northern Argentina.

There he wasted no time searching out what remnants remained of the army that disintegrated when Artigas was exiled in Paraguay. Without the Gran Caudillo, they had settled into other pursuits or wandered aimlessly around Paraguay, Corrientes, Entre Rios, and Rio Grande do Sul.

Rivera quickly worked a miracle in Corrientes. In a very short time he was riding in front of his new, if rather unprofessional looking army, standing in review. Behind them sat wagons and teams prepared for travel, the donations of local patriots.

"You have done what many said was impossible and we have built an army right under the nose of the Argentine government," Rivera said to his men. "We cannot hope to expect that every one of the good people of the Province of Corrientes wil keep our presence a secret forever. They have risked far too much already and it is now time to move."

"General Alvear has struck into southern Brazil from Cerro Largo. He has defeated the Brazilians at Bagé and São Gabriel. But now he has turned south again to confront Brazilian forces garrisoned in towns in the east of the Banda Oriental. In the west General Lavalleja is also eliminating Brazilian units, including the one in Colonia. It can no longer be a secret that the two forces are slowly moving toward each other, obviously to meet at a predetermined point near the capital."

"Orientales, Paraguayos, Guaraníes, and Charrúas, patriots all!" Rivera shouted. "My intention is that we push into southern Brazil. We shall fill the void that Alvear left behind. By our coming efforts, the patriot armies in the Banda Oriental need not fear another invasion at their rear sweeping down on them out of Rio Grande do Sul. We shall cut off any attempt of the empire to reinforce their army. Who is with me?"

A loud shout of approval rose from the men.

"Then let us move on out!"

Rivera's new lieutenants, most of whom he had not known a year ago, barked the orders and his little army began to roll.

*   *   *

From his campaign tent, General Barbacena watched with satisfaction as the men under his command set up camp on a tributary of the Santa Maria River. They had performed brilliantly to this point, and he knew it was the result of good training and good equipment. He was especially proud of his cadre of spies and scouts who had maintained a constant communication with him concerning the movements of both Alvear's and Lavalleja's forces. Now they reported that the both had converged and their movements indicated the Argentines and Orientales were as anxious to meet the Brazilians as the Brazilians were to meet the Argentines and Orientales. Now, somewhere near here, a half day's ride northwest of Montevideo, it was going to happen.

Notwithstanding all the good signs, there were still some issues causing the General concern. For one thing, never had a battle been fought in the Cisplatine Province involving so many men. Another worry was the leadership of the force that faced him. Barbacena was well aware of General Alvear. He had studied the man and had a good understanding of his strengths and weaknesses. Unfortunately most of what he studied illustrated Alvear's strengths. There seemed to be little to say concerning his weaknesses.

Regarding General Lavalleja, Barbacena had little substantive material. Almost everything was unreliable third hand reports. Much of the rest was anecdotal. He knew this sort of information invariably created legends that were almost always difficult to believe because they were almost always untrue. But in a few cases they were not.

General Barbacena was still contemplating the possible scenarios of the coming engagement when one of his scouts quickly rode up to his tent.

"What is it, Corporal?" he asked.

"The Argentines are at some distance across the arollo, General," the scout replied. "It appears they have settled in and there is no indication that they are preparing an attack soon.

"Do they know we are here?"

"I believe they do sir," the scout answered.

"Well, appearances can be deceiving," Barbacena commented, "especially if they are intentionally executed with the purpose to deceive. They may very well know we are here and they may intend to attack us as soon as we relax our defenses convinced they have settled in. Summon General Pereira to the campaign tent."

It did not take long for Pereira to arrive.

"Where exactly do you believe the enemy to be, General?" he asked.

"They are reported across the arroyo just beyond our view," Barbacena replied. "That would indicate they already know we are here. Otherwise why would they not be camped on the arroyo itself? Right now they believe they are in control of the time and place, so we must prepare to attack at dawn!"

Pereira objected. "General, the men have been force marched all the way from Montevideo. They are exhausted. If the Argentines are not disposed to fight us immediately, I believe we should rest."

"General Pereira, in this campaign the rebels have consistently been victorious," Barbacena countered. "I intend to end this thing now. Surprise is our greatest ally. The rebels know we are tired and they may believe we have not yet discovered their presence. They will be at ease. That is exactly the reason we must be prepared to attack them at dawn."

"Yes Sir," Pereira replied.

*　　*　　*

From his own campaign tent, General Alvear also held his own strategy session, meeting with his officers, Lavalleja, Oribe, and Soler, to form their own battle plan.

"Barbacena is here," Alvear announced, "and he has brought his entire army with him. We could not have asked for more good fortune!"

"To get here so quickly, his troops must be spent," Soler surmised. "After such a hard journey, an immediate attack would be most unlikely, especially since they would first have to cross water and then have it at their backs."

"Nevertheless, as improbable as it seems, we must prepare for this possibility along with the others," Alvear advised. "Barbacena is reputed to be a gambler—he depends on surprise and misdirection."

With no pre-discussion or formality, Alvear began laying out his battle plan. He understood that men would be called upon to fight on little sleep. Those with the least amount of sleep would be his officers who would labor deep into the night with the battle plan.

"I want us to be within sight of the Brazilian camp with the morning sun. We must make sure they see us and perceive us as an immediate threat. We will have the sun in our faces, so to give us back some advantage, I want them to come to us," Alvear began. "I want them to cross the arroyo. General Lavalleja, you will position your cavalry immediately on our right flank . . ."

*   *   *

—The Battle of Paso do Rosario (Ituzaingó)—

As the earliest rays of dawn began to reveal the features of the land, the Brazilian Army was already approaching the arroyo that played such a large part in the planning on both sides. General Barbacena watched as his companies began crossing the stream in good order. He called out to one of his lieutenants.

"Yes Sir," came the reply.

"Remind Pereira that he is to attack the Argentine artillery immediately," Barbacena ordered. "Speed is essential. He must secure those guns even at the high cost of casualties. Tell him if we do not silence their artillery quickly, the casualties will surely be higher"

"Right away, Sir," the lieutenant replied.

As the lieutenant rode off, Barbacena turned to his second in command, Abreu. "Marshal Abreu" he shouted, "Hit their flank hard now! I need a full attack within five minutes!"

"Yes Sir," The field marshal replied.

Assured that this part of the plan was now unfolding as it should, Barbacena rode with his staff toward General Calado's 2nd Division in the middle of his line. He looked back briefly at Pereira's infantry crossing the stream. They were already absorbing a withering fire from Soler's own infantry and artillery, the opening shots of the battle, but they pressed on in good order.

Barbacena rode right up to where Calado was seated on his horse.

"Send the men across General," he ordered. "Let us put these bastards to rout early."

"Yes Sir!" Calado replied. He turned to his aide. "Captain, Advance the division!"

The aide rode to the front of Calado's lines and within minutes they too were crossing the arroyo.

At last Barbacena took a position on a strategic rise on the Brazilian side and watched his army negotiate its advance. He could see Lavalleja's cavalry give a good account of itself against Abreu's unit but he observed the Uruguayans were outnumbered and he knew they would quickly begin to falter.

Barbacena smiled. "Finally, this is your last day, General Lavalleja."

He looked to his left toward Pereira. He also was beginning to take control against Soler. The Argentines were struggling desperately to keep their artillery from falling into Brazilian hands. The battle plan was unfolding better than Barbacena expected, but then, he had always been cautious in his estimates.

"The enemy's flanks are collapsing!" Barbacena shouted. "Now is the time to hit to the center. Give the order!"

Two preselected members of Barbacena's staff rode off to deliver it.

* * *

Paddy cursed himself. In the middle of the noise and confusion he had already lost track of Luisito, something he promised Tereza he would never do. He reaffirmed his oath after Sarandí and now this! While he searched for his son, he could see the battle around him was deteriorating quickly for the Orientales.

"Hold the line, men. Hold the line!" Lavalleja shouted. "Help is coming."

In spite of his best efforts, it was evident that Lavalleja's men were, for the first time, on the verge of faltering. For the moment, however, they still fought valiantly, but the signs of a full collapse were there.

But it was the middle of the Argentine line that actually began to falter. Confusion reigned as the Orientales' own flanks started to be pushed into the Argentine center column due to the Brazilian onslaught.

Alvear had promised to commit his reserves at this moment. That bit of knowledge was the only thing forestalling a complete collapse.

But where were they?

On the left, the Brazilian Volunteers now crossed the stream to complete the preplanned encirclement. Unaware of Alvear's units concealed in the rear, Barbacena pushed the advance brutally in order to finish off Soler's 1st Corps.

The situation worsened so rapidly that as Alvear watched he now worried he may have waited too long. He unleashed part of his hidden cavalry under Colonel Julian Laguna to counter the enemy offensive on 1st Corps. On seeing these reinforcements coming to his aid, a heartened Soler ordered his own counterattack against the Brazilian first division even though he was still outmanned. His charge was so sudden and unexpected that it struck terror into the Brazilian volunteers in spite of the fact they still held the upper hand.

Alvear examined Soler's situation and convinced himself that it was in good enough order for him to address even more serious things. He rode on to 2nd Corps and ordered a frontal assault on the Brazilians at the center of his army. If he could stabilize the chaos here, he was convinced the entire battle would turn around.

On seeing this, Barbacena suddenly became aware of Alvear's strategy. He watched the weary Brazilian infantry begin to struggle under the unexpected counterattack of the Argentine-Uruguayan center. Now the fighting was evolving into a battle that would be controlled by cavalry, and now it had become evident the Brazilians had lost the advantage. Laguna reinforced the right and Lavalleja turned his men once again on the left.

"The moment has come, men," Lavalleja yelled. "Give them hell!"

The effect of his men's response to the command overwhelmed him. Almost immediately the Uruguayans shattered the Brazilian cavalry, completely exposing the infantry of the Brazilian Volunteer Corps.

It could not have come any later for Luisito, who was wondering how much longer he could maintain the fight. His energy was sapped.

Now he watched as Juan's cavalry began to chase the Brazilians back to the arroyo. The welcomed lull gave him a bit of time to rest and reflect. He knew how lucky he had been. The Brazilian volunteers had performed admirably and beyond what would be expected from soldiers regarded as not much better than militia. But now, in spite of desperate attempts of their officers to keep them on the battlefield, they panicked and ran.

Suddenly he saw his father. To his relief he was still standing and alive. Within seconds Paddy also spotted his son.

The fighting had now diminished on the left flank, Paddy was amazed to see how close they actually had been to each other all the time. Yet in the heat of the battle he could not find him.

The fighting still raged along the rest of the line. In the center, the Brazilian 2nd Division began to drift to its right to give support to the troubled General Pereira and counter the frontal assault of Alvear's recently strengthened forces. The combined Brazilian force began to blunt the charge, maintaining a determined resistance throughout the rest of the battle. Alvear repeatedly led probing assaults, searching for a weak point along Pereira's line, but each time he was turned away by heavy fire from the Brazilian infantry.

Even so, the Argentine-Uruguayan forces on the flanks were well into cutting up the Brazilians for the first time and eliminating all their cavalry as a viable force. Lavalleja's 1st Corps surged into Bento Gonçalves' mounted corps, driving it completely from the field. 1st Corps now became the first patriot force to cross over to the Brazilian side of the stream in an effort to move to the rear of the Imperial army.

The impending disaster of encirclement suddenly became clear to Brazil's General Calado.

"Order the retreat, Sergeant!" Calado shouted.

His retreat was the beginning of a withdrawal that spread rapidly all along the Brazilian line, but it was not a groundswell. While Barbacena's forces were leaving the battlefield, the rear guard, infantry of the Brazilian 2nd Corps, continued to fight on, valiantly, and they achieved holding the Argentine and Uruguayan cavalry at a distance to secure a disciplined retreat.

A frustrated Lavalleja rode over to Alvear's position.

"We must press our pursuit against them now, General!" Juan shouted.

"They are beaten, General," Alvear replied, "and we have suffered substantial losses. We must see to our wounded now and regroup."

Alvear's response was difficult for Lavalleja. "The Brazilians are ruined as a fighting force," he cried. "I do not believe they can mount another offensive until they are reinforced."

Alvear maintained a cool unflustered presence. "And if they are reinforced, will we will be ready for them?" he asked.

*   *   *

By the afternoon the flies were already on the battlefield, doing their part in nature's plan to return dust to dust. The sound of their buzzing created a melancholy air despite the victory.

"Many good men died today," Luisito commented solemnly.

"They always do, on both sides," Paddy reminded his son.

Luisito looked at his father but made no comment. Still it was clear he was not in full agreement.

"They are just like us," Paddy explained. "They all wanted to survive this thing and get home to their families."

"But they were trying to deprive us of our freedom," Luisito countered.

"They believed they were protecting their country of the threat we posed," Paddy said.

"What threat?" Luisito asked. "Do they expect the Orientales to invade Brazil?"

"Do not forget there were more than Orientales involved in this victory today," Paddy reminded his son.

Luisito understood and nodded.

"I need to write a letter to your mother before the post rider leaves," Paddy said. "Do you want me to say anything for you?"

*   *   *

Lavalleja's fears of a Brazilian counterattack did not materialize in spite of some signs to the contrary. He regarded it as very good fortune since he did not yet understand the real reason for it.

At Melo, two months after Ituzaingó, a Uruguayan captain and his lieutenant visited his sentries at the edge of the town.

"Any activity?" asked the captain.

"Nothing at all, sir." A sentry replied.

"We should have heard reports of something stirring in Rio Grande do Sul," the captain said.

"Yes, we should have," the lieutenant said, "but the travelers we have interviewed speak of nothing on the highways, sir."

"Can their word be trusted, Lieutenant?" the captain asked.

"I believe it can, sir."

"Maintain your vigilance, men, the captain asked. "Let us know if anything appears less than usual."

"Yes sir," the sentry replied.

*   *   *

At Bagé, in Rio Grande do Sul, the people had seen so much military pass through their town the last two years that this particular force would not have evoked comment were it not for its exceptional size. It was huge, but even to the untrained eye it seemed to be missing something. The élan of previous units was gone and the officers had no swagger.

Still, it was not a typical day and the people lined the streets to watch the soldiers march through. They exited on the southwest side along the road that led into the Cisplatine province. The more knowledgeable of the people suspected that all was not well. Maybe the defeat at Paso do Rosario was more serious than had been reported. If it were, the Brazilians already in the Cisplatine would then need to be reinforced. On the other hand maybe there was nothing to worry about. Perhaps these men were simply going to replace those who would soon be on their way back home to Brazil.

The southern plain of Brazil is mainly the same grassland that extends across northern Argentina and on into the Banda Oriental and southern Paraguay. It is the great pampas country of South America. Yet there are areas where hills, small cordilleras, and even forests exist.

As it happened, a small stand of curious looking eucalyptus suddenly appeared. The Brazilian army was grateful for the grove that lie ahead and would offer some shade from the sun that now beat down so ferociously.

The eucalyptus are so different from the native trees that they naturally draw attention to themselves. This inadvertently caused the army to be less vigilant when their eyes should have been sweeping a broader area. Within the woods behind the eucalyptus trees Rivera's army of 2,000 was waiting.

Suddenly, they fell screaming upon their adversaries, covering the distance between them quickly.

"Show no mercy," Rivera cried. "These Brazilians will never reach the Banda Oriental."

The Brazilians fought back bravely, but after only a short while their leadership was not to be found. Without officers to coordinate their defense, a perception of chaos quickly enveloped the Brazilian line. Individual soldiers began to run. It only took a few before a general panic ensued and the line broke.

Now the battle turned into a full scale slaughter. Resistance withered completely minutes and the Brazilians lucky enough to still be alive fled back into Bagé.

"Excellent work, men, Rivera shouted. "Now we must regroup and prepare for our next engagement. I do not believe the Brazilians are quite ready to give up their beloved Cisplatine quite yet."

*   *   *

After the news of the victory at Ituzaingó reached Buenos Aires, Tereza decided to return to Salto. She was very happy that the Orientales had done so well, but she discovered that for her, personally, Ituzaingó was a mixed blessing. Days turned into weeks and she still did not know if her boys were dead or alive.

Finding them now could be much more difficult since individual units of men had been sent all over the Banda Oriental. These were involved in mopping up the small companies of Brazilians still to be found in the many little towns and in searching for new intruders. Alvear and Lavalleja did not want any possibility to remain that these segments might become a new viable fighting force.

"Well," Tereza thought to herself, "maybe it would not be so difficult to find her boys." It could be that wherever Juan was, Paddy and Luisito would be also – if they survived.

If they survived, they would write, and Tereza knew the only address they had for her was the one in Salto.

So she decided to return and wait.

But when she was back in Salto, after several weeks the waiting had become unbearable. She sat in her usual place staring once again at the Rio Uruguay and now allowed her overwhelming fears to finally bring her to tears. People all along the Salto Grande were continuing to celebrate the victory at Ituzaingó, but since no letter from Paddy had yet arrived, Tereza and Katy were no longer a part of it.

She knew the mail was unsure and she fought to remain resolute, but as time passed she saw herself losing hope.

She visited her friends and asked about any news they might have received in their letters, hoping that someone might have mentioned Paddy or Luisito. The chances were slim but there was always a possibility. Every time, however, the answer was no, and each did its part in contributing to her overwhelming despair.

CHAPTER FOURTEEN

The Republic East of the Uruguay

It was still dark when Paddy and Luisito left the house on their way to the livery stables. As they passed the plaza, the silhouette of the cathedral's bell towers was prominent against the moonlit sky. Paddy smiled. This was where it had all begun, where he first saw Tereza and made his feeble efforts to introduce himself. Had she refused him then, where in the world would he have been now?

But she had not refused him, and his life came to revolve around her. Even at this moment his present activities were centered on her and with her in mind.

"How long do you think it will be until we reach Salto, Pa?" Luisito asked.

"If we hurry, four or five days," Paddy answered, "more if we rest too much."

Paddy had asked for a leave to do this and he felt somewhat self conscious about it. He wondered if he would have received permission to go find Tereza had she not been Ana's good friend.

Well so what? He longed to see her and he knew any man given the same opportunity would have done likewise.

Securing the horses and preparing them for the journey required more time than Paddy had intended. It frustrated him and he wondered how many more little nuisances would bother him along the way. The first light of morning only found Paddy and Luisito at the city wall. Soon, however, they would be turning north toward San José.

* * *

In Buenos Aires, the cabildo had become a very busy place. The struggles of the past two decades had, at times, seemed without end. Then, suddenly, news of success was coming in from all over the continent. And while in the north Simón Bolivar had failed to establish his envisioned Empire of Gran Colombia, In the south Argentina was on the verge of realizing its own empire. It would be almost as large as had been planned from the beginning. That was especially true now that it appeared the last and most vexing of its provinces might finally be at the point of joining the Republic – the Banda Oriental.

Only two questions remained. How strong still was the movement Lavalleja and Rivera led to form an independent state and what problems would the Brazilians cause?

The British ambassador to Argentina hinted that he might have the answers, at least in part. So when he sent overtures to Director Rivadavia to discuss the matter, a meeting was arranged.

* * *

It seemed like hours had passed as Rivadavia sat awaiting Ambassador Canby's arrival. He was offended, of course. As head of state it should be he who determines who cools his heels. But the importance of the moment prudently directed him not to make an issue of it. Finally, the director's secretary knocked on his door. The secretary opened the door slowly just enough to stick his head in.

"Ambassador Canby is here to see you, Excellency," the secretary said.

"Thank you, Miguel," Rivadavia replied. "Send him on in."

In a matter of seconds Canby was in the room. Rivadavia rose with a broad smile on his face and courteously extended his hand. "Ambassador Canby," he greeted the emissary.

"Thank you for seeing me, Excellency, Canby said. "I presume the purpose of my visit is already known."

"To a point," Rivadavia admitted, "but until we have a better understanding of exactly what the proposal is, we may have a number of objections to it.

"The proposal is exactly what you may have perceived it to be," Canby said candidly, "complete autonomy and independence for the Banda Oriental."

A frown crossed Rivadavia's brow. "The entire purpose of our operations in the Banda Oriental was to bring it into the Argentine Republic as a full province," he said. "The Orientales themselves declared it when they rose up against the Brazilians."

"So they did," Canby countered, "but you know they do not desire it. They relented on this one point to obtain your help to defeat the Brazilians."

"Perhaps so," Rivadavia said defiantly, "but then that is the price they must pay. It was the condition under which we went into the Banda Oriental."

"My opinion is that if you continue on this path, you could have problems with the Banda Oriental for generations to come", Canby argued, "and Brazil will not abide this state of affairs for long."

Rivadavia listened without responding. He knew Canby's argument had some teeth.

"Conditions have become very difficult for both Argentina and Brazil at home," the ambassador continued. "Both have exhausted their resources in campaigns against the Spanish and Portuguese—and against each other. What's more, their citizens are tired of years of war and conflict and quite frankly are becoming justifiably restless for peace."

"Now it makes sense that Brazil does not want Argentina at its front door, so close to Bagé and Porto Alegre, and I would think Argentina would not be too happy to have Brazil just across the river once again. As of now, neither Argentina nor Brazil are really in a position to resume hostilities in spite of the suspicions each has for the other."

Ambassador Canby stopped and waited for the Director's response but none was forthcoming. It was just as well, Canby would also wait and give Rivadavia time to contemplate what he had just said.

Finally the director did speak. "What does Great Britain want from this magnificent concession?" he asked.

"What has Great Britain always wanted? Trade. The American markets are very promising. So many new nations are ready to have the things of the world. What is more, the resources here are enormous, and England wants to be part of this before the United States can step in and treat it as its own private domain.

"A very straightforward and understandable response!" Rivadavia stated. "Assuming we should agree to the independence of the Banda Oriental, what guarantee would we have that Brazil will not occupy it once again?

Of course, you know should that happen, the Orientales would call on you once again for help, just as they might call on Brazil if you invaded. They are small, and while they might be capable of delivering a nasty and permanent scar, they must know they cannot possibly achieve a final victory by themselves."

"But there is one thing more," Canby added. "England will ally itself with the Orientales immediately, regardless of who should attack."

Once again Rivadavia paused in thought. Finally he rose from his desk and extended his hand to the ambassador.

"If, as you say, England would intervene, what would keep England from simply staying as long as she wants?"

"Were we so covetous to consider such an option, it would be a most difficult task. It would almost certainly unite the different factions in South America against us. Added to that, we would also have to deal with the United States."

"The United States?"

"You have not heard of the Monroe Doctrine?" Canby asked.

"I have," Rivadavia replied. "I do not know how effective it will be."

"Effective enough," Canby said. "The North Americans intend to back it up. It should be called the Adams Doctrine. John Quincy Adams first proposed it as Madison's Secretary of State and brought it to fruition under Monroe before he himself became president."

"Well, England should not be too terrified of the United States!"

"We're not," Canby asserted, "but they can cause mischief enough to ruin everything we are trying to achieve. Already our ambassadors are in Washington explaining what we intend to do here. Hopefully any fears the United States has concerning this will be assuaged."

Again Rivadavia said nothing. He was assessing all that had been said. Suddenly he realized this plan was the only one that made sense enough to possibly bring stability to the region once and for all.

"I will discuss this proposal with the Directory," he said.

* * *

Paddy and Luisito departed the town of Trinidad on their way to Paysandú. Off in the distance they saw the wagon coming toward them on the road.

It looked so much like his old two wheel cart that Paddy's heart jumped for a moment. He had to remind himself to take it easy and not leap to conclusions. He was far too old to once again be acting like a schoolboy courting his girl for the first time.

Yet as the wagon drew closer, it was apparent that its occupants were definitely women—and finally there could be no mistake. Tereza and Katy were coming the other way.

"How about that Pa?" Luisito laughed.

Paddy just shook his head and smiled. He tapped the team lightly with his whip and they accelerated the pace. Apparently Tereza had done the same because the carts were closing much more quickly now. When they met Tereza pulled back on the reins and was jumping off the wagon even before it fully stopped. She ran to where Paddy sat and he leaned over to give her a kiss.

She almost pulled him off the wagon. Luisito looked down the road to Katy and they both smiled broadly.

Then Tereza fell by the front wheel of Paddy's wagon and knelt before it, holding onto the rim with outstretched arms. Paddy got down and stood beside her with his hand on her shoulder, allowing her time to finish her prayer of thanksgiving.

They were truly blessed, he knew. How many families, no less worthy than themselves, were not now able to enjoy such a celebration?

"I was on my way to Salto to see you," Paddy said when Tereza arose. "How about you?"

"Montevideo," Tereza smiled.

Paddy was astounded. "That's a long trip!" he said. "Why would you make it?"

"I didn't receive any news except that we had defeated the Brazilians at Ituzaingó," Tereza said. "I had to find out what happened to my family. I couldn't wait any longer."

"You didn't receive my letter? I wrote and posted it weeks ago!"

"It's true, Ma. I was there," Luisito said, thinking there might be a problem.

"Of course he did," Tereza said. It was too much. She grabbed her husband again and held him for a very long time. Luisito and Katy didn't mind waiting.

Neither did Paddy. Tereza could squeeze him for as long as she wanted. "So which way shall we go?" she finally asked.

"To Montevideo, I suppose," Paddy replied. "My leave is not indefinite and we have plenty to do. Besides, you can visit with Ana once again."

Tereza smiled.

*   *   *

People lined the docks three deep to witness the arrival of what they supposed was the English fleet. It was not a fleet really, but a squadron. Still, it had enough ships to impress. While Admiral Brown may have commanded more ships in the Argentine fleet, he had no ship like the two large frigates leading several smaller vessels coming into the harbor.

From this mass of humanity, Paddy stood studying the ships. He saw the sailors furl the sails, but they did not secure them with their own stays. Instead they tied them with two separate pieces of rope from each side of the yardarms. Either they were fastened with slip knots or could be easily cut to release the sails. He also saw that not all the ships in the squadron entered the harbor. A few sat outside guarding the entrance to the bay. He turned to Tereza.

"It does not appear the English are completely convinced their mission will come off without a snag," Paddy said. Tereza heard and nodded, but she did not fully understand what he had said or why he said it. She would ask him later in private.

But Paddy wasn't there to study the disposition of the English fleet. His eyes searched the longboats for some familiar faces – two in particular. They would not be among the officers sitting at the prow, nor would they be red jacketed marines. Unfortunately the men at the oars had their backs to him and he could not see their faces.

But that one coxswain. He almost looked like . . . no he wasn't. Wait, maybe he was. And as the boats approached Paddy suddenly realized that it was Bobby Driscoll, older for sure, but definitely Bobby.

He was almost as happy as when he saw Tereza and Katy on the road outside Trinidad. Could it be that after all the years of suffering and struggle, the rest of his life would be mostly one happy moment after another? Inwardly he laughed openly at himself for his particular folly. There would still be sadness intermingled. The death of loved ones, the pain of some friend's misfortune, these would never go away completely.

But a life where joy and happiness prevailed over hardship and pain appeared just ahead. Perhaps this is how divine providence worked. One proves himself in life's crucible and then he realizes its rewards.

Luisito interrupted Paddy's thoughts. "It is difficult to believe the people here could ever compel a force like this to leave," he said.

"And yet it happened once before," Paddy replied. "That is when I came to know your mother."

"What was life like in the English navy, Pa?" Katy asked.

Paddy smiled. "Hard, but rewarding," he said. "That is not to say the English treated their sailors kindly, but relationships were forged. In the end, when a seaman is no longer able but has become a withered broken old man, mother England rewards him with a humble but comfortable abode and enough that he will not starve."

The Englishmen were now climbing onto the wharfs. When Bobby appeared Paddy shouted out to him.

Bobby looked his direction and stared directly at Paddy. He did not acknowledge him, however.

Paddy was stunned. Surely it was Bobby – or was it? The man looked so much like him. Paddy shrugged. Well, if it wasn't him, he resembled Bobby enough to be his brother.

*　*　*

In the Brazilian court Emperor Dom Pedro took the opportunity to brief his emissaries one last time before they boarded the ship for Montevideo. He had chosen men who might not have been his most eloquent statesmen, but what he needed now were men he could trust completely to execute his will.

"Time passes quickly when men put themselves to accomplishing an eager task," he began, "and the English have certainly done that with this endeavor."

There were a few laughs, but they rang hollow. Dom Pedro decided to tell them his true opinion concerning the eminent loss of the Cisplatine.

"This treaty will mean the end of the Cisplatine province. One of its provisions is that the region will no longer be officially called by that name. For us to concede this, we have required a large concession in return. Neither will the region be officially known as the Banda Oriental. This has vexed both the Argentines and the Orientales. You will have to meet with all parties and come to a decision as to what this new state will be called. When an agreement is reached, you may concur and sign the accord."

There is an audible grumble from within the group. Dom Pedro ignored it.

"How many Brazilian patriots must lose their lives for us to secure all the goals we desire? There is a price for everything and only a small number of things demand total sacrifice. This is not one of them."

"Death comes in an instant," the emperor said, "but the consequences of a single death last throughout the lives of the ones left behind. Once the price of a goal becomes too high, it is time to reset the goal."

"The intervention of the English has raised the stakes for all of us, the Argentines, the Orientales, and ourselves. We can no longer hope to occupy the Cisplatine without the loss of many more men. Argentina also understands this. The coming of the English might be a blessing. Without them both Brazil and Argentina would have thrown their sons into the cauldron for many years to come."

"As for the empire, it can expand elsewhere, perhaps into Paraguay or Alto Peru. We can drive the remaining Europeans out of their colonies on our northern shores. Whatever course we choose to take, be confident that order and progress will not be sacrificed."

*   *   *

A knock came at the door of the Colman house.

"Who is it?" Paddy asked.

"It is Juan," came the reply outside.

Paddy opened the door cautiously. Sure enough, Juan was there, but so were two English sailors. One was the man he mistakenly identified as Bobby that afternoon. He had no idea who the other man was.

"This is unusual, Juan," Paddy said. "Why are these men with you?"

"Paddy, we need to discuss some serious issues," Juan replied. "Let me introduce Robert Driscoll . . ."

"I already know this man," Paddy interrupted. He immediately leaped forward and embraced him.

"I apologize for not acknowledging your greeting this afternoon, Paddy," Bobby said, "but the navy has charged you with desertion. I did not want to let anyone in our company know that you were the man they were looking for."

Paddy was stunned.

"Then this is very serious, Bobby" he commented solemnly. "But I never did desert. The navy deserted me when it sailed off and that was almost twenty years ago."

"Well, you know how the navy is," Bobby said, "discipline above all. Admiral Willoughby is trying to secure extradition from a man here named Suarez. He is supposed to be running the show."

"Yes, Joaquin Suarez is our president,"

"President!" Bobby laughed. "You still don't have a country."

This was Bobby for sure. His joking, that almost always bordered on insolence, never bothered Paddy before. In fact he almost always laughed with him.

Now it bothered Paddy a great deal. It was another revealing moment that he had been transformed and was now a part of this adopted land.

Juan would have been offended too, and it was then that Paddy realized Juan had no reaction to what was being said because he was the only one in the company who did not understand. The reason for the other man's presence now became clear.

"Who is this man who accompanies you? Paddy asked.

"This man? He's our translator" Bobby replied.

"Then why isn't he translating?"

"Beggin' your pardon, sir," the translator interrupted. "I did not think it necessary . . ."

"Necessary to do what?" Paddy shouted. "Do you know who this man is?"

"The man who brought us here?" the translator asked.

"May I present to you General Juan Antonio Lavalleja, the commanding officer of the army of the Orientales," Paddy said. "Now I believe he has some right to know what is transpiring here."

"Easy, Paddy!" Bobby interjected. "We here are all on your side. We intend to fight this thing." The translator needed no further prompting as he immediately told Juan what Bobby had said.

Paddy was suddenly embarrassed by his curtness. "My apologies, Bobby," he said, "I suppose the suddenness of this news has set me off a bit."

"No harm done," Bobby said.

"Please, come inside. I want you to meet my family," Paddy said as he directed them all into the front room. The men sat, but rose almost immediately when Tereza and the "children" entered.

"So, Paddy," Bobby said, "this is your lady".

"My wife now," Paddy replied.

Bobby bowed and Tereza acknowledged him with a nod.

"And this is what kept you away from the print shop so much. I see it now – such a lady. She's too good for the likes of you," Bobby laughed.

"Well, you'll get no argument from me," Paddy concurred.

"The kids are handsome too," Bobby said. "They take so much after their mum."

"Thanks once again," Paddy laughed.

"Where do we go from here?" Bobby asked.

Paddy replied with a question. "When is the hearing?"

"After the ceremony," Juan interrupted. The translator was keeping busy now and Juan, Tereza, and the children knew immediately what was being said.

'What hearing?" Tereza asked.

"England wants to try me in Portsmouth for desertion," Paddy replied

Tereza gasped. "Don't worry, it is nothing," Paddy said. "In fact, let's set this matter aside for the time being and speak of other things. Bobby, what has happened to Jimmy?"

Bobby was impressed by Paddy's coolness; or perhaps it was an act of bravado for the sake of the family.

"Jimmy!" he said loudly. "Paddy, you would not believe it. Do you remember all those times he tried to convince us he was an American?"

"Yes."

"Well, it turns out he was."

"I always suspected it."

"After the war, as part of the accord, the Americans brought a list of suspected impressments to London. He was on it and they had enough proof to repatriate him. He is a captain or something now in their merchant fleet. It is quite sizable too, for any nation, and especially for an upstart country like theirs. Perhaps you have seen their ships.

"No," Paddy said.

"I have," Luisito said.

"My son worked on the docks," Paddy said.

"They come here not so much for trade, but to refit or resupply on their way to the Pacific," Luisito added.

"We may have taught them too well," Bobby said. "They build excellent ships. During the war they won more than a few of the engagements between us."

"Over half is what I heard," Paddy remarked. Now it was Bobby's turn to be offended.

"You should see their frigates," Bobby said without pausing. "They are too big to be called frigates – somewhere between a frigate and a man of war really. They carry forty-four guns – FORTY-FOUR!"

"Sounds formidable," Paddy said.

"Since Nappy is gone, they see themselves as the only example left where republicanism can work and they intend to spread it over the entire world," Bobby said.

"We intend to be a republic," Juan interjected.

"Then be forewarned," Bobby admonished. "A democratic form of government has always been susceptible to dictatorship. Napoleon showed us that all too clearly once again."

"You may be right," Paddy said, "but we must at least try."

"I want only the best for you here," Bobby said, "so I am sharing all my knowledge and beliefs, such as they are, whether they be good or bad."

It is good to see you again, dear friend." Paddy said.

"Likewise," Bobby responded.

It appeared everyone was packing up to leave so Katy rushed in to ask a question. "Mister Driscoll, do the sailors get much time to leave the ships and visit the city?"

"I do not believe you should be with those types," Bobby said. "They are of the lowest order of men."

"Well, my father was an English sailor, and so are you."

Bobby was speechless. The evening ended well for having begun so horribly. Paddy was happy to have Bobby in his home and now Katy and Luisito had a face to identify with his old stories. Perhaps someday Jimmy might come during one of his voyages. If he held the position Bobby indicated, he could be able to choose Montevideo over Buenos Aires as his port of call should he ever be in this part of the world. It would be good to see him once again too.

*   *   *

It was a Friday, the eighteenth of July in 1828 and the plaza in front of the cathedral was packed with humanity. A large unshaded wooden stand had been erected in front of the cabildo, elevated above the heads of those needing an opportunity to see. Soon dignitaries from Brazil, Argentina, and Great Britain began arriving and searching for their assigned seats along with the elected leaders of the Orientales. Among the delegates were General Alvear of Argentina and General Barbacena of Brazil. As they warmly greeted each other it was difficult to believe that they had ever been enemies across a field of battle.

Ambassador Canby was there too, conspicuous by the finery in which he was adorned. The English surely knew how to play up importance by the way a man was dressed. Paddy stood with his family looking up at the group of men, enveloped in a sweet warm feeling as he watched Juan Lavalleja, José Rivera, Manuel Oribe, and Joaquin Suarez take their places on the front row of the stand. He was so proud of these men. There was no denying this was a hallmark moment in the events of the Rio de la Plata.

At three corners of the stand the banners of Argentina, Brazil, and Great Britain were mounted. From the fourth corner flew a new banner with alternating white and azure stripes. A square white field in the upper left corner bore the Inca sun – the same symbol Argentina had chosen for its flag to represent the new world. So there it was—the new symbol of their land. It had never been carried into battle and Paddy wondered how long it would take before people would set aside the beloved ensigns of Artigas and Lavalleja and hold to this new standard.

Lord Canby stood and began walking among his seated peers, greeting each one individually. Finally he went to the podium and prepared to address the throng.

"Orientales! We meet here today to do something that to my knowledge has never been done before. By the mutual agreement of a community of nations, a new nation—a republic I am told—is to be created."

Thundering cheers swelled from the crowd. It was euphoric. Some could hardly keep their feet. The people saw it happening before their very eyes, and still many wondered after so much suffering and hardship if it was really finally true. Others who accepted it, but used to disappointments in the past, wondered if it would last. Ambassador Canby finally had to signal to the crowd to let him proceed.

"It will not be an easy task," he continued. "Consider the difficulty encountered in simply deliberating the name of this new republic. Of course, the Banda Oriental was desired by many, but dear as it was it seemed not to have the eloquence desired for a people who are about to take their rightful place among the nations of the world."

Once again the roar rose from the crowd and once again Canby had to wait for it to die down.

"President Suarez tells me the new name will be the Republic East of the Uruguay."

A cheer swelled from the people again but it was not as forceful as before. Paddy smiled to himself. They would have to get accustomed to the new name as well as the new flag.

"We all owe much to those who have brought you here today," Canby said. "First, let me give thanks to the leaders of two great nations – Emperor Dom Pedro of Brazil and Director Rivadavia of Argentina."

The crowd applauded enthusiastically.

"And as a diplomat, I know how important and how difficult it is to achieve a ratifying vote from one government, much less two. Thanks are in order for the governments of Brazil and Argentina.

More applause.

"More difficult still is it to have two men who stood as enemies by virtue of their being called by their countries, and as patriots they heeded the call, to stand together on this same stage as friends for the good of the entire region. I give you two giants of men, General Alvear and General Barbacena."

Now the applause swelled. This was the greatest affirmation so far that maybe this great dream was actually real.

The change in Lord Canby's demeanor revealed that he knew what was coming next. "And the Orientales owe all to General Lavalleja, General Rivera, to President Joaquin Suarez, and to so many others who sacrificed everything, yes, including their lives, for us to have the joy of this moment."

The people went wild. Ana and Tereza embraced each other and Paddy could not imagine a better discourse than the one he was hearing. But Canby's final paragraph said it all.

"The greatest debt is to those who are not with us, those who paid the price of your freedom with their blood. And the Banda Oriental . . . I'm sorry, The Republic East of the Uruguay, owes most to he who remains in exile in Paraguay."

*   *   *

The messenger ran briskly up to the old man seated in front of his house sipping his yerba mate.

"I bring wonderful news from the Banda Oriental, General Artigas," the messenger said smiling. "The Orientales are free. They have established their own independent nation,"

The old General looked up and smiled back "I know," he said quietly.

"More than that, General," the messenger said. "They want you to come back."

"No! I cannot," Artigas responded. "My time is past. The Orientales remember me as a great general, and now I am a withered old man. My return would only serve to diminish the view they have of the triumph they have achieved."

The messenger looked at the General with a forlorn countenance. "I do not believe that will be a problem for them," he said. "They will still see you as their greatest general."

"Perhaps so," Artigas said, "but other things are at play here too. I had a dream of what the Banda Oriental should be once we were free. Now both Lavalleja and Rivera are fighting among themselves over what the government should be. The national hero should be the hero for all the people. I cannot go back."

Artigas took a sip from his mate and stared off into the distance. The messenger could see the old man was still collecting his thoughts so he waited patiently.

"I have a firm position in this struggle," Artigas finally said, "but if I returned and expressed it, I would be an adversary to some and no longer the example for all. I cannot allow that to happen, so my opinions must die with me here."

"Am I to tell them you are never to return, General?"

Again the old man needed time to chose the right words.

"Tell them my heart has never left," he finally replied.

CHAPTER FIFTEEN

The Accused

Less than a week had passed since the formation of an independent Republic East of the Uruguay and already she was about to enter into her first diplomatic crisis and international incident. The antagonist would be Uruguay's greatest ally toward attaining of her independence—Great Britain.

So began the hearing of able seaman Patrick Colman, as he was to be called once again throughout the ordeal. All the participants understood that the process would be difficult. The English judges and solicitors were preparing their briefs and arguments based on English military law that they regarded not only as proper, but essential. Under that law this initial process would only determine whether there were grounds for a full court martial by the Royal Navy.

But the hearing itself was already a concession to the local authorities, and while the new nation was still far from establishing its own legal procedures, trials based on Spanish law had been taking place along the Rio de la Plata almost since the Spanish first arrived.

The decision had been made to hold the hearing in the cabildo rather than on board the flagship. In doing this it was hoped there would be ample room for the large gallery that was expected. Since plenty of witnesses were anticipated, the feeling was that most who attended could not honestly deny that due process had been followed and a just decision reached based solely on testimony. Paddy would still have a naval advocate defending his case, but Joaquin Suarez and several Uruguayan jurists also would also sit at his table as counsel.

* * *

As was the custom, after a few words regarding the procedures to be followed from the chief judge and what he expected from both counsels, the hearing began with the prosecution presenting opening arguments.

"The prosecution intends to show the court how able seaman Paddy Colman left his assigned post," the judge advocate began, "and thus positioned himself to be indisposed when the fleet returned from Buenos Aires to recover the crewmen left behind. Short of this, the prosecution is prepared to reveal fully that the actions of seaman Colman constitute a gross dereliction of duty."

Paddy groaned and stirred in his chair. He felt the hand of his defense counsel on his back. He presumed it was an effort to calm him and it had that effect immediately. Paddy sat still there on out.

He looked over at his defense team. Joaquin and the Uruguayans were still taking in the last part of the translation but their faces revealed no trace of emotion.

Now Paddy understood how it was all going to be. The hearing would be brutal, full of half truth accusations, and he would be best served to sit through it stoically with little or no emotional response. He resolved to school his family to do the same when he had the opportunity.

The prosecution continued. The judge advocate was merciless. "And why was seaman Colman not at his post?" he asked. "Because he was miles away spending time with his mistress! Yet the sole reason for his remaining in Montevideo was to keep the newspaper in operation. Were it not for this, he would have been assigned to participate in the campaign.

352

But Colman now saw fit to take advantage of this good fortune, not by working at the press, but by dallying in some love affair!"

It was going to be more difficult than Paddy had imagined. It was bad enough that he was being maligned. He could bear that. But now as Tereza's reputation was coming into question, withstanding the attack without any outward emotional response was almost beyond his ability. His counsel leaned over and whispered some reassuring words into his ear.

"Opening arguments are always like this," he said. "When we respond we will show how innocent you truly are of these charges. We will make the prosecution look like ravenous wolves with no basis for their vicious attacks – and we will also show the court how virtuous your wife truly is. Take heart."

Paddy nodded.

The opening argument for the prosecution continued, ad nauseum. Paddy wondered just how often the same issues could be repeated before the judge himself would step in and say "Enough!"

His counselor reminded him that the attorneys are given the most freedom in the opening and closing arguments. Here they can say and get away with almost anything. It is hoped that the judges would hear enough in the controlled cross examination part of the hearing that they would be able to arrive at a just decision in spite of the exaggerated arguments.

The fact that the prosecution had repeated itself so often actually revealed how weak its case truly was. Had there been more substance, there surely would have been less repetition.

When the judge advocate concluded his preliminary arguments the damage had been done (irreversibly, Paddy thought, and apparently the chief judge may have thought so too). "Is the defense prepared to present its opening statements?" he asked wisely in an effort to give the team time to regroup.

"Yes, your honor," Paddy's counsel replied, but the expression on his face revealed perhaps he was not sure.

The judge wasn't buying it. "It is the opinion of this court that all parties would be better served if we recess until 0900 tomorrow morning," he said. "Is that agreeable to counsel?"

Paddy's advocate waited until Joaquin Suarez had heard the translation. When he was finished, Suarez nodded toward him affirmatively. "Yes sir," the advocate replied.

*   *   *

The Yankee merchantman weighed anchor unusually late in the day to be departing from a port so treacherous as Rio de Janeiro. Fortunately for the captain, his ship was new and state-of-the-art. It was the natural consequence of the years immediately after the Napoleonic wars when the United States and Great Britain entered into a seafaring technology race unusual for peacetime.

Both countries were developing newer ships that compromised volume for sleekness. Speed was the goal. Getting the product from one point to another quickly took precedence over everything else. The result would be ships that had pointed bows and knifed through the water. The naval architects of the day were not ignorant of the drag the stern could also present to the ship's handling, so these were designed with a gradually raked bottom that exited the water gracefully. The appendage remaining below the water that ended with the rudder also had a knife's edge, even more extreme than at the bow.

Once the design was reaching its zenith, size would again become an issue, and the ships that followed later would grow until both England and America were producing the grand clipper ships of the mid nineteenth century.

At this moment Captain James Burke was very grateful for the attributes the new design features provided his little ship. The worries of the morning were gone now, and he was confident he would be in deep open water before nightfall.

He had been troubled since he received a letter from his ex-shipmate, Bobby Driscoll. It notified him of the impending troubles that their mutual friend, Paddy Colman, was about to face.

So he requested permission to captain this particular route and did not hide his private reasons from the shipping company. His plan was to make an "unscheduled" stop at Montevideo before his ship continued on to Buenos Aires. He would take as much time as he needed to help his friend where he could, and then meet his ship in Santiago on the west side of the continent if possible.

It was a hard pill for the profit conscious board of the shipping company to swallow, but in the end Burke's story softened their hearts and he was granted permission.

*   *   *

At nightfall the defense team, together with the Lavallejas, met at the Colman house. After some thought and discussion, it was agreed that the judge had done the defense a huge favor. In not continuing with the opening arguments, there was now time for the defense to consider fully how Paddy and those dear to him should best be presented in the courtroom.

"You did well to hold your tongue today," Joaquin Suarez told Paddy.

"To tell the truth, I was very angry," Paddy said. "I considered it a very low thing for the prosecution to attack the character of my wife. Had the advocate for the defense not placed his hand on my back, I cannot say what my actions might have been. Fortunately I interpreted his signal correctly."

"We probably should have reviewed procedures more thoroughly before we entered into the opening arguments. Be assured that our response will more than clean up any blemish the prosecution intended for your wife. When we are finished she will appear to be a saint."

"One thing is certain, Joaquin." Juan Lavalleja said. "Whatever our government becomes, the citizens must have full protection in our courts of law. There has to be limitations on this sort of slander."

Joaquin nodded.

A knock came at the door and Tereza rose to answer it. It was the Englishmen coming in from the ships.

"Good evening Mrs. Colman," Bobby said.

"Good evening, Gentlemen," Tereza replied. "Won't you come in?"

"Thank you, Ma'am," Bobby said smiling. He was delighted by Tereza's accent and openly happy that things had apparently worked out so well for Paddy in spite of his present circumstances. The Englishmen entered and sat at seats already prepared for them around the dinner table.

Bobby took it upon himself to initiate the meeting. The translators droned on in a tone not so soft that Juan, Tereza and Joaquin could not hear but not too loud as to be a bother to the primary speakers. They definitely knew their vocation.

"Paddy," Bobby began, "Lieutenant Fleming here has developed, what I believe to be, an excellent defense strategy." Paddy smiled at the defense advocate. Surprisingly it was the first time he heard his name. There never was a formal introduction since they first saw each other at the defense table. When the hearing was dismissed, Paddy quickly sought out his wife and left the company at the table.

"I am not an expert in these matters," Bobby continued, "so if there are any issues that need to be brought forth, please do so."

Bobby was looking directly at Joaquin, who once he received the translation, looked back at Bobby and nodded.

"Mr. Colman, we are very fortunate that, even in the opening arguments, the prosecution has begun formulating his version of what it is you have done," Fleming said. "Right now, without hearing more testimony, his argument seems formidable to the judges, solid and without faults. But that is only because he has already provided every eventuality with a story or a reason."

"So how do we fight it?" Paddy asked.

Fleming smiled. "The opportunities will present themselves," he said, "Simply because his story is a fabrication, based only on the few facts he has. Once it unfolds, we will know where to attack it and show it for the falsehood it is. The advantage we hold is strong, because we know what actually did happen."

"We will need witnesses to validate our truths," Fleming continued. "Already Mr. Driscoll has agreed to testify and we are searching for the rider who brought the message of the return of the fleet to you in Minas. Hopefully he is still alive. May we rely on your wife to testify?"

A look of surprise crossed Tereza's face, but she quickly nodded her approval.

"Good," Fleming said. "Now, when you rode to Maldonado, did you speak to anyone?"

*   *   *

Later that night, after all the people had gone, Paddy lay next to Tereza in their bed.

"Are you worried?" Tereza asked.

"Not really," Paddy said. "Are you?"

"Yes," Tereza confided, "but only because of the uncertainty of it. Who knows really how it will finally be decided?"

"I wouldn't be too concerned," Paddy said softly. "Lieutenant Fleming appears to be a very competent man, and whatever the outcome, I do not believe Joaquin and the government will allow them to take me to England. As for me, I plan on staying here the rest of my life."

Tereza rolled over and half covered Paddy's upper torso as she lowered her head to kiss her husband's face. It wasn't a short kiss. She took her time and the message sent was not that she was being amorous so much as she did not just yet want the kiss to end. It was wonderfully sweet to Paddy and reminded him of days, now long ago, when they were in the first few years of their marriage. He raised himself against her and rolled her back toward her side of the bed, enveloping her in a sweet embrace.

Before they finally slept, Paddy was reminded once again of the marvelously magical effect lovemaking brings when it ends, one of joy, peace, and fulfillment, even in times of trial and strife – no, especially in times of trial and strife.

He suddenly realized that he had been lying to Tereza, for the feeling of contentment and consolation with him now stood in stark contrast to the fear and doubt he was denying, even to himself, only moments before.

He looked over at his wife one last time. She was already fast asleep and he was grateful for that. This last little bump in the road that worried them both just moments before now seemed very insignificant, considering all they had been through in the last twenty years. The light on the horizon was indeed the rising sun, both in his life and as it now blazoned his new nation's ensign.

* * *

"The defense plans to illustrate just how weak the argument is for the prosecution," Lieutenant Fleming began. "It has built its case around emotion, and through the tarnishing of innocent peoples' reputations. This it has done in one of the two segments of these proceedings where such outrageous claims cannot be countered by the opposition, except in the defense's statement as I am doing now. The defense will show that all the suppositions of the prosecution (and that is what they are – suppositions) are built of straw. One by one we will set a match to each."

Lieutenant Fleming sat down. The muted sound of murmuring in the courtroom revealed the level of astonishment he had achieved by this brusque and brief action. Even the chief judge's face showed a degree of surprise. The day before the prosecution used the entire time allotted in his aggressive attack against the defense. Now the response from the defense took less than a minute.

"Has the defense concluded its opening arguments?" the judge questioned.

"Yes Sir, we have," Fleming responded with a slight twinkle in his eye.

"Then the prosecution will call its first witness," the judge continued.

"The prosecution calls seaman first class Robert Driscoll," the judge advocate announced.

Bemused by Fleming's bold move, Joaquin Suarez sat in his chair with a smile he could not conceal. The man was actually in no better position than he had been in the night before, but the character of the courtroom was totally reversed. In revealing nothing by saying nothing, and simply by implying that the prosecution's case was much ado about nothing, everyone believed it, whether it was true or not.

Every aspect of Bobby revealed his trepidation as he made his way toward the stand. He had not really expected to be called by the prosecution since his friendship with Paddy was well known. Still, as a precautionary measure, he had been counseled to be completely truthful, whatever the questioning, should he be called. Fleming and Suarez both knew they would not be well served by perjury, and they advised all who might be witnesses to speak the truth, even if the testimony might seem damaging to their friend.

After being sworn in, Bobby waited on the stand while the prosecution performed some theatrical paper shuffling. Finally the judge advocate looked up and smiled, pleased at the look of concern on the sailor's face.

"Mr. Driscoll," the prosecution began, "Can you tell the court what your relationship was with Mr. Patrick Colman?"

"We were shipmates," Bobby replied.

"That was all?"

"Yes!"

"During your time as shipmates, were you and Mr. Colman ever given any particular assignment, some hazardous mission perhaps?"

Bobby looked at the defense desk and Fleming nodded affirmatively.

"We printed a newspaper," he replied, "the Montevideo Star."

A burst of laughter filled the courtroom that the judge had to bring the gavel down.

"A newspaper?!" the prosecution continued with a dramatic stifled giggle. "Did it provide any special privileges?"

"I don't know what you mean."

"Oh come now, Mr. Driscoll. Isn't it true that you, Mr. Colman, and that other chap, what was his name?"

"Jimmy Burke."

"Oh that's right, Seaman James Burke. Isn't it true that you three shared the opinion that you had it sweet, that you enjoyed staying in the warmth of the print shop while your mates endured the cold aboard ship?"

"Yes."

"And is it also true that when his Majesty's forces made their second attempt to capture Buenos Aires, you three laughed because you would not be going?."

"I would not say we were laughing."

"You were happy, then?"

"Yes."

"Even when you knew your other friends were facing dangers you would not?"

"We felt badly for them!"

"Of course."

*   *   *

The weather had been perfect and the little ship moved as quickly as it was intended when it had only been a concept on a Boston drawing board. Still it was not fast enough for Jimmy Burke. Inside he was filled with a fear he could not identify.

He suspected the proceedings in Montevideo had already begun and if so had not been going well. There was no reason for this suspicion. Things might actually be going very well and yet Jimmy could not shake the feeling.

Jimmy remembered something Paddy had told him long ago about people who have a truth confirmed to them though half a world away and without any means of having it communicated. "Messages from heaven" Paddy called it.

The first mate informed Jimmy that they were passing Porto Alegre, although the city could not be seen on the Brazilian coast as it was nestled deep within the safe confines of a lagoon.

Porto Alegre, Jimmy thought. *Just the name would want to make a man visit the place. Well, no time for that now.*

From here on Jimmy would know exactly where he was, relying on a map he had created and stored in a previously uncalled on area of his brain some twenty years earlier.

*   *   *

It was Fleming now who was cross examining Bobby.

"Mr. Driscoll," he began. "How well would you say you three men met the demand of printing a newspaper?"

"Very well, not being newspapermen. We never missed an issue!"

"And how did Mr. Colman perform?"

"Extremely well. He was our best typesetter."

"Would you say no one other than yourselves could have done as well a job?"

"Objection!" the prosecution interrupted. "Conjecture!"

"Sustained," the judge replied.

"No further questions," Fleming said. He was pleased. He knew that the court knew what Bobby's answer would have been – a resounding yes – and the prosecution by its objection did not want the court to hear it. In spite of the effort the judges would make to dutifully dismiss this incident as not a part of the testimony, it was there, awaiting its time to play its role in influencing the final judgment.

"Does the prosecution want to re-examine the witness?" the chief judge asked.

"Yes we do, your honor," the judge advocate replied, and he rose to take his place in front of the stand.

"Now Mr. Driscoll," he said, "Let us return to the day you first learned about Patrick Colman's involvement with the woman who is now his wife. Do you remember that day?"

"Yes sir."

"And how was his behavior when he announced his affair? Did he appear braggadocios?"

"No sir."

"He simply announced his conquest in passing then?"

"Oh, no sir, we had to force it out of him."

"Force it out of him? Could he not have been making vague references to it then, in an effort to playfully make you "force it out of him?"

Bobby did not like the way the cross examination was going. He could see now the devious and inescapable road the prosecutor had put him on with this line of questioning. Well, he was going to escape if he could.

He could see Paddy nervously writing a note to his defense team and he would not take part in helping convict his friend because he was not smart enough to avoid being duped.

"It was not like that at all," Bobby replied. "You set traps for me with your questions."

"Just answer the question, Mr. Driscoll!"

"The answer is no."

"Well then, Mr. Driscoll, would you relate for us how you did come to know of Mr. Colman's relationship with Miss Ferrando?"

"Paddy attended services in the cathedral, and after a while he began spending more time away from the press."

"And so you suspected he was in some relationship!"

"Not at all. It was only when he began coming in late that we knew he had a sweetheart."

"I see." The judge advocate looked back at the bench. "No further questions."

"Does the defense care to reexamine the witness?" the judge asked.

"Yes, your honor," Fleming replied. He quickly moved to the stand. It was obvious that Bobby wished more than anything to be freed from his perch.

"Mr. Driscoll, I would like you to give a little more detail about how it was revealed that Mr. Colman was seeing and speaking to Miss Ferrando, the woman who is now his wife. When he came in late, did he immediately reveal that this was the reason for his tardiness?"

"No."

"What did he do?"

"He apologized for being late."

"Was he sincere?"

"I believe he was, yes."

"So he showed remorse and contriteness."

"Well no, he was actually very cheerful."

"He was sincere in his apology, as you suppose, and yet he was quite cheerful. Did you not find this unusual?"

"I suppose so, but it was actually Jimmy who realized the reason for his behavior. He asked Paddy directly if he was seeing someone."

"By 'Jimmy' you are referring to Mr. Burke."

"Yes I am."

"Now once the cat was out of the bag, did Mr. Colman go into any details regarding his exploits with Miss Ferrando?"

"No, and when we questioned him about it he became somewhat put out with us."

"And why was that?"

"He regarded, that is, regards the woman as someone so special he dare not be the one who would alter that."

"Objection," the prosecution shouted. The judge advocate had supposed Bobby was about to hang Paddy with his own testimony. Now he saw he had been fooled into letting Fleming sneak in a conjecture.

"Granted," the judge replied.

"One last question, Mr. Driscoll. The prosecution has referred to the relationship between Mr. Colman and Miss Ferrando as an affair. That word can mean many different things in this context. In the minds of many, it only means the basest thing – sexual intercourse between the two parties. Is that what you believe was the situation here?"

"Objection!" the prosecution shouted again.

"Your honor," Fleming pleaded, "the prosecution deliberately used that word to create the impression in this court that this is exactly what Mr. Driscoll believed. Until this question is answered, the impression will remain that this is exactly what he believed and exactly what happened. Now while this is indeed conjecture, I believe in all fairness we should know what Mr. Driscoll actually believed."

The chief judge pushed his chair back from the bench and thought for a minute. Then he conferred with the other two judges on his left and right. Finally he pushed his chair forward to its original location.

"Overruled," He said.

"Answer the question, Mr. Driscoll," Fleming said.

"Paddy and Miss Ferrando had yet to know each other sexually."

"Thank you Mr. Driscoll. No further questions, your honor."

In the gallery Tereza Colman sat weeping softly and wiping tears from her eyes.

*　　*　　*

That evening, the defense team met once again at the Colman house. After sending a rider, the dock worker at Maldonado had been located and was now en route to Montevideo.

"His name is Carlos Figueroa," Juan Lavalleja said. "He was still working on the docks when we found him."

"After how many years?" Joaquin asked.

"Fifteen!" Tereza answered.

"Fifteen," Bobby laughed, "and still at the docks. Was he a young man?"

"Not really," Paddy answered, "but he was fit."

Lieutenant Fleming felt it was time to get down to business.

"I do not want to call Mr. Figueroa to the stand immediately," he announced. "We cannot count on him being here yet. Instead I want to recall you, Bobby, to tell how it was when the fleet returned to Montevideo, for the last time, to pick up the remainder of its men."

"Will you be wanting me to testify soon?" Tereza interrupted.

"No, Mrs. Colman, that testimony will come later, if at all," Fleming replied.

"Then, if you will permit, the ladies and I will retire to the kitchen to prepare some yerba mate and tortas fritas." Tereza nodded to Ana and Katy.

Lieutenant Fleming nodded back to Tereza in approval and the women rose from the table and departed.

Once they were gone, Fleming continued to lay out his strategy. Joaquin Suarez marveled at how adept this young man was, or maybe he himself had been out of the practice of law too long. He swore that he would get back into the practice soon.

But when would that actually be, now that his affairs were fully occupied in matters of state? Drafted into the presidency by the vote of the delegates at La Florida three years ago, now he realized for the first time he may have become a career politician. Surely no other man had done that more unwittingly and certainly unwillingly.

"After Bobby testifies," Fleming continued, "I want Juan Lavalleja to take the stand. General Lavalleja, you will recount the incident in Minas when Paddy and you all first learned of the return of the British fleet."

In the kitchen, the women began warming the water for the yerba mate and took out the ingredients for the tortas fritas.

"So do you believe you will still be called to testify?" Ana asked.

"I believe so."

"But the hearing is progressing so much better than it first appeared it would a few days ago."

"Yes, Lieutenant Fleming is very good. I believe he may still call me, though, if only to solidify his defense."

"Will it be embarrassing, ma?" Katy asked cautiously. "I mean, will it be revealing?"

"You need not worry, daughter," Tereza replied.

Her response put Katy's fears to rest and answered a question she had pondered for some years.

Ana smiled.

* * *

The morning session of the hearing began with the prosecution calling a surprise witness. Through an interpreter, the man recounted what a scoundrel Paddy was, as were all three who ran the print shop. His testimony ran long and had quite a few stories about the exploits of them all. As it often was with lies and falsehoods, the longer the testimony rambled the more obvious it became that it was full of errors and contradictions, a fact Fleming was sure had not been lost on the three men who sat in judgment on this court.

At the break for lunch, Suarez suggested that the citizen be cross examined and the lies exposed. Fleming countered that any more testimony from this man could be cause to increase tensions between the Uruguayans and the English and he did not want that. He felt he could achieve the same purpose through the testimony of friendly witnesses. Once again Suarez was astounded by the insight of the young Englishman and acquiesced.

That afternoon, as was his plan, Fleming rejected the judge's offer to cross examine the witness. "I want to recall Robert Driscoll to the stand," he said. The judge so ordered and Bobby returned to the witness stand once again.

"Mr. Driscoll," Fleming began, "do you remember the day the fleet returned from Buenos Aires and Mr. Colman was nowhere to be found?"

"Yes I do, sir, very well."

"Will you recount for us what happened in your own words?"

"Well, Jimmy and I were startled when we heard the knock on the door."

"And Jimmy is Mr. Burke."

"Just like yesterday, that's right sir."

"Go on!"

"Some marines came in and said we were going home. They asked for Paddy immediately."

"And did you tell them where he was?"

"Well no, we didn't know where he was actually. We did the only thing we could do. We left him a note."

"No further questions," Fleming announced.

"Does the prosecution wish to examine the witness once again?" the chief judge asked.

"Yes, your honor," the judge advocate responded and he approached Bobby as Fleming took his seat at the defense table.

"Now Mr. Driscoll", he began, "yesterday you stated that you believed Mr. Colman and, at that time, Miss Ferrando had maintained their chastity."

"Yes sir."

"In light of your current testimony are you still of a mind to maintain that opinion?"

"Yes sir, I am."

"Testimony in this courtroom, including yours, Mr. Driscoll, would indicate that Mr. Colman had been away from the print shop since the fleet departed. Where do you think he might have been?"

The question called for an answer that was pure conjecture and the judge looked toward the defense table anticipating and objection. There was none. Fleming had anticipated this line of questioning and was happy to let the prosecution dig its own pit.

"I imagine he was with his sweetheart."

"Mrs. Colman, or at that time, Miss Ferrando?"

"Yes sir."

"So he was with her all this time and nothing was going on."

"I believe so."

"How can you be so sure?"

"Just recently I asked him—out of a boorish curiosity I suppose. It was very inappropriate of me. He said no."

"And you believed him."

"If you know Paddy Colman, you know he was telling the truth."

"About a matter as serious as this?'

"Yes sir."

The prosecution paused in obvious thought. "No further questions," he finally said.

"Mr. Driscoll, you may return to your seat," the judge said. "Does the prosecution wish to call its next witness?"

"Not at this time, your honor."

"Is the defense prepared to call a witness?"

"The defense calls General Juan Antonio Lavalleja," Fleming announced.

CHAPTER SIXTEEN

Redemption

Lieutenant Fleming glanced over toward Joaquin Suarez as Juan Lavalleja approached the stand. Joaquin smiled and nodded. Short of a surprise appearance of any new witness on the part of the prosecution, it appeared now that the defense was well in control of the proceedings,

"Mr. Lavalleja, would you tell us what happened in Minas the day it was discovered that the British fleet had departed Montevideo?"

As the questioning now had to be translated from English to Spanish and back again, the testimony began to drag. But Fleming was performing masterfully. His line of questioning kept interest in the testimony from waning completely.

"A messenger rode in from the capital," Juan replied "We had just left Sunday mass and were preparing to eat."

"Was it too late to intercept the fleet?"

"I thought it was, but since the rider drove his horse so hard and the message in the print shop was discovered so quickly, Paddy thought he might have a chance to still catch it at Maldonado."

"How did the townspeople feel about that?"

"They also thought it was hopeless and they did not want him to go."

"But he went anyway?!"

"Yes."

"By what means?"

"I am sorry. I do not understand."

"How was he able to get to Maldonado?"

"I gave him a fast horse."

"Thank you Mr. Lavalleja. No further questions."

"Does the prosecution wish to question the witness?" the chief judge asked.

"Yes your honor, the judge advocate replied."

"Mr. Lavalleja," he began, "You gave Mr. Colman a horse, you say?"

"Yes Sir."

"A fast horse."

"Yes Sir."

"Even though nobody thought he had a chance and everybody wanted him to stay?"

"Yes Sir."

'Was he riding your fastest horse?"

"No."

No further questions."

"Does the defense wish to cross examine?" the chief judge asked.

"Yes, Your honor," Fleming responded.

Fleming smiled as he approached the stand. Up to now his little team had anticipated what the prosecution would do and had come up with an answer for it. It seemed their luck still held.

"General Lavalleja, you said you did not give Mr. Colman your fastest horse. Is that correct?"

"Yes."

"Then if you truly wanted him to have success in finding the fleet in Maldonado, why would you do that?"

"My fastest horse was the best horse over short distances," Juan explained, "but my best horse over long distances was the mare I gave him. She was almost as fast and she was tireless."

"No further questions," Fleming announced. As Juan was directed from the stand, Paddy reflected on how quickly time had passed since those days. Surely both horses in Juan's testimony by now had long since passed away.

"Is the prosecution prepared to call its next witness?" the chief judge asked.

"Yes we are," the judge advocate replied. "We call seaman Patrick Colman to the stand.

Paddy was surprised, but he responded immediately and went to the stand to swear the oath. The message the judge advocate sent by labeling him a seaman was not lost on Fleming. The inference, of course, was that he was still a sailor who had deserted the navy.

"Now Mr. Colman, when you rode into Maldonado, did you speak to anyone?" the prosecutor asked.

"No."

"You spoke to no one?"

"No."

"Does the name Pedro Soria mean anything to you?"

Paddy knew he was getting into trouble, but he had no idea who the man was. "No," he said.

"No further questions, your honor."

*   *   *

At the Colman home that evening the defense team all agreed. The prosecution once again had been masterful in presenting a case that in truth was not a case at all. Through skilled questioning the judge advocate had created a doubt where there had been none before. The team admitted that they had been slow to counter this strategy, and now they met to discuss how best it could be defeated.

Nobody had a clue as to who Pedro Soria might be and the chances of finding out before the next day's sessions were slim.

It was a rare thing in this hearing when the prosecution had not attempted to keep the defense off balance. But in spite of their efforts, up to now, the genius of Fleming and Suarez always had an answer.

This next day, however, the surprise was that the prosecution had no surprise, or so it appeared. They would do exactly what the defense would have wanted. They set their hopes on a single old man.

* * *

"The prosecution calls Pedro Soria to the stand."

The old man walked forward, and suddenly Paddy realized he did know him. This was the dock worker he had met in Maldonado. Whoever Carlos Figueroa was that the defense team had fished up earlier, he was definitely not the man. A large solid pit swelled in Paddy's gut.

The prosecutor began as soon as the oath was given.

"Señor Soria. What is it exactly that you do?"

"I am a dockworker in Maldonado."

"I see, and do you recall the time you saw the English fleet in Maldonado?"

"Yes, I do."

"Can you tell us what happened?"

"Lord Nelson lost his flagship. The English tried everything but they could not keep it from sinking."

The prosecutor stood dumbfounded. After a longer than usual pause, he looked over at his table where is team was desperately signaling him for a conference.

"May I have a moment to confer," he asked the judge.

"The prosecution is granted three minutes," the judge answered.

* * *

Captain James Burke was a very happy man as his little ship, the *American Vision*, pulled into its berth in Montevideo. He had never before realized just how compact the city actually was. One minute his crew was reefing the sails off Punta Carretas and the next they were rounding the peninsula and pulling into the port.

His ship was not large, but he was proud to be its captain. New England built, it was a fine example of an American merchantman. What pleased Jimmy Burke most, however, was the banner waving at its stern. Wherever in the world they pulled into port, his little band had the honor of representing the continuing hope of a republic. And at this moment they were arriving at the newest nation to embark on that grand experiment.

Jimmy was the only man to leave the ship. The crew would wait only long enough for some minor resupply and then they would depart for Buenos Aires. If he were lucky he would meet them there before they left for San Francisco. If not, he would book passage to Mendoza, cross the Andes, to hopefully catch the ship at Valparaiso. When he considered all the rigors before him, he told himself it was for a friend.

*   *   *

The only eyes not fixed on the prosecution table belonged to those who might have already been asleep before the questioning began. The discussion at that table had become very quick and animated, forcing most of those in the courtroom to wonder at just what it was that was being said.

The chief prosecutor had a difficult time restraining an intense urge to break out laughing.

"One minute," the chief judge said.

"We won't need that much time," the prosecutor smiled and he walked over to Pedro Soria. He was still smiling when he resumed the questioning.

"Señor Soria, it is true that the English fleet has visited Maldonado more than a few times in your lifetime, isn't it?"

"Yes sir!"

"Can you remember back to any one time when the fleet was actually in flight and spent only the time required to recover the garrison stationed there?"

"Yes, I remember that."

"A man came riding in from Minas. He said he was trying to catch the fleet. Do you remember that?"

"Yes."

"That man is sitting in this courtroom today. Can you identify him?"

Soria scanned the room until his eyes fell on Paddy. "He looks older but that is the man."

*   *   *

It was like Jimmy had just left Montevideo only a few weeks earlier. In five minutes he was at the cabildo. It was easy to find Bobby in the gallery. He was just about the only one wearing a royal navy dress uniform not sitting with the rest of the Royal Navy. Bobby was sitting with Tereza and her family and with Ana Lavalleja. He had them make room for Jimmy.

The judge advocate continued, "When Mr. Colman saw he had missed the fleet, what did he do?"

"He asked where the fleet might dock next."

"And what was your response?"

"I told him that I believed, if they stopped at all, perhaps it would be at Porto Alegre, but most likely they would not stop until they arrived at Rio de Janeiro."

"And what did Mr. Colman do?"

"He returned to Minas."

"No further questions."

"Does the defense wish to cross-examine?" the chief justice asked.

Fleming shook his head no.

*   *   *

Were it not for the arrival of Jimmy Burke, there would have been little joy at the Colman house that evening. Paddy was upset that the defense had not allowed him to take the stand to counter the damaging testimony Pedro Soria had given. While he acknowledged that the testimony had not been false, it had been far from complete and it left the wrong impression.

It wasn't until Joaquin Suarez spoke to him that he was able to see the reasoning behind the defense's decision. Soria was an old man. If he had remembered all he had told Paddy that fateful day, he would have mentioned it. To think otherwise would be to think the prosecution was less than honest. And if the defense pushed Soria on things that were true but that he could no longer remember, it could be disastrous.

It was Katy who kept Jimmy talking. It was a difficult conversation because Katy's English was not all that good, but she was persistent. She wanted to know what places Jimmy had visited and what they were like. She especially wanted to know about the United States and whether it was true they were realizing the success as had been reported.

"Most of it," he said.

"So now Jimmy Burke captains his own ship!" Paddy joked.

"Yep," Jimmy responded. "I suppose the shipping company knows talent when it sees it."

"Really Jimmy," Bobby said. "I know part of the story but how did fortune begin to change for you?"

"It happened right after the war, Bobby. Within a year I was dismissed from his majesty's navy wondering exactly what it was I was going to do with the rest of my life. Shortly after that an American ship arrived and took me home."

"Home?" Paddy said. "It's so hard to believe!"

"I told you both," Jimmy said, and you did not believe me. It turned out well, though. I suddenly realized I was not alone in this. There were thousands of us. I only feel sorry for the boys who never made it back. The rest of us knows how blessed we truly are!"

"What made it all possible?" Bobby asked. "I mean, the repatriation."

"I can thank President Madison for that," Jimmy said. "It was the terms of the treaty. But the men who saw it through were Monroe and Adams – the son, not his father. So I hired on as a sailor in a shipping company. I tell you boys, it is a wonderful thing living in a country without nobility. You will soon see. In a short time I was the crew leader, and then I made the move that would be impossible in most of the world. I became a third mate. It was easier after that."

"Amazing," said Paddy.

Later that night after all the guests had gone, Paddy and Tereza lay in bed talking.

"What do you think will happen?" she asked. It wasn't a question asked lightly. She was worried.

"I won't deceive you, love," Paddy said. "They might want to take me back to England. But I still do not think it likely. Joaquin would not allow it."

"Tereza's concerned expression and lack of response worried him."

"Suppose I can stay," Paddy asked "Where do we go from here?"

Tereza was surprised by the question but her answer was immediate. "Let's go to the Salto Grande."

"Tereza, I only sent you there for your safety. I did not think you would come to love the place – especially in light of the exodus."

"The exodus was difficult," Tereza admitted, "but that is where circumstances welded us together as a family. And it was the most unbearable of things that did it – Luis' death and Luisito's decision to go with the army."

Paddy nodded and smiled. "Luisito is a lot like his uncle. He must have got it from his grandfather."

"He has a lot of his father in him too," Tereza replied. "Paddy, the river is so beautiful sometime," she continued, "with the birds and especially when the sun sets on it."

"What would I do there, love?"

"You weren't such a bad gaucho," Tereza said.

"Will there be a market?"

"I know there wasn't one when we were at Ayuí, but there is now."

"I did not like you much when we were in Ayuí," Paddy confessed.

"I'm sorry about that. I thought my world had ended there. I did not realize how much I still had or had to live for. And do you remember I told you how different I felt on the other side of the river."

"The river makes all the difference?" Paddy questioned

"It surely does!"

*   *   *

The chief judge surprised everybody. As soon as he was seated he made the announcement.

"I wondered this morning what everybody was doing last night," he said. "If the prosecution and the defense were anything like the judges in this hearing, I imagine they were up planning for today's events."

He looked over his captive audience.

"Most people believe a court martial is just the military version of a civil court. It is not! Where a civil court in many countries presumes the innocence of the defendant and his guilt must be proven, in a court martial it is just the opposite. Should cause be found in this hearing, the defendant will have to extricate himself in a court martial from a presumption of guilt. That is one of the reasons the prosecutor is sometimes called the judge advocate."

"I am calling both counsels into private chambers. I am not sure how long this will take so, if the gallery chooses, it can spend a pleasant time in the plaza until we resume the hearing. We will call you in when that time comes."

*   *   *

Paddy hoped this "counsel" would not take long as the chambers were less than roomy. As soon as everyone was seated the judge started right in.

"It is the responsibility of the prosecution to show the judges where there is cause to open a full court martial. It is the opinion of all three judges that the prosecution has not done that."

"On the other hand the defense has not adequately shown where the defendant is innocent of the charge. This is not meant to cast aspersions on the abilities of either counsel. If Mr. Colman is innocent, guilt will be hard to prove. If he is not guilty, it will be difficult for the defense to prove a negative."

"The judges believe that the evidence leans toward the innocence of Mr. Colman. Still, in most cases, this would not be enough."

"However, this is not most cases. The outcome of this hearing could be enough to create the first diplomatic confrontation between England and this new nation. We would like to avoid that, so we are ending this hearing, declaring that there was not enough evidence."

"The ruling, however, will be conditional. Patrick Colman must renounce his English citizenship and declare himself fully Uruguayan. Is the prosecution fine with that?"

The judge advocate nodded.

"And the defense?"

Fleming and Suarez nodded.

"Mr.Colman?"

Paddy also nodded his approval.

"Then we will proceed with Mr. Colman's renouncement."

*   *   *

That afternoon Paddy's family and Bobby said farewell to Jimmy, who had booked passage on a ferry to Buenos Aires "just in case".

"You came all this way to testify and in the end you did not have to do anything. I'm very sorry," Paddy said.

"Not at all," Jimmy said. "I am actually glad I didn't. It showed the hearing was going well—and I am glad I had the opportunity to see my old friends again. There is one great advantage to living in the nineteenth century. Most countries have international agreements concerning the mail. We can always write."

"And we will," Paddy assured both his friends.

"Paddy, I believe you found a really good one," Jimmy said with his eyes fixed on Tereza. Then he turned to her. "And Mrs. Colman, I know you have. Good luck to you both, and to your family."

Jimmy shook Bobby and Paddy's hands one last time and gave Tereza a peck on the cheek. Then he went on board. The threesome watched as the gangplank was taken down and the ship was nudged away from its berth. Then the crew began their shanty and unfurled the topsails.

The crew and dockworkers deftly maneuvered the ship away from the wharf and out into the bay. She looked both sleek and beautiful when the other sails were unfurled and set. It quickly picked up speed and magnificently displayed the skill of its crew as it looped once around the bay, passed through the inlet and out into the Rio de la Plata.

*   *   *

It would be the last evening that the full defense team would all meet together in the Colman house. It was a party really, and a farewell to Lieutenant Fleming and the English part of the team that had served them so well. Paddy felt badly that Jimmy could not stay, but he would not let his friend's early departure spoil the festivities for the rest. There was just too much to be grateful for.

It was Juan who proposed the first toast, thanking Fleming and Joaquin Suarez for their artful defense. All were in agreement with that. Paddy followed with a toast of gratitude for the victory they had given him and his family. After several more toasts the celebration broke down into groups that mostly centered on the languages most familiar to the celebrants – the English in their groups and the Uruguayans in theirs. Paddy moved between the groups in a conscious effort to keep everybody mingling harmoniously together.

"I will not be too happy when you leave," Ana said to Tereza. "As your closest friend, I almost feel betrayed."

"You'll always be my closest friend, Ana," Tereza responded.

"You do not understand what I am saying, Tere. For almost twenty years we have been deprived of the good times most women share, when they go to the market together, or just sit and talk about their families. And always it was because of events beyond our control. Now times have improved to where it seems things might be even better than we had when we were young girls, and I began looking forward to us sharing those opportunities at last."

"You're making far too much out of this, Ana. We will see each other many times when Paddy and I come to Montevideo and we will share those times together."

"Of course," said Ana softly.

In another part of the house Katy and Luis used their limited English to find out from Bobby Driscoll a little more about their father. His Spanish was worse than their English but amazingly they communicated quite well.

"Your father loved your mother very much," Bobby told them. "At first Jimmy and I though he had found a girl just to share a little romance with, but Paddy would have none of that. He loved and respected your mother far too much."

Katy and Luis both nodded. They knew their father well enough to know Bobby was not concealing some awful truth he did not want them knowing.

"It is a tribute to both your folks," Bobby continued. "I feel you need to know how blessed you are to have them as your mom and dad."

"You haven't told us anything we have not already discovered for ourselves," Luis said. "Tell me, how was Pa as a sailor?"

"I only knew Paddy in passing before he and Jimmy and I worked on the newspaper," Bobby said, "and by then we could really not be called sailors by what we were doing. But Paddy still made himself obvious by his attention to duty. He had a lot more of the Irish in him then, but other than that, he did everything quite well."

Katy and Luis both laughed. "I know you are right about that," Luis said. "To keep our family safe, Pa was set against having anything to do with the recent conflicts. But when the exodus drew him into it, he gave everything he had."

"There you have it," Bobby said. "You know first hand the kind of man he is."

"Are there many men like my father in the English navy?" Katy asked Bobby.

"Like your dad?" Bobby said thoughtfully. "No!"

Katy's expression revealed obvious disappointment.

"Look, Katy," Bobby said. "There are good men everywhere. And while they may not appear to be in overabundance, neither are they rare. You just have to look hard until you find a good one."

* * *

Juan Lavalleja invited Paddy to the courtyard in back of the house where the conversation could be a little more private.

"What are your plans now, Paddy," Juan asked.

"Tere wants to go to the Salto Grande," Paddy replied.

"Yes, I know. Ana is not very happy about that. Have you asked your children what they want?"

"No, but I am fairly sure they prefer to stay in Montevideo. Where do you go from here, Juan? What part will you play in this new government?"

"I am not sure. There is more unrest and contention now than I would have wanted," Juan confided. "I thought we all shared the same dream the general had for our new nation, but Rivera believes the government should occupy a stronger position than many of us want. I hope this does not get out of control."

Juan's revelation convinced Paddy even more that maybe Tereza was right. He should remove his family from where the action would be if it were to come. But his children were grown now and he knew they would be making their own decisions.

"If Katy and Luis feel strongly about remaining in Montevideo," Juan said, "they can stay with Ana and me."

*   *   *

One month later Paddy and Tereza stood with their children and Juan and Ana at the city gate. The Colmans' two wheeled cart was loaded once again for a long journey, but this time their children would not accompany them. Thanks to the Lavalleja's offer, Katy and Luis had decided to remain in the city.

Ana was grateful, for it meant Tereza would truly be back visiting from time to time, especially when the grandchildren arrived.

"What more is there to be said?" Juan asked

"Nothing," Paddy replied. "This is not a farewell, just good-bye for a while."

A few more hugs and cordial good-byes were exchanged. Then Paddy and Tereza climbed into the wagon. Tereza glanced back at her children often as the little cart moved down the road toward where it forked to the north and then curved to the west around the bay. She watched them still standing at the city gate, growing smaller in the distance, and she began having second thoughts. But she put them aside and told herself that this too was a part of life.

Paddy used the time to reflect on the last twenty years. Much had been lost, but the new nation had accomplished so much more. One week earlier, Bobby left with the English fleet, committed to write. The three friends who once had been makeshift newspapermen now lived in different parts of the world, but they had become friends for life. Numbered with Jimmy and Bobby were the friends Paddy had also gained in his adopted land.

His life had taken him to a place, that in his youth, he never could have imagined. Now he lived in a totally different culture and spoke a different language.

When the little cart turned north toward Tres Cruces, Juan, Ana, Katy, and Luis waved the last of their goodbyes and went back into the city.

* * *

And so Paddy and Tereza faded quickly into the past.

The worst fears of Juan Lavalleja were realized, and arguments over how the new nation should be governed soon threw Uruguay into a bloody civil war. In the end, however, the two major belligerents in this war, led by both Lavalleja and Rivera, agreed to end the fighting. From that time forward, the Uruguayans lived under a compromise government, the two factions becoming political parties. Juan lived only long enough to see this come to pass. He renewed his friendship with Jose Rivera, and then he was gone.

The wise old General Artigas remained in Paraguay, believing his return would only bring harm to the new nation. He chose not to side with any political faction, and in spite of invitations offered him, he never again set foot in the land he loved so dearly.

But after his death, a grateful nation immediately took steps to secure his remains and carry them back to Montevideo. Today he lies within the great tomb that is also his monument in the Plaza Independencia.

Both Katy and Luis married and the unions of their two separate families produced many children. They passed down the stories of their mother and father, of Uncle Luis, and of Juan and Ana Lavalleja for many years and through many of the generations that followed. Eventually, however, the true accounts of what had happened came to be looked upon as family legends. And later on they had all but disappeared.

But Colmans still live in Uruguay even to this very day.

Epilogue

Having finished the work, I wondered if there might be any interest on where I took my background material.

Except for the Colman family, the main characters were real people. Their acts described in the book actually happened (allowing for some literary license). The surname Colman does exist in Uruguay, not because the Colmans are descended from Paddy. They are descendants of a Colman who emigrated to the country in the 1800s when the English made good their aim to open commercial markets. Many of the minor characters are fictional, but the names I gave them. all or in part, are the names of people I knew. Gubitosi and Nalerio are good examples of these.

Ana Monterroso was a real woman, but Tereza is fictitious. That being said, she is modeled after a real woman who has the qualities I described for Tereza. Katy, her daughter, gets her name from another woman I know. The modern Tereza and Katy are friends, not mother and daughter.

The friendly, genuine, and loyal nature of the Guaraní I drew from my friend Carlos, who lived in Paraguay. Unfortunately, I have no first hand reference for the Charrúa. They were virtually wiped out in subsequent Indian wars in Uruguay; the last major battle being called the Battle of Salsipuedes (translated "get out if you can").

Glossary

Alto Peru – The land roughly encompassing the area now known as Bolivia.

Banda Oriental (Bahn-dah or-dee-en-TAL [RHYMES WITH PAL]) – A province of the Viceroyalty of La Plata, bordered by Brazil on the north, the South Atlantic Ocean on the east, the Rio de la Plata on the south, and the Rio Uruguay on the west. Known worldwide as Uruguay after 1828.

Boleador (bo-leia-DOOR) – The Uruguayan name for the bolo.

Bolo – A three armed sling. The arms are tied together at one end and each weighted with a smooth stone at the other end. The bolo is thrown by grasping a single arm by its weighted stone and hurling it overhead. When released, the arms spread, and then fall into each other, wrapping themselves around the target when it is hit.

Bombachas – Traditional gaucho pants, tough and hardy. Made of heavy wool, their traditional origin is Turkey.

Bombilla (bome-BEE-zhah) – A gold tipped metal straw for sipping yerba mate, traditionally made of silver, with a silver strainer at the end to filter out fine particles.

Cabildo (cah-BEEL-dough) – Governmental headquarters building, be it city, departmental, provincial, or national.

Cisplatine – The Cisplatine Province, Brazil's name for Uruguay when it occupied the country. The name literally means "This side of the (Rio de la) Plata.

Cuartel (kwahr-TEL) – Military headquarters building.

Gaucho (GOW-cho) – The cowboy of South America. They range over the vast pampas of South America, in Argentina, Brazil, Uruguay, and Paraguay.

Lavalleja, Juan Antonio (La-vah-ZHEY-hah) – Uruguay's greatest hero next to José Artigas. In some ways he surpasses Artigas and it was he and his small band of 33 men who launched the final campaign to make Uruguay independent. Lavalleja never strayed from the philosophies Artigas championed and it is those philosophies that keep Artigas in the forefront as the national hero.

Ombú (ohm-BOO) – A tree with the peculiarity of growing alone on the pampas. They can become very large and provide plentiful shade. They themselves can be important landmarks on an otherwise featureless plain.

Oriental – (Oh-ree-en-TAL [rhymes with pal]) – The people of Uruguay back when it was a province of the viceroyalty of La Plata called La Banda Oriental, or the Eastern Strip. They still commonly refer to themselves as Orientales even today.

Pampas (PAHM-pahs) – The great rolling plain of South America. It extends from the Andes mountains across northern Argentina, throughout Uruguay and up into the southern parts of Brazil and Paraguay.

Pampero—(pahm-PEH-doh) – A great storm that blows over the pampas from out of the Antarctic. It is very similar to the norther in North America.

Parillada – Pah–dee-ZHAH-dah) _ A meal of various meets cooked on the Parilla, or grill. The method used is somewhat different from other parts of the world. The fires are huge in comparison and some distance away. Most of the cooking is done with infrared rays and very little is convective. The result is a meat with most of the juices still inside and evenly cooked throughout.

Peninsulares – (PEN-in-soo-LAHR-des) – South American Spanish born in Spain. They occupied the highest tier of society. Spaniards born in the Americas were called Criollos (Cree-OH-zhose) or Creoles and they occupied a second level tier.

Pericón – (peh-dee-KONE) – The national dance of Uruguay with old folkloric roots.

Platense – (Plah-TEN-seh) – People living along the Rio de la Plata, both Argentine and Uruguayan.

Porteño – (Por-TAIN-yo) – Citizens of Buenos Aires, literally meaning "port people". They are also called Bonairenses (Bon –aye-REN-ses).

Tortas Fritas – (TOR-tahs FDEE-tahs) Deep fried wheat flour bread very much like the Mexican sopaipilla. It is almost always served with honey.

Yerba Mate – (ZHEHR-bah MAH-tei) – The national drink of Uruguay. The mate is actually the gourd into which the yerba (grass or herb) is placed. Scalding hot water is poured over the yerba and the resulting brew is sipped through a silver straw/strainer combination called a bombilla. Traditional yerba mate is amarga (bitter) but many prefer it dulce (sweet) now.